Prototype

Best wishes

Wayne Stevens

For Carol as without your encouragement, this would not have been written and for Rachael and Sean, you know why.

"The life given us, by nature is short; but the memory of a well-spent life is eternal."

- Marcus Tullius Cicero

Chapter One

17th September, Present Day, Vatican City, Rome.

The shouting seemed out of place. A sharp exchange of male voices that resonated through the large oak panelled double doors that remained firmly shut to the full volume of the noise. It continued unabated, the strength of the words spoken confusing and loud and the quiet man studiously trying to read the dry, yet vital document in front of him had no choice but to take notice.

Cardinal Donal McGeary raised his head slowly from the report he was reading on his tablet and looked at the impressive pair of doors to his office. He sighed as he wondered what could be causing all that noise. As if the sudden breakdown of the air conditioning was not enough, this additional drain on his senses was most unwelcome.

He wiped his forehead as the first signs of perspiration became obvious. The air conditioning had malfunctioned just as the hottest part of the day arrived in full force, requiring the windows of his office to be fully ajar which did not really add any fresh breeze to the room but instead allowed just more warm, city air to enter his office. Additionally, there was the incessant clamour of thousands of tourists from hundreds of nations, milling around St Peter's and the surrounding streets, the surface dust loosened from the parched road by their impatient steps filling that same still and dry heat and finding its way through the open windows and onto every horizontal surface. Even after all that was already trying his day, what could now be making it even worse?

McGeary could quite clearly hear the raised, yet monotone voice of his Secretary, Father Bernard, trying and failing to quieten the insistent volume of his verbal opponent. McGeary heard various words in English, Italian, French and another language he was not sure of. Spanish perhaps? Bernard was clearly trying to prevent someone from seeing him, of that McGeary was certain and he quickly scanned the calendar on his tablet for any clue as to who his visitor could be. According to the lack of entries, his morning was clear so whoever this was, he had no appointment and that clearly would not do as far as Father Bernard was concerned.

McGeary smiled to himself as he knew the tenacious yet surprisingly patient Father Bernard would be using his love of rhetoric to try and calm the insistent visitor and thus McGeary was more than surprised to see the doors suddenly fly open and a portly, red-faced figure rush in followed smartly by the now less patient Father Bernard.

"Your Eminence forgive me", the man shouted in English as Father Bernard placed a restraining hand on his shoulder, "I must see you. It is of the most important matter." The man was out of breath and panting. He wore a tired suit that once screamed Italian elegance but now showed clear signs of sartorial neglect. His shirt was deep blue, made all the darker by the large sweat patches as it clung to his overweight frame. His tie was crooked and pulled down from the unbuttoned collar and his fleshy jowls wobbled as he pleaded to be seen. For all of his unpleasant demeanour and haste, McGeary realised in an instant that the man needed to be heard and raised his hand to calm the two men.

"It is alright Father," McGeary said passively, "I will see this man. Mr….?" he looked straight into the pudgy face and screwed up eyes of the sweating man.

"De Soto your Eminence." The man replied, "Doctor Eduardo De Soto". McGeary paused, trying to recollect if the name made any sense to him at all. It did not.

"I will see Dr De Soto although I am not impressed with his lack of respect by not making a suitable appointment….." he trailed off and glanced disapprovingly at De Soto, making the flustered man reactively look to the floor with instinctive reverence.

"Your Eminence," Father Bernard started, "I am afraid this man could not be restrained. I have no idea how he gained entry to this floor. He just appeared in our office and would not take no for an answer." Father Bernard shot a withering look towards De Soto and screwed his heavily lidded eyes closer together so that they resembled dark slits. The broad forehead furrowed and he tilted his head backwards slightly to stare at the fidgeting man down his long Gallic nose.

Father Bernard was Parisian born with all the hubris and disdain that would have been expected with the strict upbringing he had experienced. The son of a wealthy industrialist, his career path, predetermined within his father's company since birth, had commenced it as planned on his twenty-first birthday, but his later sudden and unexplained declaration to join the priesthood had cost him his relationship with his family. His later secondment to the Vatican had been unusually swift after taking the cloth but he had arrived with the same determination for advancement within the church as his father had expressed for business. Father Bernard stopped staring at the uninvited guest and looked again at the Cardinal as the older man spoke.

"No matter Father," McGeary responded quickly, breaking the stalemate, "Bless you for your efforts and please shut the door as you leave."

Father Bernard took his cue and retreated backwards towards the door, shutting it slowly as he left the room. Not once did his eyes leave the back of De Soto's head in the process.

"So, Dr De Soto, will you please sit," Cardinal McGeary started, pointing to the balloon backed walnut chair resting against the fresco plastered wall to his right. As De Soto sat, McGeary rose from his own more modern executive swivel high-backed tan leather chair and moved to the first large window framed by heavy gilt-rimmed gold velvet curtains. He stood between the wide-open panes and revelled in a sudden stronger breeze that thrust warm air onto his face as he looked out over the rooftops of the Vatican and on to the bustling, choked streets of Rome itself. He paused, considered his first approach and decided to look pensive before turning to face his uninvited guest.

"Will you at least fully introduce yourself?" he started, "Are you a medical doctor?"

De Soto squirmed slightly and started to rise but McGeary again raised his palm, this time as a gesture to remain seated.

"A doctor of Psychiatry," De Soto replied, "My practice is in Lisbon."

"Ah Lisbon!" McGeary expressed with sudden interest, "A city of which I have heard much but have not yet visited. Perhaps soon God willing," he smiled at the still sweating man and realised that an odour was beginning to reach his nostrils. He screwed his nose up, coughed softly and moved further away.

"Your English is very good though Dr De Soto whereas my Portuguese is non-existent. Even my Italian needs considerable work. Did you study in Britain?"

"New York," De Soto replied. "I have dual Portuguese and American citizenship but decided to reside where my mother still lives in Portugal.

"Then may I ask what brings a doctor of Psychiatry from Lisbon to Rome with such haste and alarm?" McGeary replied, raising his silver-white eyebrows as a question. He had already concluded that not all was right with this man. His agitation and clear discomfort was threatening and yet McGeary sensed that threat was not directed to him personally. The man was afraid of that there was no doubt and yet he had seemingly journeyed without packing a bag. His overall appearance clearly showed a lack of preparation, and he had insisted that he be seen despite the usual high degree of security he would have encountered to reach the Cardinal's office. McGeary was intrigued as to what could drive such fear for it was no easy path to take to enter the Vatican, even if invited.

Although McGeary had taken his post at the Vatican only three years previously and leaving his native Irish home in County Cork home to do so, the Cardinal had at once been subject to the traditions and protocol that dominated his daily life, all of which were a world away from the more relaxed environment he knew in Ireland. The transition had been long and challenging and even now, some three years later, McGeary still found matters difficult, especially in any maverick approach to what was demanded. Hence, he knew that unexpected usurpers of that process like Mr De Soto were rare indeed.

"I had a patient that has been coming to me for the last couple of months," De Soto started, breaking the elongated silence and still breathing heavily. He coughed slightly with an annoying tickle in his throat.

"Some water perhaps?" McGeary interrupted, motioning to the unopened bottle and glass on his desk.

"If I may your Eminence, that would be most welcome." De Soto replied and the Cardinal moved towards the bottle and started to unscrew the top. De Soto carried on as he did so.

"My patient was a local rich shipping business magnate, from a long line of previous family owners who have dominated the Portuguese shipping market since the late Middle Ages. RosRem Global is the modern company name," he paused to see if there was a reaction of recognition in McGeary's face. There was not so he continued. "It comes from the surname of my client Mr Rosario and the Portuguese word for shipping, Remessa." De Soto reached out his right hand to receive the glass tumbler that was now partially full of sparkling water. He took two rapid gulps and cradled the glass in his chubby hands.

"I first became involved with the family when I treated his only son a few years ago who had a serious mental disorder made much worse by his constant heroin use. His later schizoaffective diagnosis proved too much for him to handle so he sadly drowned himself. His father came to me afterwards to find out as much as he can about his son but it was clear to me that what was accentuated through drug misuse in his son was also present in a more latent form in the father. By then he was in his sixties with no other children and a widower." Paused and took another sip of water before continuing, "He had countless millions of Euros in the bank but absolutely no happiness in his life and the loss of his son was the last straw. Rapidly he started to crumble and although I prescribed therapy and medicines to help, his downward spiral was out of control." De Soto looked up at the Cardinal who was still watching him deep in thought and leaning against the front of his large mahogany desk. De Soto paused and McGeary nodded in encouragement.

"Go on my son," McGeary said with growing impatience, "I am anxious to know what this is to do with me?"

"During our regular sessions in recent weeks this man started to question something he called his 'legacy'," De Soto continued, "he said he had been tasked on the death of his own father some years previously to be active in an organisation which would dominate his life. He said that his first and only duty from the moment his father died was to maintain his legacy of responsibility towards what he called the '*Votary*'.

"The what?" McGeary replied with instant renewed interest. He recognised the word but wanted to be absolutely sure he had heard the man correctly.

"The Votary," De Soto repeated, "

"Go on," McGeary said again as he moved back around the desk to resume his seat. He needed to sit down; quickly.

"He said that the responsibility he had was too much. That it conflicted with his own faith and belief and with the loss of his son he would not now be able to complete his duties and pass on that same responsibility. He was a broken man with more than he could handle in his life, something that his money could not assist with." De Soto took two further gulps of the water.

"Yesterday he telephoned me and demanded an instant consultation. Something had happened he said. He had been contacted by someone connected to this group called the Votary whose message had sent him over the edge. He kept saying to me over and over again that he was not ready and that it was too soon. He wanted me to come to his yacht that instant and bring more SSRIs."

"What is that?" McGeary interrupted quickly.

"SSRIs – Serotonin Reputake Inhibutors," De Soto answered. "They come in many forms but I would suggest Prozac may be the best known?"

"Drugs in other words," McGeary responded with some disappointment.

"Yes, he was in a desperate state and need an instant hit as he had none left from the last prescription."

"I see," McGeary replied, "please continue."

"I replied I had other patients to see but that I would go to his boat by four that afternoon. He shouted that this would be too late and hung up so I decided to cancel my other appointments and went straight away. It took around forty minutes to arrive at the marina but as I did so, I noted that his crew were exiting the boat and walking along the jetty. I asked if he was still on board and they said that he had given them the rest of the day off and that he wished to remain alone but that he was expecting me. So, I passed the crew and boarded the vessel, calling out his name as I did so. He met me on the stern lounge area and demanded that I enter the main suite cabin where he sat on one side of the room and motioned that I sit opposite." De Soto paused again and shuffled in his seat. McGeary was staring at him intently.

"He said that time was short and that he had a job for me. He insisted that I should immediately travel here, to the Vatican to give you a message." De Soto reached into the inside of his crumpled jacket and extracted a Smartphone which he handed to McGeary after walking the four steps from his chair to the desk. He retreated back to his own chair and waited for a few seconds as McGeary held the phone.

"He was very explicit that only you, Cardinal Donal McGeary should view the video on that phone and that I should bring it to you straight after….." De Soto hesitated.

"Straight after what?" McGeary enquired.

"Perhaps you should view the video and see," De Soto responded.

McGeary placed his thumb on the button to switch the phone on and pressed. The screen lit up with a sea view obviously taken from the deck of a quality motor yacht, as part of the deck the rail of which was also visible. More of immediate interest to the Cardinal though was the run of dark small spots that were diagonally spread over the screen and which only became visible when backlight of the phone was activated. McGeary stared at what looked to be a small blood splatter and then immediately looked up at De Soto.

"Please can you press the video icon on the screen and select the first one in the list?" De Soto offered, saying nothing about the blood spots and so the Cardinal did so.

The screen immediately switched to the face of an elderly looking man with a thick-set tanned face which was heavily rutted with wrinkles. For a man in his sixties, he looked much older than his years. The hair was thinning and combed straight back giving him a pronounce widow's peak. He remained in silence looking at the camera so that McGeary had time to notice the plush interior of the yacht behind him.

"Your Eminence," the man began in deep voiced stuttering English, looking straight into the camera and McGeary flinched as he did not expect the personal nature of what he was viewing, "Please do not blame the good Doctor for his interruption of your busy day. It was vital that he sees you as soon as possible and for you, and indeed he, to understand why this is crucial. In a moment, you will see the importance I place on this message and understand why you must act on my words and I hope you can understand my English sufficiently." The man paused but kept staring straight at the camera which McGeary now realised he must have been holding out in front of him.

"Your Eminence, I am a rich man. I have more money than I can spend and whilst that has given me a life of privilege, it has also cost me very dearly in the loss of my beloved son. I am alone as my dear wife was also taken some years ago and I have no wish to engage myself with any replacement that would enjoy my money more than they would myself. My riches were partly earned myself but the vast majority came to me through inheritance and the handing down of the family business. My family has been wealthy for centuries and for those same years we have been powerful, a power we have shared with other similar families of wealth spread across the globe. This was no accident as all have been party to the same aim, to prepare for and guide the way for he who is to be announced." He took another breath, "De Soto will have told you about my legacy but he knows only part of that task and what it truly means. Over hundreds of years, some will say for far longer than that, those like me have waited and watched. It has always been the case that with the responsibility passing to eldest son upon the death of the father, we have always been in positions of influence in all the main civilised countries and continents. These families of wealth and power have also been leaders of their peoples and facilitators of their economic growth and most were or are very well known, always watching and waiting for the day that we are called upon to protect him." Another pause as the speaker kept his gaze firmly on the camera.

"But you know of this already Cardinal do you not?" The man's stare was piecing and seemed directly to penetrate the Cardinal's own pupils. "You are aware of what we are but perhaps not of who we are? You know we exist and you know our purpose. That is why you have the position you occupy now. As part of the Sodalitium Pianum? Your department is there purely to track him down – to silence him?" McGeary shot a look over to De Soto who sat expressionless, but openly sweating with rivulets of moisture running down his face in the chair before him. He had clearly already viewed the recording.

"So, my dear Cardinal, I am giving you a chance. You see I am not worthy to take on the full expectations of the legacy, I do not believe I ever was. I secretly hoped this would never come to pass and seeing my son intentionally destroy his life, I knew I could never entrust that same legacy on to him. But in any event, I now have no son, indeed I have no-one I can pass on this great responsibility to and I equally have no burning passion now to play my part. When my father told me of what was to come the sense of betrayal of all I thought I knew was too much for me to understand then and now, even years later, I choose not to believe it. I am a man who chooses to deny either truth, yours or his; religion means nothing to me. You should know that time has now run out and the hour of his announcement is near. You know what that will do and you understand what that will cause. The Catholic Church has planned for this for centuries and it will be on your watch Cardinal that all you have feared will become reality. As I speak now his timetable for action has commenced. I have received notification that his mouthpiece to the rapture has been chosen. His instruments of truth have been delivered. I have received my call to duty but I cannot complete it for the fear is too great. My doubt is too severe to be silenced. For this action, for speaking to you in this way I have already betrayed the trust that has been thrust upon me and I have failed all those ancestors before me who were loyal. I am already a dead man for this betrayal but I have nothing to live for in any event. You should know that I speak the truth and to give you this warning but just in case you doubt me, let me give you one further message. I wish you good luck Cardinal for you will need it."

The man in the video looked away and reached to the side table with his free right hand. Peering at the camera again, the large kitchen knife now in his hand was pressed hard against his neck and with a swift sideways motion, he sawed it deep into his own flesh. The action made McGeary jump in his seat and he heard the scream off camera which mixed with the gurgle now coming from the dying man. As blood shot forwards from the gaping wound, the head rolled back and sideways slightly and the hand holding the phone fell to the side. The phone spilled onto the floor and the wooden slats of the cabin ceiling filled the screen until the horrified face of Doctor De Soto appeared from above as he bent down to pick up the camera before it faded to black.

McGeary sat in silence as the video screen paused at the start of the recording again awaiting further action. Finally, he stared again at his guest as De Soto slumped as far back into the chair as he could. After a pause, McGeary forced a slight smile even though inside, he was churning.

"I understand my son, "McGeary said, "I understand your distress as that was a truly awful thing to witness." He looked at the phone before him. "Obviously this is now for me to act upon but can I ask if there is anything else expected of you Doctor? Are you to perform anything more as a request from your late patient?" De Soto shook his head to acknowledge that there was not. "Then I will ask my Secretary, Father Bernard, to ensure you are looked after and rested so that your journey home will be more pleasant that the one you took to get here.

"Thank you, your Eminence, but I must return to Portugal immediately to face the arrest warrant that is no doubt in my name. The crew will have returned to find his body and will have informed the police that I had boarded the boat in their absence. I have nothing to hide but my urgent absence will have generated suspicion. I will need that recording to prove my innocence"

McGeary paused and pondered, rubbing his temple with the forefinger of his right hand. "So, you will say you came to Italy to visit me straight after witnessing the suicide of your client and upon his last order to give me this mobile phone?" McGeary asked sternly.

"I was performing the last wishes of my client but I must still protect myself," De Soto replied, "I cannot see how I can do this without a copy of that recording your Eminence." De Soto stood as the Cardinal did also and walked with him towards the oak doors which McGeary opened for him.

"Father Bernard. Would you please look after Dr De Soto and make him comfortable? Will you arrange for food and perhaps a clean shirt for him and ensure he is transported to the airport once his flight is known?" Father Bernard gave a short nod of acknowledgement and beckoned De Soto to follow him.

"Doctor De Soto. I understand fully what you need from me and will fashion a copy for your immediately whilst you rest. I am afraid the full version cannot be seen by anyone else nor can my name be known. But the unfortunate act itself will be copied for you so that there is no doubt that this was by his own hand. You must promise to still say your panic brought you here just to get away from Lisbon rather than to see anyone in particular and now, having thought it through and with the evidence to present, you are prepared to talk to the authorities. Will that suffice?" De Soto nodded although with a confused look.

"Thank you Doctor. I am yet to fully understand why any of this has to do with me but may I wish you a safe journey home and a pleasant outcome to your troubles upon arrival. I will give you the amended recording very shortly." McGeary closed the office door once more and retreated back to his desk.

Once sat, McGeary crushed the phone tightly between his clasped hands as he placed his elbows on the desk in front of him and started to pray. From that second it all became clear and all his previous pretence of ignorance to the Votary had been well served. The day he had hoped for many years would never occur had arrived and he knew that from this moment, the very existence of all he knew and believed was at stake.

Outside the office, Father Bernard left the now more composed De Soto sat in the small staff cafeteria area on the floor below cradling a steaming black coffee and a tired looking pastry. Checking that no-one was observing, the priest extracted a Smartphone from within the hidden cassock pocket and began to send a text.

'All is completed. Instructions?' the text stated. Father Bernard waited for a few minutes before the reply was received.

'You know what to do,' it read. The priest replaced the phone and went to join De Soto again.

Chapter Two

Same Day. Exeter University Campus, England

Michael Crowe accepted the heavy leather-bound tome from the smiling Professor and dropped his arms slightly as they adjusted to the weight.

"Conrad," Crowe began, "Will you not at least give me an idea what this is about?" he asked shaking his head slightly from side to side.

"Just read Michael," the older man said softly, "just the prologue. I will be interested in what you think?" The older man sat down gingerly in the well-used fireside chair and waited for Crowe to begin.

Crowe looked at the smiling man once more before opening the thick front cover and turning the endpaper over. There was no title page as he expected. No printer's details or author's name, the page simply read, "*Prologue. Spring MDCCLXVII, England*".

Crowe looked up once more as he calculated the year in Roman numerals to be 1767 before turning the naïve title page and started to read the first page of hand-written text.

'Death can be creative in numerous ways and I have seen, experienced and delivered them all.

From the natural earth, death can come by gnawing tooth and ripping claw, or by venomous fang and poisoned sting. I have witnessed elemental death by consuming water or fire alike and by the smothering of viscous earth or the crushing of unforgiving stone. Death has come for so many at the mercy of climatic extremes that suffers hypothermia, dehydration or destruction from the terrifying power of storms onto man.

But it is humanity itself who have mastered the art of death and has wasted no time since the beginning to learn how to kill. I have seen death administered by the blow of a blunted rock or from impalement with the thrust of a sharpened stick. Man has developed and improved his tools to deliver oblivion through the slash of knapped flint and ultimately from the keen-edge of honed metal. I have seen flesh pierced by thrown spear, loosed arrow and aimed lead ball. I have heard the screams from tortures of the body so cruel as to be driven by both perversion and pleasure. Men have been stretched, boiled, roasted, drowned, crushed and crucified to extract truth or deliver punishment. I have seen the savagery of man inflict death on others in the name of their Gods or simply to satisfy their desires or basic needs. Man has killed man for water, for food, for enrichment or for love. The slaughter of thousands has been performed for possessions, for land, for minerals or just for sport. In all its variations, I have participated and sometimes enjoyed them all.

All this history of death I have witnessed and all this catalogue of pain I have undertaken. Death has been my companion, my desire, my duty, my punishment and my right. No-one can equal or contemplate the sheer volume of those I have sent from this world in numbers or method either by design of the ravages of the ages. I have seen generations of soul's spring into life and depart from it within a blink of an eye, their transient lifetime, however short, has for me been just another memory among hundreds of thousands with their death a routine act in a lifetime of the mundane that has been and will forever be my existence.

As for love, I can number thousands and have buried or burned them all. So many women and men of all colours and races have called me lover or husband before the truth exposed the monster they all adored. Their virginal bodies are now mere apparitions of memory. Their one-time fairness of face scarred, corrupted and spoiled by soil or flame. I have loved thousands but of children, I have none and the better for it as I surely would have killed them also as I watched them grow and age beyond their father. Better non-existence to centuries of shame for the actions of the beast that sired them.

I have wandered numerous arid deserts and lush forests, empty plains and windswept beaches. I have sailed untold numbers of angry seas and foaming rivers, climbed so many jagged mountains and rolling hills. I have called so many places home and have joined countless tribes of many peoples. I have been Sumerian, Hebrew, Egyptian and Greek. Amongst many others, Persians, Romans, Saxons and Franks, all have called me brother. I have been Viking,

Norman, Crusader and Saracen. Of all the peoples of the world, few have not been touched by my passing.

I have been called King, Emperor, Chief and Elder. I have been knight, warrior, general and soldier and in gentler times, I have been philosopher, poet, farmer and politician. I have been priest, bishop, Sharman and healer to Pagans, Jews, Hindus, Christians, and numerous other long forgotten and meaningless faiths.

I have created empires, dominated hundreds of thousands ravaging whole continents and destroying them, laying waste to hundreds of years of progress. I have built cities of impressive majesty and happily have stood by and seen them fall. I have been called Saviour, Messiah, Prophet, Patriarch, God and Devil.

I have seen your history as my present and I have witnessed futures arrive as the opposite of my hopes and the despair of man. I have been all things past and can be all things to yet exist. I am the forever man, the constant presence, the life in the shadows always watching, always controlling. I appear in many guises in your stories and I populate your myths and your legends. You have written my life as the actions of many not realising the truth that I have featured in them all.

This will thus be my story, an account of my life. One life that will span that of countless millions more long dead for each of you have but a short time on this Earth. It has taken countless years to create this story and it will take me many further years to document it, to write my history down and through it, describe the ages of man. My recollection is absolute. No-one can rival the memories I now offer. There is no source that can present evidence to counter the facts I state. For I have no equal, no competitor and no threat.

So be under no illusion of who I am. I am the first devised, the first conceived and the first born. I am the beginning of all, the Father of Man and the Son of God, indeed the son of all Gods. I am humanity's creation, its beginning, its far reaching past and its unimaginable future. I am the first name, the first being, the first human, the first man.

I am Adam.'

Michael Crowe read and re-read the last line over and over silently as he stared at the hand-written page before him within the large heavy leather-bound volume resting on his knees. He let out an involuntary blowing of the cheeks as his hazel eyes glanced away from tome and looked at the older man who's nodding head seemed only partially connected to his neck, so vigorously was the movement. The man was smiling through thin lips almost completely masked by the wild grey beard.

"See, I said you would react" the man said as the smile increased revealing irregular discoloured teeth. He reached out and went to lift the book from Crowe's hold with his long and bony, nicotine stained fingers but Crowe moved it away out of his reach to keep hold of it.

"What are your thoughts?" Professor Wilding stated quickly to move the conversation forwards as he sat down again, feeling rebuffed.

"It is bullshit", Crowe said quietly with some distaste. He was sad and disappointed and thought he knew Wilding to be better than this. The long car journey to Exeter University had filled his mind with the possibilities that Wilding was offering him. His email had been excitable and clear in which he had begged Crowe to visit promising a 'historical revelation' and yet all he had produced was a fairy-tale. No, Crowe was not disappointed, he was angry and was beginning to question his own reverence of the Archaeology Professor who had once been his teacher and had then become his close friend for nearly 20 years.

"You want to know my thoughts?" Crowe replied raising his thin brown eyebrows and widening the eyelids so that he presented an expression that bordered between bewilderment, fear and a slight loathing, however unwanted, towards his friend.

"I have known you for many years Conrad and I know you as a man of principled dedication to evidence. 'History is myth without evidence', that is what you made me and all your other students write as the first task on the first day of our studies. Do you remember that? I do. I have never forgotten that creed and have lived by it throughout my career since." Crowe shook his head and looked down at the page again.

"It is a fake." He quickly followed, "Surely you can see this to be total garbage? This is nothing more than an illusion from a bored, eighteenth century, aristocrat; someone with nothing more to do in his dilapidating country pile than spout this crap. A recluse who we both know at best was a particularly unpleasant and cruel individual throughout his disreputable life," Crowe stared hard at Wilding for a reaction. "Surely you are not persuaded that this…" He closed the book on his lap with some force and lifted it towards the older man "This…joke is worthy of your time or more particularly, mine?"

Wilding adjusted his bi-focal spectacles so that they sat more firmly over the pronounced bridge of his wide and rounded nose, gave a pained expression and sat back in the oxblood red leather wing backed chair, rubbing his hands over the already well-worn and scuffed sides. He looked a little crestfallen but steeled himself for the debate to come.

"If it was a simple trick," he started with a growing excitement, "Why continue to produce such a weighty script and hand-write it all? Why bind it in sumptuous leather?" As Wilding spoke, Crowe ran his hands up and down the banded spine which still felt fresh and crisp despite its supposed 250-year age. "Seems excessive for an obviously ridiculous notion? Would you not agree?" Wilding followed, his beaming smile revealing more discoloured teeth than perhaps he should have.

"Who knows what a deranged mind would consider acceptable?" Crowe spluttered, slightly frustrated. "You would try and have me believe that the infamous Earl of Barnsford penned this book to declare he was none other than Adam? As in Adam and Eve? Don't forget Conrad I know this man. You know full well that this is the man I based my dissertation and later biography on, the man I studied for years, his life, his notoriety and the theories of his demise. You now want me to believe that he was a man that had been alive for literally thousands of years? Conrad, this is beneath you!"

Crowe got up from his chair, placed the book heavily upon the desk and walked to the large bay window, staring out into the pouring rain that blew hard against the glass. They were in the ground floor study of Wilding's nineteen-thirty semi-detached house located in a small residential area behind the University of Exeter's grounds. Crowe looked at the depleted birch trees in the road, their leaves almost entirely blown away already leaving their Autumn hues in great piles where the wind had deposited them, with some hanging on to the bitter end in the face of the constant lashing rain. The memories of a short, hot summer were already fading into obscurity.

Conrad Wilding breathed noisily, let out an audible snort and then leant forward in his chair so that the aged leather creaked with the pressure change.

"How long would it take to write that tome would you say?" He tapped the book that was now just within his reach on the desk. "I mean, unless you wrote it consistently and without breaks, how long; a year perhaps... how about two?" He waited for a response from Crowe but none came so he continued, "Even if you wrote every day, would you be able to keep up a constant flow without deviation or mistake? Have you ever gone with a first draft of anything? I know I haven't" Wilding followed spreading his arms to accentuate the fact "and yet there is not one mistake, not one deleted paragraph or redacted sentence. It is like a constant dictation of events without pause or loss of momentum. Would anyone be able to keep up such a huge lie without any indication of being unsure?"

"I only saw the prologue, the first few pages." Crowe interrupted, turning to face the now serious man before him, "I assume then that you have read the whole volume?"

"I have," Wilding responded "All five hundred odd pages in one sitting and I can certainly tell you that it chilled my blood".

"So, what does it recall?" Crowe followed.

"Everything", Wilding paused for dramatic effect, "It is a history of everything, or at least the beginning of everything. Except it is not what we thought we knew, of that we can be very sure!" Wilding got up from the chair and walked towards the end of the room and placed his hand against the free-standing bookcase with a pair of long red drapes that covered it. As he did so, Crowe noticed that his gait was laboured, awkward even. His friend was clearly getting old.

"The history of man in one volume?" Crowe enquired flippantly, "The view of one clearly insane mind as to how Man developed with the author just happening to be the first man from Genesis? It is just so unbelievable!"

"Not one volume no," Wilding followed quietly and pulled the tasselled cord on the side of the free-standing bookcase that operated the curtains. The heavy velvet fabric parted to reveal the bookcase behind and the rows of books hidden within. There were five shelves and each shelf bar the top one held twenty identical leather books across. The top shelf had a hole where the volume on the desk had been previously stored. "The history of man in one hundred volumes, at least a history that has not yet been completed for obvious reasons as the future is yet to happen," Wilding spluttered waving his arm over the rows of books.

Crowe walked slowly towards the bookcase in silence, retrieving the missing book from the desk as he passed and, using the library steps, mounted them to replace it in the space from where it came. He dismounted from the steps and looked hard into Wilding's steel blue eyes.

"Don't tell me you have read them all? He started with suppressed annoyance.

"No. They have been with me only for a couple of days and there has been no time. But I have looked into each one and they follow a straight chronological order."

"Are they all hand written?" Crowe followed.

"Actually no," Wilding shot back. "Those produced in the late Nineteenth Century onwards were typed on the first such machines produced and then increased in quality as typewriters also improved. Those in more recent times were completed using a computer." Crowe looked on in astonishment as the older man gained even more enthusiasm.

"All perfectly flow from one to another despite the change of creation methods and all have been bound in exactly the same leather and indeed, of the same age. The paper used gets increasingly more modern in quality and design but the bindings are entirely the same vintage. The prose is exactly of the same style as the first and each page has been monogrammed at the bottom by hand – even those produced very recently. I have no reason to suggest otherwise to the fact that all of these have been completed by the same hand......
the same person, over the last 250 years."

Crowe began to feel hot and uncomfortable. He listened to what Wilding was saying but found it hard to accept the words. Finally, he started to speak.

"So, you are saying that Barnsford started this project in the eighteenth century and was still writing it a few years ago?" He sounded lost.

"Actually, less than a year ago," Wilding retorted, "The last volume covers the period to the end of last year but does literally end with the words, 'to be continued…he clearly saw the culmination of the last volume as some sort of threshold point"

"So Barnsford is alive now?" Crowe asked, his disbelief now overcome by enquiry, "actually living and breathing as we are." He stared hard at the professor, "If so, then where?"

"That is why you are here Michael," Wilding concluded, "that is why I asked you to drive down here as soon as you were able. That is why I have shown you the books." He was grinning widely, "You see, when they arrived I was not at home. I did not receive them personally. I just returned after lectures and the bookcase was where you see it now. Please do not ask me how anyone got into leave it here, nothing seems to have been taken and I assume burglary was not intended anyway as they left something rather than take anything! All there was with them were two letters, one addressed to me requesting that I ask you to meet with me today and for you to ready the prologue of the first volume. But the books themselves, well they were not for me – they were actually addressed for you." He paused as Crowe's eyebrows both rose in shock, "Whatever you think of Barnsford in the past or now, as we may assume, still in our present, he wants you to know about him for a reason."

"What reason? Crowe asked, the look of shock replaced with a deep expression of concern as he was about to follow with another question before Wilding produced an envelope from his tweed jacket pocket and held out his hand.

"For you Michael," he said. "The second envelope," he smiled as he started to hand it to a bemused looking Crowe. "You were always my best prodigy, the one I have always felt most pride about and more than all of that, you are my dear friend. What you have done in your career in writing and on television has been nothing less than exemplary. You have argued historical fact against all odds and come through with new concepts, theories and discoveries that have both shocked and then converted the doubters. You embrace the unusual and strive for the truth. You are rarely over-awed and always look for the challenge. Even so, I think you may want to sit down to read this." He used his free hand to push his glasses back over the bridge of his nose from where they had just fallen and held out his other hand with the letter within it.

Crowe accepted the letter and made towards the leather chair until recently occupied by his old lecturer. He sat firmly, leaning slightly forwards and fumbled with the sealed corner of the envelope fold. The envelope was clearly modern, of good quality velum and across the back was written, in hand, 'To be opened by the addressee only'. Crowe paused in the opening and looked to the front again to make sure that it did indeed state 'Michael Crowe Esquire,' before resuming. The wax seal broke with little effort and Crowe cursed that he had not taken more attention to the seal design before breaking it. He extracted the folded paper within, of which there were six sheets, all written double-sided. He placed the empty envelope on the side arm of the chair and unfolded the paper before settling back and started to read the handwriting style that was already so familiar.

"My dear Michael,

I do hope I can call you Michael as I feel we know each other very well. You produced a very fine book on one of my previous personas which, although I must say was not exactly one hundred percent accurate, was well enough informed to represent the person I was at that time. Goodness but I have a lot to answer for do I not…! Perhaps when we meet, should you wish to do so, I can correct some of the assumptions and conclusions you made, particularly about my death which as you will now understand were, well shall we say, overstated?

Professor Wilding will have already acquainted you with what I sent him. No doubt the old rogue will have already started to read my books and will thus already have an idea of what I am writing to you about but I doubt even he will have managed all one hundred volumes and I hope you have at least read the Prologue page as I requested?

If you are wondering why I have chosen you Michael it is for two reasons. Firstly, I have a certain admiration for your work notwithstanding because you produced that excellent book and secondly due to your certain 'celebrity' status as a television history presenter. What I am about to reveal is the most extraordinary history lesson ever known, one that will completely change everything the human race ever considered to be fact, or indeed even myth. You are absolutely the right person to deliver this revelation and you are indeed the best placed to offer this alternative account so the world will know the truth.

But I warn you Michael, this will destroy the established order. It has the capability to bring down world religions and philosophies resulting in potential chaos and death. It is a cruel yet exciting challenge I am setting you but I am sure you, as a student of history, would want to seek truth, however harmful that truth may be. Some will try to stop you and most will try to ridicule you. Some may even try to kill you in the name of religious fanaticism as they see their hallowed halls of belief come crashing down around them. All this you must resist if you are to follow this path.

So, your first challenge is to read on. Finish this letter and then decide but I hope and trust you will be my spokesman. I sincerely hope you will not let me down. So here goes:

Yes, I am Adam. I was the first born, the first Man. I was the Prototype.

In basic terms, I am a creation of science. An incredibly old science brought to this earth many, many years ago by others extremely advanced in genetic evolution. I was genetically engineered from a combination of indigenous earth-based early humanoid DNA as the host, spliced with genetic material taken from those that created me. For some years there have been those who believed that man is the product of alien intervention and they were dismissed as crackpots and conspiracy theorists. Cited as fanciful science fiction and yet, as you are about to discover, the truth can indeed be stranger than fiction!

As the prototype, I was engineered to be the most functional and most developed of what was seen as the perfect 'man' from inception. That required me to have vastly more DNA from the Creators than that introduced from the humanoid. The Creators wanted the finished product, something to represent what an improved 'Human' would look like. Not quite made in their image but very close shall we say? Thus, not only was I built to show what could be achieved with relative speed through science alone, I was also built to be resistant to ageing, bodily harm and indeed, death. Therefore, through the Creators technology and own infinite longevity, I am indeed, at least in human lifespan terms……immortal.

But I am not some sort of cyborg or android as you may think or as modern science-fiction would describe. I am entirely organic and made of flesh. I sweat and I eat and drink as much as the next man. Do not worry, I am not immortal through the drinking of blood and only surfacing at night – I leave those fantasies to the movies. All bodily functions exist in me just as much as they do so in you. What changes in me is how I am constructed at the atomic level and the fact that in terms of my DNA, I am over 90% Creator.

When you consider that the DNA difference between a chimpanzee and a human is only 4%, you will understand how such small differences can produce something so varied. So, imagine the difference between normal human DNA and myself - you will therefore understand what I can achieve is so infinitely more.

The secret is that my cells automatically regenerate to counter the threats from ageing or illness. Should I suffer injury, I will immediately heal. The speed at which my body can adapt is breathtakingly fast so that at the first indication of a cut for instance, the skin cells will change, mutate if you will, into a resistant layer so much stronger than the instrument inflicting the harm to prevent further damage. A cutting blade will advance only a short distance into me before the transition is completed and the metal can pierce me no further. A bullet fired will enter my body only a short distance before the force of the cell mutation will stop it completely and indeed, push it back out. Thus, I was created to always remain as first designed.

From my continued existence, the Creators would always have a model version of what they then hoped to create though natural processes and structured evolution as part of their experimentation. Having established their target being, the challenge was then to see what could be achieved with less and less direct intervention in the process. Perhaps given enough time, natural evolution of the humanoid species without intervention may well have produced something similar or recognisable to what is accepted today to be Human, but I am afraid we will never know.

I do think it is ironic that as the scientific world today debates the moral issues of genetically modified crops and cloning that they as yet remain unaware that every living human on this planet is already the result of such technology applied so very far into the past! Anyway, I digress.

Once they had perfected me, the Creators set about producing other versions, both male and female where, slowly, less of their DNA was used and more Humanoid DNA introduced. This less reliance on Creator DNA removed the immortality gene that had been placed within me. They were looking to achieve the ultimate mix that offered speed in design to reach a certain point where natural evolution could then take over though normal reproduction to result in the

Human race being modelled similar to my own prototype. But they equally wanted the natural life cycle to be maintained.

In fairness, results were mixed and the female version fared less well than the male. For whatever reason, the early directly engineered female hybrids were sickly and incomplete. They all died. The creators chose to model a second prototype similar to myself in DNA mix but entirely female. She was called Eve and like me, she was designed to be immortal but without a built-in ability to reproduce and give birth as the Creators decided that would not be comparable with everlasting life. Her ability to adapt to her status and exist in the way that pleased the Creators was compromised as a result. She rebelled and was eventually destroyed. Instead, the creators relied completely on the natural processes to produce females as the early hybrid males were able to reproduce successfully with the indigenous females that existed outside of the experimental population so that the offspring could then be assisted sufficiently to produce healthy female examples. Once this was completed after much experimentation over thousands of years and satisfied with the results, the Creators moved more to the specific development of the mind and to develop the skills man would need for the transition from simple hunter-gatherer to farmers and builders. Once that process had created a basic self-governing society in tribal units, the Creators decided to observe the development of Man without further direct involvement, however they did interfere with one or two exceptions where they wished to test the

*resilience of their creations to specific natural
disasters or introduced pestilence for instance.*

*So around ten thousand years ago and apart from
myself, other early make experimental versions lived
extremely long lives, many of them being the named
'Patriarchs' or similar in early scriptures and other
religious texts from all over the world, not just the
Hebrew versions, and being revered for their wisdom
and ability. But even though they lived far longer than
the scriptures actually suggested, they all died
eventually as the more humanoid heritage overcame
that taken from the Creators themselves. So now only I
am left from that time of creation.*

*So you see Michael, both those that argue the Creation
and those that stand for evolution and science, are
correct – but only in part. Life did indeed start
naturally on the earth and everything you know about
pre-history up to the intervention of the Creators is
correct. But everything you know or believe since that
time is wrong. Every religion is based on a false
history. Every creed is based on a lie. Perhaps now
you will understand the gravity of what this disclosure
will bring.*

*So, you are now asking yourself that if this is all true,
why do the Creators need me, Adam, to remain on the
earth? What purpose do I serve now?*

*Well it was always the intention of the Creators for
their prototype to remain, to endure and to be present
throughout history as the common denominator or the*

constant presence to man's development. I was intended to be, and have been, the guiding light, the guru, the teacher and the protector. Thus, I have performed many roles and been many things and many people. If you scan my books, you will understand just who I have actually been, both known and unknown to recorded history. I am the man behind many myths and many legends. My influence on this world has been absolute; sometimes for reason, sometimes for experimentation and sometimes for simple pleasure. The Creators looked on from above but I was always their creature and their facilitator.

Michael, you now have an unenviable challenge – how much of this should you make known? Can you only disclose some without revealing all? Indeed, you will be asking yourself further as to why I should want any of this disclosed at all?

When I started to record my history, and by definition the history of Man, 250 years ago, I calculated it would take at least that period to write it all down and prepare for the big reveal after doing so. I chose to use handwritten script at the time as I could not trust the simpler minds of the age taking it all in if being printed by others. I continued until technology allowed me to use machines to produce what could have only previously be written by hand. I finished the task only months ago and now the time is right.

The Creators want this. They feel humanity has evolved sufficiently to take it all in – to understand. They want to be accepted, revered even, as the

architects of Man. Not worshiped you understand.
There is no God complex here as there is no God – at
least not in the way that religion presents such a deity.
They have decided that evolution has produced
humanity to a point where it can co-exist with the
Creators, learn from them and through them embark
on the next great challenges for mankind.

But as the doubters will, and indeed have, debunked
any such attempts to do so in the recent past, they
want the transition to knowledge to be structured,
validated and accepted.

You are to be my chosen spokesman Michael. You are
to be the one that wakes the world up to the truth and,
when the time is right and they are ready to accept it,
you are the one who will engineer that big reveal, the
day when both Adam and the Creators are seen by all.

Meet with me. Talk this through and let us develop a
strategy together? Professor Wilding has a number for
you to call and arrange the meeting. I will expect your
call.

'Adam'

The chime of the Edwardian bracket clock on the
mantelpiece to Crowe's right broke the silence as he
finished reading the letter. He silently re-folded the
sheets and carefully placed them back into the
envelope, placing it on the side of the chair and resting
his arm on top of it. Thinking deeply, he realised that

his life had changed completely since the last hour was struck on that clock, changed beyond all measure.

"I remain to be convinced," Crowe started thoughtfully. "It is all just so fantastic a concept, so huge in the implications it would bring if true. I fully accept that to write one hundred books, largely by hand of this magnitude does indeed give weight to the theory being offered here but….." he was lost for words so Wilding interrupted.

"What did the letter say?" he said with enthusiasm prompting Crowe to hand him the envelope. The professor eagerly took out the pages and started reading, his eyebrows dancing up and down as he reacted to each revelation. Crowe remained silent as the older man read, intertwining his fingers into loose knots as he writhed them. He looked up as Wilding finished the letter and let his arm drop to his side, the hand still holding the sheets.

"You asked for evidence, we must have evidence" he started, "Well all we can search now is what is written in these books and match what we can from other documented sources. But essentially, we can only know by meeting him as suggested, or at least you can. He has not asked for me to accompany you." Wilding sounded disappointed as indeed he was. "Will you go?"

"Do I seriously have a choice?" Crowe followed with genuine acceptance of his fate and Wilding remained tight lipped to confirm that he did not.

Chapter Three

Same day, Whitehall, London

From the breast pocket of his immaculate one hundred percent wool Saville Row suit, Sir Donald Avery felt the vibration of his phone resonate against his body and heard the muffled "You're gonna need a bigger boat" text notification sound off. He had chosen the immortal line from 'Jaws' as the ironic herald of impending doom deliberately. His position as Cabinet Secretary meant that no news delivered in this method was ever good news, but an unexpected text was always especially a good reason to raise the hackles.

Effortlessly, he reached into the inside breast pocket of the jacket and retrieved the mobile. It was his job-issued Smartphone with all the usual capabilities. An essential piece of kit as it would seem no politician or member of the Civil Service could function without one now. He winced at the number of times he had seen Members of Parliament openly sending and receiving texts during debates and woe betide anyone crass enough to take their phone off vibrate. Whether they were genuinely responding to constituents, sending up-to-the-minute tweets or texting their mistresses was no suitable reason in his eyes for being so rude as to ignore the debate that was underway. During Prime Minister's questions at noon every Wednesday that Parliament was in session was the worst in Avery's opinion and if his assumed impartiality to any political party was ever revoked, he would be having his say about the matter.

His personal phone remained silent in his other jacket pocket but without even glancing at the small screen before him, he really wished it had been his private phone that had buzzed.

The one word framed by bubble on the bright white background screen made him shiver.

'Garden'

Avery knew instantly that the one message he hoped he would not have to receive in his lifetime was staring at him and he suddenly felt huge sadness envelope his body. His duty was clear and immediately he started to type the one-word reply,

'Eden'

He pressed send and replaced the phone into the jacket pocket. He got up from his revolving executive chair resting his hand lightly on the arm for an elongated few seconds before moving to the window and stared hard at the busy London street below with its heady mix of buses and cars, delivery vehicles and taxis. The pavement, as usual, was a bustling mix of office workers, tourists and others busy to be somewhere. To his right and down the street a short distance, the discarded banners and signs from an anti-Asian government protest group moved on as that country's head of state had passed, provided more detritus for the pavement fillers to dodge around as they made their daily commute.

Avery sighed, walked back to his cluttered desk and pressed the intercom to his Personal Assistant.

"Yes, Sir Donald?" Elizabeth Moon responded in her normal inquisitive but charming manner.

"Call the Prime Minister and convene a COBRA meeting." Avery barked.

"Sir, what shall I…" Elizabeth started.

"Just do it." Avery interrupted and released his finger from the intercom.

He slumped back into his chair and stared at the double photo frame on the desk in front of him. The smiling face of his plain but pleasant wife Amelia looked back at him. In the photo next to hers, two young men, both standing proud in military dress stared back. The black ribbon stretched over the corner of their photo shouted the loss that one too many tours in Afghanistan had cost his family. To lose one son to a sniper's bullet in Helmand had been devastating enough but to lose the second only months later to an I.E.D has destroyed both Avery and his wife. The matching black ribbon over the corner of Amelia's photo proved the pain to have been too much for her and the overdose of sleeping tablets she had taken days after the news had been received had stripped the one last hold on the hope of any form of normal life Avery had.

He stared at the frame with one word forming his thoughts, 'Garden'.

Reaching for his pen he wrote in large capital letters over the pink blotter before him that same word. For extra flourish, he underlined it twice before placing the pen back in its holder and opening the small drawer on his right, he extracted a key taped to the underside of the drawer. He placed the key in the lock of the larger one at the base of the pedestal and opening the drawer, withdrew the ageing Chinese pistol that his father had smuggled back from the Korean War in 1951. He cradled the cold metal in his hands, stroking it. If he chose, in a few seconds he could be dead. The last sensation he would feel would be the bitter metallic taste of gun oil as the barrel rested against his tongue. All it would take would be just one sharp pull on the trigger and then…nothing. Would he be with his lost loved ones again? Only a belief in an afterlife would offer that joy but at least he would be far removed from what he must now do. It would be such an easy option to take, death before duty. It was a question that had haunted him for months now. Suicide would be the simple solution, the avoidance of pain and the inevitable destruction of friendships and reputation that his duty would demand.

A knock on the office door before it slowly started to open made him flinch so he quickly replaced the pistol in the drawer and looked up. Perhaps he should wait a while longer before using it he thought.

"Sir, I have contacted the Prime Minister's office and he wants to know why the meeting should be called. What shall I tell him please?" Elizabeth had spent her whole career in the service. Straight from secretarial college she had progressed from the old typing pool to supervisor and then personal secretary before being hand-picked by Avery to be his P.A. She was 52, looked young for her age and pleasant rather than attractive with bottle-auburn bobbed hair that needed refreshment as grey roots were clearly spreading from her central parting. Still single, she had much more than just respect within her for Avery but knew he was still damaged by his recent losses so kept her distance. His tone on the intercom had been short and unpleasant and that had upset her.

Avery sensed the sense of displeasure and instantly smiled at her.

"Elizabeth, I am sorry for being an arse," he started, "just some bad news I am afraid, nothing you have done I assure you." She smiled back and looked downwards slightly. "Tell the Prime Minister that perhaps we should speak privately first and then, if he deemed it necessary, we can call COBRA together afterwards."

"Of course, sir," Elizabeth responded with a sense of relief, "Shall I tell him you are going to number 10?"

"No," he decided quickly. "Ask him if he would not mind meeting me at the club. I will arrange a private room for supper." She nodded as she retreated from the office. "Oh, and Elizabeth?" she turned and smiled, "Thank you." As she closed the door she beamed widely. Elizabeth felt that perhaps soon, she should make her move after all.

Avery looked down at the word he had written in large letters on the blotter and immediately ripped it from the holder, screwing it up as tightly as he could and throwing it in the metal bin under the table. So, the time had come. The legacy of duty handed down to him from his father as all Avery patriarchs had done for generations had now fallen upon him. His was the chosen generation and as both his sons had gone before him, at least he was around to complete that duty. He could no longer pass on the responsibility so it was right and just, he concluded, that the time was now.

The Votary demanded total obedience. Avery knew that instructions would now come frequently as they would to all other members equally placed in positions of authority in many of the major countries of the world. He knew that the Votary had developed their network over many centuries, adapting to political change and trying to maintain influence without actually having the responsibility of the top office of state. Making sure that the power behind the throne always rested within them and through the use of the legacies of past fortunes, vast inherited wealth, large profits from new and established industries and even benefiting from the proceeds of organised and systematic crime, the Votary held the real power. Their existence and secrecy was ancient, predating more well-known brotherhoods like the Masons and now they acted as a counterfoil to them. Their aims had evolved over the centuries, spawning other, cruel short-lived sects that saw carnal pleasure and racial hatred as the main crux of their beliefs but as these imposter groups rose and fell, the Votary remained, ever observant, always ready.

Avery knew that, like himself, the word Garden would have been communicated by text, email or voice in numerous different languages to the eleven other senior disciples, men of influence. Like him, all would be now planning their designated first task, their first action to prepare each State to be ready to receive the announcement.

Andrew Stubbs would be his first action although this was equally from Avery's sense of deep friendship as much as it was from his duty as a member of the Votary. The Prime Minister would need to know why Avery had to immediately act. He will have to understand that, despite their past association, why he was letting him down. He knew that Stubbs would see it that way, that what Avery was doing would shock him to the core. Avery had no doubt that what he would need to speak to Stubbs about had the potential to destroy their friendship. But he had no choice and he knew it.

Such a change was about to envelop this country, he thought, indeed the whole world was going to change but at least he and his fellow Votary members would no longer need to exist only in the shadows, denying their true purpose and eventual destiny. The time for their establishment subterfuge was over. There was a new dawn approaching and Avery would be one of the new Disciples; one of the chosen in the age of the new world, the Age of Adam.

Chapter Four

Same day, Downing Street, London

Prime Minister Andrew Stubbs was confused as he held the secure phone to his right ear. He listened intently to Elizabeth as she spoke on the other end of the line but he was not taking it all in.

"Thank you, Elizabeth. But for clarity, is he asking for a full Cabinet or just COBRA at this stage?"

"Either if need be Prime Minister but first he would like you to join him for supper at the club this evening if you can to explain. Will eight o'clock sit well with you?"

"So, it is not urgent then. Why on earth would Avery call for a COBRA meeting and then change his mind and ask to speak to me first?" Stubbs asked.

"I am sorry Prime Minister, I am confused also," Elizabeth added, "I am not sure he is one hundred percent himself at the moment."

Stubbs consulted his diary. "I will have to move the Justice Secretary but yes, please tell him I will meet him there at eight but cannot be a long night as I am flying to Paris tomorrow. Thank you Elizabeth." He replaced the handset on the phone cradle and placed both hands on the desk before him, flexing and extending his fingers back and forth. He sensed movement and looked up to see the Home Secretary standing in her usual elegance but with a concerned look on her face. Although the office door was open, Stubbs could not remember seeing or hearing her enter so he jumped slightly when she spoke.

"Prime Minister?" Anne Melton asked slowly, "There was no response. "Prime Minister? Andrew?".

"I am sorry Anne," he blurted, "I was miles away... Can this wait?"

Anne Melton looked slightly indignant. "We have a booked appointment but I can postpone if it suits?"

"That would be better Anne. Would you mind? Can you liaise with my team and let me know?"

"Yes Prime Minister," Melton confirmed as she made for the door, "of course." She stopped in her tracks and turned awkwardly so that rather too revealing split in her pencil skirt exposed more thigh than was necessary, "I am sorry Andrew but I forgot to give you this." She moved over to the desk and handed Stubbs a small package. "New phone, I assume from Procurement," she said briskly, "Nothing arrived yet for me but this was in your tray outside." She looked awkward as she waited for Stubbs to respond.

"Thank you Anne," Stubbs said, taking the package from her, "I was not expecting it." She smiled thinly and made for the door again, this time exiting without further comment.

As the Home Secretary shut the door, Stubbs slumped back in his chair. He felt a cold sweat down his back yet his cheeks felt flushed. His mind was unable to focus on what he had been told. Avery would never normally bluster his way into the schedule. And why would he ask for a COBRA meeting only to back-track minutes later? Was there a crisis or not? Half-way through the Parliament, the economy turning into positive territory despite the world fall in oil price, capital expenditure on new transport links nearing completion, the Opposition in leadership disarray, Stubbs had every reason to believe that a third term was his for the taking so anything unexpected would be most unwelcome indeed! Stubbs obviously knew the catalogue of grief that had befallen Avery would have been crushing for him but they had dined and joked only yesterday, reminiscing about their Eton and Oxford days together. Stubbs thought he knew the man thoroughly but this request was out of the ordinary.

A remote buzzing distracted Stubbs from his inward thoughts and for a moment he could not decide where the sound was coming from. He listened to try and pin-point it and after a short period, he realised that it was coming from the package the Home Secretary had just given him. As the sound continued unabated, the package was visibly moving over the polished mahogany as if inhabited by a swarm of angry bees. Stubbs' current state of mind did not contemplate that there could be a sinister motive behind the buzzing and under different circumstances his first move would have been to exit from the office and call a security guard but somehow he was enthusiastic to look into it himself.

Stubbs quickly tore the end of the bubble-bag instantly realising that could have been a stupid action to take but dismissed his folly with equal speed and retrieved the now shaking box from the envelope. Clearly the phone within was ringing but in vibration mode only. He opened the box as quickly as he could and took out the vibrating phone with a brief shock when he saw it was not the upgraded replacement he expected it to be but instead it was practically a vintage Nokia, similar to one he had used almost 15 years ago. Recovering quickly from his confusion, he put the old mobile to his ear and pressed the call acceptance button.

"Yes?" He asked quietly.

"Prime Minister Stubbs?" a voice enquired.

"It is," Stubbs responded, "how did you contact me? How did this phone get here?"

"Prime Minister, please be advised that at this time, most leaders of all G20 countries are being contacted in a similar fashion. The U.K. is not alone." Stubbs furrowed his eyebrows and looked to make sure no-one else had entered the room.

"Go on," he said gingerly.

"Prime Minister, forgive this interruption and the secrecy around but what I have to say requires your complete attention and I cannot risk using known numbers. At the end of the conversation, if you will allow me to continue, I hope you will understand."

"Go on," Stubbs said slowly, clearly intrigued.

"I represent the Council of World Faiths of which I suspect you have heard of."

"I have," Stubbs confirmed.

"Specifically, on that forum, I represent the Church of Rome with the full authorisation and blessing on the Holy Father himself. On his behalf, I regret to advise you that we are aware of a great threat to our civilisation, something that will affect every nation, every faith and every person on this planet. We expect there to be widespread violence, reaction and death and we want to forewarn you that this will happen." The speaker paused.

"Before I consider anything further," Stubbs replied, "and before I ask you to prove who you are and who you represent. You said nearly all the G20 countries leaders are being contacted. Why nearly all?"

"Prime Minister, you need to be aware that there are certain forces within the Governments of all G20 countries which mean we cannot be exactly sure of the security involved. The wrong conversation can be a further threat to what is coming. We suspect that there may be some powerful leaders amongst the G20 countries who are part of the conspiracy we wish to combat. As we now suspect that the catalyst for this problem may occur in the UK, we feel it is imperative that you are made aware."

"You are saying that there are seditious forces at work within all Governments? On what basis?" Stubbs was both intrigued and slightly angry. Who was this person calling on a secret phone predicting world chaos? It was too surreal and he needed a name.

"I am not going to continue this conversation without your name." the statement was clear.

"My name is Cardinal Donal McGeary. You may not remember me but I had the honour of being at the reception held in your honour when you visited the Holy Father here at the Vatican eighteen months ago."

"Actually, I do remember you," Stubbs stated as he put the soft Irish lilt he was hearing to a half-recalled face.

"Prime Minister, who I am is not important but I hope you will take the knowledge that you do recognise me and therefore take what I have to say with importance for I cannot express strongly enough that you should prepare for the chaos that will come from within so that lives can be spared. We ask this in the name of all faiths and on behalf of all peoples. The forces of the Antichrist have been activated and his followers are on the move."

"Antichrist? Now look!" Stubbs demanded, "Indeed I can accept you for who you are and I can even overlook the bizarre way you have chosen to contact me." He paused as his mind raced, "But if this is some sort of sick joke I can tell you now that I am not laughing! A positively ancient mobile phone that arrives out of the blue and immediately rings with a Cardinal calling from the Vatican warning of the apocalypse......It is so cheesy to actually be anything more than a prank and this Government; this Prime Minister has much better things to do than fall for that."

"I assure you Prime Minister that this is no joke. Mrs Melton, the Home Secretary is well known to us and has been involved in the inter-faith gatherings she organised to assist recent divisions in the United Kingdom, to support our calls for tolerance and healing. It was a personal favour to me that she agreed to pass the package to you so that there would not be any unnecessary checks made. Please do not remonstrate with her after this call as I would not have asked her had it not been of the most serious nature. Being a minister of faith, I am prone to speak in Biblical terms but the threat is real. I apologise for the subterfuge but I........."

"No, enough!" Stubbs shouted with anger. "I am calling the Home Secretary to explain this phone and then I am going to get the security services to track you down and arrest you." Stubbs exploded.

"Prime Minister," McGeary followed, "I have not hidden my number."

Stubbs looked at the screen to see that the caller ID was fully working and the number was displayed.

"By all means do whatever checks you need to do but please keep hold of this telephone and call me back as soon as you feel comfortable. All I would ask at this time is that you refrain from speaking to any other G20 leaders until you have done so. I will look forward to hearing from you."

The phone went dead as McGeary ended the call and Stubbs was left staring at the small basic green screen. He sat upright and turned on the laptop. Selecting Google, he put in Cardinal Donal McGeary and pressed enter. The results steamed back with several articles and photos showing a smiling white-haired man in his sixties with the latest entry noting his appointment as Cardinal with special responsibilities appointed to the Holy See. Stubbs recognised the face and despite the unusual method of communication, something was telling him that the face he was looking at had been the man on the phone

Stubbs decided to forgo the taking Anne Melton to task and concentrated on the perceived threat of which he had just been warned. He got out of the chair and moved slowly to the portrait of Queen Elizabeth hanging over the fireplace.

"Antichrist," he murmured quietly to himself and chuckled as he looked into the eyes of the smiling monarch. A wry and wide grin spread across his face. He glanced around at the phone on the desk and moved towards it, picking it up and placing the phone in his jacket pocket, he was going to need this, he though with relish.

Chapter Five

Later that evening, Pall Mall, London

The cold front that had swept over Britain from the
Atlantic to the North Sea was now retreating south east
towards France taking the excitement of the sharp,
sudden deluges that had plagued the capital all day
away into the night. As darkness fell, London settled
down to a gentle drizzle and light winds that followed
the weather system so that it was necessary for the
large fireplace to be fully occupied by an active and
warming log fire that crackled and spit with the recent
addition of copious seasoned wood.

Avery admired the intricate carving that made up the
mahogany surround with its representation of African
animals superbly crafted into the grain, rising
majestically to a tall mantle shelf and a huge Regency
bevelled mirrored frame above. The whole room at the
Southern Empire Club just off Pall Mall positively
shrieked Victorian elegance and design. Revivalist
rococo architraves and pelmets in the same rich red
mahogany dominated the small space that the private
room offered. The faint lingering smell of aromatic
shag tobacco and long smoked cheroots permeated the
soft furnishings of Stuart tartan and plush reds and
golds. The room looked like, as indeed it was,
unchanged for over one hundred years. To cap off the
longing for past glories, each wall had a single huge
oil painting of famous battles from the Zulu war of
1879 and the later Boer conflict at the turn of the

nineteenth century. Although dedicated to lofty empire days and conquests south of the Equator, it was clearly the South African sphere that dominated, especially in the Natal room as the room where Avery now sat quietly had been named. Such feats of bravery for Queen and Country Avery thought and wondered what would be said of his duty to the Votary in later years. Would his portrait hang in some future temple to the faithful? He looked around the room which apart from the small dining table immaculately laid out with place setting for two only, this private supper room he had ordered had two Stuart tartan high back armchairs facing the fireplace with an accompanying wine table each and a long table with warming plates and other dinner accessories along its length which rested against the back wall.

Stubbs was late. It was now almost a quarter past eight and Avery, above all other considerations, was hungry. When the door finally opened a few minutes later to reveal an apologetic and slightly flustered Prime Minister rushing towards him with his arm extended, Avery was at least pleased that supper would now not be too long.

"Prime Minister," Avery said as he stood and took the extended palm to shake it.

"Andrew, please Donald," Stubbs replied, "We are off-duty now." Avery allowed himself a wry smile as if he was anything at all, he was never going to be off-duty for some time.

"Shall we order straight away?" Stubbs followed, making his way to the table and sitting down. He picked up the small brass bell with the mahogany colour wooden handle and shook it. Avery joined him at the table and took his seat to face him. Stubbs was busy reading the beautifully encased Menu as the door opened again and the waiter entered. Stubbs' eyes were flitting up and down repeatedly as if he was anxious about the choice he was making.

"Got to try and eat more healthily," Stubbs said. "This Head of State business is far too easy to put on the pounds!" Avery smiled but stayed silent.

"The pate', and then the salmon for me I think!" Stubbs announced gleefully and replaced the menu on the table looking at Avery and expecting an instant response. Avery took his time before deciding but then also discarded the menu and looked at the waiter who seemed at least in his late seventies with his sergeant stripes on his immaculate white jacket a testament to past service, but who now stood ramrod straight and precise at his side.

"The soup and the beef please," he stated, "and the Domaine de Chassorney Saint Romain 'Sous Roche' I think for me," he requested quoting off the wine list without reading it and shifting his gaze to Stubbs. "Prime Minister?"

"No, I am having fish anyway but I think just water tonight, bearing in mind I am on the early flight tomorrow." The waiter marched off and closed the door silently behind him.

"So Donald," Stubbs began," Why the urgency? We only saw each other, when was it?"

"A week ago last Saturday", Avery responded, "at the Chequers reception for the Dutch Prime Minister."

"Of course." Stubbs continued. "Now Donald, indulge me. Why did you ask me to meet you this evening? I had to cancel the Justice Secretary to be here and you know how much of a prick he can be when he is disappointed!" Stubbs sat back in his chair and relaxed a little.

"Andrew," Avery started, "We have known each other for many years. Prep school, Harrow, Oxford and over twenty years now at Westminster. Our families have been associated for centuries and despite all that we have shared in the past, I have always maintained my neutrality and remain unbiased politically in my latest position."

"Never in question Donald," Stubbs responded with an expression that sensed concern. He suddenly looked up and into Avery's eyes. "You are not going to resign, are you?" He asked quickly.

"I need time to concentrate on something away from the Cabinet Office," Avery replied. "Whether I resign or simply take extended leave will be up to you Andrew but it will happen either way." The door opened and the waiter re-entered with the wine for Avery and water for Stubbs. As he served and poured both, Stubbs and Avery remained quiet. Avery tasted the red wine, confirmed that it was good and the waiter again left the room.

"What has happened?" Stubbs asked, "What is so pressing that you need to do this Donald?"

"We both come from titled ancestry Andrew." Avery began, "We both live in inherited estates with pictures of our dead ancestors on the walls as is expected of us. We both can boast long and dutiful family service throughout history to this country and what it stands for."

"Of course, I know all that to be true Donald but I am still unsure what you are getting at?" Stubbs interrupted.

"We both exist, as our families did before us, from a sense of duty to this country," Donald paused and stared fully into Stubbs face. "But I have been tasked with something else that I must follow without question and place the success of this instruction above all others. Please understand Andrew, I am telling you this out of a duty to our friendship and the good of the country for we need to prepare the people for their own protection and you should be aware of what will come."

Stubbs sat silently for a few moments but the expression changed on his face from concern to sudden realisation. Inside, his excitement grew. Avery slowly sipped from his wine glass and maintained his gaze upon the Prime Minister.

"Donald, forgive me." Stubbs said sharply. "It has been a very strange day thus far and I have had my fair share of doom mongers yet I am getting a sense of foreboding from your comments. What exactly are you saying? Is there a threat to this country that I do not know about? If so, what is it?"

The door opened and once again the waiter entered, this time with the chicken liver pate' for Stubbs and the tomato and basil soup for Avery. He elegantly served both and retrieved the bread basket from the side table before leaving. Nothing was said until the door was closed.

"Very soon, there will be an announcement, a revelation that will dominate the news, and social media across the world," Avery started. "This shock will cause disbelief and arguments at all levels from the local pub to the highest levels of Government. Most of all it will question the faiths of millions. No country will be immune, no religion spared. It will expose the crackpots and the academics alike. It will question everything we know or thought we knew to be historical fact. Whilst no harm is intended in any way, we will need to be prepared for possible civil unrest and potentially racial and ethnic divides causing violence and even death on our streets. Violence is not promoted or wanted in any way from what will be revealed but human nature and fear may simply make that inevitable. As your friend, I do not want you to be seen as just another reactionary to the chaos but to be at the forefront of the change and be prepared." Avery paused as Stubbs raised his hand and was about to speak.

"Let me finish Andrew," Avery quickly said to stop Stubbs before he started. "You and I are friends Prime Minister so I can say this to you with passion but you should know that the heads of government in all major industrial nations will be receiving the same warning at this time. This is a global event that will need a unified, worldwide response and Britain can be instrumental in achieving that. We need to prepare for the Rapture."

Avery stopped, selected a large piece of rustic granary from the basket and proceeded to spoon soup into his mouth. Stubbs left the pate' untouched and sat rigid in his chair. He considered his reaction after some moments before responding.

"What the fuck do you mean the Rapture?" He exploded, "Are you threatening this country?" Stubbs continued sternly. "I am not sure I fully understand what this is about but if you are dirty in any way Avery I will have you arrested, despite our friendship. Is it the Russians? The Chinese?"

"Ha!" Avery blurted, "If only it was a simple as basic treachery. No Prime Minister, it is not the actions of any foreign power although I suspect each will react in the same way as you have done. This is, as I said, a worldwide phenomenon, a global event. Only those that have kept the secret for centuries, the best among us, have waited for this time to arrive. The time when he will be revealed to us all and to save us from ourselves."

Stubbs suddenly stood away from the table and pointed at Avery. "Rapture?," he shouted and pointed at the slightly shocked Avery, "You are mad Donald if you think I am going to be threatened by some sort of happy-clappy, born again philosophy you suddenly seem to have acquired! First, I get a bizarre call from a deranged priest predicting the end of the world and now you? I thought I knew you but this shit has nothing to do with me or my Government. You have always been my friend Avery but you are testing me here and I will not have it! Resign if you must. Destroy yourself if you think you need to, but do not assume for one moment that you will drag me or the British people down with you. I have no time for this or indeed for you. Give me your intention about your position in the morning but only to me, is that clear? Donald, I can only pray that the severe losses you have suffered these past years have not addled your brain and I cannot imagine that depth of despair you have had to deal with but some wacky, self-imagined, second-coming complex is not the way, of that I assure you. I want your letter of resignation in the morning and only to me. One word to the press or online and I will destroy your name utterly, of that you can be assured. Goodnight!"

Avery slowly continued with his soup and broke a further piece of bread as the infuriated Prime Minister of Great Britain stormed from the room, slamming the door behind him. So, the Church had already begun its assault, Avery thought. Pray if you must Andrew, but you will come to understand soon. Avery took a sip of wine and eagerly awaited the arrival of the beef. His first act was completed and he felt strangely relieved.

Stubbs swore to himself as the slammed door echoed behind him and the startled waiter moved to let him pass. His security detail was waiting to escort him at the end of the corridor and with raised eyebrows, they quickly followed after Stubbs as he stormed past heading for the front door where his car was waiting. He got straight into the back seat and sat fuming as the security man got in as well, sitting next to Stubbs.

"Number 10 Parkinson," Stubbs barked to the driver and turned to the window looking out onto the damp pavements and huddled pedestrians as they drove. He put his hand into his jacket pocket and cradled the mobile phone within. First McGeary and now Avery he thought. One a man he had met only once and the other he had known for most of his life yet both with the same warning on the same day. But Avery had been…different, not the man Stubbs thought he knew and he was troubled by what he had seen in him. Perhaps, just perhaps he would have to think the unthinkable at last. Perhaps the time had indeed come. Stubbs reached into the other pocket of his suit jacket and retrieved his official phone. He pushed the quick dial for the office and put the phone to his ear.

"Cancel Paris," he said firmly as the call was answered. "Say I have been taken unwell." He hung upon and replaced the phone as the car reached Trafalgar Square and turned down into Whitehall. The opportunity he had sought for many years was happening. He leaned over slightly to the security man next to him.

"Would you mind awfully walking from here?" he said before turning to Parkinson, the driver, "Stop here will you?" The car came to a gradual stop and the man beside Stubbs got out without complaint. As he shut the door, Stubbs turned to Parkinson again.

"I have changed my mind. I need a little stress relief. Usual place but call him as we travel. Ask what he has in nice and fresh." Stubbs settled back and smiled.

Chapter Six

Summer evening 1791

Augustus Percival, Third Earl of Barnsford, at least that was the name that Adam had created for himself to live the life of an English aristocrat for the past thirty years, dismounted from the grey mare and handed the reins to the young African stable boy who had run quickly to meet him when he arrived. The horse whinnied and tossed her head in anticipation of water and feed following the four-hour ride, most of it at a punishing pace from the overnight coaching inn where Barnsford had stayed the night before. The boy struggled to get control of the skittish animal and glanced nervously towards Barnsford as he did so. The Earl looked on with a hard stare and then a thin smile which the boy could not read sufficiently to give comfort. He had seen that look before and made an instant mental note to sleep away from the stable block when darkness fell, somewhere he could feel safe when the screaming started as he knew it surely would. He gave a small bow and quickly led the still nervous animal away towards the stables and some sort of safety.

Adam stood and watched him go before turning to look at the manor house before him. He marvelled at the stone façade with its architectural nods to classical grandeur and the many tall, multi-planed glass windows. The whole building screamed elegance and above all else, wealth and Adam looked with a satisfied grin that in this life at least, he had gained some semblance of security and safety, even respect. There was something about the persona of a titled English country gentleman that he thoroughly enjoyed, something comforting, relaxing even. Perhaps for so few times in his long, long life, he was living now in some place he could really call a home. A house though that served more than a simple residence for it also had its secrets and Adam remembered that another chapter in that silenced use was due.

The 'Third Earl' removed his oilskin cloak which had left him humid and sweating beneath and placed it over his left arm. He ached for a change of clothes as the dank summer drizzle delivered by a rush of a southern wind provided the worst possible combination of heat and rain. His clothes stank of sweat, both his and that of the horse from the ride and his normally luscious black hair was damp, matted and tangled under his brushed wool black tri-corn hat. He checked his gold fob watch extracted from his waistcoat pocket and grunted as he realised that his much-needed bath would have to be curtailed in length for his guests would start to arrive to less than two hours. He marched swiftly towards the main doors and as he entered the ornate hallway with the extravagant marble staircase sweeping majestically up to the galleried landing, he shouted for the water to be made ready. There was much to be done if he was to be ready on time and he did not want to be keeping his guests waiting simply due to the lack of sufficient boiled water. He cursed when there was no immediate reply. And stormed towards the staircase in an irritated mood.

Adam walked briskly up the polished stairs and along the landing to the left passing the closed doors to the rooms where his guests would reside for the night. As he reached the junction with the corridor that led to his right and down the private back stairs to the entertainment area his irritation was bettered by the inner demon and he smiled broadly, his darting eyes peering into the gloom of the unlit space before him. In only a few hours' time, after he and his guests had feasted, the games would begin.

A sudden small light in the gloom from the distant dark hallway and then the rapidly expanding illumination of a moving single candle on the walls and ceiling of the corridor announced the arrival of the man he wanted to see. Acting also as Adam's personal valet, Kamal Atakan had been with Adam for all of the years he had acted as the Earl of Barnsford and for several years previously. Of Albanian descent, Kamal's journey from that rugged and impoverished land had been arduous and not without danger. Orphaned young by a division of passing Janissary soldiers of the Ottoman Empire, he witnessed the cruel massacre of his family, neighbours and friends amongst the northern Geg tribe that made up his village, his parents amongst them. Fleeing into the rugged mountain passes of northern Albania with the screams of his family echoing though the jagged valleys, Kamal had made his way, tired and hungry over several weeks to the shores of Lake Scutari before stealing a small rowing boat to cross the water and into neighbouring Montenegro. He followed the direction of the setting sun each day, taking food from remote farmhouses and always hiding at the sound of footsteps or horses until he reached the coast at Ulcinj. Facing daily abuse whilst begging on the streets of that dangerous port, Kamal finally gained the courage to conceal himself upon a small cargo xebec that had taken shelter in the port during a vicious swell. He hid amongst the barrels of Greek wine and bales of wool the ship had picked up from Corfu only the day before and tried to sleep, hoping that the ship would leave port before he was discovered. He did not care at that point as to which destination the ship was bound, just as long as it was outside of the control of the hated Turks.

As dawn broke the next morning and after a night of fretful bouts of snatched sleep, Kamal took his chance to peek up over the barrels before him. He knew that the vessel had left port with the earlier tide and had started out into the Adriatic which, to his relief, had not been too rough. But now as the sun fully started to soar over the mountains to his right and the Dalmatian islands started to appear, he started to feel queasy and knew at some point, he would succumb. As he peered over the barrels his heart sank as the first person he saw was a fine Turkish nobleman who was looking straight at him smiling. The man approached Kamal and beckoned him to come out as he smiled with perfect white teeth that seemed to reflect the already strong morning sunlight. Kamal did as he was asked for he had no other choice but to approach the stranger but he was rewarded with kindness and a willingness of the man to explain that he had purchased the ship in the port in return for direct passage to Venice. He was the only passenger and was eager to hear Kamal's story.

Adam, dressed in his finest satirical elegance as a Turkish Governor living as Lazari Beg instantly saw the potential that the young Kamal offered and being without a manservant having fled the Ottoman judiciary's persecution of his inability to age, accepted Kamal as his body servant and allowed him to stay in his cabin until they reached Venice. For many months they travelling across Italy, the Alps and France, until finally the pair docked at Southampton with Adam now dressed as, and taking the mantle of, an English Aristocrat. Since that first day, Kamal had stayed with him ever since and now, over fifty years later, his loyalty to his never aging master was absolute and unquestionable.

Adam held out his oilskin cape to Kamal, the manservant's once midnight black hair as Adam had found him on that ship so many years ago now grey and lank. As he approached Adam barked his question. "Did you hear me shout for my water?" he asked sternly. "Where are the servants?" he followed.

"I did sir," Kamal replied, "and as usual on nights of the gathering, they have been discharged from their duties and banished from the house. So, I will get that bath for you immediately. Will there be the usual number this evening?" he asked, raising his thick eyebrows, wild and grey.

"Yes. Are the women here?" Adam responded curtly, "all of them?"

"They are sir," Kamal confirmed, "There are seven in all. Two are local as only five could be supplied in time directly from London and I know five alone would not be enough."

"Damn!" Adam exploded with widened eyes, "How local? You know we never seek our cattle from the nearest markets." He turned and paced towards his private rooms with Kamal scuttling behind and trying the fold the cape under his arm with one hand. "Next time, make sure you are better prepared to make up the shortfall from villages further away, do I make myself clear Kamal!"

"Yes sir," Kamal offered weakly, "It will not happen again."

"Make sure it does not else I take your daughter to make up the numbers next time!" Adam shouted and slammed the door to his room behind him leaving the trembling Kamal alone in the candle-lit hallway. As he watched his master retreat into the room, Kamal mouthed a curse under his breath and raised a scowl on his face. There was much he could be thankful for from the man who have saved him as a child but had made him a slave for the rest of his life to this day. But Kamal had long since ceased to revere the man who refused to age and had also not remained afraid of him. Kamal had asked Adam many times why his youth never changed yet even the truth he could not believe.

He was sure that one day, Adam's death would be his to see, perhaps to take. Whatever sorcery sat behind his eternal youth, Kamal knew that a greater power must exist to deny him everlasting life. All he had to do was discover it.

Three hours later the huddle of wealthy men sat silently in the darkened room, staring as each of the gagged and weeping women were led out one by one by Kamal and forced to stand, naked and shivering on the small platform against the back, damp stained wall.

Adam appeared from the door to the right that was opened slowly and walked past the line of terrified women, pausing by each and taking furtive glances to the seated audience of salivating judges, politicians and land owners. He turned to face them.

"Gentlemen, as members of the Hades Society, let us now partake of the rites of our order!" The assembled men cheered and raised tankards. "You know the rules….. There are no rules!" Adam shouted, "But woe betide any of you who blab of what we do for the purge of your person will be a thousand times more painful than what you intend for these poor wretches!" he pointed to the whimpering women behind him.

Adam moved towards the men and walked behind the semi-circle of chairs. "Gentlemen, please proceed." He barked and watched as each man, politicians, judges and other erstwhile worthies enthusiastically got up from their chairs and made their choice.

In the still night air within the wood behind the main house, the stable boy started to hear the screams and placed both hands over his ears to try and drown out the noise. He began to weep and shake until he could take the sounds no more and started to run deeper into the woods, trying to get as far away as possible from what he could hear. He ran at full pelt through the trees and the darkness as he had done so many times before but this time, he would keep on running.

Chapter Seven

Evening, September 17th, Present Day, the Vatican Rome.

De Soto finished his coffee and all that remained of his pastry were a few flakes on the small gold-rimmed plate with the papal motif in the middle. He was feeling more relaxed that his message had been successfully delivered and yet the vision in his head of Rosario slicing deep into his own throat whilst he watched in horror and filming the whole act just for effect would not leave his mind. All his years of experience with mental trauma and yet that had taken him completely and utterly by surprise, an unexpected act of savagery. De Soto knew Rosario was depressed, perhaps one of the worse cases he had seen and self-harm was always going to be a risk in such cases but the determined resolve of it all, this was what he simply could not fathom.

He heard the scrape of a chair leg to his left and saw the approaching shape of Father Bernard. He was holding a brown paper package and was smiling as he made his way past the other tables to where De Soto was sat.

"Did you enjoy your coffee Doctor?" Father Bernard asked as he stood beside De Soto but did not sit down and carried on speaking before De Soto could answer. "I apologise this has taken so long but I sent out for a shirt for you as his Eminence requested. It says XXL as the size which I hope will suffice." He handed the plastic wrapped shirt to De Soto who took it. It was plain pale blue, lighter in tone than the stained one he was still wearing.

"I am sure that will be perfectly acceptable, thank you" De Soto replied, "and my copy of the recording?" he asked.

"On this," Bernard replied holding a small USB stick which he also gave to the man who still remained seated. Father Bernard placed the memory stick on the table and De Soto picked it up.

"Thank you," De Soto said, "Where can I plug this in to view it?"

"Not necessary Doctor, it only shows the final seconds of that unfortunate man's life. It will suffice completely to show your innocence," Bernard responded with a half-smile, "You have my word."

De Soto felt uneasy but the expression on the priest's face shouted that nothing more would be gained by pressing the point and in any event, if the USB stick was not enough, he would have no choice but to include the Cardinal's name and he knew that was not going to be an option as far as McGeary was concerned. He concluded that there was no chance of that being risked so he chose to accept the situation as it was presented.

Standing, De Soto started to look around. "Where can I change?" he asked.

"Of course." Bernard responded, "Probably best not here in the restaurant so please follow me and I will guide you to the toilets. I am sure they will suffice." The priest started to walk towards the double doors that allowed an exit from the café and into a marbled hallway beyond. De Soto followed him in silence as they walked the length of the corridor and turned right at the end, following the small sign and to where the toilets were located opposite the door to the fire escape. Father Bernard went first into the toilet and De Soto followed him. The priest scanned the room before turning to De Soto.

"Will one of the cubicles suffice?" Father Bernard asked, pointing to the two open cubicles to the right as they entered. "I shall wait outside for you."

"Thank you," De Soto followed and started to make his way towards the first cubicle as the Priest turned away from him. As the fat man reached the door of the first cubicle, Father Bernard launched himself strongly into the man's back, knocking the wind out of him and pushing his weighty bulk forcibly against the cubicle door which crashed open inwards on it hinges and smashed against the dividing wall with the next. De Soto's weight continued to propel him forwards with greater force and his shins cracked against the bowl of the toilet making him howl with the pain as it jarred up his legs. Seizing the opportunity, the priest punched the fat man hard in the right kidney twice and as he arched with the searing pain in his side, Bernard held the back of De Soto's head with both hands and smashed it into the porcelain cistern. De Soto went as limp as a rag-doll and became instantly unconscious. Taking advantage of the man's flaccid weight now bending over the bowl, the priest shifted his head and forced it downwards into the toilet so that the water covered his face. Father Bernard held it there with all his strength for as long as he could and continuously operated the flush so that the bowl filled without draining past the unconscious man's head. He held the position until the laboured breathing of the drowning man became shallow and then stopped. He was grateful for De Soto's unconscious state for although he was a fit man, the priest would have had a challenge on his hands to restrain him if fully awake. Now as pure dead weight, Father Bernard could not move him very much at all and he sighed with the effort. He withdrew from the cubicle and reached for his mobile phone from his cassock pocket, starting to type a text,

'It is done. West wing, first floor restrooms. Use the fire escape and come now.'

He received the response only a few seconds later and left the corpse of De Soto where it lay as he exited from the toilet and stood guard by the outside door. There was no going back now, he thought and he rubbed the suddenly aching knuckles of his right hand. His instruction had been clear. De Soto had to be silenced and his duty had been carried out. Now he had one more task to complete. He retrieved the phone

again and scanned the contacts list before selecting
one and ringing the number. It answered after six rings
and a low male voice stated simply, "Oui?"

Bernard spoke in French to the man on the other end
of the phone. "The meeting has been called for
tomorrow night. The rendezvous is not decided but
will be known soon. I will send you the co-ordinates
when I have them. The Cardinal leaves this evening on
a scheduled flight. Make it look like another act of
terrorism as discussed but make sure you get the
timing right." Bernard stopped talking and awaited the
response.

"Understood," the man growled and hung up.

Five minutes later two men dressed as paramedics
entered from the fire escape door and nodded to the
priest, one was pushing a wheelchair.

"In there," the priest pointed to the toilet. "Be as quick
as you can and I will stand at the end of the corridor to
deter anyone who comes." He started to walk away
from the two men as they entered the toilet door. "The
river," Father Bernard said after them. "Put him in it –
downstream and outside of the city!"

As one decision to cancel a Paris flight had been taken
by the British Prime Minister, another flight to the
same city was taxiing ready for take-off at the
Leonardo da Vinci airport at Fiumicino, Rome.
McGeary sat back in his Air Italia business class seat
and mouthed the same small prayer for a safe flight as

he did every time he flew, something which he totally detested.

He whispered into his clutched hands. "*My Holy Angel Guardian, ask the Lord to bless the journey which I undertake, that it may profit the health of my soul and my body; that I may reach its end, and that, returning safe and sound, I may remain in good health. Do thou guard, guide and preserve us, Amen.*"

He settled back in the knowledge that he needed the words of his prayer to ring true now more than ever before. The calls had been made and the invitations given. The warnings had been passed on, giving the meeting additional gravitas and so he was not surprised that all had agreed to attend with him despite the short notice. The aircraft stopped taxiing and the engines were being pushed to full throttle as he started to put his mobile phone on flight mode. Just before successfully doing so a message came through which he selected immediately, it was from Father Bernard.

'Terrible news your Eminence. De Soto is dead. Found in the Tiber. How terrible that he should also take his own life so soon after witnessing the same act of another. Is there anything you wish me to do?'

McGeary did not bother to reply but closed the text facility and completed the aircraft mode requirement. He shut his eyes and now prayed for the man whose visit had changed his immediate purpose entirely.

Chapter Eight

Late evening of September 17ᵗʰ, Present Day, Exeter, England

Crowe knew there was no choice and that he would have to meet the man who was claiming such an unimaginable heritage. But the seeds of doubt remained strong within him and he needed further comfort.

"Let us assume, just for one moment, that this is all truth," he started, looking towards the professor. "If this man is indeed the first human, if we can really call him human in any event, then as he says, this revelation, however preposterous, is world shattering."

"I can only…..," the professor started to speak but was muted by Crowe speaking louder to interrupt.

"But if this is one huge, well thought out and developed joke," Crowe spat, "then anyone purporting to represent this as truth will be ridiculed to the point of being professionally destroyed for ever. We need proof and the word of one man – even these 100 alternative history books mean nothing without it." He waved his arm in the direction of the bookcase as he delivered the final sentence.

"I can only agree" Wilding followed successfully this time, "Adam speaks wisely that his words, if indeed truth, would mean the end of world order as we know it. The great religions would be neutered, accepted philosophy challenged, history debunked and politics influenced by blind faith destroyed. I have spent many hours since receiving these books debating with myself what a future world would look like should what they contain be accepted as truth. Thus we, as academics and investigators of history, have a crucial decision to make – most of all, is the truth worth what would come afterwards?" Wilding suddenly felt his seventy-four years fully and sought the rail of the library steps as a support to regain his balance.

"Sit down Conrad" Crowe said quickly, getting up from his chair and offering his arm to the Professor to guide him back to it. As Wilding sat down and rested fully into the back of the ageing leather, Crowe pulled the desk chair towards himself, spun it around and sat down, leaning forward with his elbows on his knees and his hands clasped as if in prayer.

"Okay," he started. "Let us start with the assumption that he is who he says he is and I am going to meet Adam. In fact, let's just call him Adam for ease of reference although I really need to be persuaded here!" Crowe turned on the seat swivel and pointed at the bookshelf containing the 100 volumes, "Let's assume that Adam has been alive since the inception of Man, is indeed the product of alien genetic engineering with a sub-human variant, has lived for thousands of years; let us say for all recorded human history. Has lived many lives during that time, some with historical significance we know of and many we do not. He does not age, does not become ill and can cheat death." He paused and waited for Wilding's acknowledgement but received only a thoughtful nod in response.

"Then we can assume, without birth or the normal life as an infant or growing child, or indeed as elder in any of his numerous personas, he must have literally just appeared in any given community as a grown man and subsequently disappeared without years of ageing in-between. In ancient times, he would have thus seemed extraordinary, a magician or wizard, at the very least, someone of special significance. He would have risked much through the fear of less-developed minds who would have equated his abilities as evil, something to be feared. Therefore, he would have most likely travelled widely, staying in each area only for a short time before his lack of ageing became too noticeable. Do you agree?" Crowe looked once more for a response from his friend.

"I concur," Wilding replied. "The volume I read completely, the first volume, centres entirely on his creation and the various experiments being conducted by the Creators themselves. It explains their influence in various parts of the world, providing their knowledge to assist their hybrid products of their experiments to assume the abilities to farm and become less reliant on hunter-gathering, how to build etcetera, but ends with Adam starting his own solo journey into the world. I suggest between us we study further volumes to gain a better understanding." Wilding started to rise but Crowe raised an open palm to stop him.

"In good time," he said sharply, "yes we should read as much as we are able from the books. If nothing else, we need to find the flaw, assuming one exists, that exposes Adam as a fraud. Part of me hopes we do as then our choice is much easier! But understanding the man will require extensive research and if no such flaw exists, then I for one will want to be absolutely convinced beyond all doubt that he is genuine. There is no way that my reputation and career, or yours for that matter, should be destroyed by a charlatan with some unknown grievance with the world that requires its destruction on the basis of a lie. I understand why he has chosen me to be his mouthpiece but at the end of the day, I am only a historian and television presenter. I am not a world leader or senior politician – I have no clout."

"I think that is his point," Professor Wilding responded," with you being the person to front this, it first becomes a hypothesis, then a statement of perceived truth from the evidence you present on the television. Social media will pick up the chatter the programme creates and it will go viral very quickly, expanding and increasing in depth by other academics offering counter views and arguments. If such a world leader or politician were to first announce it, then the headlines created would be more about politics and personal ambition or intent. Adam is playing cleverly here into the power of Twitter and the like, letting the people control the argument and through that, creating followers in huge numbers to carry the day. The 'Adamists' perhaps?" Wilding smiled broadly.

"Ha! Adamists! With you and I the chief Prophets?" Crowe spat. "How very appealing." Crowe got up again and started to pace the room.

"So, Adam is constantly on the move spending only a number of years as each person he becomes before moving on. He would have to be fluent in many languages to do so…" Crowe paused as Wilding interrupted.

"Perhaps." Wilding suggested, "'much of the first volume offers similarities to Genesis and the early books of the Old Testament with references to what we can be believe was written, or at least handed down verbally before being recorded at the time. He mentions Eve…"

"As he does in that letter," Crowe interrupted.

"Indeed. And he also mentions division by language, think Tower of Babel for example and other impositions by the 'Creators' which mirrors those actions by 'God' upon man in the earliest years by way of education or punishment. But can we assume Adam is Caucasian in appearance? With all the colours of humanity to choose from and as clearly the Creators were active in various parts of the globe, what will he look like? Also, if we assume he has no means of changing appearance like some sort of chameleon, will he not have taken at least perhaps an olive hue if his history is to mirror where the Bible, for instance, is centred geographically? I am assuming also that this would have been around the ancient city of Ur?" Wilding raised his bushy greying eyebrows in a questioning manner, reverting to his lecturing past.

"Why not Negroid, Chinese or perhaps from Central America?" Crowe suggested, "Although I agree that Adam was most likely modelled based on the region of the world in which the Creators first engaged in their work. So, would Adam have to be fluent in all languages of his travels if he did not criss-cross continents? Perhaps not, he may have limited his travels to areas of similar language, perhaps learning linguistic differences as he went. Who knows, he may have even influenced much of language still in existence today?" Now Crowe raised his own, thinner eyebrows awaiting acknowledgement.

"Actually Michael, I think he may have travelled more widely than you think!" Wilding reached for a folder on the floor between the seat and the hearth and opened it. "After reading the first volume, and I do suggest you do so also, Adam refers to how his travels would ultimately influence the wider world and that would be his purpose. I am sure if we read the earlier volumes between us we will find such references but before doing so, I took the liberty of researching the similarities between the great world religions at the creation stage and the results are quite....intriguing."

"Go on" Crowe said with interest.

"May I read verbatim?" Wilding continued clearing his throat before starting to read his research.

"It is somewhat difficult to fathom that even though ancient cultures of wide geographical spread are most likely not to have had any contact with each other, their individual religious structures, their legends, stories, and most significant gods in ancient mythology show remarkably similar traits from each culture to culture.

We see in every culture there are very similar patterns and other indicators which encompass their individual specific beliefs. For instance, such patterns will include the existence of not a single god as such, but multiple god-like deities who interact with people in all aspects of their daily lives. There will be the creation itself by a supernatural being who influences existence of all who follow. Other deities born or created from the first, plus a supernatural explanation for the creation of the earth and particularly, the human species are also common to all. There are also strong indications of a relationship between the created humans and their creator 'God' requiring worship and in many cases, sacrifice." Wilding paused and looked up at Crowe. "The next bit I think is particularly thought provoking", as he resumed to read the work before him.

"There are also multiple references to a figure known as the 'Dying and Reviving God', who is often a powerful entity himself, and who is killed or dies naturally and yet will revive and, you will like this bit especially Michael," Wilding said looking up, "for our particular interest, comes back to life for the good of his people. This entity is given many names and is recorded as Tammuz in Mesopotamia, Osiris in Egypt, Krishna in India, the Maize God in Mesoamerica, Bacchus in Rome, Attis in Greece and of course, Jesus Christ." Wilding stopped as Crowe interrupted his flow.

"So, could the ancient scribes have reflected on this ability to be resurrected as an explanation for an inability to die... in other words, immortality?" He offered. "You are suggesting that Adam was, or at least could have been any or all of these myths – or at least he was the origin of them all for word of mouth and later recording of his story with changes made to reflect the area of the world that each religion grew? The Chinese whispers of theology perhaps?" Crowe summarised.

"It is a synopsis worth exploring," Wilding suggested, "And I suspect the volumes may offer some references to suggest it is reasonable. There are other references which we may wish to consider also," Wilding looked up before continuing and Crowe nodded approval.

"The Phoenician myth of Baal, the great god who dies and returns to life to battle the god Yamm and his chaos and who was apparently already ancient as far back as 2750 BCE, back when the city of Tyre was founded according to Herodotus for example. Similarly, the Greek story of the dying and reviving god Adonis which derives from around 600 BCE was a version from earlier Phoenician tales based on Tammuz, tales that were borrowed by the Sumerians and also later by the Persians in the famous Descent of

Innana myth. So you see, stories are recycled, adapted and changed to fit a new people, belief or civilisation. In times of simple word of mouth or basic scribes recording these stories, the opportunity to simply re-write a different version of the same tale is overpowering.

This theme of life-after-death and life coming from death and, of course, the judgement after death, gained greatest prominence in early Christianity and in the figure of Jesus, the anointed son of God whose death was an act of sacrifice to redeem humanity. This was most likely drawn from earlier belief systems and influenced the understanding of the later scribes who would write the books which make up the Bible.

The religion of Christianity made standard a belief in an afterlife. But the early Christians were simply following in the footsteps of the Egyptians, the Sumerians, the Phoenicians, the Greeks, and the Romans all of whom had their own stylised rituals for the worship of their gods. Judaism or any of the older 'pagan' religions, served the same purpose as the rituals once practiced in worship of the Egyptian goddess Hathor over five thousand years ago. All suggest that human beings are told that they are not alone in their struggles. The religions of the ancient world provided answers to people's questions about life and death and Adam is, if we are to believe him, the one being upon whom the world's great religions who have developed their teachings based upon the 'Son of God' who suffers for them and supports them in their lives." Wilding paused for breath and awaited Crowe to respond.

"But Christ was two thousand years ago where as some of the other ancient deities we know of are twice or three times as far back than that if not more?" Crowe sounded quizzical, "not sure that computes if Adam is the origin of all?"

"We only have ancient scriptures to base this on – some of which were written many years after the events they describe and by men still ignorant of relatively basic science. Who is to say that the draw of an enigmatic traveller in Roman Judea two thousand odd years ago did not evoke similarities of more ancient stories and were adapted accordingly? Take any street magician in modern times, particularly those seemingly able to bear superhuman extremes in full view of the public, or those able to perform seemingly impossible illusions in the name of so called magic. Are these not examples of something if performed in ancient times with no scientific explanation to be miracles? I would think it the easy option to describe such feats as the actions of gods." Wilding finished with flourish and with strength of conviction.

"You know," Crowe started, "if true, this will destroy not just established religious thinking but the deeply held personal beliefs of millions. Who are we to sweep away the innermost thoughts of the devout? Do we have that power or that right?"

"I am sure we will find that despite all we may say or anything Adam may do to prove he is who he says he is will not be enough to change the beliefs of many." He paused, "Perhaps all that would be achieved will be the strengthening of those with no faith. In any event, even if Adam is proved to be the architect of all world religions by nature of his existence alone, will that only destroy the history of religion but not the basis of faith? Will the argument not shift from if the Creators made man, who made the Creators?"

"That is a fair point Conrad," Crowe considered, "People will want to believe in faith because they *need* that ability to believe in something bigger than all of us. But you cannot deny that there would still be a backlash against the structure of established religion, the rules by which the traditions of faith have been impressed upon the people for countless centuries. How will they accept that all they have been taught is factually wrong? Will they not seek someone to blame?"

"I am sure Adam will have prepared the way for such hurdles and will have a suitable answer," Wilding suggested softly.

Crowe remained silent and stared at the older man. He widened his eyes, raised his eyebrows and exhaled strongly. "You already believe him," Crowe half shouted with effortless realisation, "You already accept Adam for what he says and who he is. You agree that he is the founding being for all world myths that mention the dying and reviving God. You believe he is Krishna, Baal, Osiris, Jesus and others. You accept that ancient scriptures are all bastardised forms of the same story and that all religions are based on the same creation, being the manipulation of the human species through genetic engineering and that Adam is the immortal prototype. Professor Conrad Wilding, the renowned scholar and leading academic of the past is putting his name to the alternative history to dwarf all established philosophic thinking and recorded thought. Is that truly your position Conrad?" Crowe was flushed in the face as he had now realised that Wilding was already convinced.

"Part of me wants to remain sceptical," Wilding started, "but I have to say, what Adam is offering does explain much. I suggest we organise some food and spend the rest of this evening being re-educated Hand me volume two would you?"

Crowe was lost for words and robotically mounted the library steps once more and extracted the first two volumes. He gave volume two to Wilding and took the other to the desk before him.

Neither made any move to organise food.

Chapter Nine

Later that evening, September 17th, Present day, Exeter, England.

Crowe looked up from the volume he was reading to see Wilding had quietly fallen asleep in the large wing-backed chair. It was hot and the electric bar fire was on full. Crowe considered it extremely odd that despite a perfectly useable fireplace behind it that Wilding insisted on his trusty old electric appliance. Indeed, Crowe was sure it was already old when he was a student himself and he first visited the Professor's house over 20 years previously.

Volume two of the one hundred volumes that comprised Adam's work lay open about a quarter of the way through on Wildings lap. His glasses were dangerously close to falling off the old man's nose and his head was starting to loll about in his slumber. Crowe considered for perhaps the first time that his friend was clearly in the autumn of his life and for that he was genuinely sorry. Had the ravages of time clouded his judgement to accept the writings of Adam purely on face value? Crowe sincerely wished not.

He turned to look again at volume one before him on the desk which he had managed to read through to about a third of its volume of pages. All that he wanted to know about the early days of man, the first days of Adam, had been clearly plotted in the measured, detailed and flowing script. As a writer, Adam had considerable skill, very descriptive and engaging, writing almost as a novel in its own right. He described his feelings as well as his actions. His own desire to learn and grow, to acquire new skills and improve was apparent in his prose and in many ways; Crowe was beginning to respect the author. Clearly the Creators had produced the body prototype as a blank canvas before filling the mind with incredible amounts of information in a relatively short period of time and Crowe surmised that something similar had been deployed in various locations over the world with at the same time to create the new farming and animal husbandry outlook from that of simple hunter-gatherer. He concluded that this would explain at lot of the issues around the agricultural revolution of around ten thousand years ago where all the evidence suggests a worldwide withdrawal of reliance on hunting and a new science almost in the cultivation of crops. That was the question that plagued historians. The evidence that this happened was quite clear but the almost simultaneous event, at least in terms of relatively short periods of years, of it happening in all the main population centres around the world, civilisations that could not possibly have communicated, was an enduring enigma. Was he really looking at the answer to that mystery?

He was tired now and hungry. The food never materialised and looking at his watch, he realised that at thirteen minutes past ten, it was getting too late to eat much anyway. He resolved that the research needed fresh eyes and a full stomach to and decided it was time to leave. As Crowe pushed his chair back from the desk it scraped past the small Indian rug and onto the floorboards, making then squeak. The sound was enough for Wilding to jump and, taking a few seconds to realise where he was, he composed himself and sat upright. He saw Crowe moving across the room.

"How did you do?" he asked, making Crowe pause.

"Well let's just say it is either a very well thought out piece of science fiction by a master of his craft or you and I have a lot to talk about and decide." Crowe said and continued towards the bookcase, mounting the library steps but then stopped mid-way and turned.

"It has just struck me. Who else knows about these books Conrad?" He asked quickly. "How did they arrive?"

"By courier," Wilding replied, "The bookcase and curtains arrived at the same time"

"Private courier or a national company?"

"Private. At least I assume so as the van did not have any livery on it. Why do you ask?" Wilding sounded concerned with the last question.

"I see. So it was the complete package and not just the books themselves?" Crowe asked as Wilding nodded, "Did the courier leave a card or anything?" Crowe continued, completely ignoring the older man's question.

"Well actually I was quite late answering the door and they had already posted a 'sorry we missed you' card and they were standing by the back of the van when I opened the door and shouted after them."

"They?" Crowe asked with a frown, "more than one?"

"Yes, three of them. One more smartly dressed and two who eventually did all the lifting and carrying."

"Unusual for a courier to come so mob-handed," Crowe followed, "The card...do you still have it?"

"Yes, I think so. On the shelf by the telephone in the hall," Wilding said as he started to rise, "shall I get it".

"No, you stay put and leave it to me", Crowe stated firmly and left the room, walking into the gloomy hallway that, like Wilding's study, had not seen fresh paint for decades. He moved a pile of receipts to find the card tucked beneath them and turned it over. All it stated was a hand-written mobile number and a simple 'Sorry we missed you' message. Crowe sighed as he realised it was a generic cheap shop-bought card and not a bespoke printed business card version. The number was legible though so he placed the card into his top jacket pocket and started to walk back into the study.

"Right, I have it," he announced as he re-entered. "Just a number handwritten on a cheap card so Adam didn't want anything registered through a national company. Took a chance with his work of 250 years going missing though by using an unregistered service. Odd."

"Can I see that please?" Wilding asked quickly, holding out his hand. Crowe gave him the card and watched as Wilding fished about in his inside jacket pocket for a battered wallet he subsequently produced. Taking out a folded piece of paper he examined the card and the letter he now held, his eyes darting from one to another. "Oh, dear God!" He exclaimed.

"Possibly a poor turn of phrase given the circumstances," Crowe quipped.

"It was him." Wilding said slowly, "the smartly dressed courier……it must have been him. Adam. The numbers are the same!"

Crowe was surprised but kept his cool. " Makes sense I guess. If you trust no-one then who better than yourself to entrust the delivery to. If not the man himself then at least it was someone he could trust. I assume that is a letter from him to you? Can I read it?"

Wilding turned the letter to show Crowe. It had only two lines upon it.

'Give these books and the letter to Michael Crowe as soon as possible.

Once he has read the letter, ask him to call the number below.'

"The same number of the card," Wilding followed.

"So, we can assume that Adam is in this country, possibly near, but gives only a mobile number. Do you recall what he looked like?" Crowe asked hopefully.

"For obvious reasons I did not take much notice!" Wilding started. "Maybe thirties, swarthy. He wore a baseball cap and dark sunglasses but now you come to mention it, I do recall that his dress sense was more refined than perhaps you would see for your average delivery driver. His clothes were of some quality."

"Look Conrad," Crowe started, "We could be reading these books for weeks and debate the whole scenario of Adam still being amongst us and in any rate; you do not seem to need to be persuaded at all!"

"Yes, but at least we can discover his journey and may yet find, as you suggested, the flaw in his argument."

"Well, volume one could read as fact or fiction depending on which way one leans," Crowe followed. "It is so far in the past that we have nothing to compare with it and even if you suggest the Bible or the Torah for example as suitable reference, in all cases we are not looking at anything that offers real proof." Wilding nodded in agreement, "I think it serves no purpose researching the distant past but perhaps we should be looking at the last volume to discover what we can find out about Adam today? I mean who is he? Will we know him? Can we look online for photos of his life in the twentieth century or indeed this one perhaps? Will we not find out more about who he has become rather than who he has been?" Crowe finished and waited for Wilding to think it through.

"Call him," he said handing the note over, "Call him and arrange to meet as he has asked. Look him in the eyes and read his expressions. Listen to his voice and observe his movements. Offer him a polygraph test or a medical examination, or both. Yes, I may think he could be for real, I still have some doubt but I do think there is enough in the research for me to consider he is genuine. But then, it is not me he has to convince if you are to stand up and declare his authenticity and nothing we do here in my rooms will produce an absolute truth. You have to meet him." His eyes were fixed and staring and Crowe knew the time was upon him.

"I will make the call," he said and reached into his trouser pocket for his phone.

"Use my landline," Wilding said, "Just in case."

"Just in case what?" Crowe responded.

"I just think it would be more secure perhaps?" Wilding followed and Crowe moved to the hallway and picked up the receiver. He dialled the number on the letter and waited as it rang. There was no response until the voicemail message kicked in except there was no invitation to leave a message, just a voice that said 'GPS 50, 42, 10 North, 3, 31, 49 West. 18 September

10 am'. The message repeated itself once finished and Crowe beckoned Wilding who had appeared in the doorway to bring a pad and paper for him to write the numbers down. Once he had checked what he had written he finished the call and replaced the receiver.

"No answer, no way to leave a message. Just this." He handed the pad to Wilding.

"Co-ordinates to meet," Wilding stated in surprise, "and I assume he means tomorrow as that is the 18th!"

"Looks like it," Crowe responded, "Conrad, I have booked a room at the local motorway services for tonight…"

"You could have stayed here," Wilding protested.

"I thought you might offer but I was not sure and it is too late to cancel now. Besides I need to eat!" Crowe exclaimed. "I am going to get some food and some sleep and I need to check back with Jessica before it is too late. I have an errand to run tomorrow anyway but it seemed like my day is now spoken for. I will come around again tomorrow night and let you know what happened if ok with you?"

"Absolutely." Wilding said quickly, "Yes a good night's sleep will be best."

"You are going to continue reading aren't you," Crowe said with a smile.

"You know me too well Michael," Wilding responded and held out his hand which Crowe shook before leaving the Professor to his research.

Forty minutes later, Crowe checked into the cheap motorway services hotel and despite the lateness of the hour, the noise from the motorway alongside was still loud enough to be annoying. He decided not to unpack his case but instead looked at his watch and decided that despite the fact it was nearly midnight, he would call Jessica anyway. He lay on the bed as it rang before a tired and disorientated voice replied.

"You better be in need of an ambulance or something equally pressing to wake me up now," the irritated voice of Jessica Russell said with clear annoyance.

"Love you too!" Crowe said cheekily, "I'm sorry baby but just wanted you to know I am ok."

"Thank you," Jessica said, "and you have but I need to get up early tomorrow for a breakfast meeting before class so I will love you and leave you for now if you don't mind."

"I am sorry darling," Crowe responded, "I will call you at a more acceptable hour tomorrow. I promise. Miss you!"

"Miss you too," Jessica replied, "night, night". The call ended and Crowe lay fully back on the pillows. The takeaway he had on the way from Wilding's house was already lying heavy on his stomach but he realised he was very tired and closed his eyes to rest them. Almost instantly, he was asleep.

Chapter Ten

Mid-morning 18th September, present day, outside of Exeter, England.

Michael Crowe felt extremely ill at ease. Not the best passenger in the backseat of a car at the best of times anyway, the general feeling of nausea had been exaggerated by the use of the rough hood that the two men had forced him to wear throughout the journey. The weave of the cloth was particularly thick form of hessian and dyed black so he only had a small amount of light to view under his chin, giving no indication of his location.

He had absolutely no idea where he was, only that he knew they had been travelling for about forty minutes and the general smoothness of the journey after the first ten minutes suggested that at least part of the way must have been on at least a dual carriage-way road, the M5 or the A30 being the most likely out of Exeter, but whether North or South, he had no clue. The sharp twists and clear sense of climbing after coming off the larger road did suggest that the remainder of the journey had been on smaller country roads which meant Exmoor to the north or perhaps the Quantock hills offered the best possibility for their final destination. Alternatively, if south, then Dartmoor was the best guess. The journey had not been long enough for the Welsh hills or the Cotswolds to be alternatives so if it was to be any of the three former possibilities, there was the most likely and bizarre possibility that Adam was residing in the West Country of England.

The instructions had been clear to wait at the designated spot using the GPS co-ordinates which Crowe was surprised to see was by the car auction offices on the large industrial estate to the South of Exeter. He was equally perturbed when the two men approached him after alighting from a car that they must have just purchased as it still sported the lot number on the windscreen. The vehicle was an old-style Ford Mondeo with a 'T' prefix number plate in a dark electric blue colour that had certainly seen better days and as such, would not have been expensive.

The two men seemed to be both in their late thirties or early forties. One tall and muscular, the other short and more rotund. Crowe had already made up his mind to label them Tall Man and Squat Man respectively as neither had been forthcoming with their actual names. He got into the back seat as he was invited to do so whilst they drove to a nearby garage, purchased fuel and oil which they put into the vehicle, checked the water and tyre pressure and for good measure, mounted a hanging air freshener in the shape of a pine tree from the rear-view mirror. Crowe was at least grateful for that as the smell of stale smoke was well imbedded into the ageing upholstery. Other than the first instruction to get into the back, not a word was exchanged between the two men or to Crowe himself until they were ready to set off from the garage and then one spoke.

"Mr Crowe, you will need to put this on," Tall Man said, who was sat beside him holding out the hood. "He apologises for the need but would rather you do not know his exact location at this time, you understand of course." It was not a question. Crowe had accepted the hood and put it over his head, thankful that it was odourless.

The Mondeo, which had proved relatively smooth overall throughout the first part of the journey when they were gliding along at a constant speed had now developed an occasional loud cranking sound as the uphill gradient became steeper, suggesting that perhaps more than just the addition of the air freshener would be needed in the near future. The car took some acute turns and on one occasion braked hard, causing the driver to swear in a foreign tongue that Crowe could not identify. The vehicle carried on quite slowly for a few more largely uphill miles before it came to a measured stop with a crunch of gravel clearly present under the tyres as it did so. Crowe moved to take off the hood but was stopped by the man next to him who placed his hand on Crowe's head to block him.

"Not just yet Mr Crowe thank you." He said firmly before exiting the car and coming around the Crowe's side, opening the door and holding his arm to assist Crowe to get out. Looking through the gap at the base of the hood, Crowe could make out the grey stone drive made up from granite chippings and a turf edge which had not been cut for some time. It was windy and relatively cold so Crowe assumed they were at elevation, He resigned himself to the fact that he would simply have to wait until Adam was ready to reveal himself and where they were.

"Two steps Mr Crowe," The tall man said as he led him away from the car and sure enough, Crowe could see the steps made of the same grey/blue granite near his feet. He over-compensated the height required to mount the steps and his foot fell heavily onto the tread of the first. Squat Man chortled at his obvious imbalance and Crowe came to the conclusion that out of the two men, Tall Man would perhaps be the most reasonable. The hurdle of the entrance steps over, he was led into the house where two things were immediately apparent, the musty smell that assaulted his nostrils and the disgustingly stained old patterned carpet he was treading on visible beneath the hood. At least he was out of the wind now but he was already missing the fresh air.

He felt the hood being removed and suddenly free of it, he blinked and tried to focus on his new surroundings. The carpet was indeed fit for burning only and the damp corridor he was in had very yellowed paint on top of old, flock wallpaper with a dado rail at chest height. Several doors led off the central hallway and Crowe did not have to investigate further to realise that this was a simple bungalow of modest size and scope that had been allowed to fester. If this was the Adam's residence then Crowe doubts were suddenly magnified.

"In here Michael". It was a new voice, thin and soft, almost lyrical that he heard coming from the room behind him. Crowe turned and walked into the room where there was a large wide window with no curtains offering a quite splendid view of a barren Tor in the distance. The desolate moorland vegetation leading up to the Tor left him in no doubt that he was somewhere on Dartmoor after all.

"So very pleased to meet you at last," the voice said from his side and he turned to see a figure sat in a basic wooden chair in the corner of the room. There was no other furniture. "I am very sorry about the condition of this abode and as you may assume, I do not live here, but I needed somewhere remote and away from prying eyes for our first meeting. Therefore, please forgive me Michael for not accepting you into my presence in more fitting surroundings but I do have to be sure about you. You see, if I do leave my home, I do have to spend most of my time on the move from place to place as too long in one location can bring its own challenges."

"You are Adam?" Crowe said observing the man and ignoring the words spoken. He was quite extraordinary to behold. Dusky olive skin with piecing black eyes, thick voluminous hair that was perhaps longer than it was absolutely necessary to be yet perfectly brushed and with long waves. The face was slightly round but not chubby and the nose thin. As he rose from the chair, Crowe could see that he was of middle height and relatively slight in his frame. His clothes were expensive with a fine steel blue suit, crisp white shirt which was open down to the third button. There was something that Crowe could not define that troubled him until it hit him with a rush. He was perfect, not a line or a blemish, just silky looking skin with no discolouration. No moles or any other surface flaw. He was a beautiful man, but not at all rugged. Crowe chuckled at what he knew Jessica would call him, a 'pretty boy'.

Adam approached him and held out his hand, "yes, I am he," he said with a smile that clearly showed the milky white perfect teeth. Despite all his mystery, Crowe felt totally inadequate against this Adonis that shook his hand.

"And you are Michael Terence Crowe," he followed, "Age 42, born in the village of Hurstbourne Tarrant," he emphasised the last syllable contrary to how Crowe would have said the name of the village he was raised which placed the emphasis on the 'Tar' prefix rather than the 'rant', but he decided to let it go unchallenged.

"County of Hampshire," Adam continued. "Family moved a few miles away to the town of Andover when you were four and then Fareham when you were nine. Father was a Lieutenant Colonel in the British Army and your mother was an aspiring lawyer until your birth. Parents divorced three years afterwards and you were raised by your mother alone together with your younger brother and sister until she remarried the year you started at Exeter. First class honours in Archaeology and ancient history followed by two years field work before gaining a position of authority on the Taw Valley settlement site and the uncovering of the burial ship dating back to the Viking raids of the Tenth Century and equal in majesty to that discovered at Sutton Hoo. Published your first work on the Vinland settlements on the east coast of North America by the Vikings at age 29 followed by other renowned studies on early British settlements and the Roman invasion. You departed from your area of expertise to write the biography of the Earl of Barnsford six years ago which was made into a short successful TV series due to the salacious and downright naughty activities of that terrible man which developed a voyeuristic audience following ," Adam forced back a huge smile to himself and winked at Crowe before he continued, "You were later commissioned to present a well-received series on your core areas of Ancient Britain and have been seen many times in the newspapers on account of your, how did they term it? 'TV History Hunk' status. Currently fronting the 'History Live' broadcasts of archaeology as it happens with a large Twitter and Facebook following, not just in this country but with admirers globally. Currently un-married but in a long-term relationship with your girlfriend Jessica Russell, a teacher in Wokingham, Berkshire, affectionately known as 'Jack' and where you live together in the town. No children." Adam stopped and stared at Crowe waiting for a reaction.

"It appears you know of me quite well," Crowe responded, "and I hope to be able to find everything out about you in the same fashion."

Adam paused and just looked at Crowe without speaking. Crowe delved deep into his mind to resolve the nagging feeling that he had seen this man before. He was absolutely sure they had met but remembering where was becoming impossible. It was almost as if he could identify with him only partially, something was different to putting together the whole story as to where and when.

"I would ask you to sit but as you can see, there is little by way of furniture here." Adam suddenly said and smiled again as he walked towards the window. "Join me would you?" he asked and waved the two men standing in the doorway out of the room. "I will call you when ready," he said.

Crowe heard the door close behind him with a defined squeak that suggested the damp atmosphere had expanded the wood. He looked at the man before him as he gazed deep in thought towards the rugged moor through the window. His breath was steaming the window slightly as his chest rose and fell in measured pauses.

"You know Michael," Adam started, "I have seen so many wonderful sights over the centuries, so many beautiful views of lush meadows, thick green forests and snowy mountains and in all that time, I have not seen those same vistas truly change. I may have been on this earth for many millennia but the earth itself is much, much older and it takes an unimaginable amount of time to change how it looks. Every year we see the seasons change, the renewal of Spring, the bounty that is Summer and the fading away that is the Fall," he paused suddenly, "I am sorry Michael, too long in North America can affect your speech. I mean of course, the Autumn and then the death that is Winter. Whilst the seasons may merge as each year repeats the one that went before, there are some things that seemingly do not change except in incredible long periods of time. Take that rock up there," He pointed an elegant thin finger towards the Tor," Rounded and shaped by wind for how long? Millions of years..... many millions," he answered himself, "That rock has seen so much more than I have ever done in my own incredibly long time on this earth, so much more. The time that rock has seen I can never catch up and yet will I see the landscapes change around me far into the future just like that rock has done over the past? It is an interesting thought."

Adam suddenly turned and looked Crowe straight in the eyes catching him slight unaware. "So, Michael, have I convinced you of who I am?" He smiled, exposing the perfect teeth once more.

"Conrad seems convinced at least," Crowe started, "I think you will have a harder job with most, including me, although the whole concept is compelling to say the least."

Adam let out a sudden shrill laugh, cupping both hands to his face which he then opened and closed repeatedly like he was playing peek-a-boo with a baby.

"Well I have never been described as compelling," he laughed. "You amuse me Michael. Oh, I do hope you and I are going to be great friends."

Crowe was taken aback by this sudden infantile outburst and had an instant rush of doubt as to whether the striking individual in front of him was even sane. He was troubled and fascinated by this man at the same time. Crowe was not entirely sure of what to expect from meeting Adam, particularly as to what he would look like or how he would act. The person before him now did not fit any pre-conception he had considered.

"Now then Michael, we must meet again and in distinctly more comfort than I have offered you today. This was never meant to be the location for our great discourse but I just needed to know you were prepared to meet in the first place and to accept me as I am. I wanted you to be genuine Michael and whilst the theatrics of making you wear a hood was perhaps over the top, it seemed somewhat playful for me and perhaps would have added to your sense of the unknown." He again paused to no effect. "I am pleased and happy to answer any and all of your questions so there remains no doubt in your mind that I speak the truth and in doing so, offer the best hope for mankind." Adam paused but Crowe remained silent. "So, I will have my colleagues take you back to where you started from, unless you have a preference for somewhere else?"

"That will be fine, thank you." Crowe responded. "Do I need to be hooded again?" He asked.

"Not necessary as I will leave first. But I will not be returning to this place, it was only a temporary location although I cannot understand why anyone would want to live so remotely and in such a bleak landscape. When we next meet it will be in more applicable surroundings and I have ensured there is enough security so that we will not be disturbed. I will send for you Michael in the next few days and please pack a bag so you can stay for a few nights as I mean to convince you utterly and I sense you may need longer than I hoped. Se la vie. Once I have convinced you Michael, then we will plan how we will announce to the world of my coming. I will wish you goodbye for now." Adam shook Crowe's hand once more, enthusiastically this time, and moved to leave the room. He opened the door and disappeared in to the corridor. Crowe made to follow him but the form of the burly Squat Man blocked the entrance.

"If you want to remain un-hooded then please wait until he has left," he said without emotion. Crowe moved backwards but could immediately hear the sound of a helicopter starting up and then the loud, dominating booming of the rotors gaining speed. Although he could not see the aircraft outside of the window, the deafening noise and sudden vibration announced that the chopper had left the ground and was hovering over the building. The sound slowly diminished as the aircraft moved away and once it was more difficult to hear, the burly man moved and beckoned Crowe to follow him.

They left the building and Crowe was able to fully see the remoteness of their location. The bungalow was indeed in a poor state and had clearly not been lived in for some time. Surrounded by moorland, a single short track led away from the building to a single asphalt road at the end of which Crowe could see the 'For Sale' board. Of any sort of main road, there was no sign. Adam was clearly not taking any chances for this first meeting Crowe concluded.

The two men indicated he should get back into the car and they started the journey back with the clunking noise getting louder with every mile. Joining the A30 at Whiddon Down, they travelled East and were soon in Exeter and at the pick-up point where Crowe had met the two men. Parking the car at the side of the entrance to the auction house, the men remained silent as they had done so for the entirety of the journey and Crowe was surprised as they simply walked away, leaving the Mondeo where it was, the keys still in the ignition. He called after them but they ignored him and marched around the corner and out of sight.

Crowe paused for a few moments and then started to walk in the other direction to where his own car had been parked and considered what had happened over the last two hours. It seemed like an anti-climax how the encounter with Adam had ended but if nothing else, he was now even more intrigued and looking forward to the invitation to meet arriving.

Chapter Eleven

Afternoon, 18th September Present Day, outside Exeter, England.

Crowe woke with a start and an aching head. His sleep had been short and without any genuine rest as the effects of the strange hotel bed and an over-active mind battled with the need to peacefully drift off. Returning to the hotel after the meeting with Adam, he head was spinning over the possibilities that were now exposed. He cursed slightly as he returned to his room to see that the bed had not yet been re-made or the room cleaned for his second night booked but decided to put the 'do not disturb' sign on the exterior door knob to ensure he could get some rest. Now awake again, he lay with his head screaming for a better position on the hard pillows but made no attempt to adjust them and instead rubbed his neck enthusiastically to try and relieve the strain that had developed as he slept.

Finally fed up with the ache, he launched himself out of the bed flinging the duvet to one side and went over to the window to open the curtains fully. The sudden rush of sunlight that filled the room as he parted the fabric made him wince and he turned away to walk towards the bathroom. His head felt like he had enjoyed a heavy night drinking but he had not and felt a little cheated. He passed his phone which had been charging since he had returned and he pressed the on button to awaken the screen.

There was a message notification showing. Crowe could not remember even hearing the tone for an incoming message so assumed it had arrived during the brief hours of sleep he had enjoyed. Assuming it would be from Jessica chastising him further for his late-night interruption of her slumbers, he was surprised to see it was from a withheld number but the words in the text that greeted him were clear enough.

'Michael, I enjoyed our little meeting earlier so I would like to continue our talk tonight if you can? As I mentioned, bring an overnight bag and drive to the co-coordinates that will follow later. You will be picked up at 17.00. Safe journey.'

Crowe looked at the time at the top of the screen and again at his watch, it was 14.57. Not wishing to waste any time with the rendezvous for pick up not yet disclosed, Crowe rushed into the bathroom and then, suitable freshened, dressed and packed, he checked out of the hotel and went into the shop area to purchase coffee which he took back to his car to drink.

It was 15.26 when the text notification sounded and Crowe looked down to see a set of GPS co-ordinates on the screen but with no other instructions. He copied the text and then pasted it into the Satellite navigation app to see where the co-ordinates related to. Realising that the location was just over an hour away, Crowe immediately started the engine and followed the exit signs from the services onto the M5 motorway, heading North. He realised he was speeding and chose to reduce his urgency to ensure he reached the location in time and not to risk not reaching it at all if pulled over by the police, but still soon reached junction 27 where the M5 met the A361 and came off at the intersection, heading West. He was heading towards North Devon but knew that the satellite navigation would ultimately take him to the coast close to Exmoor. Crowe was sure he had been to the rendezvous location before whilst on holiday in the area as a child but was reaching as far back as he could to remember what was there, and failed. Forty minutes later and at he arrived at the location and immediately remembered what had played on his mind. Goats; wild goats that wandered the jagged and wild area known as the Valley of the Rocks that towered above him but of these infamous residents, he could now see no sign.

Crowe parked the car in the designated area and was surprised to see his was the only one there. What also was not there was anything other than the small cottage used as a tea rooms and a stone built public toilet, but both were closed. Crowe was murmuring to himself about Adam enjoying meeting in places far from signs of major human activity when the distant sound of helicopter rotors could be heard, ever coming closer. Crowe strained his head to discern where the sound was coming from but could not place it as the tall rocks between him and the sea and the rolling hills behind created a natural amphitheatre which distorted the sound. He was surprised as the chopper suddenly appeared from the seaward side and vaulted over the highest peaks of the rocks with their slopes of shale standing menacing above him.

The pilot skilfully guided the Bell 429 with striking blue and silver livery into the valley bowl and brought it to a rest at the other end of the car park, the rotors still running. The door opened and Squat Man from the car journey the day before got out and beckoned Crowe over.

Crowe went back to his car, took out his bag and pressed the locking button on the key. He then half ran to the waiting helicopter keeping his head unrealistically bent forwards to avoid the rotors even though he had plenty of room to spare.

"If you would Mr Crowe," Squat Man said and took Crowe's bag as he climbed into the rear passenger seat. Tall Man was inside waiting and handed Crowe the hood he had worn the day before in the car plus pair of ear mufflers.

"I thought Adam said there would be no need for the hood?" Crowe said disapprovingly.

"Change of plan." Tall Man said and motioned that he should put it on which Crowe did with reluctance followed by the ear mufflers on top.

Once squat man had got in and shut the door the rotors started to quicken their revolutions and the helicopter took off, hovered for a short while before moving quickly away.

Inside the hood, Crowe had no sense of direction or speed of travel. The ear mufflers stopped some of the sound but several attempts to speak went unanswered. Instead, he decided to settle back as comfortably as he could.

The feeling of enclosure inside the hood combined with the heat and the rhythmic throbbing of the rotor blades dulled by the ear defenders made Crowe feel sleepy again as he dozed between the two men pressed against him either side of his body. Their weight and pressure wedged him into the seat so that his body could not move but his head lolled around forcing him to correct his head position several times when the pressure on his neck became too much.

As he started to come around, he had absolutely no idea of how long they had been flying or in which direction. It was simply impossible to see anything to assist beneath the hood so he gave up trying. Just when he started to drift off once again he could feel the Bell start to bank and then descend slowly before rearing up to hover for a short period before finally and gradually touching down. The pilot turned the engine off and the rotors started to slow but taking some time to become silent.

The hood was pulled off and Crowe once again found himself blinking wildly and adjusting to the sudden half-light of an Autumn evening after a long period of darkness. Squat Man opened the door and exited from the aircraft beckoning Crowe to come with him which, after a short pause, he did. As he alighted from the helicopter, a light and cold typical September breeze blew in his face and he heard the rustle of leaves as they danced and skipped around him. He looked about and saw that the helicopter had landed in a glade which was completely surrounded by trees in glorious browns, yellows and reds as their leaves resigned to the colours of the season. The setting sun was sending beams of orange and red through the trees accentuating the colour display. It was a worthy view commensurate with anything Crowe had seen for Autumn and brought to mind his research years in New England and maritime Eastern Canada as he sought the mythical Vinland Viking settlements.

"Mr Crowe?" Tall Man asked and pointed to three Segways that were parked at the edge of the glade behind him. Crowe was surprised to see the strange vehicles but also delighted as he had experienced using them before. The three men walked to the Segways and Squat Man mounted one and waited. Tall Man turned to Crowe and again pointed to the machine.

"Do you know how to ride it Mr Crowe?" he asked with an expressionless face.

"I do," Crowe responded and mounted the one nearest to him, immediately engaging the steering stick forwards and backwards to get his bearings and test the agility.

"Please follow me Mr Crowe," Squat Man said and started to steer his Segway between the trees where a thin path could now be seen in the advancing gloom. Crowe realised that only using this vehicle or walking was the only way out of the glade as he did not see any access roads for larger vehicles. Tall Man took up the position at the rear so that Crowe was between the two men and the three of them sped quite quickly through the trees with few turns required as the path was both mostly straight and free of protruding roots. A well-worn path Crowe thought to himself.

The three men rode their vehicles for at least five minutes before the trees started to thin on each side and the forest floor showed signs of greater ground dwelling vegetation as the gaps between the trees would have allowed more sunlight to reach the soil. Finally, the trees thinned to almost nothing and Crowe could see vast lawns before him leading down to an impressive country house several hundred yards away. Squat Man led the three to a small shed by the side of the wood which served as a housing and charging area for the Segways and dismounted his vehicle with Crowe and Tall Man following suit. A third man appeared from the shed and took charge of the vehicles as Squat Man led Crowe to the waiting golf buggy that was parked behind it.

"Any reason why we couldn't land in all this space?" Crowe asked, waving his hands at the expansive lawns.

"He doesn't like his herds to be frightened," Tall Man said pointing towards what Crowe realised was an impressive herd of Red deer grazing in the distance, taking their evening meal before returning to the woods for the night.

"Quite the menagerie," Crowe exclaimed, "but no fences I see?"

Tall Man came over to Crowe and pointed beyond the deer. "Electric fences in the trees over there," he waved his arm towards the far forest, "and a Ha Ha in the lawns separating the deer from the house."

Crowe raised his eyebrows as the dry and unfriendly man had uttered the 'ha-ha' description. He would have expected him to have resorted to deep ditch as the adjective used and he was surprised that the man went for the correct term.

Crowe continued to take the view in with a smile but suddenly realised he had forgotten his bag and reacted with a start.

"My bag," he began, "I have left it on the helicopter."

"Not a problem Mr Crowe," Squat Man answered, "He will get that for you." He pointed to the man taking care of the Segways who swore under his breath and mounted the last one not yet housed to begin the return journey to the helicopter.

The golf buggy was driven by Tall Man and the three of them started towards the house, first on the grass and then on a narrow, gravelled path. As they approached the building something was troubling

Crowe as it looked so familiar and yet out of place at the same time. It also looked newer than he first imagined. The yellow stone was cleaner than it should have been and there was no real indication of weathering or erosion of the stone faces. Statues they passed on the path also showed no age to them and yet the whole property exuded a style and look that from a distance would have been several hundred years old. Also, there seemed not to be anything approaching a road or wide path suitable for larger vehicles. He scanned the trees surrounding the whole area but there was no break in the forest edge.

As the buggy pulled up in front of the columned entrance canopy Crowe was sure that what he was looking at was a modern reproduction of a classical style house, and one he thought he recognised. It was very odd. As he alighted from the buggy, the two great oak doors to the entrance of the house opened and a figure emerged with a large smile on his perfect face, it was Adam.

"Michael!" He exclaimed. "Delighted you were able to come. Do you like my house? I can tell you all about it over supper, will you join me?" He held out his hand and Crowe shook it.

"It looks familiar," Crowe said, "But I am not sure why."

"I can explain Michael as we have much to talk about. Please, walk with me will you. We have a wonderful supper prepared and I hope you will not mind the vegetarian menu, I am afraid I cannot abide the eating of flesh, my diet has changed radically since the early days I can assure you."

Adam seemed to be almost skipping as he led Crowe through the entrance doors and into the reception hallway with its wide imposing staircase in front of him with galleries above on both sides. The walls were packed with brooding oils paintings, some portraits and others land and seascapes with miniatures dotted amongst the large frames. A huge and wide chandelier with hundreds of crystal glass droplets dominated and illuminated the ceiling directly above the entrance hall and Crowe noticed the large colourful lidded ceramic urns and marble topped side tables that sat in pairs on opposite sides of the several doors leading off from the central hall. The floor was entirely of marble in rich hues and polished to a mirror finish and extended to even the staircase itself where the rich gilt banisters gleamed in the light through the swirls and curves of their carved design. It was indeed an expression of great wealth and opulent taste yet seemed exactly right for the style of house, even if the house itself appeared much younger than its contents.

"I see you are taking in my collection?" Adam asked. "It is the product of many years as you may understand." Adam walked towards the door way to their right and Crowe followed. As they entered, a large and long ornate table which sat against the wall to their left was full of silver domed platters and also copper pans sitting on warmers. A round mahogany table with space for twelve placements was set for just two with shiny white ceramic plates, glistening silver cutlery and crisp white napkins. There were several different glasses in crystal on one placement setting only plus a large crystal glass jug of water with lemons in the centre of the table. It was a sumptuous supper table indeed.

Please Michael, "Adam asked. Will you take a seat? Over there." He pointed to the setting with the many glasses. "I was not sure what you would like to drink so I planned for everything," he said. "Champagne, wine, beer. A soft drink of some kind? I very much recommend the rhubarb presses; my particular favourite."

Crowe looked at the jug of water and pointed. That will be fine thank you." He said.

"Perhaps later," Adam followed. I am not an alcohol drinker myself so water is my drink of choice most of the time.

They both sat and immediately Adam clapped his hands twice. The door behind them opened and three staff emerged, two young women and a tall young man. All three busied themselves removing the domed lids of the serving platters to reveal a selection of salads, rice and pasta dishes which they took turns to spoon onto the plates as requested. Crowe let his eyes control his stomach as he did not know when he would eat next and thus wanted to take advantage of what was being offered. The young dark-haired girl looked at him with stolen glances and a determined expression as if she wanted to say something but she met Adam's eyes and swiftly departed.

They ate silently and Crowe kept expecting Adam to start a conversation but he just maintained his gaze on his guest and munched slowly. After many minutes, he took a sip of water and finally spoke.

"So Michael, when we have eaten our fill I suggest we retire to my study and begin. I will be happy to answer any question you wish to pose. If we achieve nothing else over these few days, I want you to eventually leave in absolutely no doubt of the truth." He paused and started to fill his fork again.

"Before we start," Crowe said between chewing, "What if I remain doubtful, even after everything we discuss? What if I want to leave because I simply do not accept you or your premise? What then?" Crowe rested his cutlery and sat back.

"Michael, I am sensing some resentment here." Adam said quietly, "Let us not talk of such things, such pessimistic outlooks. You have not even questioned me yet. You are my guest, not my prisoner and you are free to leave at any time. Knowing you as I do though, your desire for historical truth will keep you here as long as you need to discover that truth. Of that I am sure." Adam smiled again and continued to eat. Crowe furrowed his brow and wondered how safe his return journey would actually be if he did decide not to play Adam's game.

Once their plates were cleared, the servants appeared again and removed all the savoury platters and lids, replacing them with further platters of cut fruit and impressive cheeses, two of each which were placed either side of both diners. Coffee appeared and Crowe accepted a cup being poured. It was deep and aromatic and very strong.

Crowe cut some blue cheese and some Applewood from the platter, took a few crackers from the plate alongside and a spoonful of quince jelly. Adam picked at the cut pieces of melon and apple.

"You keep a good table," Crowe said to break the silence; "this has been an excellent supper, thank you."

"The pleasure is all mine," Adam replied and once you have finished your cheese we will retire to my study. You can have more coffee in there if you wish."

Crowe noticed that Adam's plate was empty whilst his still had cheese upon it but sensing that supper was over, he wiped his mouth with the napkin, folded it and placed it next to his plate, downing the dregs of the coffee at the same time.

"I am ready when you are," Crowe said enthusiastically and saw that Adam was already halfway out of his chair. Adam stood beside his chair and motioned that Crowe should follow him back out the same doors they had entered and across the impressive hallway to the door opposite. Whatever happens now, Crowe thought, is going to affect him

for the rest of his life. He was genuinely excited and
hesitant at the same time.

Chapter Twelve

Rue Le Tasse, Paris, France. 19.15 hours, September 18th Present day.

The room was poorly lit with more than several bulbs blown on both of the large ornate yet dusty glass chandeliers that had been previously converted from nineteenth century candelabras. The irregular light cast from the gilt, multi-branched light formed strange shadows amongst the panelled walls and large gilt framed portraits of past worthies looking stiffly down on the assembled group. Where once the overall baroque feel of the room would have once been splendid and dazzling, subsequent years of neglect and lack of ongoing investment now presented just gaudy sadness.

In the centre of the room was a huge, coffin shaped mahogany table with eighteen high-backed seats around it of which eleven were filled with silent men. Each sat stony-faced looking intently at those sat opposite as if to represent a forgotten scene fit for another of the ancient oil paintings that surrounded them. The bizarre differences in dress would make such a painting full of colour and style and yet in this gloomy room, the most vivid colours in particular would now seem drab and lost.

A tall door, one of a pair at the end of the room, opened with a defined creak and all eleven heads turned in unison to investigate who had entered. The man at the door entrance stopped to take in the faces but acknowledged none of them. He turned to swing the door shut again with some effort and having done so, he moved purposely to the empty seat at the head of the table and sat down. Eleven pairs of eyes followed him as he approached and sat.

Cardinal Donal McGeary gave a short thin smile to the assembled men and nodded. His hair was fully white yet his face seemed to have suffered little by way of wrinkles and his eyes were large and clear and in better light would have sparkled blue. He raised his hand.

"God be with you all" he started and was surprised as almost in unison, each man delivered a similar greeting from their individual faiths. "I sincerely apologise for my tardiness in arrival and I hope I have not kept you waiting too long." It was not really a question and none of the group answered.

Cardinal McGeary looked at each pair of eyes in turn. In some small way, the fact that they had all come to this place at the same time without rancour or expressed difficulty was in itself, a miracle. Apart from himself representing Christianity, each of the other eleven men sat around the table represented a major world religion. The representatives from Baha'i, Buddhism, Confucianism, Hinduism, Islam, Jainism, Judaism, Shinto, Sikhism, Taoism, and Zoroastrianism all sat silently looking at him until the Cardinal raised his hand once more.

"I thank you for coming, especially as you only received the invitation yesterday and for waiting so patiently," McGeary smiled, paused and then started. "Between us we represent the twelve great world religions. Whilst many of us will have separate sects and branches of our respective faiths, we are the founding churches and thus we must speak for all at this time. We have all travelled far and for one purpose and I do not have to surprise any of you with the background reason for this meeting as each of you will be aware already to some extent. What I do have to tell you is that the rumours are without doubt. The Catholic Church has been informed that the one person we all fear is ready to present himself to the world and thus, we are forced to act. The senior members of each religion have known the secret passed down by word of mouth for hundreds if not thousands of years that this day would come, the day that our very survival as world faiths will be in question. That what we all hold dear in our separate faiths is under extreme threat. He that would destroy our faith is ready and so should we be." McGeary looked around the table and saw the concern in each of the eleven other faces.

"I need not remind you of what this means for us all. We must look to try and settle the petty squabbles that have consumed us in the past and work together if we are to resist this menace. No one religion is safe or can profit from his lies. Separate, we become lone voices against the tide of anger that will arise. Together we can seek to calm the faithful and turn the power of the antichrist upon himself."

"We should start by not labelling him which means something to only a few of us" the senior Rabi to McGeary's immediate left interrupted. "Let us just call him the Beast."

"The Beast it is then," McGeary agreed without comment. "In him we have someone who, if he is to be believed will destroy us all. We agree that he must be a false prophet and that his untruths will bring immense harm to the world. He is no God, no son of God, no angel. He is evil and sustains himself through evil ways which we must seek to thwart. That in itself is not something we will find easy. We must achieve all this by destroying the one myth that he will seek to use to prove his lies."

"Which is?" the Japanese Shinto representative asked in a thin reedy voice.

"We must destroy the myth of immortality, the legend that he has lived forever. Through that deception he will seek to enslave the world."

"Just how do you kill that which cannot be killed?" The Sikh asked plainly, "and if we fail, will we not reinforce that myth and make him all the stronger?"

"We are men of faith!" The Confucianism member shouted. "Are we to become murderers? Let him announce himself and let us start to battle him with words and tested argument. Let us destroy him with reason and logic."

"You forget," McGeary followed, "what he represents predates all of us. All of our faiths rely on the basic concept that our God existed as creationist and developer of man. He will argue the same but will replace the word God with a species of being not at all holy, but of science and experiment. In this age of technology and future thought, his words will be accepted far easier than ever before. He has chosen this time and whilst we have all known that he exists, we have also all known that one day we must face him. Always moving, always changing, we have tried for millennia to find him. Many of all of our revered Patriarchs or Prophets are based on him and whilst we may now question the sense of our ancestral scribes placing his deeds upon the pedestals of our individual faiths, we also now know that to challenge that thought is to betray all those of faith who have believed what we have given them over the centuries. Can any of you imagine what would happen if we do not defend what we have taught to be truth? Whilst we all seek higher enlightenment in the presence of our individual Gods and we all accept the divine presence of him, much we have written and taught in praise of our Gods have been through the interpretations of strange deeds and actions of ancient man or the expectations and traditions of individual religions." McGeary paused for reaction but the room was silent so he continued.

"All of us ultimately believe in a greater purpose, a creed by which to live by. Yet everything we teach is the product of man's thought and indeed of ancient men crude in speech and worldly knowledge, men who viewed science as magic and invention as diabolical. If we are to promote the purity of God we will be forced to defend the reasoning of ancient man, however unreal they appear in a twenty-first century world. He, on the other hand will offer a view that is so far back in history that we cannot debate with confidence. He will do so on the premise that millions may accept purely on the basis of science fiction being a mainstream genre and thus, easy to sign up to. No my friends, debate is not in our favour and it is what he wants as he will relish the confrontation. We have no choice but to remove his threat and unless any of you seriously question your own faith in the light of his coming then I suggest you agree to how best this is to be done."

The room was silent when the Cardinal stopped speaking. McGeary waited for a whole minute before starting to speak again.

"In the Catholic Church we have for many years invested in specialists; an off-shoot team of which I now control to counter this threat. I have no doubt that we will be successful in finding him and eliminating the threat but just in case we do not, I know we all have various…'assets' we can call upon I understand," he offered a wry smile. "But our task is indeed to discover how you eliminate someone who will not die. In the meantime, we also need to find him and in that at least, we have a chance."

"How?" The reedy voice from the Japanese man spoke again.

"You will be aware that he started to compile the history of Man, including his own supposed creation, over two centuries ago. We know this from the reports of previous attempts to capture him, one of which resulted in a partially completed book being obtained. It was clear from reading this unfinished book that many went before it and we can assume many more, including a rewritten version of the one in our possession was written since. The infamous journals that he has produced over so many years were delivered to an English Professor two days ago. We heard this from a messenger sent yesterday by a member of those that guard him who could not take the responsibility that had been thrust upon his tortured mind. He sent me a video message which ended with his bloody death by his own hand to reinforce what he wanted to say. I have no reason to believe his angst against that unholy brotherhood was not real. He killed himself as he knew his life was forfeit in any event so we cannot doubt him. I have also been informed that the messenger himself was found dead, apparently he fell into the Tiber and was drowned but I severely doubt that is the truth of it," McGeary recalled the text he had received from Father Bernard the previous evening. "

"We have reason to believe that the Professor," he looked at his notes, "Wilding of Exeter University is a history academic and we assume our foe is seeking authoritative, academic backing before he makes himself public. We know little else about this

Professor at this time so do not know how deeply he is ingrained within this."

"So, our plan is to watch and wait. Use this a professor to find the Beast and then take him?" The Indian Hindu representative suggested.

"It is," the Cardinal replied. "And destroy those books at the same time. Once we have him we can discover how best to kill him and whilst we hold him securely, he cannot peddle his lies. We can agree the formalities and procedures for co-operation separately but with a show of hands, can we at least agree that we must work together here?"

A few hands rose immediately. Three more rose more slowly and without enthusiasm and two more after that, even slower. Only the representative for Islam remained unmoved.

"Books burn. Flesh corrupts," the man started, "but ideas you cannot kill," he started to rise and pushed the chair back, standing upright. "We are leaders of men both in thought and deed. We have shunned non-believers and encouraged sacrifice in all its forms in the name of our faiths. Yes, we argue against an idea that predates the establishment dates of all our religions but have we not been already doing that for thousands of years? Call it atheism, evolutionism, witchcraft, science or whatever you wish, the fact remains that we have never been the only argument for man to consider. Whilst we have argued, shouted, fought and bled in the name of our faiths against each other, the battle is never won. He is but another creed, another idea that we must add to the list of those who would oppose our own." The tall bearded man stopped but nobody spoke so he continued.

"Disillusioned fanatics in my own religion have killed with bomb, bullet and knife in the false name of Islam but for what? What does it bring but shame and hatred ten times over. We condemn such acts as those of the deluded with a perverse view of what it is to be a true Muslim yet it does not stop. The fact is my brothers that once an idea has taken root, it does not matter who you kill as whilst the idea exists, others will always pick up the fallen flag and charge again." The man paused and knitted his fingers of both hands together in a tight ball as if starting to pray, "So we kidnap and perhaps kill the beast but what then? Will the ideas he has spouted simply go away? Or will they grow, pushed ever forwards by the cries of those who swear vengeance. Killing the beast will prove nothing as it will be assumed he will return as he says he has already done countless times. We do not rid the world of the beast by killing him, we give sustenance to many others to claim his heritage and power. I vote against this action and agree with my Chinese brother, "he pointed to the delegate from Confucianism who nodded in response. The Imam resumed his seat and rested his hands on the table face down.

McGeary silently cursed. Even now, he thought, even now they cannot see it. This was going to be much harder than he could have imagined.

"My Muslim brother speaks wise words and is said with all our best intentions at heart," McGeary started. "Indeed, I have thought similar thoughts these past hours on the way here. Which is why our first act must be to simply capture him. If his death is actually impossible, then to thwart the myth of resurrection we must not give succour to even the rumour of his death. If he is seen to die and is resurrected then his argument is won. But if he is seen to disappear and never resurface, then his argument cannot be proved – indeed that will allow us to go on the debate offensive and suggest he was a fraud who, when found out, abandoned mankind and disappeared into obscurity. His legacy will wither on the vine and those that supported him would be ridiculed. Our intent should therefore be to capture him only and then throw him into the deepest, darkest and most secure hole on this planet that anyone around this table can offer. Immortality confined underground with no hope of discovery of escape would be a very lonely and long time to exist." McGeary ended as eleven nodding heads confirmed the support was there.

"Can I thus say my friends," the Cardinal continued, "that we are in agreement? If so, our first task is to locate the Beast before we deploy our teams to capture him. It is likely that he is in the United Kingdom at this time in order to liaise with his publicity backers, of that we can safely assume. But we still do not have a modern picture of him, no photograph or film we can refer to. He has been clever in using his huge amassed wealth from centuries of investment plus the support of his super-rich brotherhood friends to ensure he maintains his secrecy. All we have to go with as to what he looks like are in these." McGeary stood and walked towards a small table near the main entrance to the room upon which there was a small cardboard box. He extracted a pile of thin folders from the box and walked back to the table splitting half to he left and half to his right to be distributed.

"These are images captured from known art," he started, "You will see these paintings represent impressions of Adam himself from mostly renaissance artists but also later works." As he spoke the eleven other men slowly sorted through the series of blown-up section of various paintings depicting the face of a man assumed to be Adam. "However, mixed in amongst them are other depictions of various historical figures, kings, generals and the like. All have been selected through an intense computer face recognition programme that scanned all the known classical paintings to select those most alike." McGeary stopped as he was interrupted by the Rabi again.

"Forgive me Cardinal," he started, "but none of these artists painted from life. What use is this as they could not possibly have known what he looks like?"

McGeary looked up and placed his folder on the table before him. "You are quite right of course that these are representatives of his features only but do not forget that it would have been nearly impossible to use an older painting as the inspiration for a copy. These artists were from different ages, different times and indeed, different countries. The fact that so many of

Adam himself being similar is odd in itself bearing that in mind, plus the fact that the facial features are also very similar to other great historical figures, also painted by different artists at different times, even down to sculpture and relief moulding to metalwork is extremely strange would you not say?" The assembled representatives of each faith nodded in silence. "Who is to say that some were actually modelled on a life study at the time not knowing that the model they were using was actually the man himself?"

"You are saying the Beast actually sat for some of these?" The Rabi exploded with indignation.

"Why not?" McGeary confirmed, "No doubt such risk would have given him a certain pleasure." He suggested. "I am sure his sense of fun will have stopped when photography became mainstream as the risk of discovery would have been much greater. Which is why the images are getting much fewer as time goes on." He paused again. "The last image in the sleeve at the back of your folders is a computer-generated composite of all the images used to give an approximate representation of what we believe he looks like, or could look like now. We know he does not age so will look to be in his thirties and of Middle Eastern appearance as shown." The men were all looking for or extracting the last image from the folder to look at. "I appreciate that this is an approximation of what he may look like but it is all we have."

"But will we not know exactly what he looks like once he has made his presence known anyway?" The Sikh stated.

"By then we may already be too late," McGeary followed. "May I suggest we speak regularly, until we have him?" The other nodded. "Thank you, Gentlemen. Let us make this a new beginning for all of us by working together as much as we can. I thank you for your attendance tonight and may I wish you a safe journey home."

Each delegate collected their personal items and made for the exit bowing and shaking hands as they left. McGeary watched then leave before moving himself. "Oh God," he murmured to himself, "give us the strength."

Outside the building on the opposite side of the Rue de Tasse across from the Moroccan Embassy, the man kept in the shadows of the deep doorway away from the streetlight. He looked up at the dim glow from the first-floor window and waited. He had witnessed all twelve arrive with the Cardinal arriving last and he would wait until all had left before carrying out his task. The night air was turning chilly and he put his hands in his trouser pockets for warmth so that his right hand cradled the small mobile phone within and the man smiled broadly. This was going to actually be fun he decided.

As the doors opened, he watched as each of the faith leaders left and got into their respective vehicles parked up along the street and each departed orderly one after another. Only the Cardinal was left and he walked furthest up the street and away from the building towards his car which started to inch forwards towards him. The man pulled the mobile phone out of his trouser pocket and slowly selected the speed dial number, pressing send. The signal travelled in an instant to the receiving phone attached to the device under the Cardinal's car which exploded in a rush of flame, flipping the car into a forward somersault so that it crashed down roof first onto the street, a burning and ruined shell. Windows around the blast zone fractured and blew inwards and masonry chips peppered the street like a sudden shower of hail. Cardinal McGeary was forcibly thrown backwards and slid flailing along the pavement until his head connected with a railing to secure bicycles and he was instantly knocked unconscious.

To the background accompaniment of car and property alarms set off by the blast and the consuming fire that engulfed the blackened car, the man smiled as he rushed down the alleyway to his rear and made for the Seine to make good his escape.

Chapter Thirteen

*19.23 hours, September 18th, Present day,
somewhere in England*

Adam led the way into a room that was much larger than the one they had just left. It was twice the length and had two bay windows with stone frames along its length as opposed to the one window in the room where they had eaten. On the opposite wall facing the space between the two windows was an enormous stone mantled fireplace within which a large log fire was burning enthusiastically. Around the room, the walls were completely filled from floor to ceiling with books, thousands of them ranging from large antiquarian tomes in rich multi-coloured leather to simple more modern paperback novels. There had been a degree of order in their filing, but it seemed to become much less structured the further into the room as Crowe walked. Above him, the ceiling was frescoed with rich classical scenes separated by plaster relief garlands of vine leaf designs. Crowe strained his neck to look up and recognised the paintings to be representing stories of antiquity including, somewhat ironically he thought, a clear representation of the Garden of Eden. He looked down and saw that Adam was staring at him.

"You are wondering after all I have told you why I choose the classical Garden of Eden scene as part of my decoration?" He asked with a smile. "Call it self-imposed irony," he waved his arm upwards, "indeed most of the scenes you see have some relevance to my life. It took eight artists to complete this in three months you know. I know how hard it can be to paint at height on your back, it is not a natural position to be creative. Michelangelo taught me that. He never really did so you know," Adam continued softly," He sort of leaned at an angle, not quite horizontal. All part of clever scaffolding design really. He really was a very special human being and," he paused and looked at Crowe directly, "a good a friend to me as I hope you will also be Michael," he said with a wide and welcoming smile.

Crowe also smiled, but to himself with the casual name-dropping and chose to ignore it. He looked at each fresco in turn and marvelled at the quality of the artistry. His eyes fell on a scene that clearly represented the great flood and the building of the ark. He pointed to it as he asked Adam the question. "I suppose you will tell me that you were on the Ark?" he enquired in a half-mocking tone, "Are you going to tell me you were Noah?" He half grinned to himself as he looked at Adam.

"Yes, I was there," Adam started, "but no, I was not Noah. He was a great man you know, a true visionary. He saw what was happening to man all around him and strove to keep his family protected from the mayhem of the time. He took me in to his family and treated me as one of his own. I lived with him for several years and helped build the Ark itself together with his real sons Shem and Ham. At that time, I was known to him and the rest of his family as Japheth and I enjoyed their company. His house was a place or peace in a land of human torment. Despite my already advanced age, I had not yet developed any sense of anger or resentment with humanity but I relished the quiet and simplicity of family life. It helped me think." Adam looked as if his thoughts were elsewhere as he fixed his stare on the fresco above. Crowe looked deeper himself and realised that the character portrayed as part of the family group yet just far enough away from the others to seem distant. That character had more than a little resemblance to the young man that revelled in the painting next to him. "Noah always regarded me with enquiring eyes but obviously did not know my true heritage," Adam continued, "or the fact that despite his appearance of great age and my youthful demeanour, I was already thousands of years older than he." Adam looked at Crowe once more, his face now more studious and focussed.

"The time of Noah was when the products of many earlier generations had successfully produced children without Creator intervention. Although many new humans then existed, it was clear that most were not complete. Physically the Human form was well advanced. The amount of Creator DNA at that point within the Human body was diminishing rapidly and although Noah himself lived a very long life, I understand the bible speaks of around 950 years, although I regret to say that most of these great ages were wrong anyway, he did age considerably during that time and was able to sire children well into the later periods of his life." Adam stopped speaking and waited for Crowe to make a comment.

"If memory serves, did not Japheth sire his own lineage? I thought you stated in the prologue to your books that you were unable to produce children?" Crowe asked genuinely.

"Ah yes, that is true," Adam responded smiling," I did take a wife but she mourned the inability for me to fertilise her so she took lovers. Certainly, Shem and Ham. Possibly even Noah himself!" Adam laughed enthusiastically, "It was of no consequence to me and I had very little to do with the upbringing as I had already left them once the waters receded."

"So, the flood then," Crowe started to ask. "It actually happened, as the story is known?" He made towards one of the armchairs facing the fireplace and sat down. Adam copied his move and sat opposite in another similar chair. It creaked as he sat.

"You remember in my letter that I mentioned the Creators sometimes tested Humanity?" Crowe nodded in agreement, "The flood was one of those tests although they also saw it as an opportunity to destroy many of the less successful results from their engineering. As I said, physically the tests were successful but many minds were weak or distorted. The Creators realised that whilst the flesh was easy to manipulate, conscious thought was not. Thus, the people were more inclined to base instincts than intellectual progress. It was a time of chaos"

"And the animals, did they really enter the Ark two by two, from all over the world?" Crowe followed.

"Only examples from the immediate area of the flood itself," Adam replied, "It was more about safeguarding the ability to start again with farming and animal husbandry than saving whole species. In any event, it was not all over the world. You have to remember that the cradle of civilisation at that time was still quite localised to the eastern Mediterranean and indeed, Mesopotamia in particular. As you know, the area is bordered by the Euphrates and the Tigris rivers and the poor drainage caused by low gradients in the area causes frequent flooding."

"So, the Creators," Crowe grimaced as he found himself using Adam's own terminology, "Brought the flood to what was then largely a dry area by…" he stalled, "By…..how exactly?"

"They had the technology to effectively 'seed' rain clouds on a massive scale over the northern heights that feed the two great rivers so that it rained for a sustained period in extensive amounts."

"Forty days and forty nights?" Crowe interrupted with a sly grin.

"No, that is biblical embellishment I'm afraid. It was as long as sufficient for the two rivers to be hugely overwhelmed in a short time. The flood surge reached far across Mesopotamia covering everything before it. The rains continued unabated and the Ark, actually just a flat-bottomed wooden platform with shoulder-height sides, floated until the waters settled sufficiently to allow the highest hillocks to poke through the waters once more. It was through me that Noah was advised of what would happen. Taking the animals was more about saving Noah's livelihood than the rescue of all natural life" Adam paused. "You see Michael, most stories are based on some truth and all will be made even more dramatic by the imagination of the author, but sometimes you have to wait for the real truth to be disclosed, something I hope you will help me with." He sat back in the chair and waited for Crowe's reaction.

"Then you are saying Noah and his sons became the fathers of man after the flood? There were no others left?" Crowe asked following quickly with another thought that rushed into his head. "And Atlantis? Was that consumed by the flood?"

Adam laughed and shook his head. "Oh no, there was no Atlantis. Just another myth of misplaced hope." There were others that survived and established settlements and cultures and who had previously migrated East, South or North to beyond where the flood reached. Plus, there were already independent civilisations in other parts of the world where the Creators were working. The descendants of Noah and his sons primarily spread themselves further to repopulate the Middle East and to join those that had gone before them. My journeys after that time was partly to find them and guide them accordingly." Adam replied, "Which of course is what I did and in doing so, I became the myth behind much of the legends you will know about."

Crowe looked up at the ceiling again and spoke without looking at his host.

"I see a painting here that looks Norse in its heritage. One there that is clearly Ancient Greece, another early Egypt. One seems to be Indian in style. So, you are saying that each are episodes of your life?" He looked down again as his neck muscles started to strain.

"Indeed, each do represent some of my travels, perhaps the most important ones that contributed to the myths of history shall we say. I will have played some part in all and in many cases, it is the same story that has changed and morphed into something else depending on the culture base of the civilisation adopting it." He stared straight into Crowe's bemused eyes, "Michael, I need you to accept that I am who I say I am. If you can at least accept that I am the first man then everything else will fall into place. I hope you can understand that."

Crowe felt uneasy. Every conscious argument in his brain screamed that he could not possibly be sitting opposite a man who had lived since the dawn of humanity. A man impossibly old in years and yet not having aged older than Crowe himself. It just didn't ring true and yet Wilding was already convinced, potentially the last person Crowe would have thought to be susceptible to wild theories. Adam could just be a rich eccentric with a persuasive argument and the money to make things happen to 'prove' his wild boasts. Crowe knew he would need something more.

"I need proof Adam," he said bluntly. "You spin a great yarn but you look like ordinary flesh and blood to me as you will to billions around the world. How exactly are you going to prove you are genuine, despite all the academic backing you may or may not get?" Crowe maintained a concerned look on his face as he leaned forwards, resting his elbows on his knees and his chin against his clasped hands.

Adam smiled a cheeky grin and raised his eyebrows. His eyes positively sparkled and reflected the dancing flames of the fire.

"This house," he began, "you thought you recognised it?" He raised his arms wide as Crowe nodded. "Well you should as it is a stone by stone copy of my estate when I lived the life of your biography subject." He waited as Crowe eyes widened because he knew Barnsford House had been completely destroyed by the baying mob that attacked it in 1791. It had been razed to the ground, the blackened stone scattered and lost.

"I kept the original plans and had it re-created here as my refuge. Here, let me show you." He got out of the chair and went to a large chest by the door that had a stack of thin drawers, the top one of which he drew back and extracted a large parchment sheet. He beckoned Crowe to join him by the low table between the two chairs and spread the sheet for him to see. It was Barnsford House, of that there was no doubt and was drawn in profile and plan to show the dimensions together with a pictorial representation of the finished building in the lower right-hand corner complete, Crowe noted, with a small herd of deer grazing on the lawns.

Adam pointed to the West wing of the house and the upper storey plan which would have been above the room where they now stood. "As you can see Michael," he started, this was my bedroom and these," his long elegant finger drew an imaginary line across the rooms that all interconnected from the master bedroom, "These were the rooms for my 'guests'," He smiled again and for the first time, Crowe noted the slightly musky smell he had about him. Not an unpleasant smell by any means but something unknown, something of quality and of age.

"You are referring to your club participants?" Crowe responded knowing that Adam was indeed referring to his hedonistic pursuits that had shamed and disgusted the people. Even in the century of promiscuity and excess, the debauchery of Barnsford's notorious 'Hades Society' was an ever-present scandal. The 'Hellfire Club' paled into relative insignificance in comparison. Nothing was taboo, nothing untried. Even claims of sacrifice and ritual murder had been waved away at the time as exaggerations of simple pleasures of the body and mind. The whole reputation of the man had been the inspiration for Crowe to base his thesis on social immorality of the eighteenth century and his later published biographical work.

"You know me for who I was," Adam started, "You know in your heart that this is who I am now," he continued. "Why fight the truth Michael? Are you not intrigued? Are you not excited!" Adam placed his hand on Michaels shoulder and squeezed it slightly, making him feel uncomfortable with the apparent warmth of the gesture.

"If you were Barnsford, then do you wish to be him again? Create a new society on the back of your elevated position as a new Messiah?" Crowe walked back to the chair and sat. Adam looked annoyed and his mood darkened.

"What happened then was exciting and it was pure pleasure I can assure you but the two matters are not the same. I know certain supporters of mine still like to carry on the heritage of those times but for myself, I want to bring mankind hope. I want to guide, to lead."

"To control?" Crowe interrupted.

"I want to bring truth!" Adam exploded shocking Crowe with the sudden ferocity. "I am the saviour of man, the chosen one! The creation of those that made humanity what it is! Know this. I can do this with or without you Michael but I would much rather you were my Prophet than that fool Wilding. I see I must offer you the proof you need and so be it."

Adam moved to another chest with four deep drawers opposite the fireplace and opened the third drawer down. He took out a flat wooden box and opened it to show Crowe the fine pair of duelling pistols within. He took out the lower of the two guns and proceeded to use the powder flask to prepare the gun to fire. He rammed the ball home with the rod followed by a small piece of wadding. He then drew back the cocked flint, reversed the pistol and handed it to Crowe butt first. Crowe firstly refused the pistol but with Adam's clear insistence, took the gun gingerly.

"What you are holding there Michael, is one half of an exquisite pair of duelling pistols that I have owned for the past twenty years. I assume you are not an expert on guns, Michael but I can tell you that if you were holding a standard flintlock pistol then you most likely would notice a delay between pulling that trigger and the ball being fired. What makes this pistol and its twin so special is the hair trigger that will send death speeding towards a victim a split second faster so I would advise caution to keep your finger away at this time." Adam stood upright and stiff. "The barrel is smoothly bored and the calibre is slightly larger than the normal flintlock. The ball itself will be a perfect sphere and smooth so that its velocity and ejection from the barrel will not be compromised by a shoddy finish. Believe me when I say Michael, what you possess there will be amongst the most efficient killing machines of the age."

"But I don't understand," Crowe started, "what do you want me to do?"

"Kill me." Adam said calmly. Point it at my chest and kill me." He undid his quality silk shirt to the navel and pulled apart the two sides to reveal a muscular and honed hairless chest. "What are you waiting for Michael, this is your chance. Pull the trigger."

"But I can't," Crowe said weakly, "Surely you don't want me to do this just to make a point? There has to be another way!"

"Just pull the trigger," Adam shouted and moving even closer.

"I can't," Crowe argued, "This is crazy."

"KILL ME!" Adam screamed, his face a sudden mask of rage and loathing as he pushed his chest against the muzzle of the flintlock causing Crowe to retract in horror.

The sound of the explosion from the pistol hardly registered with Crowe as his finger involuntarily pressed the hair trigger mechanism. The gun bucked in his hand and he felt his wrist strain with the backlash. A cloud of grey-white smoke filled the space between the two men and Crowe's eyes began to sting from the acrid particles that attacked them. He had the sense that Adam had pitched backwards for he was no longer standing close to him and could see that he now slumped back against the chair, sitting on the floor with his legs splayed. As the smoke cleared, Crowe could see he was conscious and staring at him. His face was a picture of agony but as only seconds ticked by, his expression quickly changed and was once again serene and at peace. Above his heart, his once perfect skin was a scene of black, bloody ruin but as Crowe stared, the ruptured flesh began to move, ripple and flow around the hole where the lead ball had entered. The blood stopped flowing and the charred, red edges were dulling in colour as the skin started to pucker around the wound. Crowe could see the gunmetal grey of the lead ball suddenly become visible, getting larger until the ball itself emerged from the entry wound and fell into Adam's lap. Once out of the body, the hole healed completely before Crowe's eyes, the red skin turning back to the olive fleshy colour it originally had been until there was nothing to show there had ever been a wound in the first place.

Adam sighed and started to move. "You see Michael," I cannot be killed but goodness me, it still hurts to prove it!" He smiled once more as he rubbed where the wound had been and took the gun from Crowe's shaking hand before cleaning it and replacing it into the case, placing the box back into the drawer and closing it.

"Michael," he said as he turned to face him, "Do I have your belief now?"

Crowe looked down at his shoes as his mind was everywhere at once and he could not look into Adam's mesmerising eyes. One thought tore through the confusion, Crowe realised that despite all his misgivings, he had just witnessed the impossible. Whoever Adam truly was, whether he was indeed

Adam anyway, he was clearly someone, something special. Adam smiled broadly as Crowe started to nod his head up and down, his ears still ringing form the pistol shot.

Although the smoke was now gone, the acrid smell still hung heavy in the air. In front of him, Adam remained silent and thoughtful. The brief anger he had shown with passionate ferocity had totally abated and he was once again the very example of calm. Whatever he thought of this man Adam, Crowe could not help but be concerned at the relative speed and efficiency at which his moods seemingly changed. Could it be that the oldest 'human' alive had developed multiple personalities or schizophrenic tendencies he considered?

Crowe's mind was still racing but he could not escape the fact that he had witnessed a complete reversal of death. More than that, he had seen the wound independently repel the ball that had penetrated Adam's body and subsequently heal itself with alarming speed. Although Adam had clearly felt the pain and for very short time his body looked to be in death, now here he was, unharmed, uninjured and as if nothing had happened.

"You know, recalling the total number of times I have died for my journals was the hardest thing," Adam said flippantly, "Once you have been killed in the same way so many times it is much harder to be precise of exactly when, where and by whom." He paced the room until coming back to the chair opposite Crowe and resumed his seat.

"Do you have further questions Michael?" he asked with another of his perfect smiles.

"Adam, you have proved you cannot be harmed for I have seen that with my own eyes – although I find it hard to accept," Crowe started, "But I am persuaded that you have proved either a fantastic skill of illusion, or you are indeed immortal and I am prepared to accept the latter for the purpose of further discussion at this time."

"Excellent!" Adam exclaimed with a flourish and clapped his hands in glee.

"Therefore, if we can assume you are indeed capable of immortality, or at least you can show an extremely strong resistance to harm, whilst fantastic enough in scientific terms, that alone does not prove you are Adam, the original Adam, or that you have been all you claim to be. If I must go public with this, if you wish me to endorse you as the very embodiment of history itself and with every apple cart that is going to upset, then I am going to need more. The world is going to need more." Crowe sat back in his seat once again and started to wring his hands slightly, the shock was still taking its toll.

"And being immortal is not enough?" Adam asked, raising his eyebrows.

"I am sure we can devise multiple ways to kill you in public and hear the gasps as you regenerate but again, how does that prove you are Adam? How does that prove beyond doubt the Creators exist? That you are not just a brilliant illusionist?"

"If I could be harmed then you have just cut me Michael, to the quick." Adam responded disappointedly. "For my public appearance I will endure any form of death, or attempts at killing me as you like. Perhaps more than one will prove beyond doubt in any event. Can I suggest being burned at the stake perhaps? Always popular in the Middle Ages I recall, or perhaps beheading? Many of times the axe man's blade has bounced back with force and once I remember it took a chunk out of the priest's leg who was there to give me the last rights. It was he who died on that scaffold that day." Adam laughed. He was making a joke but Crowe failed to see the funny side.

"Michael, put together whatever circus you see fit to make this point. Arrange it in the most public place if you wish. I certainly have one in mind. Use blades, bullets, fire, the choice is yours. Make it as spectacular as you like! For I guarantee this, if the world sees me die and come back time and time again in real time, in full public view it will be on every news channel, every online blog, every social network page. The act of immortality alone will sell my authenticity. All you have to do is to add the substance, present the back-story, explain the facts so that there can be no mistake. I am Adam and the people of the world will accept that." Adam raised one eyebrow only now as he looked hard into Crowe's face.

"When I asked this earlier it angered you," Crowe said quietly, "But I must ask it again. What will you gain from this? What is it you want?"

"As I said before, I wish to be recognised and to lead." Adam replied with restraint.

"As a God?" Crowe suggested.

"As a teacher," Adam responded with a glare, "A guide, a wise man if you like. If man has developed anything over thousands of years it has been resilience. Man is afraid of change. I am not asking humanity to give up their gods in favour of me. What would I do with all that worship?" he laughed quietly, "there will be those that will resist and perhaps the world faiths will have a challenge on their hands to defend all they have purported to be their truth over millennia but perhaps not all. I am not going to stand up and say that Christians or Muslims, Jews or Hindus are wrong to believe what they do. They have all spent centuries saying that to each other and going to war to defend it but I wish no ill on any religion or believer within it. My purpose is clear, I want to show that Humans are who they are today because nature was given a genetic boost when it needed it, nothing more." He paused but Crowe was waiting for more so he continued.

"Michael, early man worshiped the sun and the moon. They believed in forest spirits and deities that existed within the natural world in water, earth or in animals. Why was that? Because they had no scientific explanation for why the moon changes shape over the lunar cycle, why the sun goes dark during an eclipse, why plants die and are then reborn with the spring. They made up their gods because it was the easy explanation in the absence of the truth. Modern religion is also ultimately based on the pre-science age. It involves characters and actions that revolve around the activities of the gods that were created to explain the message they wanted the believers to accept. But do you know what Michael," he paused again but Crowe did not respond so he continued. "despite centuries of indoctrination and evolution of faith, the old gods of the earth, the spirits of the forests are still worshiped by some, although they are now designated as 'new age' or pagan. The point I am making Michael is that faith adapts and in some cases regresses. I do not seek to be the God of all, or indeed the God of any and despite whatever we show people, whilst they may accept my immortality, many will not be persuaded that their faith is wrong." Crowe nodded in agreement as he realised Adam had a point.

"They do not have to give up the old ways to welcome the new," Adam continued, "The great churches will adapt their messages. They will say that an Almighty God still exists for who created the Creators? They will say the great Prophets and wise men of the Bible for instance were similar to myself, a product given to man by God through the Creators. The will say that the Creators were simply the facilitators of a higher God and that my appearance now proves that process is continuing. Who will say that is not a clever compromise to keep them relevant? Yes, I will change history back to the truth but is that not a bonanza of opportunity for you as a historian to rewrite thousands of years of supposed historical fact? Will the peoples of the world accept religious inspired terrorism and death when the big reveal shows how futile that approach is? Once the doom merchants and the doubters are silenced, will there not be a new age of enlightenment and peace? Will that not be the true essence of the Rapture?"

Adam paused one last time before standing again. He completed the two steps to Crowe's chair and placed both hands on it, one on each arm so that his face was only a few inches from Crowe's.

"Believe me Michael, this is yours for the taking. The opportunity is exclusive to you. Only you will have the books of my life to publish as your own work. This is your only chance for your own brand or immortality. Please take it?" He straitened himself and walked to the door.

"And now we should retire for the evening. Karl will show you to you room and we will resume tomorrow." He left the room silently and Crowe remained sitting until Tall Man, now known as Karl entered.

"This way Mr Crowe he said and moved back to the door. Crowe followed silently, his mind still deep in thought as they moved towards the grand staircase. Adam, Crowe noted was already at the top of the steps and was proceeding across the landing to the left above the hallway. As Tall Man and Crowe reached the top of the staircase, he was led in the opposite direction, across the length of the gallery and then right into a short corridor towards a door at the end. For some reason, the spacing of the corridor seemed wrong. There was no other branch of it from the gallery and although they passed other doors to his left as they walked, the symmetry just felt wrong. Crowe would have expected an opposite corridor to the one they were one that accessed the back of the house but it did not exist.

The room they entered that was to be his accommodation for the night was of reasonable size and although it was now already dark, Michael was sure the room would have a wide view of the front lawns and thin gravel path that led away towards the tree-line where they have previously left the segways. There were tall ivory curtains surrounding the large sash windows with a matching pelmet. The walls were painted a deep Wedgwood blue with classic plaster relief dado and picture rails. A white plaster fire surround housed yet another roaring log fire which Tall Man added a large log to before leaving the room and closing the door.

Crowe examined the relatively small half-tester bed in with the antique oak frame. It was higher off the floor than modern beds but the mattress seemed comfortable enough if not a little soft. The bedding was of high thread count white cotton with a silk bedspread with matching bolster and scatter cushions. A door next to the bed led into a small but beautifully tiled en-suite that looked brand new and unused. Crowe decided to christen the toilet bowl accordingly and the resulting flush seemed to generate a series of gurgles and knocks in the feeder pipe to suggest it had been some time, if ever, since it had been used. He washed his hands and dried them on the sumptuous cotton towel noting that there was a stack of six quality towels of various sizes at his disposal. Moving back into the main room, he searched in vain for an obvious television but there was none. The cabinet opposite the bed was modern in contrast to the other furniture in the room and he opened it expecting to find the television within but he found only a kettle, cups and a range of hot drink options. Bottled water, three bottles in all with one sparkling and two still variants stood alongside the kettle and on a tray beneath on a separate shelf, there was a fruit bowl with apples, bananas and pears plus a large selection of individually wrapped biscuits. If nothing else, Crowe realised that Adam lived in luxury and expected his guests to experience the same, even if Crowe himself was possibly the first.

Crowe walked to the entrance door and turned the knob. Nothing happened. The door was locked and despite his attempts, he was not going anywhere. With suitable alarm, Crowe moved to the window to note that locks were also present on the frame. At the top of the window a ventilation grill was open to allow fresh air but clearly, he was just as much a prisoner and he was a guest, despite the luxury and despite Adam's assurances.

Reaching into his jacket for his mobile, Crowe thought it would be the best time to call Jessica and explain why he had not text or called her previously. He was already two days later than expected with only the short, slightly strained late-night call in the early hours of the morning. So much had happened since then and Crowe needed to speak to somebody. The lack of signal coverage was apparent by the message the phone was giving. Crowe tried to seek a suitable Wi-Fi connection in order to Skype or email her but there was none. With sudden realisation, Crowe understood that he was both unable to leave his room or contact anyone outside of the house. He had no means to see what was going on in the outside world and was being restrained by a man of which he neither trusted nor really understood. He suddenly felt thirsty and, not wishing to go to the trouble of making a hot drink, he chose one of the bottles of still water to quench that thirst. He unscrewed the top and put the bottle to his lips, drinking lustily. Only after gulping the water down did he think there was a slightly strange aftertaste that he could not discern. Within a minute he felt weary and weak, suddenly very tired. Blaming the heaviness of the supper, the disturbed sleep, the long helicopter journey and the stress of what had transpired earlier that evening being too much. Crowe mounted the bed and within seconds, he was sleeping deeply.

Chapter Fourteen

21.17 pm 18th September, Present day, Hospital Armand Trousseau, Paris, France

Cardinal McGeary awoke slowly and with some difficulty. The very act of normal movement seemed restricted as if he was being restrained. He blinked hard as his eyes became accustomed to the light and slowly turned his head to take stock of his surroundings. The strange light and cream hue of the walls to the room masked any recognition and the thumping rhythm in his head was oppressive and constant.

His face felt strange, heavy somehow and he moved his right arm to feel out what was troubling him but it was strangely heavy and unresponsive so he tried the left. That arm moved more freely but still felt like a dead weight. He reached his face and explored with his fingers as they found the cause of the strange sensation and he realise that there was gauze taped to his cheek. His face was painful and he understood as his body slowly recovered from his slumbers that both legs and his back ached and were heavy to move. Despite the pain, he shifted his body as best he could to try and find a more comfortable position and in doing so, he became aware of the fact that he was not alone.

"Your Eminence?" a voice spoke to his left and McGeary slowly turned his head to see the dark shape of a tall and thin man in a crumpled brown coat with fur lapels looking down at him. The man wore a battered brown trilby and was unshaven. His expression was one of cheerlessness and fatigue. McGeary wondered how long he had been waiting for him to come around from his sleep.

"Your Eminence, "The voice followed in heavily accented English, "I am Inspector Claude Fournier of the Police Nationale. You are in the Hospital Armand Trousseau in Paris. Do you know who you are? Are you aware of what has happened to you," Fournier's voice remained monotone and without expression.

"I am Cardinal Donal McGeary. I am an Irish citizen but appointed with special responsibilities as Cardinal to the Holy See in the Vatican," McGeary answered, "I believe I have been involved in some sort of 'incident'," he paused, "but do not be troubled my son, I do not think I am badly injured other than muscular aches and a few cuts. Can you tell me what happened?"

"A bomb. A car bomb," Fournier responded, "You were caught up in the blast and you suffered unconsciousness. You were lucky." He had not improved his bedside manner and gave no sign of encouragement in his voice.

"My driver? Pascal?" McGeary followed.

"Non," Fournier answered, "il est Morte." He said before realising he had answered in French, "He is dead."

"Oh no," McGeary exclaimed with genuine sadness," He was a good man, a family man. I am saddened to hear this terrible news." Fournier nodded his agreement.

"We think you were the target your Eminence although the media are saying it was a terrorist act aimed at the Moroccan Embassy in that street. Do you know why you would be a target?" Fournier asked directly.

"I am sorry my son but I do not. Are you sure the bomb was meant for me?" McGeary asked sympathetically.

"It was your car that was destroyed your Eminence," the Captain responded with a shrug, "You were approaching it when it exploded. Who else would it have been for?" He asked hypothetically. "We know that it was a device that was set off by a mobile phone signal so the bomber would have been close to know when to send that signal. He may even have been watching you." The Captain paused and waited for a reaction from the Cardinal.

"Surely if he had been watching and wanted me dead then he would have waited for me to enter the car before blowing it up?" McGeary answered.

"A warning then?" Fournier responded, "A message perhaps? A threat?"

"I really cannot imagine why someone would want to warn me or indeed kill me Captain but I will await your thoughts from your investigation." McGeary closed his eyes, "Will you forgive me my son and allow me to sleep. I feel weary." He waited as the policeman fumbled with his notebook, placing it in his coat pocket.

"Of course your Eminence," he started, "forgive me, you must be tired. I will return when you are more recovered." He started to make for the door.

"Thank you," McGeary whispered and made out he was slipping into slumber.

Once the policeman was clear of the door McGeary counted to one hundred and then reached for the cord above the bed, pulling it. He hoped that would be sufficient to call a nurse and was surprised as one appeared almost instantly.

"Oui monsieur?" A young attractive nurse of West African descent entered and walked to beside the bed.

McGeary started to speak in his best French which was as good as Fournier's English but he did not want the policeman to know that. He asked for some painkillers and his mobile phone, both of which turned out to be in the cabinet next to his bed and the nurse took out the small plastic container with two pills inside which he took with a little water. Once she had left the room, McGeary turned the mobile phone on and viewed his 47 messages, nearly all of which were sentiments to his wellbeing. He scrolled through each knowing he would have to respond to all until he came to the one he had hoped he would find. It was timed only a few hours after he had left the meeting and the bomb having been detonated and was from the phone he had called and conversed with Prime Minister Andrew Stubbs before. The message was short and to the point.

'You have my interest. Please contact me.'

Cardinal Donal McGeary smiled and grimaced at the same time as it stretched the gauze supports to his cheek. At least there was something of a breakthrough there, he thought. Stubbs was going to be vital as McGeary was sure that Adam was in Britain and at least there, the reach of the Votary had not scaled the heights of the ultimate power base, at least he hoped not.

McGeary thought hard and realised that the bomb could have been nothing else but a warning to him that the Votary were active. If anything, more than the bomb could have been detonated to kill, perhaps not just him but all the attendees at the meeting. No, the Votary were being clever. They were making the point that their reach was wide and powerful. Killing the faith representatives would have sent the wrong message, one of hate that would have damaged their cause. They exist to protect Adam, to nurture his reveal and keep him safe. By labelling the bomb as yet another act of religious fanaticism they strengthen the argument that the old faiths are weak and divided. McGeary knew that the rumours of their power were true and he and his team would need to be vigilant to be able to combat their aims.

A sudden thought rushed into his head. How did they know he was going to be there? Indeed, that all the faith representatives would be in that building and on that street at the time on that day? McGeary himself only knew the venue had been confirmed a few hours before. They had hired that room for the convenience of speed and secrecy and even the drivers, including poor Pascal, had been hired within 90 minutes of the meeting starting.

Firstly, the Votary had known about De Soto being the messenger about Rosario's suicide almost at the same time as he had done and had quickly despatched the Portuguese man, he assumed, afterwards and now, McGeary's own movements had been known. McGeary had the quick realisation that their tendrils must have reached even inside the Vatican. How destabilising could it be that at the heart of the Catholic faith, the creed of many millions across the planet that even in that place, the exponents of the destroyer of faith had support?

McGeary knew that he needed allies and without hesitation picked up the phone again and began to text. He needed to be out of this hospital as soon as he possible could so despite the protestations of his doctor, McGeary insisted that he should be immediately discharged and had organised assistance from the Vatican Embassy to provide manual help to do so. With the assistance of two men assigned to the task. McGeary left the hospital after a short period into a waiting car and was soon convalescing in rooms made available to him in the Embassy for the Holy See on the Avenue du President Wilson.

Despite the pain he was now feeling, as the movements made to get him to his new location had jarred and rubbed his various bruises and cuts, he refused the medication issued by the hospital upon his departure and instead asked for his tablet to be fully charged so he could work whilst propped up in his bed. He asked for some orange juice and, once received, requested a period of non-disturbance so he could make the long-awaited call he needed to complete.

Waiting until the door to the whitewashed room was closed, McGeary reached for his mobile phone and pressed the recall button to the number of the phone kept by Stubbs. It continuously rang without going to voicemail without being answered so McGeary pressed end and waited a few minutes. He rang one more time and was rewarded with an immediate answer.

"Yes?" it was Stubbs.

"Prime Minister, it is McGeary," the Cardinal replied.

"I am pleased to hear you are alive and not too seriously hurt I hope?" Stubbs started. "It looks like it was a close-run thing."

"I am as well as can be expected thank you, "McGeary replied," although I am convinced the purpose of the bomb was not to kill me in any event. Sadly, my driver Pascal was not so privileged"

"A warning perhaps?" Stubbs continued. "If what you are saying to me is correct, then you will have enemies I suspect."

The Cardinal furrowed his brow as he replied. "Perhaps in places I thought I need not look. I am afraid I may have an agent of the Votary close to me; something I had not prepared for."

"We all have our own version of rats to consider", Stubbs stated mournfully. "Cardinal McGeary," Stubbs exclaimed, "You have asked me to consider a threat to the United Kingdom. You have done so in a rather underhand way without going through the proper channels and whilst I have no doubt that this conversation will register on word recognition software within my own intelligence services, I am drawn to what you have said directly and wish to know more simply because you are not the only person who has said it to me in recent days."

McGeary started to speak but Stubbs interrupted him as he continued. "From a very unexpected source and a trusted friend. Someone who I thought I knew but I find myself questioning many years of friendship as a result. It is that sense of personal betrayal that has prompted me to respond to you now and as such I need to speak to you face to face as soon as possible. How feasible is that given your current situation?"

"I will make it happen. When were you thinking?" McGeary replied quickly.

"Tomorrow, I will be in Paris as part of a meeting with French officials that was cancelled previously. I will also be taking the opportunity to have dinner with my late wife's sister and family who live just outside the city after the meeting. Something can be arranged then."

"Just tell me where and when and I will be there," McGeary replied, "But Mr Stubbs, to me only please?"

"Understood," Stubbs replied solemnly and hung up.

McGeary settled back upon the nest of pillows supporting his back and closed his eyes. If Stubbs had been contacted with the same message at the same time as his own then that could have only come from the Votary he concluded. As Stubbs confirmed, someone well known and trusted to the Prime Minister himself, indeed a friend. It would fit the profile, McGeary considered, a person of authority and of the establishment. A personal friend of the decision maker of independent and considerable means, possibly a power-broker or facilitator. A 'fear cumhachtach' as his Gaelic speaking grandfather would have said; a powerful man.

McGeary afforded himself a wry smile as this thought drifted back to his tenacious and forthright grandfather. What would he have made of his grandson now he thought? So anti-establishment in his outlook with a distrust of the Catholic church in general and with his anti-British sentiments resulting in a brother lost to an army bullet in the 1916 Easter Rising within the General Post Office siege, the fact that his grandson was now a Cardinal and instrumental to warning the British about a possible threat to the United Kingdom would have been too much. He would have used his limited English to state his thoughts in his best Anglo-Saxon McGeary concluded. Perhaps it was just as well the man head been dead these thirty-five years past he thought.

Despite his desire to consider the situation further, the exertions of the short journey and settling into his new place of residence was catching up on the Cardinal and his relaxed posture soon brought about involuntary slumber. Within seconds, McGeary was asleep.

"Merde!" Captain Fournier exclaimed as he put the receiver down. He had just telephoned the hospital to be advised that McGeary had discharged himself. Whilst the hospital had declined to advise the policeman where the Cardinal had gone to, Fournier was in no doubt that it would be the Vatican Embassy and that made matters difficult. He could not get access without a very long-winded diplomatic process and therefore, he has no means to keep an eye on him. He sat and thought deeply about his next plans of action but in his heart, he already knew what he had to do.

Reaching into his coat pocket that hung on a stand next to his desk, Fournier retrieved the mobile phone and pressed the button sequence to show the history of the calls he had made. He scrolled down the list until he reached the one he was looking for. He hesitated for a moment before selecting the number and the options button. He waited a few more seconds before pressing delete and consigning the call to history that had destroyed many windows and peppered building with shrapnel in a quite Paris street, obliterated numerous cars, killed an innocent driver and badly injured a Roman Catholic Cardinal. The Captain was taking no chances and needed to know there would be no record. He then sent one text to the number used the most, 'Position compromised, target out of reach. Will lose phone and move to contact point B.' he pressed send and then proceeded to delete all numbers in the call list under the 'delete all' option. Standing, he turned the phone off before removing the back plate and detaching the battery. He put all parts back in the pocket of his coat which he then put on and headed for the exit. Fournier was scared. Failure was not an option as had been drilled into him many times. McGeary now being in the Embassy was nothing he could have controlled but the loss of the Cardinal to daily observance was a failure that would come calling in the fullness of time. The Captain decided immediately that contact point B was the last place he would be going to.

Chapter Fifteen

07.41 am 19th September, Present Day, the River Test, Hampshire, England

Donald Avery read the message over and over again but realised the content was not going to change.

'Nine of Twelve is dead. Suicide. His cowardice and betrayal will be forever damned through the future ages of Adam. You are to assume his duties and position as required until we can replace him. You will continue to be referred to as Four of Twelve. Continue to await further instructions as your location now confirmed for announcement'

Avery grimaced knowing that his own contemplated ending of it all would have produced the same damning response but the vintage Chinese copy of the Mauser C96 revolver was safely back in his house and locked away. Indeed, all his possessions, photographs, books and personal papers once in the Cabinet Office were now in boxes in his private study. His resignation the day before had been public and brutal, spawning various conspiracy theories as to why such a personal friend of Andrew Stubbs would quit on him at the height of the Government's success. Hounded by the Press, Avery had retreated to the fishing lodge hidden within his Test Valley estate and there he sat now contemplating what had happened as the crystal-clear River Test bubbled and sluiced over the gavel beds and long dancing tendrils of weed. A large brown trout shimmied over the central bank of gravel and stayed quietly in the current waiting for the next insect to conveniently drop onto the surface ahead of it. Avery watched the fish as it waited before being rewarded by a long-legged fly that delayed taking to the air again by one vital, fatal second. The surface rippled and thrashed as the trout took the fly and swam quickly to the deeper pool back to finish its meal.

Stubbs had remained angry after their dinner meeting. He had blocked all attempts Avery had made to contact him and had returned none of the voice messages he had sent. Even Elizabeth had become concerned at the lack of response but had already reacted badly to the news Avery had given her that he was about to resign. The hug she had given him as he started to pack his contents into the storage boxes had been genuine and with affection and Avery, for a moment, had reprimanded himself for not seeing how she felt after all this time working together. As Elizabeth had allowed the embrace to last a few seconds longer than protocol would have allowed for, Avery had responded, pressing her into him and rubbing her back gently. Elizabeth had looked up and after a few more seconds, the kiss had been long, delicate and meaningful.

A noise from outside the office resulted in an immediate disentanglement of their embrace but the line had been crossed and Elizabeth had left the room beaming. Avery had reacted also and knew immediately that this was absolutely the wrong time to start a relationship, but knew also that he would still do so. He had already been too long alone and in mourning plus who knew what would be happening in future days and weeks. Would he even still be alive? Perhaps, he thought, this is exactly the time to enjoy the company of someone with genuine feelings for him.

He looked at the message once more which had been sent via the private texting app created especially for him and the others making up the Votary. Until now, all had remained anonymous of each other. All each knew is that they made up the high council and at the time of his presentation to the world, Adam would call upon them. Avery knew he was Four of Twelve with each of his council colleagues named similarly with numbered prefixes although none denoted any rank over the others. No one member of the Votary seemingly controlled the others as it was Adam himself who took that role so each had been kept in isolation of the other eleven until the call would come. Only One of Twelve assumed the position of deputy but like the others, his identity remained secret. The name each took had remained unchanged as it had been held by all first born male ancestors of each bloodline with the secret and the duty that came with it passing to the eldest son. If the line was broken through the lack of a naturally born son or the death of the first-born son before the father, or if no other son reached maturity before the father's own death, then the line would cease. In that event a replacement lineage would be chosen by Adam who would use his influence and control to induce that family into the fold. Many of the Votary could trace their ancestral membership back beyond publicly recorded history, before parish records and it was known to the council as a whole that most of their lineage was ancient but of the names involved, all remained secret amongst them. The only link that was known is that throughout recorded history, Adam had been instrumental in supporting and in many cases, funding the original business enterprise that had created their individual empires.

All Avery knew is that generally only one member of the Votary existed in any one major country or general geographical area that made up the 'Old World'. The full network of the Votary extended in every country to include those that did the bidding of the Votary but only one authority existed to cover each. Avery was the designated council member of the Votary for the British Isles, including the Irish Republic as the council made no allowances for geo-political changes, preferring instead to base each of the Votary's areas of responsibility on more ancient boundaries. So, Avery remained Four of Twelve and by default, he was now temporarily responsible for Nine of Twelve's area as well which he knew to be the Iberian Peninsula comprising Spain and Portugal plus the various island groups applicable to both. Narrowing this down, Avery had poured over English translated news reports from the two countries to try and get a clue about who Nine of Twelve could have been. It served no real purpose to him personally as through the man's suicidal action to rid himself of the responsibilities to come, any financial or other connections with the council or the Votary would have already been deleted, but he simply wanted to know, if he could, what another council member could look like in establishment terms.

In the end, he was drawn to the small news report he eventually found online which reported the mysterious death of the leading Portuguese shipping magnate. The report stated that the Portuguese police were seeking a man known to be the deceased's psychiatrist but that evidence had emerged which suggested that the death was self-inflicted. Whilst not interested in the investigation that had since started, it struck Avery that the profile of the dead man would make him a likely subject. Vastly wealthy from 'old money' investment and business ownership spanning hundreds of years in the same family and with business contacts in satellite companies spanning the whole of the Portuguese/Spanish sphere. But the name meant nothing to Avery himself, Heitor Guilherme Iago Rosario. He was in his sixties, a widower with one son who had pre-deceased him. Avery suddenly considered that the similarities between him and this Rosario were becoming all too clear. Both had long established family businesses going back hundreds of years, in Avery's case it was exporting and international trade, both extremely wealthy and both widowers who had lost sons, in Avery's case, both of them.

Avery continued to search on the name and came across the report of the death of the son, also called Heitor, a few months earlier from drowning after entering the sea under the influence of drugs. An accident surely Avery thought, although in a state of induced confusion no doubt. The mother had died of cancer some years before and Heitor senior was noted as being a widower in this report also.

He considered this further. What if the profile of all the Votary were men who were alone? Tasked themselves with the duties of protection for Adam's return, had their son or sons also died before them? Were their wives no longer living or perhaps separated through divorce? Could it be that with it being his generation of council membership actually required to perform the duties assigned to them that this was all pre-planned? Would it benefit the cause if each council member had no-one in their lives, no family to which they would turn to with greater importance than the establishment of the age of Adam?

Avery's mind began to race. He must be mistaken surely? Both his sons died on active service in Afghanistan from the actions of the Taliban unless…..Avery considered a thought which caused actual pain in his head as he concentrated. Could the shot that was fired into his eldest son's brain have come from a sniper not actually in the Taliban. Could the IED which blew up his second son have been planted deliberately with his patrol in mind? In both cases, had the intention been murder then where better to plan and enact the killing than in the middle of a wider war? With his wife, taking pills was unnatural to her at the best of times. She always preferred pain killers in solvable form and yet had swallowed enough sleeping pills to kill herself, something which she would have found extremely hard to do. In Rosario's case, he read that the wife had died of cancer but the online translation seemed wrong. He separated the words and tried the translator to each separately. It stated that she died of 'complications' linked to cancer. Could that have been due to outside intervention? Was the son's drug fuelled drowning also innocent?

Avery sat back and exhaled deeply. Was he really considering that his family had been killed? Would the same have happened to Nine of Twelve and perhaps the other ten of the council also? Was it all simply to make sure that it was this generation of the council that would be ready to act with no ties to worry about?

The notions were too fantastic to contemplate but he decided the thought had merit. For the world-shattering announcement that was about to be made would change very many lives and having an organisation ready and willing to support the transition would indeed be something that required pre-planning and selection. By not being known to one another until the crucial time, none would know the history of each. No comparisons would be made and no conclusion drawn in the way that Avery was now thinking. If all this was true then it was monstrous and would question the whole endeavour to which they had been committed. Was Adam the real saviour of the world, the new Messiah? Or was he something else? Part of a huge, expansive conspiracy for who knows what?

Avery knew he must not take it all at face value. Yes, he knew that his duty remained clear, he must use his influence and power, both by association and wealth, to help promote the coming of Adam, especially if indeed the announcement was to be made in Britain. But he needed to know, he needed to be sure that his theories were fanciful only. He needed to know the identities of the ten remaining council of the Votary.

All he had to go on was the known geographical areas of each, the fact that they would be wealthy and that they would most likely, if his theory was correct, to be without living family and especially had suffered the loss of an eldest or all sons.

Immediately, Avery started to search the Internet with increased enthusiasm.

Chapter Sixteen

16.34 pm, 19th September, Present Day, Embassy of the Holy See, Avenue de President Wilson, Paris, France

McGeary paced the small room in the Vatican Embassy and went to the tall window looking out to the Paris street below. The double glass doors onto the balcony with its black iron ornate design were locked but the ventilation light above was open so that the sounds and smells of the French capital were clearly apparent. The yellow and white flag of the Vatican fluttered from the flagpole behind the coat of arms in the light breeze that whistled up the street.

He now felt his full sixty-seven years. The muscular aches and the small cuts and bruises he had sustained in the bomb attack were starting to dull but he was not yet close to being a well man. The dressing to his face had been removed to leave a ragged stitched and throbbing scar where glass had been catapulted into his cheek. He was fully dressed in casual clothes whilst he awaited a replacement cassock and robes, both of which has been damaged beyond repair in the blast as he was flung along the street.

Cardinal McGeary was impatient. Time was moving very slowly and he did not wish to be kept within the embassy much longer. The unimpressive French policeman had made several attempts at contact but McGeary had made it very clear that he had no time, or desire, to talk with him again. It was clear that there had been no intent to kill him or the other faith leaders. It would have been easy to place a car bomb under the very window where they had met if the intention had been to kill them all, or simply to have allowed him to reach his car before it exploded if he alone was the target. No. the intent was to warn. But in doing so, McGeary knew that someone at the Vatican, possibly even probably in his own team, was supplying information to those that wish to protect Adam.

Apart from sleeping long periods, McGeary had spent much of the preceding night in thought about the conspiracy within. For the first time since taking on the position he now held, he felt vulnerable. De Soto had come upon him unannounced and with dramatic suddenness. The message he brought was clear and graphic and the man who had resiliently slit his own throat gave more than one bloody message to McGeary. Yes, he was announcing that the coming of Adam was soon, but he was also committing an act of defiance, his own act of treachery to the Votary. His suicide was the first indication McGeary had known, possibly the first act of outright resistance to the creed of expected duty passed from father to son for countless generations that any of the long line of his predecessors had known, that those they oppose were fallible. In that, McGeary took some comfort. If one of their number, possible a senior member at that, could refuse the expectations the organisation had upon him then perhaps others would follow. Just how committed would their members be? Could a clear sense of loyalty and commitment be maintained simply from the legacy of empowerment to repay what was given hundreds or years ago to acquire that sense of duty? It was an intriguing question.

Of more obvious clarity though was the fact that whilst those entrusted with the everlasting duty may have their doubters, those whom they employ to carry out what they wish to be done are much less swayed by anything deeper than simply cash. McGeary was convinced that the foot soldiers employed to murder De Soto, for he could not bring himself to consider any other reason for his death, or to plant a car bomb in the French Capital would be motivated not by some higher expectation of faith for the Messiah to come, but only by the price they could demand. What is more, that money would be limitless. The number of mercenaries and other specialists in killing would be equally as limitless as long as the money flowed their way. One factor that linked every single member of the Votary was their wealth, of that fact McGeary was sure. But in an age where so many Billionaires exist, the majority of which had numerous international deals in progress to maintain and increase their wealth at any one time; that alone would not pinpoint who the Votary actually were. But someone close to him was already in their pay and he needed to know who.

The sharp knocking on the door roused McGeary from his thoughts and caused him to turn around away from the window.

"Yes?" he said weakly. The door opened and the young man who had acted as valet and waiter since he arrived entered.

"Your Eminence, the car is waiting. I must ask you to use the rear exit if I may" He gave the briefest of nodded bows and left the room. McGeary picked up the long wool coat he had been given earlier and put it on before following the retreating man as he led the Cardinal to the rear of the building and down the service staircase. As they exited the emergency fire door on the ground floor, the breeze tore into the building making McGeary gasp slightly. The car was indeed waiting at the end of a short, cobbled path, the engine was running and the passenger door was open.

"Good afternoon," McGeary uttered as he sat down and closed the door.

"Please buckle up your Eminence," The driver, a man of small stature and impressive comb-over bald patch facing the Cardinal said quickly. "You know what Paris driving can be like and you do not want to exasperate your injuries."

"Wise advice my son," McGeary said with a smile and did what he was told as the car pulled out of the small driveway and entered the main streets, busy with early afternoon traffic.

The driver had been pre-advised of where they were going and McGeary was pleased to see the packed main thoroughfares of the city centre give way to more suburban streets and finally the hint of the French countryside. They drove for a further thirty-five minutes along tree lined roads before coming up to a large chateau behind a gated entrance with impressive statues of hinds on each pillar. The gravelled drive was twisting and wide and the lights of the house looked inviting with the advancing darkness. McGeary noted that several cars were waiting for them and that three suited burley men stood on the entrance steps to which the car swung alongside. One of the men came to the passenger door and opened it.

"Good afternoon your Eminence," he said and beckoned that McGeary get out of the car. "This way please".

McGeary noted with some surprise that the man was speaking English and in a profound North-Eastern accent. He also noted the wired earpiece he wore and the smart gait which he employed to mount the stone steps. He was clearly ex-forces and now part of the security detail that Stubbs would have brought with him so at least McGeary could rest assured that the Prime Minister was within. The man led him straight through the entrance doors and on past the staircase. He could hear a female voice laughing in the room they passed to his right and further comments from a male voice that brought about more laughter from the lady present. The security officer stopped at a painted door in front of them both and knocked it. McGeary heard somebody say enter and the man opened the door but stayed outside of the room, indicating that McGeary should enter.

"Come in Cardinal," a voice sounded in English and McGeary walked in to be met by the gaze of Andrew Stubbs, the British Prime Minister. "Sit down please."

Stubbs moved to shake McGeary's hand and then pointed to the two simple dining chairs positioned either side of a small hall table.

"Can I offer you a drink?" Stubbs started, "Our hosts keep a particularly good 20-year Malt which I can highly recommend. I am pleased to see you are at least a little bit recovered from your ordeal."

McGeary did not have to think for long before he accepted with a graceful acknowledgement with his head. "Our hosts?" he asked.

"In the next room," Stubbs replied. "My late wife, Jane's sister and her somewhat boring French husband. I am grateful for your visit your Eminence as, if nothing else, I have managed to escape for a short while before I have to endure hours of small talk and an unimpressive supper!"

"I thank you for this opportunity Prime Minister," McGeary said. "Although I think we both now know the importance of this needing to happen."

"Forgive me Cardinal," Stubbs replied whilst pouring a generous measure of scotch into the crystal tumblers before both of them on the table, "But my reason to be here is not so much because I take you at face value, although I have no reason to believe you have any malicious intent. It is because my most trusted friend and colleague, a man I have grown up with, spent time with at schools and university and perhaps the only person I could trust in politics generally. That man told me out of the blue that he was bound by a higher purpose than serving his country and that I, the Prime Minister should be ready to receive some sort of saviour by ensuring the country does not collapse from the announcement of his coming. That same day, I get a similar call from you via a phone secreted into my office to say more or less the same thing. So, excuse me Cardinal for what I am about to say to you. But what the fuck is going on?" Stubbs sat down and took a large slug from the tumbler draining half the contents in one swig.

"Your concern is well founded Prime Minister," McGeary followed, taking small sips. "I can even forgive your colourful language," he smiled, "but your friend comes to the same destination as I, but from a different path." He paused and settled himself into the chair to prepare.

"Go on," Stubbs indicated.

"I was brought into the Vatican specifically to head up a specialist team whose sole function was to monitor the globe for signs that he would be announced. By 'he' I mean the one figure throughout history with the potential to do the most harm to the world in general and religion, specifically in my case the Roman Catholic religion, in particular. Other faiths, not all, have adopted similar approaches but up to now, he has evaded all efforts to be found, captured or killed."

"Who is 'he'?" Stubbs enquired.

"In the Christian faith and others, we would term him as Adam but he has been known by many, many other names. Do you know your bible Mr Stubbs?" McGeary paused, took another sip and waited.

"I know the basic stories of course," Stubbs responded sharply, "please tell me you are not referring to 'the' Adam, as in the Garden of Eden?" He was indignant and titled his head so that he was looking down his nose at the Cardinal.

"I am very sorry to say that I am," McGeary followed. "Throughout history there have been legends of an immortal. A man who has lived since the Creation. A man who cannot be killed. A man who was created from, and is thus a son of, God; not specifically the Christian God Mr Stubbs as his story has been adopted by many of the world faiths." McGeary looked at Stubbs who sat expressionless as he returned the stare.

"Imagine what would happen if such a man suddenly proclaimed himself to be that immortal. That he predates all world religions and indeed, is the inspiration behind some of them. What if the whole religious stories taken as fact by so many billions are wrong? What if the whole basis for faith is challenged?" He paused again for another sip of whisky but Stubbs remained silent. "Can you imagine what effect that would have on our modern world?" McGeary sat back and waited for a response.

"So, you are saying," Stubbs started after a pause, "that this Adam will proclaim himself the true God and expect the world to follow him?

"Not exactly no," McGeary interrupted, "Although we cannot be sure of the true motive at this stage and perhaps it will be become clear if he should announce himself before we have the chance to find him, but even the threat of his appearance should be enough to cause irredeemable fear and chaos."

"I understand the threat of what might happen," Stubbs continued, "and we can do what we can to maintain order in the streets accordingly, but there is more to this than you are telling me Cardinal, isn't there? For instance, where does he come from? How can he still be alive after so many thousands of years and why now?"

"I have learned to question my faith many times with the responsibilities that have been placed upon me," McGeary said. "For a man of a faith to be told that all I have lived my life by may be based on erroneous scribbling of men mishearing or deliberately fabricating fact to fit a creed or creeds is challenging to say the least. To believe in Adam is to believe there is no God as man has described him since we have been able to write. Whilst I will always think that above everything, including those that created Adam in the first place, there will always be a kind and everlasting almighty and nothing will dissuade me of that belief, that will not help the Catholic church or indeed any religion who have told people how to live and who to kill for thousands of years because it suited a particular doctrine to do so. How do you defend centuries of religious motivated killing Mr Stubbs? How can you if all that was thought to be true, simply was not? Would you not want to shout your anger at anyone who would listen? Would you not want to tear down the symbols of what will be seen to have oppressed you?"

"I do understand you Cardinal but I am finding it hard to accept all this and I suppose there would need to be unassailable proof of this man, or whatever he is, and what he stands for if there is to be any action to prevent it. You must understand that the people will expect to know why the troops are on the streets and with respect, this is a slim prospect for an answer." Stubbs drained the last drops from his glass and placed it rather too firmly back on the table with a bang. "And what of Avery?" he followed, "what links you both?"

"Proof can only come from the man himself and with respect Prime Minister," McGeary said with resignation, "once the genie is out of the bottle, we will not be able to put him back in." He paused, "As for…. Avery was it? This would be Sir Donald Avery who resigned the other day? I had my suspicions from the timing and have been doing quite a bit of research whilst bed ridden."

"Indeed," Stubbs confirmed.

"Prime Minister, it pains me to say this but your friend Mr Avery may well be a party to this conspiracy at the highest level. We have known for centuries of a brotherhood who support and protect Adam, awaiting the time they would be called upon to stand beside him. Men who are wealthy and powerful in their own countries and as I said before, some may well be actual leaders in their countries however, more likely they may be the power behind the throne shall we say. The responsibility is hereditary based on some solemn pact centuries ago and in reward for financial or other assistance to build vast business empires. We believe the methods to maintain this trust are hard and cruel, including murder to make sure the duty passes as it should. We also believe that they have networks of paid men who will do what they are instructed to protect them and the man they serve. The bomb under my car was a warning not to get to close, not to prevent the coming of Adam."

"Okay I get the secret society bit and in fairness, it does not surprise me that Avery would get involved in that sort of thing, he is the type," Stubbs concluded. "I even get the violent conspiracy to protect those that subscribe to this cult, because I take it that this is indeed some sort of cult, but I do not get the immortality thing frankly or the replacement of a God by what, aliens? Forgive me Cardinal but I must return to my boring in-laws soon. We will need to bring this to a close now." Stubbs got up from the chair and motioned the Cardinal to follow him.

"Prime Minister will you at least put your security forces on the highest level of alert, perhaps you can blame intelligence of imminent terrorism for instance? Can you also detain Mr Avery so that I may ask questions of him? I know one of the group is already dead by his own hand and Avery is probably the only other known member so it is vital I speak with him and perhaps can find out where Adam is hidden. Will you please at least do that? McGeary stared at Stubbs without blinking.

"The first request is already happening on my order yesterday," Stubbs responded curtly. "I cannot just arrest Avery but," he paused, thinking, "I can engineer a tripartite meeting. I will need to be there myself Cardinal, you understand that?" Stubbs made directly for the door as McGeary nodded in agreement and followed, "Goodbye your Eminence, you will hear from me again."

Stubbs shook the Cardinal's hand and left the room. The security man re-entered and led the Cardinal back through the hallway and outside to the waiting car. As he got into the car and it drove off, McGeary thought that maybe this time, he had an ally and a powerful one at that.

16.47 19ᵗʰ September, Present Day, Exeter University Campus, England

Professor Conrad Wilding sighed loudly and rubbed his forehead above the wild eyebrows as the strain of the past forty-eight hours began to take its toll. He yawned enthusiastically and glanced at the mantle clock with a confused look as it clearly showed the hour incorrectly. He could not remember the last time he had wound the vintage timepiece to full capacity so he had no idea if he was looking at the time in the morning or at night, nor indeed, which day. He sighed again and used the arms of the leather chair to hoist himself out so he could stretch and get the circulation going again.

The fourth volume of Adam lay on the floor next to the chair opened approximately half of the way through. As a professor of ancient history, Wilding had become both entranced and concerned at what he had been reading. Clearly almost everything he had ever taught in historical theory was now up for further debate. At no time had academics ever considered what they had studied had been from first-hand recollection from the earliest ages of man. Only partial later scrolls and stone tablets offered insights to early history and the finds from numerous digs suggested possible migration scenarios and natural events, but in the Adam chronicles, Wilding was reading almost a diarised account. It was the constant revelations that continually challenged modern thinking which had kept him reading, missing meals and leaving toilet breaks to the last possible minute. Sleep had been snatched rather than planned and he still wore the same clothes he had worn when he first welcomed Michael Crowe to his house.

Thinking of Crowe, Wilding suddenly felt a pang of disappointment that he had not heard anything more from him since their previous parting. There had certainly been some words of discomfort as the full realisation of what was being debated had resonated with Crowe and perhaps Wilding had not been at his best during that discussion, but since Crowe had followed up on the first meeting with Adam, nothing more had been discussed between them. No call and no text. Wilding picked up his mobile to check he had not missed anything from Crowe but no messages or missed calls were registered. He did note the time though and rubbed his stomach in realisation that he should finally cater for himself. Wilding concluded that Crowe would call once his head was in the right space to carry on the discussion and to force that would be wrong. He would give it until the next morning and if nothing had been heard from him by then, he would call Crowe himself.

The professor left his study behind and walked into practically the next room from the hallway which was the kitchen. The blind was down in the window as he made his way to the fridge, opening the door so that the light within illuminated his dishevelled state. He was greeted by almost bare shelves and what was there was clearly passed their prime of being useful ingredients. Wilding raised both eyebrows in indignation and concluded that a necessary walk to the local corner shop would be required if he was to eat at all.

Leaving the kitchen, he reached for his coat which was hanging on a hook along the hallway and checked the pocket for his wallet. Grunting in satisfaction when he found it, he started to put on the coat when the doorbell sounded loudly above him, making him jump. He looked ahead and saw the dark silhouette of a figure in the glass of the front door. Although first impressions suggested it did not look like the outline of Crowe, Wilding assumed it would be him in any event and beamed widely. He removed the coat and made his way to the door, opening it enthusiastically and standing back.

The smile faded almost immediately when he saw that the man was not Crowe. He did not recognise him at all and the round pudgy face with the cold, almost lifeless eyes did nothing to alleviate his concern. A glance down the fat man's body to the pistol that he held out in front of him dispersed any hope of a welcome and Wilding stared at the gun barrel with wide-eyed shock.

"Now Professor," Squat Man said quietly, "We do not need to make this any harder than it needs to be," he followed raising the barrel slightly two times to indicate that Wilding should retreat back into the hallway. This he did, letting go of the edge of the door and paced backwards whilst Squat Man followed him until his was clear of the door which he pushed shut with a backwards movement of his right foot.

"A bit further professor please," he breathed menacingly and suddenly thrust his arm forwards so that the gun barrel connected with Wilding's stomach causing him to bend double and let out an audible wheeze, the pain etched deeply into his face.

"Time for a talk professor, "Squat Man said with a reptilian smile as he pushed the shaking old man into the study.

Chapter Seventeen

17.45 19th September, Present Day, Wokingham, Berkshire, England

Jessica paced the room with growing anxiety. She was kicking herself at the curt and impatient way she had spoken to Crowe in the early hours of the previous day, especially as the promised follow-up call had never arrived. It was now late afternoon and still nothing, no contact at all. She had been texting Crowe all afternoon since lunchtime but every one, all seven of them showed that it had not been delivered, meaning he was either out of signal or his phone was not switched on. Jessica strained to remember if she had been unduly harsh or had said something that he would have upset him but could not recall anything specific. Crowe was never the sort of man to possessively call or text her at all hours, indeed she had sometimes wondered if she was ever on his mind, but on this occasion, it just simply did not feel right and Jessica was now beginning to despair.

Jessica's long strawberry blonde hair was tied up in a ponytail but still reached halfway down her back. The British Summer just gone had been reasonable warm and long coastline walks with Crowe in recent weeks had given the sunshine every opportunity to bring out the numerous freckles that were her trademark and her charm. With her deep green eyes, thin nose and full, still freckled lips, which were in perfect symmetry to her face, Jessica 'Jack' Russell was indeed a beautiful woman and had been immediately attracted to Crowe whilst they studied together, staying at each other's side ever since. Childless and having never married, Crowe and Jessica were inseparable whilst together and yet she ached when his archaeological investigations had taken him away for some months at a time. She desperately wanted a child and they had discussed it at length many times but as always, he had insisted that the long periods apart were not fair on her as a new mother and to the child itself. They each had their own lives but with a deep understanding and enthusiasm for life together as one. She understood Crowe completely and that is why her fears were growing now so strongly.

The school day had finished as normal and her Year Four pupils had been collected and had dispersed from the school grounds as with every other normal day. She had text surreptitiously during lessons away from the view of the children or the classroom assistant so not to be frowned upon but the constant lack of the response had just built up the angst within her. The journey home had been eventful as her concerned daydreaming meant that he failed to see a cyclist emerge from behind as she stopped at traffic light and as the lights changed, she made her left-hand turn without indicating so that the man was forced into the verge and fell over the kerb. Realising what had just happened, Jessica stopped the car and clambered out apologising loudly and asking if the man was hurt. To her relief, he rose from the ground with ease with nothing more than his pride suitably damaged. He had sworn at her though and pointed to his helmet camera with threats of reporting her before mounting his bike and setting off again, leaving Jessica even more shocked so that all she could do was to raise her middle finger towards the back of the fast disappearing cyclist and swear loudly. The rest of the journey home was at a measured and careful pace but she channelled her anger from the incident into a rational debate within herself as to what the long drive to Exeter could offer by way of comfort if nothing was received from Crowe soon. Whatever was needed, she could not continue not knowing.

By six o'clock the decision was made and Jessica tore around the house to grab clothes and toiletries to be packed roughly into her holdall before putting everything in the car. Exeter was just under three hours away so she set out with the intention to eat something from a filling station or roadside fast-food restaurant during the journey. She had decided to check with Conrad Wilding first as that was the only person she knew that Crowe was going to visit but already ten miles from home, she realised she had not called in advance to say she was coming. Additionally, she was sure she did not have Wilding's number in her phone as Crowe had always been the one to call in the past. She knew where he lived in Exeter though from past visits, or at least would hope that she would recognise the house when she arrived for she knew the general area at the back of the university where his home was.

Throughout the journey she kept checking her phone for that elusive proof that he had received her texts, let alone actually replying to them She had stopped for petrol on the M4 and later when the hunger pains became too strong, for a disappointing and over-priced burger and fries, the relish for which she had managed to drop onto the front of her top. After just over three hours with an ever-reducing traffic volume on the southbound M5, the exit junction for Exeter was suddenly upon her and she drove past the out of town office complex and the park and ride station onto the main route into the city centre. It was now very dark but the streets were well lit and she followed the signs for the university until she came to the junction with the old prison close by which she remembered that Wilding lived in one of the side roads further on.

Turning into the second cul-de-sac, having made the mistake of first going into the one before it, Jessica drove the car slowly up the residential tree-lined street of detached 1930's artisan homes until she came upon the one she was sure was where Wilding lived. She brought the car to a guided stop and parked a little further up the road on the opposite side before turning off the engine and looking back. The house was in darkness and Jessica cursed to herself before checking her watch. It was a few minutes past nine, still early for Wilding to retire to bed Jessica thought so she got out of the car hoping that he was perhaps working in a back room, the light for which she would not have been able to see from the road. She had a sudden pang of doubt that he was in at all and did not quickly consider what that would mean for her that evening. Going home would be too long and tiring so if nobody was in the house now, she would find local accommodation and try again in the morning.

She approached the house by crossing the quiet street. The houses either side were fully lit up with residents and Jessica looked into the main window of the one to the left, into the sitting room where a middle-aged couple were curled up together on a sofa watching an oversize television. The curtains were wide open and the light blazed brightly outwards from the room inviting anyone to see everything within. Not so the professor's house which showed no signs of life at all. She opened the small pedestrian iron gate that led to the gravelled path and was slightly relieved to notice the black van that was parked partially over the entrance to the house, not enough to stop another vehicle entering the driveway but still a tad inconsiderate. Perhaps the vehicle belonged to Conrad and he was in after all.

The rounded brick arch above the porch loomed over her as she mounted the two brick steps up the front door. The doorbell was illuminated so she pressed it hard and long and heard the bell sound inside the house. Jessica waited for a light to come on to indicate Wilding was coming to the door but none did. She pressed again, longer this time but still nothing. Finally, she knocked hard on the door itself and was surprised to feel the weight of the door shift away from her and open a little. Pushing lightly, the door swung into the hallway with little effort and Jessica peered into the gloom of the house.

"Hello," she called lightly before increasing the strength of the words, "HELLO!" she said forcibly. "Hello, Conrad? Are you in? HELLO?" she said again.

Moving into the hallway she probed the wall to her right with her finger for a light switch and, finding it, switched it on. The hall and stairs were immediately bathed in a bright yellow light and she was momentarily blinded. As her eyes adjusted to the sudden light, she moved slowly along the hall and towards the far door which she remembered led into the kitchen. A further door to her left led into the front room which she knew Wilding used as his study as it offered the greatest wall space for his immense collection of books. Indeed, he hardly used much of the large house, she remembered, choosing to keep his activities to the one room for heat conservation and convenience. They had eaten from trays on their laps on mismatched chairs the last time they had visited despite there being a perfectly serviceable dining room off the kitchen, such was the preference the professor had.

The door to the study was open slightly and Jessica pushed it open wider to look into the room. The light from the hall escaped into the study as the door stood further ajar but she could not see much. Reaching around the doorframe, she found the light switch for the room where she expected it would be and pushed it down. The scene of devastation that greeted the sudden explosion of light in the room made her gasp. The desk was on its side, all papers and pens that had once lain upon it were strewn across the floor. Books lay in heaps as they had been torn from their shelves in every direction apart from a tall freestanding bookcase set in front of the wall shelves behind which stood empty. There were no books either on it or on the floor below it.

Jessica entered the room fully and turned towards the fireplace expecting to see more chaos but was suddenly jolted by the sight of a figure sat motionless in the red leather chair by the fireplace. The figure did not move and Jessica suddenly felt a wave of panic overtake her. She gingerly walked towards the chair, realising even before she got close that it was Conrad Wilding who was sitting there. He was dead. Her hand raced to her mouth to stifle a scream as she realised that the top of Wilding's skull was missing. A deep red and black cavity occupied the space where the top of his head should have been and as she averted her gazed to the wall behind, she saw the long and wide splatter of blood and gore that covered it.

Around Wilding's mouth the skin was blackened and torn and she noticed shards of broken teeth in his grey and thick beard which was matted with dark blood. There were bruises and cuts to his face and hands and Jessica realised that he must have put up a fight or had been deliberately abused, possibly both. Clearly a gun had been forced into his mouth and fired.

Jessica felt cold and numb. She was rooted in fear to the spot simply staring at the ruin of what had once been a gentle and kind man. Her mind raced but could not find a rational thought other than the fear that

Crowe may also be somewhere in the house and may be dead himself. She forced herself to make a turn, not knowing whether to run or look further but her thoughts were brought to an abrupt end as she saw the shadow of the man coming towards her with his arm raised. She uttered a short scream as the raised gun barrel met the side of her head and everything turned immediately black as she fell unconscious next to the chair.

The man wasted no time in picking Jessica up with one strong arm to carry her under his armpit. He switched the light off to the room with his gloved hand and then again to the hallway as he exited. He checked the area ahead of him and to both sides before, still carrying the unconscious woman and sure he was alone, he moved quickly down the short drive way to the vehicle and along the pavement to the rear. Opening the back of the van door, he placed Jessica roughly inside and slammed it shut, engaging a small padlock to a bolt retro-fitted to the bodywork. The man started to return to the house to close the front door but belatedly changed his mind and returned to the van, starting the engine and moving into the road before speeding off. In the adjoining house where the couple still sat clutched together watching the television. Nothing and no-one had been disturbed.

The man drove the van as quickly as he could out of the city without tripping the speed cameras or exceeding the limit. He was soon onto the A30 heading west. At the first roadside lay-by, he stopped, got out of the van and opened the rear door before getting inside. Everything he needed was already there and he set about securing the woman who remained unconscious. Satisfied with an audible grunt at his handiwork, he re-locked the rear door with the bolt and padlock and returned to the cab before setting off once more.

When Jessica finally came around from unconsciousness, her first thought was the searing pain from her wrists and ankles. Both were tightly bound and her fingers in particular were numb and throbbing. Her head was also pounding where the butt of the gun had struck her. She was lying on her side with her bound limbs being further tied together so she formed a foetal position. A foul-smelling cloth was in her mouth and the tightness she felt over both cheeks confirmed that strong tape had been placed over her face to secure the cloth in place. She could breathe freely through her nose but the smell that assaulted her nostrils was from something rotten and in the darkness of the moving van, she had little in the way of light to observe much around her. The motion of the van and the smell made her nauseas so she tried with all her mental might to stop herself from vomiting and choking herself to death.

Jessica stretched slightly to see if any lights were rushing past through the darkened rear windows of the van but the effect was fleeting and useless to aid her get her bearings. She had no idea how long she had been unconscious or who had hit her. The pain in her head was beginning to increase as she managed to flex her muscles around where she was tied to bring some relief at least to those pressure points.

Soon, any lights she glimpsed became much less numerous until they disappeared altogether and all became complete blackness. The van was travelling at speed and the ride became as smooth as it could be given her hog-tied position. Shifting to find as much comfort as she could, Jessica tried to rest but her panic was building. What she had seen in that house, the sight of Conrad brutally killed, his room ransacked and now the attack on herself was too much. It was like a film she was living in. It couldn't be real life and she prayed the dream would soon end and she would be in her bed with Michael safely next to her before another normal day at school with her pupils. The more she willed it all to end the more the pain in her head and along her numbed limbs ached and she started to shake as the fear overcame the longing for the nightmare to come to its conclusion.

Suddenly, the van swung to the left and after a short distance, started to climb as the roads became twisty and irregular. The nausea was back and once again she found herself fighting the impulse to retch. How much longer, she thought, when will the journey end and what awaited her when it did? To compound her fear, she thought that Michael must also be injured or possibly already dead, but why? She tried to think what could possibly be so bad that one academic was already dead and the other missing? What was it Michael had got himself involved in? He was just a history presenter for fucks sake!

The van started to slow before turning a sharp right and Jessica heard the crunch of loose stone under the tyres. As the van came to a stop, she heard the driver's door open and then be slammed shut. She listened to the footsteps on the gravel as the driver came around to the back of the van and the doors started to open. She gasped as the burly frame filled the doorway silhouetted against a poor yellow light behind the figure. The man grunted as he climbed into the van and roughly started to pull Jessica's body with him as he retreated back to the lip of the van floor and down onto the gravel. As he gave a final strong pull to remove her from the van, Jessica screamed a sound muffled by the rag in her mouth as she felt herself fall.

Chapter Eighteen

22.54 15th *June 1791, Barnsford House, England*

Kamal instinctively threw the first punch but missed badly and overbalanced as the slightly taller man ducked to his right so that the Albanian's fist skimmed only his long hair. The attacker followed quickly with a kick to Kamal's shin which made him howl in pain before the man's accomplice grabbed Kamal around the waist and used his own bodyweight to overbalance him fully, forcing the flailing Valet to fall onto his back on the marble floor. He lay there, bruised and unresisting as the man who had tackled him disengaged roughly and immediately joined the other shouting men and women of the village as they stormed through the entrance hall and dispersed into the various rooms that surrounded it. Some split into the library and dining room whilst others made straight for the staircase and ran up it, filling the wide steps as the surge continued until the most immediate doors to rooms on the landing behind the elaborate balustrade were also being forced open. Kamal saw his chance once the main volume of people had passed to sneak quickly away. He was grateful and relieved that none of the mob had made for the kitchen so Kamal had a free passage to move silently into the kitchen and through the pantry to the outside courtyard at the back of the building where the log store was situated. He glanced back and was comforted by the fact that the mob were still more concerned about invading the living space of the master of the house rather than the servant's quarters and quickly set about opening the small latch door beside the logs. He entered shouting for Sophia, his twelve-year-old daughter who he had hidden there only hours before, to come into the light. She did so and looked up at him with frightened eyes as Kamal wasted no time in scooping her up and leaving the log store area to make a dash for the trees a few hundred feet away at the back of the house leaving the shouts and screams that disturbed the night.

The mob had been hastily assembled when the search party for the two missing girls from the village intercepted the young black stable boy fleeing through the woods. After calming him down and giving him water, the boy blurted out his story and his fear of what was happening again at Barnsford Manor. Incensed, the village search party wasted no time in assuming their missing girls were involved and rounded up as many of the villagers as they could to march on the manor, flaming torches leading the way through the darkness. Upon arriving at the house, they screamed their revolt and stormed the doors, forcing their way past Kamal in the process.

Now that they were inside the house, a new batch of screaming began. Instead of the hysterical wailing of the abused girls, those that had inflicted the torture were being set upon. As each bludgeoned door revealed more horror, the hapless torturer was overpowered by the baying mob. Ineffectual protestations of rank or status fell on deaf ears as the evidence of their crimes was plain to see in the flickering candlelight. Dead and dying young girls, some mutilated beyond recognitions inflamed the raging crowd so that they ripped the men to pieces, tearing off flesh with probing fingers and clenched teeth. Chair legs, candlesticks and anything that could be used to inflict harm were greedily picked up and fashioned into tools of misery as each member of the Hades Society fell bloodily under their blows. Room by room they searched and probed, seeking out the cowering men who tried and failed to hide from the mob.

Of all the members, only two kept their distance. The young Lord who upon hearing the first shouts of the mob immediately donned his riding boots and opened the window to his room which faced the rear of the building, clambering naked through the opening and dropping to the ground where he lay momentarily, winded from the fall. Regaining his senses, he ran immediately towards the trees, hopeful that the blackness of the night and the darkness of the dried blood covering him would shield his escape. Animalistic screams emanated from the room he had just left as the mob had burst in to find one of their own, one of their missing girls, dismembered and dead. Further shouts echoed out of the window as the pursuers strained to see their prey in the night but he was already amongst the relative safety of the trees and allowed himself a short pause to regain his breath. The snapped twig behind him caused the man to twirl around and he gasped as the face of Kamal loomed out of the darkness. The man almost collapsed with relief as he recognised Adam's manservant but then caught a brief look at the wicked Sica Kamal had placed point first above his exposed midriff. The young Lord looked in astonishment into the dark eyes of the older man as they returned his stare with hate and anger.

"For my daughter," Kamal hissed as he thrust the long-curved blade of his father's dagger up to the hilt in the young Lord's stomach, twisting the full width of the blade before pulling it upwards to the sternum, gutting the man so that he died screeching in pain as the sudden release of heat from his exposed intestines clouding his vision in the cold night air. As the dead man fell, Kamal spat upon his face then collected his daughter once more before moving silently to where he expected Adam to eventually appear.

The other escapee of the mob's revenge was the Earl of Barnsford himself who calmly came out of his room with a candlestick in hand and presented himself, causing the crowd of villages in the hallway to stop suddenly and go quiet. He said nothing but simply smiled and raised one eyebrow. As one, the crowd surged towards him and grabbed his bodily, pushing him along the landing and down the marble stairs, into the main library, pummelling and kicking him as hard as they could as they went. Once in the room, they dragged the unprotestingly prostrate man towards a large high-backed armchair. There they sat Adam down and bound him to it using the tasselled tie-backs from the ornate gold velvet curtains which they had ripped from the windows and were now creating a pyre around his chair, added to by as many of the books that they could take from the surrounding shelves. Satisfied that their pyre was ready, the crowd stood back and two torch bearers came forward to start the blaze.

The two men hesitated as the Adam looked at each of them in turn with a salacious grin. One of the men, a burly ploughman with immense ham-fisted hands backhanded Adam with all his might, grazing the sitting man's cheek which even in the muted light of the torches looked raw. The ploughman waited just long enough to note that the cheek was quickly healing itself before his eyes until prompted by a sudden fear, he thrust the torch into the books below, quickly followed by that of the other villagers. They retreated as the flames took hold, which spat and roared towards the writhing Earl. Satisfied that the fire had fully taken, the villages turned their backs on Adam and left the room before the fire could take hold of the building itself.

Helping the one disorientated survivor amongst the captured girls they could find, the crowd left the building and stood at the front to watch the flames consume it. Faster and faster the fire built until all the windows first showed orange flashes and then full flames that shattered the glass and fed hungrily from the contents. Once the building was totally consumed, the mob finally turned away from the collapsing walls and walked away in silence, their grief just commencing but their revenge complete.

Adam timed his departure from the chair once the bindings had burned away and the mob had left. His blackened skin had already developed the asbestos type coating to prevent further damage but the pain was still real and he winced with every step on his exposed charred feet. He made for the kitchen and exited the building as the sound of failing wooden floors and falling masonry filled the night behind him. The light from the flames lit up the yards to the trees and he could just see the figure of Kamal waving to him. As his ruined skin renewed enough to calm the pain, Adam looked back upon the destruction that had been his most recent life and contemplated where the next would take him. He looked at Kamal.

"The books?" he asked, enquiring about the two volumes he had completed thus far.

"Hidden safely from the house as instructed in the Folly," Kamal said, "all is well."

"Well done, I knew I could rely on your foresight," Adam said and smiled at the young girl who was attempting not to notice his nakedness.

"Come," Adam said abruptly, "To the Folly and the provisions we have there. In the morning we will start again."

Chapter Nineteen

08.05, 20th September Present Day, Dartmoor, Devon, England

Jessica awoke from a short but disturbed sleep brought upon her by the constant pain and stress that her body had been in all night forcing it to shut down, at least temporally. She lay on the slightly damp but grubby and musty carpet on her left side still in the hog-tied position. The room she was in was old in style and decoration and void of any furniture save a single wooden dining chair upon which her captor sat leering at her. Her tongue was dry and swollen and moved around inside her mouth with difficulty suppressed as it was by the disgusting rag that had been thrust inside. She was desperate for water and strained inside the gag to shout at the man. Her bladder was screaming for relief but she held it, masking the pain.

Squat Man remained silent and still as he watched the woman squirm and emit muted sounds. Her eyes were wide and red-rimmed whilst her cheeks were stained with mascara that had run with her tears. He licked his lips and smiled for when the time came, he had already decided what he would be doing to her and he knew that her screams would then be long and loud.

Squat Man got up from the chair and walked over to where Jessica was lying. With no effort at all he picked her up and moved her to the edge of the wall. He took out a small penknife and cut the cord connecting her bound hands and feet. The sudden release of the tension made her cry out but the gag reduced the scream to a muffled groan. Squat Man moved her into a sitting position with her back against the wall and her legs bent in front of her. The sudden rush of blood to the previously restricted areas was both excruciating and a blessed relief. Jessica fought through the pain as she willed her limbs to relax and take advantage of the improved position. With a sudden strong swipe, the man removed the tape across her face so that she was able to splutter out the rag that had filled her mouth. Her moans were audible now but she had only one thing on her mind with the sudden freedom to breathe through her parched lips.

"Water," she croaked weakly, "Please. Some water?"

The man smirked on one side of his mouth and walked out of the room returning a few seconds later with a plastic bottle of water. He unscrewed the top and offered the neck of the bottle up to Jessica's parched lips. She took a sip and immediately reacted as the bitter aftertaste of the cloth that had been in her mouth mixed with the cool water. She swallowed hesitantly at first and then more greedily until he pulled the bottle away again.

"Enough," he said, replacing the screw cap and placing the bottle on the floor next to her. Jessica looked up at the man with eyes filled with hate.

"Why am I here?" Jessica asked meekly, "Where is Michael? What have you done with him?" she followed.

"Sorry," Squat Man started, "No talking else I will replace the gag. Understand?" The last word was breathed almost into Jessica's face and she reacted to the pungent halitosis that filled her nostrils.

"But I…." she started but was abruptly silenced by the back of Squat Man's hand as he swiped it hard against her cheek. She cried out in shock and pain.

"I said silence!" he spat before starting to smirk again as his hand dropped to her left breast and started to squeeze.

Jessica shook involuntarily as she tried in vain to retreat from the pawing monster before her but she was trapped against the wall. His tongue was slightly poking out from the thin lips as he pawed both breasts and his eyebrows rose up and down rhythmically.

"Oh, I am going to enjoy you," he whispered giving the right breast one final squeeze that sent ripples of pain through Jessica's body. Squat Man moved away back to the chair and sat down again. He maintained his stare at the petrified woman whilst she desperately looked for something, anything in the room that offered her a chance. Any semblance of hope.

08.15, 20th September, Present Day, Exeter England

District Detective Sergeant Carol Davis stood silently in the Professor's study and scratched her left arm which had suddenly started to itch. The protective white overall was never her most favourite look and she was sure it irritated her exposed skin. The plastic overshoes did not fit her boots so she had removed them and, being now barefoot, her feet were beginning to sweat. With no heels, even the squared off boot heels, her five feet one height became quite noticeable in a room where taller forensic officers were now working. She now scratched her right arm and became committed to getting out of this house and removing the overalls as soon as possible.

The call for her to attend was automatic. She was on shift and as it was clearly an unexplained and very violent death, a category two death, the District Detective Sergeant was required and as of eight a.m. earlier this morning, that was her. The scene that confronted her upon arrival looked strange in what would normally be a very quiet city in terms of violent crime. Crime Scene officers had already sealed off the area and prepared the front of the house to screen it off from prying neighbourly eyes. Two uniformed officers stood guard at the entrance to the short driveway and another handed her the protective clothing to put on before she entered the house. As she had walked into the front study, she was not sure what to expect but was shocked at the sight that greeted her all the same.

In front of her, the corpse of Conrad Wilding remained sat in the chair within which he had died. The large and obvious hole in the back of his head and the black cavity where his brain, no doubt a very intelligent and knowledgeable brain she concluded, had once been was already the target for a few brave flies that had to be constantly waved away by Oliver Rivers, the Crime Scene Investigator taking samples from the body.

Carol scratched again and then pushed an errant strand of blonde hair that had escaped from the severe pulled back style kept in place with a rubber band to form the short pony-tail. Her glasses had slipped down her nose as they were want to do on the wrong side of the prominent bridge at the top and she pushed down on the bridge of the glasses to try and find additional purchase. She kicked herself for running out of her daily contact lenses yet again and made a mental note to stop by the opticians later in the day for an emergency prescription. Her green eyes still sparkled behind the thick lenses and she felt a little flushed in the face. She looked at the man attending to the body.

"Thoughts?" Carol said, directing the comment to the man as he was carefully applying tweezers to a remnant of brain matter.

"Well he didn't starve to death," Rivers said with typical gallows humour that always seemed to creep into similar scenes. "Gun forced into his mouth breaking his front teeth, if you look, his beard caught some of the fragments. Not sure of the model yet but most likely a pistol of course. Nine millimetre I suspect" Carol bent towards the corpse but decided that the officer's words were sufficient. "Gun fired inside the mouth. Two shots fired upwards, taking the top of the head off and blowing anything that was in the way all to Hell." He pointed to the wall behind the chair that was covered in dried blood and gore. "Bullets are up there," he pointed to the ceiling, "have not got them out yet." He looked at the corpse, "Signs of a struggle with pressure on the arms. See that bruising?" He pointed to some angry purple and black colouring with his pen. "Further signs of inflicted torture to the face and arms. My guess is that whoever did this actually enjoyed it. A true sadist. Close quarter stuff" Rivers turned and smiled at Carol who looked away without comment and moved to the other side of the room where a forensics officer was dusting the surfaces around the empty bookcase.

"Do you think these shelves were as full as the rest," Carol said pointing towards the shelves upon which Adam's volumes had once been stored.

"Likely," the dusting officer said, "on the basis that all the others are stacked with so many books, I cannot imagine why he would have left these empty. All the others on the floor seemed to have just been pulled from the shelves without much finesse but if there were any on these shelves, they must have been removed."

"Why steal books?" Carol said in a puzzled manner, "and what the hell were they worth to cost an old man his life?"

"Who knows," the officer said, "perhaps they were all first folio Shakespeare's." He suggested as Carol turned and walked back out into the hallway and out into the front garden. Detective Constable Jonathan

Stone was walking up the short drive as she started to remove the overall and plastic overshoes. The rush of fresh air on her exposed feet was welcome indeed.

"Neighbour called it in. Didn't like the fact the front door was open so called and walked in to see him. With the female constable over there," he pointed to a huddle of people in a front garden a few doors down the road, "I have knocked up the street," Stone said, "Nobody saw or heard anything. Apparently, he kept himself pretty much to himself other than casual greetings etcetera but everyone seemed to know of him and those that had met him had liked him."

Carol looked up the street at all the parked vehicles and pointed.

"Are they all accounted for?" she asked.

"Yes Sarge. All bar one belongs to the residents apart from that one. Nobody recognises it and it has been there since last night apparently." He pointed to the blue Astra parked on the opposite side of the road just up from the Professor's house. "I have had a look. It is locked but I can see some women's scarves on the back seat so we are assuming it belongs to a female. We are running the plates now."

"An unknown female visitor to a lonely male in the street perhaps?" Carol suggested whimsically, "anyone of interest amongst the residents?"

"No Boss," Stone replied. "All families or retired couples. The Professor here was the only single man living on his own."

"Okay, let me know about the car as soon as you do," Carol followed, "It could just be a car belonging to a University student not resident in this street at all." As Carol finished speaking Stone's mobile rang and he started talking. Once finished he put the phone back in his pocket and looked towards Carol.

"It's not local," he said, "Belongs to a Jessica Russell. Registered at an address in Wokingham, Berkshire."

"Student?" Carol asked quickly.

"Possibly, if mature," Stone replied. "The office reported that the date of birth on the licence details shows she was born in 1982. I will get on to this and speak with Thames Valley Police to go around to the house."

"Check with the University as well," Carol replied, "I want a report back here in an hour is that clear?"

"Crystal Boss," Stone replied as he started to walk towards the police car blocking the road, blue lights flashing. Carol walked into the road ducking under the yellow crime scene tape and went over to the Astra. She looked through the window of the driver's seat and saw the detritus of abandoned fast food wrappings on the seat, the scarves on the back seat as Stone as reported together with a make-up bag that was partially open. On the floor behind the back of the driver's seat, she could just make out the back dust-jacket cover of a hardback book. On the cover, the handsome face of the author was pictured in black and white. The man was holding a sword and Carol was sure she recognised the face but could not place it. Recognisable or not, it seemed out of place.

Carol walked back to her car and decided to wait until Stone came back with the report. What was really on her mind was the savagery of what she had just seen. It was unnecessary cruelty if the motive was just robbery. Also, why kill so obviously and with such relish? Why risk the sound of the shots being heard in a suburban street in the heart of a major city when a knife or club could have done so just as well, be it quietly. Whilst she pondered the motive for the murder, her thoughts strayed to the empty bookcase. Why steal books? Apart from a perceived value, even if they were rare early editions of something, they would be difficult to fence. There were no signs of general ransacking outside of the murder room and she had noticed obviously valuable ornaments in full view that remained undisturbed. No, she thought, this was a targeted raid for something specific, something in the books themselves. The murder was not so much the act of panic but a deliberate sustained action. This was a planned and perfectly executed act by someone who had no fear of discovery, almost as if it did not matter if the perpetrator was found. Almost like he had nothing to lose and was going to make the best of the opportunity he had to inflict as much pain as possible. Carol shivered as she realised that this was in no way, a normal murder, if any murder could be labelled as such.

Chapter Twenty

09.12 am 20th September Present Day, Test Bank House, Hampshire, England

Avery was jarred from his slumber with a start at the sound of his dog, Cromwell, barking at his feet. The Cairn terrier showed endless enthusiasm to make a point as he bounded relentlessly, placing his two front paws on Avery's legs with every jump. Confused as he tried to make sense of where he was, Avery slowly realised he had slumbered all night in his favourite old armchair. He strained and stretched the best he could but knew instantly that the odd position he had adopted sat upright when he should have been horizontal in his own bed would tell on his body for some hours yet. He looked and saw that his laptop was still beside him on a small table and, like him, it had remained in sleep mode throughout the night so he drew his finger across the mouse pad to awaken it. The Google page that came up was where his research had ended when the urge to sleep had been too much.

He was now back in the study of the main house having spent all the previous day in the fishing hut, breaking only for a short lunch and to post the envelope. It had been essential to do so following what he had discovered through his research for there were too many similarities between the filtered names remaining to suggest anything other than his worst fears. He knew in his heart what that meant for him personally and had sought and found some blank writing paper to begin the letter he knew had to be written. He settled down to explain himself in flowing yet inwardly unwanted words. It was an explanation, a confession. Something to remain if he was to disappear, something he knew had to be known if his full fears were to be realised. He wrote continuously in long flowing script for ten minutes without deviation before reading the contents back to himself with a huge sigh as he finished the last word. Searching for an A4 sized envelope and addressing it, he had reached into the desk drawer and extracted the photographs contained in the unmarked and untitled blue folder. He looked at each in turn slowly before carefully placing them in the same envelope and sealed it. He then placed a self-adhesive first class large letter stamp on the envelope and stood up before he walked towards the shiplap door with the landing net hung over a hook at the top on the back and went to leave the hut. He collected Cromwell's lead from the same hook as the excited dog yapped at his heels and connected it to the thin leather collar. He walked the short distance to the private foot bridge over the silvery fast-flowing river and then followed the path on the far side of the bank to the main road and turned left, Cromwell pulling on the lead to get wherever they were going even faster. The post box was soon reached at the junction with the Whewell road and he had placed the letter in the slot grunting with satisfaction that the last collection time was still and hour away. He was pleased that because of the short distance, Elizabeth would receive the letter in good time the next day. He had then returned to the main house, eaten a light salad lunch before continuing with this investigation. After a full afternoon's work laced with the contents of a good claret and a re-heated beef stew from the freezer, he switched to his favourite ten-year-old single malt and finally falling asleep in his chair soon after dark.

Now, some thirteen hours later, Cromwell was still uttering a series of short yelps and having given up the tiring consistency of jumping up and down, sat staring at his master in anticipation. Avery looked at his watch and realised he was already twenty-five minutes late for Cromwell's breakfast to be in his bowl and smiled to himself. He was amazed at the time-keeping abilities of dogs who seemed to know the exact time every day that meals would be prepared and even continued to do so when time was artificially altered twice a year to move the hour forwards or backwards for British Summer Time. Perhaps we still do not truly understand the value and aptitudes of dogs he thought as he busied himself to get ready to take the dog outside before feeding him.

Avery opened the back door and the two of them went out into the bright morning sunshine. As they walked the autumn air had taken a very pronounced sudden chill and he was grateful for the thick fleece he was wearing. The weak sunshine of morning was now growing slowly to his left. Cromwell bounded ahead whilst momentarily being distracted by the sudden flight of a startled blackbird or robin on the path between the shrubs that Avery was taking. As he got nearer to the end of the garden and just before the path down to the fishing hut, he could see a black Lexus pull into the drive from the side entrance that opened up on the Kings Somborne road and saw it slowly make its way up the gravelled driveway before parking close to the house under the large sycamore. Avery called after Cromwell and started to make his way back on the path and upon reaching the house, continued in through the French doors to his study knowing that he would make the front door easier by going through the detached Georgian built property than going around the side.

He reached the door just as a shadow could be seen through the small glass window at the top of the door approaching the threshold. He opened it before the bell was pushed and saw the form of a man in his early forties with slicked-back hair and an expensive suit standing there.

"Sir Donald," the man said, "The Prime Minister asks that you accompany me to Middle Wallop, the army base, I am sure you know it."

"I do," Avery said politely, "Is the Prime Minister there?"

"He is on his way now."

"And you are?" Avery asked raising both eyebrows.

"Parkinson, Sir Donald. MI5" The man produced his ID and held it up in front of Avery who scanned it.

"I need ten minutes to get ready and I must feed my dog," Avery continued as the man looked at Cromwell who was panting at Avery's feet.

"Please make it five sir," he answered and walked back to his car.

Avery shut the door and immediately went into the kitchen and to the cupboard housing cans of dog food. He opened one and spooned the contents into the bowl on the floor. Cromwell started eating before he had finished spooning and he pushed the dog's head away slightly for more room. He checked Cromwell had enough water and then left the kitchen closing the door behind him. He quickly sent a text to Cathy his cleaner to check on Cromwell in a few hours and then went to his bedroom to freshen up and change into a suit. In just under ten minutes he exited the front door, locking it behind him and walked over to the car where Parkinson was standing and smoking,

"Please put that out before we set off," Avery said with some disgust and got into the back seat.

Parkinson made a meal of performing a three-point turn in the narrow, gravelled drive but once clear of the stones and onto the road, he impatiently sped away. Middle Wallop was not far but he did not want to arrive too late before Stubbs arrived.

Avery watched the green Hampshire fields and hedgerows speed past as he looked out of the side window of the car. Flashes of berried colour and

Autumn leaves from the hawthorn, hazel, ash and oak sped by as he pondered on what his research had uncovered. He had been prompted by a sudden rush of doubt that his duty was as his father had explained. His life had been marred by such tragic loss and thus his sense of being the chosen generation to oversee the coming of the Age of Adam had initially been exciting and in some small way, a justification of what he had lost. With no male descendant to pass on the responsibility, it seemed right that it would be up to him, the last of his line, to do his duty. And yet......what had driven Nine of Twelve to take his life so needlessly when the time of regeneration was so near? Was it fear or perhaps a lack of self-confidence? There had been many moments when Avery himself had thought about it, but that was before the call had come. To do so now would be out of the question. Such a betrayal of everything his father, grandfather and all male ancestors before him had stood for would be inexcusable – so why did his Portuguese opposite number not feel the same?

Avery had tried to filter his searches to men of wealth, considerable wealth, who were without either wife or surviving children as that was the only thing that was common both to him and Nine of Twelve. Surprisingly, the list had been huge, far more than the ten names he was looking for and even after grouping the names into geographical regions that could have represented the specific territories similar to those both he and Nine of Twelve were responsible for, he had more names than he could discernibly reduce to likely suspects.

What he had found, however, was that the premise of the Votary being made up of very wealthy widowers or single men who had suffered the deaths of their male offspring was entirely credible as all areas could field likely candidates. But at that point, he had nowhere else to go with his enquiries. He could not exactly call each and ask outright what number of Twelve they were. In any event, his father had made is quite clear that only upon the announcement of Adam would the Votary be revealed to show global support for his presentation. Until then, to protect them all individually and together, each should remain unknown to each other. Avery decided that, for the time being at least, he would keep his innermost doubts to himself as clearly the time of revelation was close enough at hand for the issue to be resolved in any event.

The relatively quiet roads were devoured by the sleek Lexus in double quick time and Avery could see the outer fence of the Middle Wallop base and the building housing the Museum of Army Flying coming ever closer. At the entrance Parkinson showed his credentials and an armed corporal checked with the Gatehouse before raising the barrier and letting the car in. Parkinson drove the Lexus around the main buildings to the wide-open expanse of grass with the concrete strip splitting it in two and parked facing the main runway. He opened the window then turned the engine off.

"Are we not getting out," Avery asked enquiringly.

"Sorry sir," Parkinson replied, "shouldn't be too long sir."

Avery sighed and looked over the airfield wondering how long the Hurricane pilots had sat and waited before this very view until the order to scramble and head for their planes was given each time German aircraft were spotted heading this way during the Second World War. His thoughts drifted to his father who had been just too young to participate in either the German or Japanese conflicts, despite his enthusiasm to do so and instead had experienced the mud and gore and the onslaughts of massed Chinese infantry on the Korean peninsula five years later. Would war be a thing of the past under the new enlightenment Avery thought? Would all those years pretending to fit into the establishment, doing what was expected as an English Gentleman in a world where the secret truth was not yet known. Would it all be worth it? His late wife had seen through him, realising that his heart was not in the actions he had been asked to complete. Many times she had raised it and many times, he had dismissed her concerns as fantasy but she knew he had been distracted. When the loss of their second son had strained her Christian faith to the very limit he thought about telling her, revealing who he was and what he had been told he may have to do but in the end, he could not. Days later she was dead whilst he was working late in Whitehall, the strain had been too much and in hindsight, he now wished he had spoken of it all.

The sound of rotors made him look up and he saw the clear outline of the helicopter approaching from the South, silhouetted against a lucid light of crimsons and gold. The aircraft made a measured approach and started to descend until it touched down thirty yards from the car. As Avery watched, the door opened and Stubbs got out. Avery opened the car door and stepped out. As he closed it behind him a second figure alighted from the helicopter. He was an older man with sheer white hair wearing a long coat that perhaps looked a little big for him. Both men started to walk towards the car as the helicopter rotors started to reduce velocity. As the two men got closer, Stubbs shouted over the reducing noise of the chopper and pointed to the older man.
.
"Donald," he started, "This is Cardinal McGeary. He wants to talk to you and so do I. Shall we go inside?" He pointed to the old building to their left. McGeary held out his hand and Avery shook it.

"I am very pleased to meet you Sir Donald," McGeary said with a wide smile, "I have been waiting to meet someone like you for many years."

The three men walked in silence until they reached the door of the building which was held open for them by a young soldier in camouflage trousers and shirt. The soldier did not enter behind them but locked the door from the outside as they entered the room. Avery noticed the table, three chairs and the video camera on a tripod at the end of the table facing one of the chairs at the other end.

"Forgive me Donald but I have no choice. I hope you can see that," Stubbs said without emotion and pointed to the chair opposite the camera. "Sit there," he said as he and McGeary occupied the other two chairs.

"Now Sir Donald," McGeary said immediately, "Shall we begin?"

Chapter Twenty-One

10.38 20th September, Present Day, Middle Wallop, Hampshire, England

Parkinson re-entered the old one-room building that had now become an interrogation room and shut the door firmly behind him. He stayed motionless and ramrod straight with his back against the door. Stubbs had taken his seat to the side of the table at which Avery now sat uncomfortably while McGeary stood in front of the metal framed single glass window and looked out onto the airfield where the helicopter's rotors were now spinning very slowly. The room was cold, a relic of the wartime past where most attention, quite rightly, was paid to the well-being of the aircraft and support required to counter the Luftwaffe threat than the office comforts of those that fought it. The walls were of single skin brick which countless subsequent layers of yellowing paint and later internal dry-lining had failed to keep out the damp. The air smelt musty and in need of ventilation but all the windows seemed stuck fast. It was a soulless and miserable room and one McGeary wanted to get out of as soon as possible.

McGeary suddenly did not have a clue what to say to the seated man that Stubbs was positively glaring at behind him. The drive back from the chateau the previous day had not even reached the main outskirts of Paris before the call came from Stubbs. The message was short and to the point.

"Cardinal, please board the 06.37 Paris Charles de Gaul to Exeter flight tomorrow. Tickets can be collected at the desk. You will be met at Exeter when you land and your return flight is arranged for later in the evening. Goodbye." Stubbs had quickly hung up the phone and McGeary guessed that his parting from the meeting was already being noticed and as such did not want to give rise to any unnecessary questions. The Cardinal was surprised by the speed of response in setting up the meeting with Avery but even more shocked that matters were coming to a head and beyond his control. He was delighted that the Prime Minster of Great Britain of all people was driving that speed and assumed, probably correctly, that his motives were more about political damage limitation from any involvement Avery had with what would be coming rather than countering the threat itself.

He had arrived at Charles De Gaul airport and collected the tickets which were waiting for him as promised. The FlyBe flight was relatively quick and eventless and upon landing and after going through customs, he was directed by a member of the airline's staff to a reception lounge where he waited. He passed a smaller room on the way where he could see Prime Minister Stubbs and others sitting in conversation. Soon the personal guard from the château the day before, the one he remembered with the Newcastle accent approached him. McGeary was offered refreshments and asked to wait as the Prime Minister was busy working on a stack of paperwork until their transport arrived. The Cardinal accepted the room without complaint knowing that even with the crisis nearly upon them, Stubbs still had a Government to run and enjoyed a pot of steaming black coffee and a plate of breakfast pastries whilst he waited. They were fresh and very delicious and as it was almost forty minutes before he heard the arrival of a helicopter so he had used considerable self-control not to finish them all. He went to the bathroom to prepare for the journey and came out to find Stubbs waiting near the main entrance doors and led him outside towards a helicopter waiting on the side of the main runway.

"I have set up the meeting," Stubbs started, "Hampshire. I have asked MI5 to collect Avery and bring him to us. We will travel directly by helicopter from here. When we are finished the helicopter will bring you back here and I will go by car back to London. This will literally be a flying visit."

As they took off, McGeary tried to speak with Stubbs through the headsets they each had but he was not in the mood to talk. He is going to test me, McGeary concluded. We are going to interrogate his lifelong friend and Stubbs was going to observe as part of making up his mind just who he could trust. McGeary thought it best to allow this to happen. Interviewing Avery was the first, possibly only, chance anyone had had to speak directly to the Votary and McGeary wondered just how far the level of duty would go in preventing that discussion being useful to him. Thus, the air journey to Middle Wallop had remained silent apart from the noise of the rotors and McGeary settled himself to viewing the green and brown fields passing below.

Now McGeary gave the view of the airfield one more glance through the glass of the old hut window and turned back into the room to face Avery. Both he and Stubbs remained silent.

"Sir Donald," McGeary started, "Please forgive the urgency of this meeting and whilst you expected only to see the Prime Minister," McGeary nodded in acknowledgement to Stubbs, "I regret the subterfuge in suggesting he was all you were going to meet." McGeary moved to the table and sat on the empty chair facing Avery.

"Mr Stubbs's very kindly arranged this to happen as he and I have been discussing something over the last few days that is of supreme concern to us both, indeed to many others," McGeary paused to gather his thoughts. "Sir Donald…"

"Look," Avery said suddenly, "we can dispense with the 'Sir' bit. I see no need for formality here. I suspect the honour will have little or no significance soon anyway"

"As you wish," McGeary continued, "Donald, I know you and Andrew here have been friends for very many years and it is out of that friendship that he wanted us to have this chat. You came to him the other night and announced something that shocked him to the core. You have since resigned your position to, as you claim, concentrate on your duties elsewhere but that you felt you owed Andrew an explanation exactly because of your long history together. Mr Stubbs had taken your announcement with some derision and perhaps the matter would have ended acrimoniously between you both there and then had it not been for the fact that very day I had spoken to the Prime Minister to say practically the same thing as you did." McGeary paused again and, remembering the presence of Parkinson by the door, he looked towards Stubbs.

"Prime Minister," He started, how much of this should I be saying with others within earshot?" Stubbs paused for a second before replying.

"Parkinson," Stubbs said, looking up at the guard, "Would you please resume your post outside of the door. I am sorry, but this needs to remain confidential."

Parkinson moved without questioning the request, unlocked the door and went outside. The three men heard the key being engaged from the outside immediately afterwards. They were now locked in and McGeary continued where he left off.

"I believe it is without any doubt that you are involved in the organisation that seeks to shield the man who calls himself Adam. The brotherhood known as the Votary. Do you deny it?" McGeary looked hard into Avery's eyes. His scar was quietly pulsating on his cheek and the stitches were starting to strain.

"Of course, I do not deny it," Avery responded, "By nature of the responsibilities placed upon me by long and noble tradition throughout centuries of duty, I am tasked with whatever I am instructed to do, and that includes whatever interrogation I may have to endure," Avery was calm and relaxed. He even smiled. "As I said to Andrew, He is coming, and although I never thought I would be of the chosen generation to help proclaim his coming, I am thankful that it has fallen upon me."

"What drives this duty of yours?" McGeary asked quickly.

"What drives it?" Avery said," What drives anyone to follow what they believe in?" he smiled again as he answered McGeary's question with another. "I did not choose this path but was born to it. My Father took me aside when I was old enough to understand and explained how it would be. He was my father and I loved him so why would I challenge that?"

"So, you simply chose to ignore all the teachings of the world you knew simply because your father said everyone else was wrong and he was right?" McGeary followed.

"I challenged him and I have challenged myself many times since," Avery said but when you consider the facts, when you think on the truth, my mind is clear. My family would not be where we are today if the Age of Adam was never going to be a possibility…."

"Age of Adam?" McGeary interrupted concerned.

"Yes, the Age of Adam is why we are here now here in discussion. I assumed you specifically brought me here to talk about that" Avery continued. "That is what we, his disciples, we of the Votary, are tasked to usher into the world. The ultimate resurrection of the first man. The Rapture" Avery paused for a reaction but the others remained in silence, "I have obviously surprised you with my candour. When I spoke with Andrew it was out of love for a dear friend who I did not want to see suffer politically or personally when He is announced." Avery paused.

"So you admit you seek a new world order? A revolution against the establishment and modern religion? Replacing all that has gone before with a new creed?" McGeary posed.

"Adam is the oldest constant to this world. His message is not one of revolution or violence. All violence and death that happens from the time that He is announced will be by man's own hand, not his. Adam is a man of peace and love and most of all, truth. He wants us to embrace our beginnings, believe our origins and revel in our future opportunities. All religions have a book of their creed. Their Bible, Torah and others. Adam has as his book of faith the history of man, the journey of Human development, the diagram of the Human body as modelled by Creators through ages of old and immense scientific discovery. Adam has created all of this through his life story that has been written down ready for the world to receive it. He offers not one bible but one hundred, all of which have been written with his own first-hand knowledge of historical truth. Not by observers or later interpreters of tales passed down vocally only" Avery paused for breath and glanced at both Stubbs and McGeary in turn. Both men remained silent.

"I know you wish to stop his message before it starts," Avery continued, "You know that the power of social media and twenty-four-hour news will eclipse your efforts at stifling it at birth. That is why I choose not to deny the truth to you. Once it is out, it will be unstoppable and self-fulfilling. All Adam has to do is announce himself with the backing of trusted disciples, men of influence and power. Men of wealth to ensure the process is flawless and effective with their vast resources"

"Like yourself?" McGeary said sharply, "Men of unquestionable loyalty and devotion to the cause? Men of ultimate belief in your truth?"

"Of course," Avery responded.

"And what of…" McGeary fished in the pocket of his trousers and brought out a slip of paper before putting on his reading glassed which he extracted from the other pocket, "What of Heitor Guilherme Iago Rosario?" McGeary said, reading the name from the paper. He paused and looked at Avery over the top of the thinly framed glasses, "What of this man who killed himself on camera to betray the coming of your master to me. Was his loyalty unquestionable? Did he possess ultimate belief?" McGeary took his glasses off and placed them on the table next to the note.

"Not a name of which I have heard," Avery lied, his voice noticeably quieter.

"You know," McGeary started with a flourish, sensing the mood change in the room. "You know it is surprising the similarities between the two of you. Did you know Donald that Rosario was also a widower? That he had lost his eldest, indeed his only son to an unfortunate accident? That he lived alone apart from staff, in his case on his luxury executive yacht? That he was ridiculously rich, had a global business empire that had been started centuries before? Are you beginning to recognise anyone else with this description?" He paused and got up to pace the room. "You know that once I had been made aware of this man I did some deep investigation into him and his companies. The Internet is a wonderful tool, isn't it?" McGeary smiled at both men and continued to pace. "Did you know that his modern shipping empire was based on a simple single route, indeed a single ship, that transported Madeira wine from Funchal to Lisbon in the fourteenth century. That one small carriage service grew in the space of one hundred years only, to one that covered all Southern Europe and North Africa and followed by the main routes to the newly discovered Southern American outposts in the two centuries that followed. The Rosario shipping empire never stopped expanding, never stopped to pause or to consolidate. Never suffered from wars or disease interrupting their business. It was as if some unseen hand was protecting them with generous finance and other incentives." He stopped pacing and turned to Avery. "And yet despite that immense and impressive pedigree. Despite everything that had been done to keep the Rosario name on side for centuries. When it came to the crucial moment in history, the reason why all that help had been guaranteed in the first place, the man upon which the responsibility fell to help announce the coming of Adam preferred to draw a kitchen knife along his willing throat as the camera watched to warn me that the 'Age of Adam' was upon us. Why do you think that happened Mr Avery?" McGeary was leaning on the table with two hands splayed before Avery, his face inches away from the silent man.

Avery looked uncertain and strained. He glanced quickly to Stubbs who had remained silent throughout the exchange but his face was cold and without expression.

"Perhaps he had lost his faith or considered himself unworthy to complete his duty," Avery offered but did not do so with conviction.

"Something else my research uncovered was that the cause of death for Rosario's son was 'inconclusive'," McGeary followed, "The Portuguese coroner could not decide if the drowning was foul play or accidental. There were traces of hallucinogenic drugs in the boy's blood and unexplained bruising on the back of his neck. Perhaps the boy had been deliberately drugged and then held down in water to drown him before dumping the body at sea to make it look like an accident? Perhaps it had been murder to remove the last thing Rosario had in this world to care about? Perhaps all that was done to ensure his loyalty at the appropriate time but instead of reinforcing his beliefs, what if he had known the death was deliberate, that it was murder? What if he had discovered that the murder was linked to his duty as one of the Votary? What if his last act of his life was to give time to myself and others to stop Adam before he has the opportunity for his great reveal? McGeary remained very close to Avery who visibly seemed to retreat into his chair.

"I am sorry if this is making you uncomfortable Donald but you see I am wondering if in the same position as Rosario, which of course in a way you are with the sad deaths you have experienced, whether you would also question your own belief in the great undertaking you have been awarded? McGeary resumed his seat and nodded to Stubbs who cleared his throat.

"Donald," Stubbs started, "I am dreadfully sorry about this but you need to read these. He reached into his bag that was on the floor next to the seat and extracted two manila card folders. He reached across the table and placed them front side up in front of Avery who looked at the names on each. Both read 'Ministry of Defence inquest into the death of" followed by the handwritten names or each of his sons, one for each file.

Avery looked up at the two unsmiling men and knew immediately what he was going to read in these files. His heart sank.

Whilst Avery started to open the first of the two manila card folders he had been handed, McGeary suggested that the three of them be given refreshments and Stubbs had called Parkinson to re-enter. McGeary made the request for coffee to Parkinson who radioed it in and resumed his post outside keeping the door closed behind him. McGeary resumed his standing position at the window whist Stubbs fiddled with his Smartphone and let out the occasional tut and a plainly audible,

"Shit!"

Avery read the first file carefully and with a growing emotional fear. As he thought, the official enquiry into the first son's death by a sniper's bullet concluded that the type of gun used was not known to be in the possession of the Taliban. A similar model of the Accuracy International L11543 had been responsible for the deaths of two Taliban soldiers only a few years ago at a distance of over eight thousand feet, delivered by the trigger finger of a British corporal trained in long distance kills. So, it was known that the weapon type was in the combat area, just not facing coalition troops. Either the Taliban had a very efficient and specific source of new generation armaments or they did not fire the fatal shot. Additionally, the shot had been made from almost a mile distant and from a direction away from known Taliban territory held.

Whilst no conclusive verdict had been stated other than death by shooting, the file offered nothing by way of proof as to who or which organisation had fired the deadly bullet.

Avery placed the first folder back on the table and reached for the other. This one explained the death of his other son by a suspected improvised explosive device left at the side of the road travelled by his son's platoon. But this also cast some doubt on the perpetrators as the device did not follow the normal pattern of those known to be favoured by the Taliban and indeed, it suggested a more sophisticated explosive was used. The blast zone was not as extensive as usual and was specifically targeted to take out one man on foot only as opposed to all in the vicinity. Again, the file concluded that death was from a detonated device but did not draw a conclusion as to who was most likely to have planted it. Bearing in mind all such incidents were normally attributed to the Taliban, this was unusual.

Placing the second file back on the table, Avery came to his own inevitable conclusion that what Stubbs was suggesting was that both of his sons had been specifically targeted by assailants unknown. In other words, they had been murdered. He paused for a short while and looked up at the two men who were both now staring at him. He was about to speak when there was a knock at the door and it was opened by Parkinson from the outside to let in another man, younger and in army fatigues, carrying a tray upon which three Styrofoam cups, some small containers of

UHT milk and a few packets of sugar were displayed. No one spoke as he placed the tray on the table, turned and saluted the Prime Minister and left the room. Parkinson closed and locked the door from the outside once more.

"I know what you are trying to do," Avery said to break the silence. "You are saying that the evidence shows that both my sons were killed deliberately and not as an act of war, not by the Taliban. You want me to believe that the killings were done on behalf of, or at the behest of, Adam. That all of the Votary will have suffered the same sort of loss both as a means to ensure there would be no conflict with family concerns at the time of His coming and also because there would be no need for the sons to then take over the duties of the father. Am I correct?" He sat back in his chair and made no attempt to reach for one of the cups steaming in front of him.

"You have seen the evidence," Stubbs spoke first as he did reach for a coffee, ignored the milk cartons and the sugar packets and sat back down.

"Andrew," Avery started, "we both know the power of dodgy dossiers concerning the Middle East as history will confirm. At least the history of what came before the Age of Adam in any event, but I can choose not to believe what I have been shown."

"But you cannot ignore it either," McGeary followed, "If it was me in your position being offered such information from a man I had known all my life, I would at least think first that it had been done so with the best intentions for my well-being."

Avery remained quiet again and thought of what they were trying to achieve from him in this room. He did not want to believe the files and what they suggested but as his own doubts and concerns had proved only a few hours before, this did indeed cast doubt on the roots of what he thought had been his destiny to complete.

"What do you want from me," he said quietly, looking hard at the coffee tray.

McGeary walked towards the table and picked up a cup of coffee which he placed in front of Avery. He followed with two cartons of milk and two packets of sugar. As Avery broke open the cartons, pouring the contents into his cup, McGeary took the last cup and performed the same action.

"Donald, I am frightened," McGeary said in a low tone. "The Prime Minister may well be here for different reasons based on concern for this country but I am here with even greater concerns for the well-being of this whole world." McGeary resumed his seat the right of Avery and opposite Stubbs.

"You have lived your life with an expectation, actually probably you thought it would never come to pass which is why I suspect you were more easily swayed to accept it, but nevertheless, you have lived your adult life where everything you have said and done as part of society has been a lie. You have participated in rituals and celebrations that you knew in your heart were based on lies, at least you saw them as such. You could not, at any time, consult any of your friends or family about what you had been tasked with and therefore, your life has actually been quite lonely. Would you agree?" He sipped the coffee and grimaced. Years of quality Italian espresso had developed his palate for something that this brown liquid was not offering.

"It has been hard to remain quiet when wanting to shout out, yes," Avery answered.

"And in all that time, you have never had contact with anyone else, no other member of the Votary for instance, until recently?" McGeary followed, raising one eyebrow.

"Not until a few days ago. The day I asked Andrew to meet me at the Southern Empire Club that evening." Avery replied.

"How," McGeary asked.

"How what?"

"How were you contacted?" McGeary repeated his question.

"A text. One word. The one word that my father said to me would come by whatever method possible. The word that would say that He was coming. That the Age of Adam was upon us." Avery confirmed.

"And that word was?" McGeary followed quickly before taking another sip. Avery paused briefly before answering but concluded that it did not matter now what he did or did not say.

"Garden," he answered, "and before you ask. Yes, there was a response required which was 'Eden."

"This came on your personal phone?" McGeary asked, deliberately not acknowledging the information that Avery had provided.

"One of them, yes. One that had been sent to me some years ago." Avery answered.

"And you still have that phone?" McGeary asked tentatively.

"No, destroyed as per the instructions that came with its delivery." He lied, choosing not to reveal the later message about Nine of Twelve.

"Not a problem," Stubbs interrupted, "We know the date and location. Avery here can give us the time. It will not be too much of an ask to get GCHQ to filter through the traffic and track it down although it may take a while."

"Thank you," McGeary said and drained the last of the coffee from his cup despite the desire not to bother.

"The main point is that you were contacted. Do you know who would have sent that text?"

"Look," Avery said with impatience, "I know you are looking to find out who else is involved, who the other ten members of the Votary are but you will already be too late I'm afraid. In any event, I simply do not know. One of the main rules of the Votary is that no one member has knowledge of the others. They do not need to do so as they will never meet until after He is proclaimed. Each of us has a country or Geo-political area that is considered to be our responsibility and within which we become the spokesperson, the prophet of His coming. Only after He is announced will we sit as a council, a world forum. I am responsible for the British Isles and I assume that poor unfortunate man in Portugal, Mr Rosario, was responsible for the Iberian Peninsula and associated Spanish and Portuguese islands in the region. Other than that, I know nothing. No names, no areas. Nothing." Avery finally started to drink his coffee.

Stubbs reached once more into his bag and withdrew a stack of A4 papers. He cast his eyes down the pages and raised his eyebrows before speaking.

"Donald, you spent most yesterday researching the internet using random filters to find out list of names. You searched by continent and country. Then by wealth statistics, industries, nationalities and finally family history."

"You hacked me?" Avery shouted with indignation.

"Why are you surprised Donald," Stubbs followed. "You make a guarded threat against this country and resign to follow some unknown Messiah. What would you have expected me to do with anyone else that had done so. You are not immune from investigation."

"Fuck you Stubbs," Avery shouted in defiance.

"Come, come Donald. We are all grown up men here. Surely you are not surprised by this?" McGeary concluded. "You clearly had the mind to research other possible members of the Votary based on the very assumptions I have suggested today yet you did so even before I suggested them. I must conclude therefore, that you have had subsequent contact with somebody after the 'Garden' text and that conversation changed your perception. Had you been advised perhaps of the demise of Mr Rosario? What was his designation in the Votary? Do you all have titles?"

Avery thought hard on his next response. He hated the knowledge that his computer had been hacked and blamed himself for not thinking that would happen in the first place. He had nowhere to go with this as the proof would already be in the papers Stubbs was holding. Both men had known he already had his doubts about the coming of Adam and what that had meant for his own family and possibly those of the rest of the Votary which prompted his research in the first place. Above all, Avery knew that he was cornered but unlike a rodent in the same position, he had absolutely no wish to come out fighting. In his heart, he wished now that he had not put that souvenir for the Korean War back in his desk drawer. He looked up at the two men, each in turn before answering.

"I am Four of Twelve. Rosario had been Nine of Twelve. After his suicide, I was told to assume responsibility for his area in the short term until a replacement can be advised. There are always two potential members of the Votary for each region but the reserve list, if you can call it such, would have a different code word for activation. Therefore, the second group would have no knowledge of the first although we always knew that there could be a replacement in case of an early death that destroyed the family line before the duty could be passed on. I will get confirmation once that code word has been sent to the replacement for Iberia and he is in place." Avery sat back again, strangely relieved.

"So potentially," McGeary started, "Potentially there is a network of at least twenty-four rich men spread around the world ready for activation, of which the first Twelve, the original 'Votary' have all already been activated?"

"Yes," Avery agreed.

"And these men," McGeary followed, "each will have lieutenants that they can call upon to perform whatever actions or deeds are required to maintain the secrecy and promote the cause?"

"Not that I am aware of," Avery said, "I have no such contacts. My brief is to make myself known as the Prophet of Adam in Britain and be seen to promote Him. I have never been asked, nor have needed, anything done to want to use such people."

McGeary looked puzzled. He had expected the reverse situation to be the case. He knew about the Votary, but assumed they also were responsible for direction of the actions taken to protect the cause. The Paris car bomb and the murder of De Soto, each would have been directed by somebody with the connections to those able and willing to take orders. The reality hit with a sudden rush of sense.

"When you speak of a reserve Votary, I doubt that is indeed the case," McGeary stated forcibly, "I think those that stand ready to replace a member of the Votary have a more hands-on role shall we say to trying to prevent the need for any replacement to be made. Natural death cannot be prevented but all and any actions need to protect Adam and the Votary, especially violent action, will be commanded and overseen by the sub-network. It is these men that direct the money to the thugs and mercenaries that keep the pretence going. My God, I see it all now. The wars and atrocities that have been done to protect commercial interests prompted by the business interests involved, completed so that those businesses, the very empires built around the Votary themselves, have been committed to ensure the underlying wealth of the future Age of Adam is protected. Personal threats to the Votary eliminated and business threats neutered. I believe we are dealing here with nothing less than a global conspiracy that reaches into the very heart of the economic, political and religious interests of every country, of every person on this planet." He stopped, exhausted and strained.

"And you think this is all directed by Adam alone?" Stubbs offered.

"Possibly," McGeary responded, "but his profile would need to be kept relatively low until the right time. No, I think there is another who fulfils the post of Commander here and given the need to always be in place, I would assume that is also an inherited role. 'One of Twelve' perhaps?

The three men paused to reflect until Avery piped up.

"What will happen to me now?" he asked.

"I think there is nothing more you can offer Donald but I must tell you that you will not be allowed to promote this Adam in any way." Stubbs said, "You have to understand that. You will be kept under house arrest until further notice. Parkinson will take you home and you will find that guards are already there waiting for you."

McGeary looked at the crestfallen Avery and reached to squeeze his arm. "The truth is my son that even you can now see this is the wrong path. You thought that yesterday and you must see it now. I implore you not to do anything stupid. Do not end your life. There is no shame here. You are not in the wrong."

"But if I am inoperative, will the replacement member of the Votary not just be activated in my place?" Avery offered.

"Let me deal with that possibility," Stubbs said. "Parkinson!" He shouted. The big man entered and Stubbs told him to take Avery back. The cardinal shook Avery's hand but neither Avery nor Stubbs made an effort to say goodbye in a similar fashion. Avery left the room a broken man as Parkinson shut the door once more.

"What will you do now?" Stubbs asked the Cardinal.

"How much of those papers are you willing to share?" McGeary asked.

"Forgive me Cardinal but I must put this country first, "Stubbs followed. "I cannot stop you doing similar research but Donald is right. If I lock him up then another will take his place. At the moment, all I have to go on is in this research and straight after this meeting, the whole Government machine and associated agencies will be focussed on this. I want this closed down as far as Britain is concerned. Now Cardinal, your helicopter awaits to take you back to Exeter and then your flight back to Paris." He got out of his chair, "If you please your Eminence."

Chapter Twenty-Two

Early afternoon, 20th September, Present Day, The English Channel

The parting from Stubbs had been convivial and respectful. A simple handshake and appreciative words for what had been completed and yet McGeary remained unsure as to exactly what had been achieved. He was obviously appreciative of the Prime Minister's interest and assistance but he still did not feel that Stubbs had fully committed to anything wider than the interests of the United Kingdom alone and that was troublesome. The last thing McGeary needed at this time was inward navel-gazing in the national interest, the threat was simply to vast to accommodate individual concerns.

Avery had been made to see the real possibility that his life and, most importantly, the deaths of his two sons had been planned and carried out with murderous intent by agents acting on behalf of the very Messiah he had been taught all his life he should revere. He was clearly a broken man and despite McGeary's parting words of encouragement, the Cardinal was convinced that Avery would remain in a depressed state. He hopes that would not be the case for McGeary had actually liked the well-bred Englishman, the very essence of all that his Grandfather had fought and died to reject on the streets of Dublin. Yet despite that respect, McGeary knew that if a genuinely good man like Avery at heart could have been so brainwashed until considerable doubt had been planted then more ambitious or vicious followers undoubtedly did still exist.

As the aircraft from Exeter yet again crossed the Channel for the return journey, McGeary was focussed but not fulfilled as a result of the interrogation that had taken place. All he had really achieved had been confirmation of the existence of the Votary, that the profile of each member would likely be similar now that the presentation of Adam was near and that there was an additional organisational tier whose function was to both protect the Votary with all means necessary and also be ready to supplement the council where required. McGeary now knew that his job had been made harder, despite the revelations made, as the depth and reach of the organisation beneath the Votary was unknown. He concentrated his thoughts on the under-organisation. Who controlled them? Who directed operations? Was is likely to be a global direction or left to local decision makers, perhaps directly linked to their respective member of the Votary?

The rhythmic hum of the engines had faded away as McGeary thought more deeply on the organisation he would now be facing. He accepted that those likely to commit whatever action was required would not also be those in charge. That made complete sense. The foot-soldiers would most likely be professional paid assassins and mercenaries, perhaps not even knowing why they had been instructed to kill someone or create mayhem. Indeed, they would not need to know anything other than the fact that their actions demanded a payment, most likely in cash to be untraceable. That would require access to cash deposits and a suitable method of delivery, both needing secure storage of the money and the means to transport it in ways not to arouse suspicion. Alternatively, masked computerised financial transactions would be cleaner and speedier to pay the hired guns as required but each one, however well disguised, could eventually be found out though persistent digital accounting. The Cardinal preferred the cash approach. It may be old-school but nothing, simply nothing would be as vintage as Adam himself. After centuries of amassing huge wealth and through the business he had supported and controlled, his own cash vaults would be immense. It made sense that payments made by easily transportable cash by the suitcase-load was the most basic but equally more secure method without third-party banks to worry about.

McGeary knew he now faced a double threat. He still needed to identify the unknown members of the Votary in the hope that the specific location of Adam himself could be obtained but in doing so, the shadowy hand of the organisation beneath the Votary was an ever-present danger. The car bomb that was timed to ensure he would not be killed was evidence that their reach was already around him. The death of De Soto was just too convenient not to be at their hand. Plus, if they had been able to both fake a death through drugs and drowning of the Rosario boy as well as being in an active war zone to deal out their own special version of death in such a specific manner to Avery's sons at the same time suggested that their scope was sophisticated at the very least. These were dangerous people and McGeary suddenly felt vulnerable. He had resolved himself to get back to Rome on the first available flight or would drive if need be. All the research he now needed to complete meant using the assets at his disposal in the Vatican. More than that perhaps, if there was a traitor in his staff then he needed to be where he could keep a closer watch and that required him to be on hand in the Eternal City. He had willed the plane to go faster as the darkened shape of the French coastline approached.

Early afternoon, 20th September, Present Day. Hampshire, England

Parkinson had remained quiet in the driver's seat throughout the journey back to Avery's home. Avery himself had spent the journey simply staring at the lush countryside as it sped by. It did not occur to him that the route they were taking was not the more direct one they had journeyed on to meet Stubbs and McGeary at Middle Wallop. As they passed through Stockbridge, his eyes did not focus on the people or buildings they passed but he simply concentrated on his own thoughts, his own deep personal regrets.

He had known the moment the two folders had been placed before him that his own fears had been proved. His sons had been deliberately murdered and had not just simply been battlefield casualties. His wife's suicide had been a simple reaction to their deaths, thus saving the killers from doing it themselves but he had no doubt that under different circumstances, they would have taken her life too. All had been simply to ensure he would not be diverted from his duty when the call came. His family had died to order so that he could be the Prophet of Adam. The thought was horrible. An obscene act of betrayal to the entire history of his family for as long as they had followed the cause of Adam's arrival. The cause that had driven his father and grandfather and all male patriarchs of his entire line had been false, a creed dominated by corruption and death. All were simply pawns in Adam's great game. Everything had been manipulated specifically to fit a pre-determined timetable. He despised himself for not questioning it all earlier and more deeply. For not standing up to his father when he had been told to disregard all that he had been taught up to that day.

Avery contemplated where he could go from here. His career was over, of that there was no doubt. He could not possibly follow his duty as the protector of Adam, of that he was resolutely convinced. His family was gone and he now faced house arrest for an undeterminable time whilst the chaos that could descend on his country and indeed the world commenced. Avery closed his eyes and fought back bitter tears as he realised all was lost. In his heart he knew that there was really now nothing more to do.

The crunch of gravel made him look up as he realised they had arrived back at his house. The car moved slowly along the drive and Avery could see that there were already two other cars waiting. He assumed they belonged to his guards, his captors in his own house. The vehicle came to a stop and Avery got out of his seat and shut the door as he walked slowly to the house. As he entered the hallway, voices inside the main living room distracted him and he moved to enter the room. He was instantly dumbfounded by the sight of Andrew Stubbs waiting in the room together with two other men.

"Andrew…..what?" Avery began but his senses could not figure it out. How could Stubbs have been there before him? He was sure they had not been passed on the journey.

"Sorry Donald," Stubbs began, "but it was necessary to use a few short-cuts to beat you here and Parkinson had already been briefed about the route he should take." He paced towards Avery but stopped a few feet away.

"Other than earlier," Stubbs started, "have you been in contact with the Cardinal or indeed anyone else about this matter before?" Stubbs waited for a second before continuing, "I need to know Donald that this remains confidential."

"Nobody," he said assuredly. Stubbs waited in silence for a few seconds and then sucked air noisily between his teeth whilst his eyes widened.

"Good. It really does not change matters but I had to ask. I really had hoped there would not be the need for this. Believe me I really did." He said not meeting Avery's eyes. "But you leave me no choice. You see, I was not exactly that surprised when you came to me the other night about your supposed duty. I have known for a very long time actually. From the moment my father told me of the legacy that was his to hand down." Stubbs paused and waited for a reaction from Avery.

"What...?" Avery said, his face a mask of confusion.

"It is quite simple really," Stubbs continued, "The old priest now knows of the full structure that surrounds the Votary and it obviously does surprise you to know of my position in connection with it." He started to pace around the room, picking up selected ornaments for examination as if interested in their style and finesse before replacing them, "You see Donald, with your removal, I will replace you." The statement came out in a simple matter of fact way and Avery's eyes widened with shock. "It is all quite logical really you see as the right was always supposed to be mine to be Four of Twelve but the first male line of the Stubbs family died without issue in 1791, on the night of the great fire of Barnsford Manor. Have you heard of it?" Stubbs looked up to see that Avery neither acknowledged or understood.

"Ah I see a small history lesson is required," Stubbs continued. "Simply put, the last real Lord Stubbs had, how can I put it, unusual tastes," He smiled and slightly whetted his lips. "He was Four of Twelve for the last half of the Eighteenth Century and a founder member of the Hades Society, the chairman of which was none other than Adam himself in the persona of the Earl of Barnsford. The same Earl of Barnsford who was tied to a chair and burned alive in his own mansion together with several other senior members of the Hades Society, Lord Stubbs with him, when their cult of blood was discovered and stopped by men of the local village looking for their missing girls. But of course, Adam walked away from the flames to begin anew with only his Valet and that man's daughter. The same girl who had been made pregnant by my ancestor after he forced himself upon her weeks before at a previous gathering. The original Lord Stubbs never saw the product of his lust enter the world and grow but the girl indeed had a healthy male child. Adam saw an opportunity and though a sense of loyalty to the girl's father, was quick to formulate the iron and later steel business empire around the infant using himself as benefactor until what became The Stubbs Steel Company grew as the young man also matured until it became the bedrock of the global business for which my family is now known. The young man became Kamal Stubbs as a direct nod to his grandfather's Albanian roots and was my direct paternal ancestor. You have always thought my middle name was Keith and I had no reason to contradict that thought, but it is and always was Kamal, Andrew Kamal Stubbs, Prime Minister of the United Kingdom, facilitator of and soon to be the new Four of Twelve in the Age of Adam." Stubbs stopped and glared at Avery before he motioned to Parkinson who immediately grasped

Avery's arms and held them tight against his body. Avery's eyes widened as he stared with icy determination at the now chuckling Stubbs.

"You always were a bastard, Stubbs," he spat, "Always needed to be the centre of attention, the one who would not lose well. How it must have pained you to see the Avery's ascend at your expense." He felt the grip on his arms grow stronger and a sudden panic overcame his loathing.

"Stubbs! What are you doing?" he shouted as the other two men behind Stubbs approached. One had something in his hand and Avery gasped as he realised it was a length of gold coloured electrical flex. The standard lamp that normally stood behind the reading chair in the corner was now on its side on the floor with the flex ripped from its housing and removed. Avery screamed and shook his head as one of the other men also held him whilst the third placed a makeshift noose made from the flex over his head and pulled the slip knot tight. Avery chocked for breath as the trio manhandled him out of the room whilst maintaining the tension on the flex and started to ascend the staircase. He struggled and kicked as much as he could but the gripped hands upon him were too strong.

Stubbs followed the panicking man and his three assailants and spoke in muted tones.

"You see Donald, the Avery's were only ever the substitute for the Votary after the murder of Lord Stubbs and the moment you came to me about His coming I knew you would not be up to your duty. You were always the enthusiast who developed such considerable self-doubt when it mattered. All throughout our lives together you were the first to suggest something and equally the first to back out and indeed you have again showed it now. Your family was always the second-best choice really but my own ancestral reliance on the macabre pursuits of carnal desire cost my family dear over two centuries ago as it still plagues me now. Your family prospered whilst ours started again through sheer will and through that, the Stubbs name was able to recover our importance to His will. To be on hand to monitor your family, to protect you and, yes, to remove your reasons of distraction when it was needed to be done. I bitterly regret having to order the death of your two sons but I knew it was inevitable when the call came and the time for His coming was so soon. Nothing must get in the way of His rise. Not even my dear departed wife could escape her fate. We are the chosen generation Donald. We should relish the opportunity we have been presented with and as Prime Minister, I am uniquely placed to do a far better job than you could ever hope for and with your cowardice through your 'suicide', I will fully resume my family's true place with a seat on His High Council. I shall become the new Four of Twelve and will sit at His right hand."

Stubbs followed the three men as they managed to get Avery to the top of the stairs and held him tight as Stubbs himself took the loose end of the flex and tied it securely to the ornate metal balustrade.

"You were always the weaker man Avery," Stubbs said as he finished his knot and looked into the Avery's face as it turned a deep red and purple hue, his eyes bulging. "At least you leave this world with some honour." He stepped back and nodded to the three men as they heaved Avery over the banister and let him go. The fall was insufficient to break the hanging man's neck so he danced and shook as the flex bit even deeper into his flesh. He clawed at the flex as it tightened even further until his strength all but left him and his enforced jog stopped until he swung silently, the air filled with the stench of his bowels relaxing through the strangulation trauma.

Stubbs and the three men descended the stairs before he made for the door with his driver.

"Give me five minutes then call it in," he said to Parkinson. "File the report to say that you were both checking the grounds and were outside for only a few minutes before coming in and finding him like this." Stubbs looked down as Avery's dog Cromwell sat silently looking at his master swinging above his head.

"Feed the dog," Stubbs said as he started to walk outside. He got into his car and shut the door followed by the driver. Within seconds the car was gone.

Chapter Twenty-Three

15.05, 20ᵗʰ September Present Day, Somewhere in England

Crowe had not experienced such sleep before. He awoke to streaming sunshine though the bedroom window which had made him jolt with a flurry of blinks as his eyes became familiar with the sudden strong light. The room was bathed with the illumination and his head was directly in the beams of sunlight that shone upon the head of the bed he had been sleeping on.

He remained fully dressed, even his shoes were still on his feet. His mouth was exceptionally dry and his tongue was difficult to move around as it searched for moisture. His eyes felt weary and tired still but he had clearly slept for a very long time. He looked at his watch and saw that it was 15:05 am. He had slept for nearly 18 hours.

Moving slowly to the edge of the bed, he suddenly felt an urgent need to urinate and made his way on unsteady legs to the bathroom using the edge of the bed to hold on to for stability. He pissed for almost a full minute as his stretched bladder relished the immediate release of tension and once finished, he washed his hands, face and splashed water over his hair to help wake himself up.

His head was now pounding and Crowe knew for certainty that his long sleep had been induced rather than natural – he had been drugged. Hooded, locked in his room and now drugged, Crowe was both concerned yet fascinated by what was happening to him.

Looking towards what he expected to still be a locked door, he saw that for first time and to his astonishment that it was ajar. He moved swiftly as he could towards it before peering through the gap into the corridor beyond. Seeing it was empty, he pulled the door open a little more and slipped out into the corridor, moving silently as he could to retrace his steps from the afternoon before. Reaching the corner with the staircase gallery, he peered around the corner into the entrance hall below. He breathed a sigh of relief to see it was empty and so he made his way further along the landing sticking tightly to the wall on his right separated by a number of similar doors of the same style as the one to his bedroom. A sudden noise below made him stop and slightly overbalance as his still fuddled brain sought to compensate for the surprise change in momentum. He fell sideways into the wall and was immediately surprised by the flexibility of what should have been a stone structure. The wall moved with his weight and whilst steadying himself, he afforded a light knock on the surface to double check. Sure enough, instead of a dull thud of knuckle on stone, the clear report of the blow on wood was evident. The wall was a fake. It was not a solid structure and immediately Crowe understood the lack of symmetry in the corridor that had confused him the previous day. There was no opposite hallway to the one taking him to his room as would be expected of a great house simply because there was nothing to access. The house consisted of the front half only, a mere shadow of the original it was supposed to replicate. Crowe moved to the nearest door and crouched to peer through the keyhole. As expected, although there was a space behind the door but it was too gloomy to see anything distinct. Instinctively, Crowe selected an app on his smart phone that delivered a torch-light from the back and positioned the phone so that the light shone under the base of the door. Looking again though the keyhole, the soft light that made it into the room showed it not to be a room at all, but the size of a cupboard space only, totally empty and backed by what looked to be simple bare breeze blocks. Crowe moved to the next door and repeated the procedure to be met with exactly the same view. The whole wall was a facade to hide the plain supporting block wall beyond.

A further sound from below made Crowe reach for the phone, disengaging the light app and replace it into his pocket. He considered his options. He could try and make it to the front door and simply leave but with Squat Man and Tall Man, the latter being who he now knew as Karl, could still be around and Crowe did not fancy his chances of taking on either of them, let alone both. He thought about returning to his room and await being called but then reasoned that the door had been left as his invitation to come down at some point anyway. The third option was to play along and go downstairs as if nothing had changed, apologise that his weariness had enforced an extended sleep whilst not giving anything away that he thought he had been drugged and not mentioning the subterfuge that the half-finished building represented. Crowe came to the conclusion that he had to play Adam's game, at least until he had a better chance to get out and….. well, what? Crowe had no idea of his location and the lack of any sort of access road to the building through the trees meant he could stumble off completely in the wrong direction of any assistance. Adam may have installed additional security measures to keep him safe, cameras, wire, perhaps even traps. There were simply too many unknowns and Crowe knew that his best chance of escape had not yet presented itself. He would have to wait.

Crowe recovered himself into a full standing position, stretched and flexed his limbs and purposely started to descend the stairs. As he reached the bottom, he let out what he hoped would be a booming greeting but the dryness of his mouth muted it to an arid crackle. He swallowed hard, strained to find some moisture and coughed.

"Hello!" he said in the best raised voice he could muster and started to move towards the large library room where the flintlock test had been completed the day before. A sound from within stopped him in his tracks.

"Ah Michael, you are up," came the familiar voice of Adam from the room, "Come in! Come in."

Michael entered the room to find Adam seated and wearing a long robe type garment in red and gold. He beckoned Crowe to join him and pointed to the same chair that Crowe had occupied previously.

"I am so sorry to have missed breakfast this morning and indeed lunch," Crowe started, "I was clearly much more exhausted than I thought.

Adam smiled a knowing smile and did not respond to Crowe's apology but gestured to the table next to him which held a variety of fruit and a jug of orange juice.

"Then you must be hungry Michael," He said quietly, "Please, help yourself."

Michael first poured himself a glass of juice which he first sipped, then gulped to quench his thirst. He then took a banana and some dates before sitting down to start consuming them.

"I do not sleep much," Adam said, "Perhaps a few hours each night at the most. My body does not require excessive rest. But I love the night. In some ways I find the mysteries of the night more enthralling than the day." He leaned forward. "Consider this Michael, when you have seen practically all the beauties there are to see in the light, is it not more exciting to imagine even more splendid sights you can only imagine in the blackness of the dark?"

Crowe was not really listening. His head screamed to shout at the man before him and demand to know why his house was little more than a movie set, a fake. Whatever he was, Adam was a fraud of that Crowe was sure but for what reason? He had witnessed up close and personal the ability of the man to be immortal. He was charismatic and beguiling, of that there was no doubt and perhaps he was, however slim the probability, the actual Adam. But what was his endgame? That was the question that both troubled and in a perverse way, excited Crowe.

"So, Michael," Adam started, "What else can I tell you or are you convinced already?"

"I am convinced you could be Adam," Crowe started, "you are certainly someone, or something special of that I do not doubt. But I am looking into the future and the possible challenges I, or anyone will have in explaining that." He took a date into this mouth and chewed slowly as he continued to speak. "If you have influenced history and possibly religion as you say, what more can you offer in proof?"

"Do you mean who can I claim to be?" Adam replied raising his eyebrows.

"Exactly," Crowe responded as he started to peel the banana.

"Well, where to start," Adam followed as he sat back in the chair. "We have already discussed the flood and my involvement there so let me see." Adam pondered and paused. Crowe was puzzled by the delay. He was expecting Adam to reveal a string of names that Crowe would recognise and some he would not but the longer the pause went on, the more he was urging Adam to say something.

"Don't forget Michael," Adam started finally, "I have been the inspiration of many as opposed to actually being the person. However, in equally many cases, I was instrumental in the deeds that created the fame in the first place. So rather than me giving you a list which will not convince anyone I would suggest, why don't you ask me specific questions and I will do my best to answer them."

"Okay," Crowe responded, "Let's start with the big ones. Which Gods are based on you?"

"Ha!" Adam cried, "I would have won a bet with myself on that one!" He clapped his hands gleefully. "Many of the ancient deities are actually the same legends that have been altered by numerous civilisations but were ultimately based on my deeds. There is no value in discussing these as what man has made of the stories vary so widely that there is nothing to be gained. But let me tell you who I was not," he continued, "I was not Jesus Christ," he paused and stared wide-eyed at Crowe, his dark pupils seemingly burning through the Historian's head, "Although I knew him well," he continued, "Whilst much of the stories and myths of his life were based on fact, much was also fabricated. But he was an amazing man who deserved the adulation and it is of no surprise to me that an entire religious creed was developed from his meaning. Again, the human desire for divinity required

285

his story to be moulded over time and few will know the truth of that time in Judea. But I was there so I know him to have been real."

"Not the Son of God though?" Crowe asked.

"Depends on what you believe as in all things Michael," Adam replied with a wry smile. "From my point of view though, I could see the level of following that he achieved and from him I realised what would be necessary to create the sort of mass persuasion required to become a Messiah. But I could not let it go on forever. He had to be stopped at the right time to elevate my own myth for future generations."

"I don't understand," Crowe said genuinely.

"In him I saw the opportunity to maintain the old legends of resurrection. If he could be killed whilst still young, the blessings that would be seen from his perceived restoration to life would serve very well to renew the older legends, the ones that had previously been based on my own exploits. If he had been allowed to die an old man, those legends would not have been revived. I knew the scribes of the age would want to embellish the old stories into this one, to elevate their own importance and involvement and I was right. So, whether you consider Krishna, Osiris or even Bacchus, all of whom have their roots of my involvement in the earliest cultures and you will see the similarities in the later story of Christ." He paused allowing Crowe to speak.

"So, you manipulated the situation to allow the older legends based on you to be effectively repeated, to keep the myth of the immortal man going?" he breathed heavily, "Thus you were not Jesus Christ, I understand that, but you said you knew him?"

"Of course, and I was instrumental in his capture and later execution," Adam continued, "You will know of me as the whole Christian world now does. You will know me as Judas Iscariot." He rested back in his chair again as Crowe's eyes widened as he breathed a barely audible,

"Fuck."

"Indeed," Adam replied with a smile. "You should applaud me with my ingenuity at the very least." He said. "My 'hanging' was duly staged and from which I obviously walked away from later and everything that has now been written about his resurrection and the whole creation of the Christian church is down to me. You see Michael, once you start to probe, who knows what you will uncover!"

From that moment Crowe was absolutely convinced. Any thoughts he had of presenting this man as Adam for purposes of historical fact were impossible. Truth or not, Crowe knew that his only purpose now was to escape from this mock house and make sure Adam could never cause the ultimate human crisis, one that would cost countless lives as the backlash took hold. At all costs, Crowe knew Adam had to be stopped.

The man was insane, of that he was sure, and dangerous with it.

Adam's phone rang quietly on the table next to the fruit bowl and he immediately looked at it as the vibration made it skip and jump across the French polished walnut. He reached for it and put it to his ear whilst pressing the green button.

"Yes," he said a little muffled.

Crowe could not hear what was being said but the expressions on Adam's face made him wonder what the man was being advised of. Adam said nothing and replaced the phone on the table after the caller had finished. He pondered for a moment before looking up at Crowe.

"I see you have signal," Crowe said sternly. "I have not. No Wi-Fi either?" he followed, "I would like to be able to call my partner to let her know I am safe and well. Is there a landline I can use please?"

Adam ignored Crowe's request and stared hard into his eyes. His expression was stony, cold.

"When I told you that I was Judas Iscariot you reacted strangely Michael. The look on your face changed and if there is one thing that I can read after all these years of looking at people is that the eyes say far more than the mouth ever does." He paused and rested his chin on one cupped palm as his elbow was placed on his knee. "Have I lost your trust Michael? Have I said something which means you can no longer place your faith in me?"

Crowe moved awkwardly in his chair and started to reason with himself as to how to play this sudden threat. His plan had been to go along with Adam until he was in a position to make good an escape and, if necessary, seek assistance from wherever he could to guarantee his safety and that of those he cared about but Adam's sudden change in tone was concerning.

"You shocked me, I cannot deny it," Crowe blurted, shifting in his chair awkwardly, "Perhaps I was not ready for such a revelation or perhaps the callous way which you tried to manipulate a whole new religion to fit your own longer-term ends disturbed me. Did you really think over two thousand years ago that it was necessary to betray Christ simply to effectively steal his crown when the time suited?" Crowe doubted his last sentence suddenly as being too provocative but it was too late, the words could not be un-said.

Adam remained quiet for a few moments whilst he boyishly moved his chin as it rested on his upturned palm side to side, moving his jaw rhythmically with the movement.

"Hmmm," he started, "You know Michael I am beginning to think you are not wishing to be my friend. I sense that your doubts outweigh your beliefs. I am correct?" He moved his head away from his palm and sat back into the chair. "Is that it?" he followed, "despite all I have told you and shown you. Despite all that Professor Wilding has spoken with you and despite the evidence of your own eyes to this reconstructed monument to the man you studied for years," He waved his arms around to indicate the house, "and despite the fact that you saw first-hand that my immortality is real. Despite all this you still fail to understand? To believe that I am the truth? I must say Michael, you do disappoint me, you really do."

Crowe realised in an instant that he was exposed. The mood had changed and Adam was unpredictable so he decided to go for broke.

"You have kept me hooded to prevent me from seeing where I travelled. You have kept me locked up in this farce of a building," Adam looked up at Crowe, "Yes, I know it is a mock-up, a half mansion. The front is modelled on the old Barnsford estate house but it ends there. The old plans you showed me of the original house with its upstairs club rooms where you held your orgies and God knows what else over two hundred years ago have not been reproduced here. There is nothing behind those doors up there but the rooms you and I retired to after dinner yesterday. You then locked me in that room and drugged me so please tell me why I should want to trust you?" Crowe drew breath and slumped back down.

"I see," Adam responded with sudden calmness, "You have found me out… Well Michael, I cannot contest your summary about this house for it is indeed merely a mock-up of how the Barnsford house used to be.

Think of it as a film set Michael in which you are the star. Indeed, I suppose it is exactly that. You see one of my supporters, the one responsible for North America to be exact, is a tremendously wealthy film studio mogul as well as a leading politician. It was his set designers and builders that produced this for me, all in the guise of a future costume drama to be filmed. The very land we stand upon was once just covered in trees. The film company bought the forest, cleared the space within which the house was to be built and used helicopters to bring in the materials and men to build it, all in the name of privacy for a fictitious production. Rather brilliant when you think about it!" Adam had a sneer on his face that rattled Crowe, "You see, I thought you would be better convinced of me, more trusting of me if I presented what was familiar to you. Oh, the antiques, the art and everything you see around us is quite genuine I assure you. But the fabric of the house is a mere shell, a folly if you will. You see, Michael, I considered that my cause would be best served if worthies like yourself and Wilding to a degree were amongst the first to proclaim my rising. Such a popular man like yourself would add a sense of contemporary wisdom, a foil to the political and religious establishments that would seek to bring me down. Perhaps I was wrong? But I thought that immersed in the familiar would open you up to the reality of what must happen." He paused momentarily before continuing.

"Maybe I was wrong to be over protective, to keep you hooded or locked away. But as you seem to remain unconvinced perhaps then it was advantageous foresight on my part after all." Adam got up and went to the mantelpiece above the fire. He reached for a small bell that was positioned there and rang it before returning to his seat.

"You see Michael, I must be in control. I have always been in control. For centuries I have controlled the wealthy and powerful, mostly easily corruptible men willing and able to put their own riches first, money I was able to shower them with from my endless coffers in return for their loyalty. All of this you see around you was my attempt to bring you on my side with a new strategy, one simply based on reason. On earned trust and respect, but I see I failed. My persuasion was insufficient and perhaps I must now try another approach." The door opened and Karl a.k.a. Tall Man entered. He stood by the door.

"Did he send it?" Adam asked plainly and Karl nodded slowly. "Send it to me." He followed.

Karl extracted his phone and pressed a few buttons before waiting for Adam's phone to register a text. He replaced the phone in his pocket and remained by the door. Adam in return picked up his own phone and looked at the text received. He got up out of the chair and walked the short distance to Crowe holding out the phone before him.

"As you can see," he started, "Where reason and trust fails, then one is left only with what works even better…. fear." Crowe looked at the photo on the form and exhaled deeply as he visibly slumped. The terrified and bloodied face of Jessica, a rough gag over her mouth held in place by wide tape, her eyes red and wet with tears stared back.

"You fucking bastard," Crowe shouted as he moved to grab Adam. The now laughing man side stepped with effortless grace so that Crowe stumbled and crashed into the small table scattering the remaining fruit. He regained his composure and lunged once again at Adam but his arm was caught in the vice-like grip of Tall Man's hand. Karl's free hand came up to connect with Crowe's left cheek and he crumpled beneath it, falling to the floor. Karl was about to deliver a savage kick to Crowe's midriff when Adam shouted.

"No!" he said, "restrain him only."

Karl wrenched Crowe's arms behind his back and used a cable tie he extracted from his jacket pocket to bind his wrists. He then forcibly manhandled Crowe back to his seat and threw him in it.

"Such aggression Michael, you surprise me. I thought you were a man of learning, not fighting." Adam resumed his seat.

"So, this is how it will be," He started. "You will willingly proclaim me as Adam, the metamorphosis of all things that is human. The gift of the creators to this world. The immortal man. You will do so by way of a live transmission where you will kill me many times and I shall arise from each. You will allow the viral explosion of that event to be transmitted across all social media outlets and respond to any who ask you that the truth is how you state it. You will do all this Michael for I have Jessica in the less than caring clutches of Pavel, you have met him of course. He came to me with a particular set of skills that have proved very useful in interrogation. He loves it you see. The ability to use pain to bend anyone's will to his own. It is a rare skill indeed to be so ruthless and yet so precise in the application. You would also probably expect his social skills with the ladies to be as efficient as his ability to see right from wrong. Do I make myself clear Michael?"

Crowe nodded through a realisation of fear and loathing and his own stupidity for even considering the prospect that had been offered to him.

"You bastard," he repeated, "What of Wilding, is he part of this?"

"Oh, Professor Wilding is dead Michael. I am sorry, I forgot to say." He shook his head as if to remonstrate with himself for the oversight. "And the books are gone. Stolen. Well, re-acquired shall we say." He smiled broadly. "It will look like the actions of some deranged fundamentalist looking to stop me before I even start. But you know, the books will be re-discovered in the hands of the man tasked to find me. The same man who will be linked to the gruesome death of one of my followers, a man hounded by the Catholic Church to commit the ultimate sin of suicide as penance for supporting me who they will brand as the Devil himself. The world will see that at the same time I am announced as the true bringer of faith and love with hope for a future world where the Creators can elevate Humanity even further, those that purport to represent the old, tired and discredited ways will be seen increasingly as desperate zealots, happy to endorse murder and religious fundamentalism through violence. The content of the books will be then taken as gospel, *the* Gospel. The Gospel of Adam heralding in a new age for Humanity." Adam rested from his rant and relaxed staring at Crowe.

"You are a madman," Crowe spluttered, "no one will ever fall for your lies."

"They will Michael," Adam followed, "When they see what I can offer, what power I can bestow." He paused. "You need to know Michael, that I will not lose here. You cannot kill me. Nobody can kill me. Nobody can stop me. The timing is perfect, the mood of man is ripe to offer something new when so much of the old is left to backward thinkers and murderous maniacs who kill for faith as if theirs is the only path to their God. I offer the future, not the past. The beginning of the new. You will play your part and announce the Age of Adam and afterwards Michael, you will also be its first real martyr, that is the offer I make to you. If you do this right, your death will be seen as an act of cowardice by a desperate group of faiths clutching at theological straws to remain important. I promise you a clean and painless departure and the total restoration of health and long life of your dear Jessica. Her kidnapping will be seen as another act to persuade you not to support me and nothing more so do it right and she goes free. I offer you her life. Refuse and you both die and it will be my duty to order Pavel to do so in a way that gives him the most pleasure, do I make myself clear?"

Crowe remained tight lipped but merely nodded. There was nothing more he could do.

Crowe's mind was racing. Adam had made his intention very clear and if nothing else, Crowe was most definitely now his prisoner. More worryingly, he had taken Jessica and if Tall Man was here alone in the house, then it must mean her captor was Squat Man, or Pavel as Adam had called him. The thought of Jessica suffering at his hands sent waves of revulsion and hatred through Crowes body. He strained against the cable tie holding his wrists but all he achieved was additional pain as they bit into his already scoured skin. Adam remained silent in front on him and Tall Man's heavy grip on his shoulders was keeping Crowe firmly in his place in the chair.

"So, you intend to force me to announce you, to kill you as proof of your immortality, or should I say divinity you sick fuck! What sort of god seeks respect from threats and death. If you think you can control the world this way then you are very much mistaken." Crowe curled his top lip in anger.

"Name any god you humans have dreamt up," Adam responded," Have they all not controlled you by promoting the killing of others and by threatening retribution on those that do not believe? Is not the threat of Hell, the torture of everlasting damnation reserved for those that refuse the Ten Commandments? You are wrong Michael for I bring the world freedom, freedom from the old gods and the old ways. Those that follow me will know true enlightenment."

"And what of the 'Creators' as you call them? Do you not still answer to them? Will they not just return and relegate you to what? A demigod?"

"Oh, I forgot Michael. I did not tell you something I should have." Adam laughed slightly and placed his hand over his mouth, his eyes wide. "The Creators are not coming back. That was a little lie I threw in there to make the story more palatable. They abandoned the Earth many thousands of years ago as they considered the experiment a failed one. They realised that the perfection they created in me could never be matched by simple natural evolution alone. The prototype was just too perfect to be replicated by any other means than simple manufactured production. Humanity you see, was a failure as far as they were concerned. You were not worth the effort and they left to seek more success elsewhere. I was abandoned just as much as you were but I knew that, given enough time and development, my age would come. I have been patient for a very, very long time Michael."

"You are mad and deluded. I will have nothing to do with you or your perverted ambition. Fuck you!" Crowe spat.

"Then the lovely Jessica dies before you Michael. Visibly before your own eyes. I will ask Pavel to film the whole thing and I will force you to watch it before you die. I will still become who I must be whatever you decide so do you truly wish to put her through all that suffering? What will that achieve? Yes, I do not need you for I have friends in very high places indeed, but I would still prefer the reasoned and academic announcement of my coming. The arrival of my Age through a non-political route." Adam paused and stared at Crowe intently. "Help me achieve this Michael and she lives. Of this I promise you. She will be released completely unharmed, totally untouched."

Crowe thought for a few seconds and came to an easy conclusion. Comply and he had a chance to save Jessica, however slim that may be. Resist and she would die as well as him and Adam could just as well succeed in any event. If he showed reluctant compliance, at least it would mean he would get away from the house and even if under strict supervision, there may be a chance to escape and, or expose Adam whilst hopefully save Jessica in the meantime.

"How will I know she is still safe?" Crowe asked.

"I can get Pavel to send hourly proof if you so wish Michael. You have my word that as long as you are with me, she is safe."

Crowe took that pledge with considerable doubt but realised he was cornered. He paused a few moments before speaking.

"Bring her to me. At least if she is with me then there can be no doubt."

"I will think on that Michael. But I see no reason why not if I have your word you will cooperate?" Michael sensed an opportunity and decided to press further.

"And my death," he said slowly, "Is that……. negotiable?"

"Well Michael, it could just well be, could just well be…." Adam tailored the words off, "But that is down to you. Any attempt to escape or to disrupt what I need from you and you both die. I hope you understand?"

"Then I will do as you ask but I will need to know she is safe at all times. Do I have your word?"

"You do Michael," Adam smiled broadly.

"And when will this all happen?" Crowe asked.

"Tomorrow," Adam replied. "Tomorrow is the first day of the new Age. My associates are preparing the ground as we speak. We leave at first light. I will give you full details in the morning Michael. In the meantime, I will have food sent up to your room. You will be locked in of course but at least you can freshen up and change to be ready. I promise you that Jessica will be fed and looked after. She will also be brought here," He nodded to Tall Man who started to make a call, "Thank you Michael. I am sorry we cannot do this as friends but you must understand that I have no choice. There has been far too much done in the planning for this to fail now." He smiled once more. "Now I must get my rest for the remainder of the day and try and sleep for as long as possible for tomorrow I die!" he winked at Crowe, "Many times!"

Chapter Twenty-Four

17.14, 20th September Present Day, Embassy of the Holy See, Paris, France

McGeary breezed through his room at the Embassy as fast as he could to collect his possessions. His injuries still offered some pain but adrenaline was overcoming any discomfort far more effectively that the pain killers had. A knock on the door heralded the fact that his aide was outside.

"Come in," McGeary said as he continued to pack.

"Your Eminence, I am pleased to say your replacement robes have arrived from Rome. Will you wear them now?" The young man placed the robes on the bed.

"I shall, thank you Albert. Have the car ready for twenty minutes from now. Did you manage to get me on the next flight to Rome?" McGeary started to inspect the robes.

"I did your Eminence," Albert said happily, "Business class, Air France as you requested."

"Ideal," the Cardinal replied. "Now Albert, if that irritating French policeman calls again, you are to direct him through the proper channels straight to the Vatican. Is that understood?" Albert looked suddenly confused and worried.

"Did you mean Captain Fournier your Eminence?" He said hesitantly. McGeary nodded a little impatiently so Albert continued, "Your Eminence, I regret to say that Captain Fournier was found dead last night. It is all over the news today. He was apparently stabbed, murdered, somewhere in Montmartre. They think it was a gang-related killing according to the press." Albert looked to his shoes and wondered if he should have just have given the news without further details.

"How very unfortunate," McGeary replied. "I cannot say I liked the man but still, how sad." He started to take off his casual clothes as Albert left the room and dressed deep in thought. Surely there was no connection? The Captain had seemed very insistent in his questioning, pushing McGeary on whether he had been a deliberate target. It was almost as if he had discounted any other explanation, concentrating on McGeary alone, and now he was dead. Coincidence? McGeary was unsure and wondered if there could possibly be a connection between his death and that of De Soto's? Both had been insistent on talking to McGeary and both mysteriously killed less than 24 hours later. But the connection, if there was one at all, was weak. Unless…. His thoughts were interrupted as his mobile phone rang. It was Father Bernard so McGeary took the call.

"Yes, Father Bernard, how are you?"

"I am fair your Eminence thank you. I was just checking to see if you are ready to return to the Vatican and that you are fully restored to health?"

"I am recovering well thank you Father Bernard. I will be there after supper this evening but do not feel you have to wait up."

"Thank you, your Eminence, but there is another reason for my call. The Holy Father has asked for an audience tomorrow morning."

"The Holy Father?" McGeary repeated surprised. "But of course. At what time?"
"late morning. Will you be able to attend? I fear I alone will be insufficient." Father Bernard said.

"Not a problem Bernard, I will see you in the office tomorrow morning and we will go together." McGeary replied.

"Thank You your Eminence, have a safe flight." Father Bernard responded.

"Thank you Bernard. Goodbye." McGeary pressed the red button on the phone and replaced it. This he had not allowed for. An audience at the request of the Pope could only mean one thing, he was aware of Adam's imminent arrival already and needed to know what was being done.

McGeary thought back to the first audience with Pope Pius the thirteenth less than two years previously.

Despite the Pope's Mexican place of birth, making
him the first Pontiff from Central America, Manuel
Oswaldo Palencia spoke flawless English from having
studied much of his adult life in the United States and
the two had laughed with the new Pope still having an
issue with McGeary's thick Irish accent. The meeting
had been strained though coming so soon after the
unexpected election following the unexplained death
of his predecessor and Pius had realised he had a huge
task in pacifying a shaken church rife with conspiracy
theories and spurious accusations. Pope Pius had
sought to tackle the charge of conspiracy against the
previous Pope's modern views by carrying on much of
his proposed reforms and had laughed off the threats
that came with it. Pius was a man of his times and his
election had been based just as much on his close
friendship with his predecessor with whom he had
studied and worked together for many years as it was
his own vision for the future of Catholicism.

Therefore, the Pope had given McGeary his blessing in
his appointment to head up the task force within the
church to tackle all threats, chief amongst them the
vast problem that an announced Adam could bring. At
the mention of the request for the Pontiff for another
audience now received, McGeary's thoughts reached
back to that first meeting and to something that Pius
had said, something which at the time he had paid no
heed but now understood. The Pope had almost
whispered in the Cardinal's ear,

"When faced with God, not all understand his truth."

The Pope had smiled broadly and wished him well and the audience was at an end. McGeary wondered now what he could have meant. Perhaps he would now elaborate.

17.23 20th September Present Day, Dartmoor England.

The phone vibrated in Squat Man's pocket and he reached inside his trousers to retrieve it. Jessica could not hear what was being said but her captor's expression changed from expectant to disappointment very quickly. He grunted and as he replaced the mobile he swore loudly.

"Fuck!" he shouted as he stood up and walked towards Jessica. "It seems you have a friend," he said as he pulled her up to a standing position and steadied her as she wobbled. His hand went straight to the top button of her jeans and unbuttoned it. As his hand forced the zipper down he cruelly let his fingers rub against her, moulding her flesh. His hand lingered and she moaned in horror rather than pleasure, but was instantly grateful as he withdrew the hand.

"Shame," he said with a sneer, "That felt nice. I would have enjoyed that." She turned as his nauseating breath enveloped her nostril once more.

"You need to piss before the chopper gets here," He said. "You are going on a little trip."

"Um…where?" Jessica asked meekly, "where can I go to the toilet?"

"Where you stand." Squat Man replied, "Do you need me to pull your trousers right down or can you do it? I have orders not to hurt you but what the eye doesn't see eh?"

"I can do it," Jessica replied knowing that her tied hands would allow her to do so with difficulty. "Is privacy too much to ask?"

"Ha!" Squat Man replied. "Don't you want to give me a show then?" He waited for an answer but saw that Jessica's pained face already presented him with the answer.

"Stupid Bitch," He said as he moved towards the door. "I will go to the car to get you something to eat. You have two minutes." He exited from the room and Jessica heard the outside door open a few seconds later. Quickly she pushed her jeans and underwear down to her knees in staged actions with her tied hands and squatted. She relieved herself with care to rest her back against the wall but still assumed some of the splash back would hit her jeans. She didn't care as the relief from being not able to pee for so long was too good. Once finished she used her weight against the wall to haul herself upright and reversed the movements to pull up her clothes. With her hand tied behind her back she would not be able to do the jeans up again though and baulked at the thought of his probing fingers on her crotch again to do so.

Squat Man came back into the room holding a plastic supermarket bag which he placed on the chair. He moved towards Jessica and bodily picked her up and away from the urine soaked carpet placing her on the chair after lifting the bag up. Extracting a knife from his pocket, Jessica started to scream but he just laughed as he reached behind her back to cut the cords holding her wrists. Her hands started to ache as the blood rushed back and she brought her arms around to flex them.

"The feet stay tied," he said but you can use your hands to eat," he motioned towards the carrier bag which he placed on her lap. Jessica looked inside to see a selection of packed shop bought sandwiches and a can of Diet Coke.

Once her hand became flexible enough to function, the first thing she did was do up her trousers which brought forth hoots of laughter form the watching man.

"Eat," he urged," the helicopter will be here soon. It is the last chance today you will have for food."

Jessica accepted that she was hungry and without reading what was in the first sandwich she tore open the packaging and started to devourer the contents.

17.40 20th September, Present Day, Exeter, England

Carol Davis felt the phone ring before she heard it and reached into her pocket to get it. Stone was calling so she pressed the green button and placed it to her ear.

"Davis" she said smartly.

"Hi boss, Stone here," the Detective Constable said," Got that update for you."

"Go ahead," Carol replied.

"Thames Valley Police have been around to the girl's house. No one there and all locked up. They asked neighbours and found out she is a teacher at the local primary. Phoned them and they said she did not turn up for work today, very out of character. Looks like we may have a missing person boss?"

"Yes, looks like we may have. Any connection with the corpse?"

"Well boss, Thames Valley told me that the neighbours know them quite well. She is the partner of that TV historian, Crowe. Michael Crowe. Do you know who I mean boss?"

Carol suddenly remembered the face on the back of the book in the missing woman's car. Now she knew who he was.

"Yes, absolutely. His book is in the back of her car. What was the Professor an academic in? Did you call the University?" she asked Stone.

"I did boss. He was an Archaeology and History professor. Been there thirty years apparently. They are really upset."

"Understandable." Carol replied. "Okay, we have a connection and something concrete to go on. The girl is the partner of a history presenter and author and her car is left outside of a deceased history professor's house. The girl is a missing person and while we are at it, we need to establish the whereabouts of Crowe at the same time. He can be both suspect and possible missing person at the same time. Get the team together back at the station, I am on my way". She pressed the off button and threw the phone onto the seat in the car next to her.

DDS Carol Davis turned the ignition key and put the car into first gear. She roared off towards the end of the road, her mind racing in unison with the car. Instantly, she knew this case was going to be career defining.

Chapter Twenty-Five

18.24 20th September Present Day, Over England

Jessica hated the hood over her head. It made her feel weak and vulnerable but one thing gave her hope, the faint residual smell of the after-shave scent she had given Crowe the previous Christmas was embedded in the material. She would recognise that brand anywhere and although not necessarily an obscure fragrance, she was absolutely convinced that Crowe had worn the same hood, hopefully not too long ago. That could mean that he was still alive, at least he had been, and possibly he would be wherever she was now being taken.

Her hands had been re-bound but her legs were now free of the ropes so that her ability to get up into the helicopter had not been compromised. The hood had been placed upon her before the chopper landed so she had not seen the pilot but the other unassailable stink in the aircraft was that of Squat Man's foul breath so she knew he was sitting beside her. Despite the faint glimmer of kindness she had been offered, the instructions to stay silent during the flight or risk the back of Squat Man's hand was enough for her to keep quiet. She had no idea where they were going and did not ask. Her main comfort was that she was not now alone with the disgusting, leering monster who had threatened her. She hoped that wherever they were now going, he would not be part of whatever it was she was here for.

The helicopter banked suddenly and caught Jessica unawares so she overbalanced into Squat Man who laughed loudly. She straitened herself as the chopper started to descend and sat in anticipation until the bump of the rails connecting with the ground sent shockwaves through the cab. As the engine noise gradually reduced, Squat Man had leant over and pulled the hood off so that she jumped with the sudden explosion of light.

"Get out when I tell you and keep your head low," he breathed with foul-smelling accuracy over her face, making her recoil. The door opened at her side and he motioned for her to alight which she did so with some difficulty as her hands strained against the ties. As she landed on the recently cut grass, she noticed the slight young man in an ivory linen suit waiving to her from in front of a large stone house. The man was extremely good looking and bore a wide welcoming smile, both of which unnerved the disorientated Jessica. She felt the bindings to her wrists being cut and relished the blood flowing fully to her hands once more which she hastily rubbed together to increase the circulation. She felt Squat Man's meaty hand push her in the small of her back and she started walking forwards. The young man in front of her waved her inside frantically.

Crowe watched the helicopter land in front of the house from his bedroom window. So much for not frightening the livestock, Crowe thought remembering that his own arrival had required a landing on the other side of the large surrounding forest in a small glade where the Segways waited. He looked to see if the deer were still grazing but all had retreated into the trees. Once the helicopter door had been opened, Crowe cried out in relief to see Jessica, dishevelled and dirty, looking vulnerable and scared but most of all, alive, jump out of the chopper. She was looking and reacting to something Crowe could not see to his right and below the base of his window, surmising that Adam was waiting there.

Jessica was being accompanied by Squat Man and Crowe developed pained thoughts as to what, if anything the man had done to her. But at least she was alive and Adam had been good to his word of bringing her to him so for that, Crowe was thankful.
The arrival party disappeared from view as Crowe moved away from the window and towards the door to his room. He tried it but it was still locked so he retraced his steps and looked out again at the rapidly cooling helicopter. As the rotors stopped completely, Crowe could make out muffled voices from below and felt like banging on the door demanding to be let out to see Jessica. He decided, however, that he should now play Adam's game and wait until he brought her to him. He did not have to wait long. The knock on the door was forceful and immediately followed by the sound of the lock being worked. The door swung open and Tall Man stood there smiling before moving to one side to allow Jessica to enter. Seeing Crowe, she immediately burst into tears with long loud sobs and ran across the room to put her arms around him, crying constantly.

"You are to remain here until you are both collected. Fresh clothes for the woman will be provided at that time." The door closed on Tall Man's last word and for the first time in days, Crowe and Jessica were alone, their embrace and showered kisses urgent and passionate.

"I thought I had lost you," Crowe breathed as she hugged him incredibly tightly. "I am so sorry you have been dragged into this," he followed. "Are you hurt? Did he……did he touch you?" he asked hesitantly.

"He didn't touch me," she lied, "at least not in that way. He hit me a bit and I was tied up for most of the time but I knew I would see you again. I felt it!" They kissed again and after a prolonged period of just holding each other, Crowe finally disentangled there embrace and led Jessica by her hand to the bed.

"What is this all about Michael?" she asked in a sudden panic. "Conrad is…. he's…."

"Dead. Yes, I know," Crowe replied.

"That fat bastard killed him." She drilled the sentence with passionate hatred, "why did he kill him Michael? What is this about? I don't understand."

Crowe sat on the bed and pulled Jessica down so that she sat next to him. He considered for a moment whether the best thing would be to just tell her everything that had happened or not. He decided on the former.

"You have met him; Adam?" Crowe started, "The man you probably saw as you landed?"

"Yes, he introduced himself to me. Apologised for my treatment and then said that I would soon join you. He then asked the other man, Karl, was it?" Tall Man Crowe thought, "to bring me to you. That is all I know. What has he got to do with all of this?"

"Everything, I'm afraid," Crowe replied, Absolutely everything." Crowe began with the call from Wilding, the request to visit him and the revelation about the books, about who Adam truly was and what he wanted. He explained the meetings, the shot from the flintlock re-emerging from Adam's body, the fake house they now sat in, everything. He explained how Jessica's kidnap was the insurance Adam needed to get Crowe on-side and what Crowe had to promise so that Jessica could now sit beside him. When he had finished, Jessica looked on stunned and disbelieving. She did not know what to say.

"It may take a while to sink in," Crowe summarised, "it is a lot to consider."

"You are right Michael, it is…..well…..a lot to accept. Do you truly believe that man is the actual Adam?"

"It is about as believable as anything else that defies description but yes, I really think I do. Okay, I loathe what he has done or commanded be done in his name. What happened to you and to poor Conrad but I can see what will happen once he is announced and is proved to be immortal, the chaos that will ensue. I do not want to be party to that but I don't think I have any choice." Crowe sighed heavily and slumped back.

"Because he will kill us both if you don't," Jessica surmised.

"And he may still kill me if I do," Crowe followed and Jessica shot him a concerned look.

"What do you mean?" she said in panic, "What has he said?"

"Conrad's death was planned to look like the established faiths are trying to stop Adam before he starts. To remove the books from being used as another source of proof, to suggest Conrad was tortured to reveal where Adam was, assuming he ever knew which I sincerely doubt. Adam confirmed that the books will be found in the possession of the Catholic Church, more specifically within a team dedicated to finding and eliminating him, at least as much as they can, bearing in mind his immortality. All this will bring discredit upon a desperate faith trying to suppress his truth eclipsing their own historical dominance. Conrad will be lauded as the first martyr to Adam's cause and I, being the spokesman that introduces him to the world, will be apparently assassinated by another world faith to become the second." He paused and breathed. Jessica looked on in astonishment.

"But he can't do that. You said you would help."

"And in doing so I write my own death warrant. But you will be safe, I have his word and despite everything, I believe him about that."

"Well I won't allow it, I can't allow it. I would rather die than see that madman use you like this!" She shook visibly. "Refuse to help him and let us die together if we must."

"It won't stop him Jess, there is far more at stake here than my life. If I refuse he will do it himself. He will forget any academic endorsement and just go for the spectacular. He said he has friends who will help, powerful men on his side. He can do this without me yet he created all of this," Crowe looked around the room, "This house, the gardens, even the fucking deer herds to recreate something I could relate to. Something of the world I lived in when I wrote the book on Barnsford. He wanted me to be his friend for fuck's sake and all of this was to win me over by reasoned debate. He would not have done all this if he thought he would fail in that persuasion, but he did and what happened to you was the result of that. He is a very dangerous man darling, and one with powerful allies that will stop at nothing." Jessica got up and started towards the bathroom.

"We need help," she said, "Someone must be able to help us. We can't just let him lead us like lambs to the slaughter. I still think we should tell him go fuck himself and see what happens." She entered the bathroom but kept the door open. Crowe heard the flush and then the basin taps.

"Christ, I stink," Jessica shouted. "I am going to have a shower then let's see what our options are." Crowe heard the shower come on as he laid back on the bed and started to think. What options did they have?

Chapter Twenty-Six

18.57 20th September Present Day, Downing Street, London, England

Andrew Stubbs walked solemnly and silently up the main staircase in Number Ten past the portraits and photographs of his many predecessors. He briefly looked into the eyes of each as he passed and wondered if they were looking down upon him now in silent anger at what he had done and in whose name. He doubted that any of the framed pictures would remain after the Age of Adam has truly begun. What need would there be for titles or Government in such a small island when the whole world would be united under the future direction of Adam and through the direct rule of his council, the Votary. Stubbs afforded himself a cruel smile that his elevation to that venerable body was now assured. Avery's death was necessary and right. Stubbs had insisted to Parkinson that he should participate personally and there was a cruel irony in the fact that the last thing Avery would have known is that his lifelong friend had been the ultimate betrayer.

Avery may well have spent much of his adult life as a lie, always hiding his true vision and beliefs, always thinking that only he would rise should Adam be proclaimed in his lifetime. Yet throughout all that time, Stubbs had observed and waited. His father had relayed the tale handed down throughout the patriarchal line that the Avery family possessed the power that truly should have been theirs. That the time would come when a Stubbs would regain the rightful standing and reclaim their position with the Votary. So, knowing that if the time did indeed come within his generation, that he would ensure Avery never claimed the throne he believed only he would be destined for. Stubbs was, as all those that gone before him, tired of merely being the facilitator, the organiser of the chaos required to elevate Avery to his position of power, Stubbs had played the long game and now he had won.

He reached the door to his office and entered closing it behind him. There was an immediate knock on the door but Stubbs shouted for whoever it was to leave him in peace. He removed his jacket, took a small key out of the internal loose change pocket and rather than hang it on the coat-stand, he clumsily placed the jacket over the back of his chair. Sitting down, he placed the key in the third drawer down lock and turned it. He opened the drawer and reached under a stack of files, all of which were entitled D.A. for Donald Avery. Under the files he found what he was looking for. It was an unused Sim-card still in its delivered form with an unbroken attachment. He now removed the card from the surrounding holder and held it between his thumb and forefinger and looked at it before placing it on the desk. He then retrieved the phone left for him by the Home Secretary and dismantled it, removing the battery and the used Sim-card within it before replacing it with the new one. He reconstructed the phone and turned it on, going through the installation procedure as he was prompted. Finally, he started to press the keys for the number he wanted. The connection seemed to take a longer time that he was expecting but finally the call was answered.

"Yes"," the voice was monotone and distant.

"Eden," Stubbs said and waited. There was a long pause. "I said Eden," he repeated as impatience got the better of him, "Four is dead and I now assume his place as was agreed." There was a long pause.

"Garden?" the answer came back with the voice giving inclination the word to be a question. Stubbs was suddenly confused and did not answer immediately.

"Garden?" the voice said again, a little impatiently this time. Stubbs decided to answer immediately.

"Gethsemane," he replied. Clearly his contact was suspicious of something to have wanted the confirmation code. The voice began speaking in measured tones.

"You will be required to deliver your address to the British nation and through them, the world tomorrow at Ten o'clock in the morning. Arrange for multi-network, multi-media coverage from outside Number Ten. Inform the networks that all programming is to be changed to accommodate you. Advise them also to install their Outside Broadcast units near Speaker's Corner in Hyde Park. All other arrangements are in place. Do you understand for there will be no further communication?"

"I understand," Stubbs replied. "May I say…." The line went dead and Stubbs was left holding the phone in silence. He replaced it back into his pocket and closed the open drawer, locking it again and replacing the key in the change pocket of his jacket.

If all had worked according to plan then Avery's death by apparent suicide will be public knowledge within hours and the media will assume that the address he intended to give tomorrow will be to cover that breaking news. The media will have no idea of the true message he would be giving.

He pressed the intercom. "Can you come in please?" He said and settled back in his chair. The time had come.

20.59 20th September Present Day, Vatican City

As Cardinal Donal McGeary alighted from the official car and made his way quickly up to his offices, his mind was already confused and flitting wildly between thoughts of what more he could do and who he could trust. His instructions to Father Bernard were succinct and direct. He wanted the entire team of five priests in the office to start replicating the research that Avery had suggested. They were to filter the names of known billionaires worldwide who had all suffered family tragedies in recent years and months, who were childless, at least from a male offspring point of view, lived alone and were the product of 'old money'. He explained that what he was looking for were those who had amassed their wealth based on family companies that had originated centuries ago as opposed to those reliant on new business ventures. He gave the instructions before he left Paris and despite the relative shortness of the journey, he wanted a list of names, at least potential candidates based on the filters used that could suggest possible members of the Votary. McGeary reasoned that if Avery could unearth sufficient data from his own efforts alone in less than a day, sufficient to get Stubbs over excited and want to retain the data for his own Government's use, then five priests working at top speed to research the Internet could do so in a couple of hours. As he entered the office, he was pleased to see all five still busy typing away at their keyboards and to a man, they all instantly rose to welcome the rushing Cardinal and to enquire about his health. McGeary thanked the men and retreated into his private office quickly followed by Father Bernard.

"So, Father Bernard, His Holiness still requires my presence tomorrow morning?" he asked briskly.

"He does your Eminence," Father Bernard replied.

McGeary turned to see the stack of boxes in the corner of the room. There were five in total, all of similar size and each were numbered. The one nearest to McGeary had a large hand-written note to the front, 'Open first.'

"What are these?" McGeary said pointing at the boxes.

"They arrived a couple of hours ago," Father Bernard said, "Express air freight from England. They are addressed to you." Father Bernard took a step back to allow the Cardinal to inspect the boxes.

"Shall I get you a knife your eminence?" Father Bernard enquired.

"Yes, if you please my son," McGeary responded and waited until the Frenchman returned with the blade. He used it to slit open the packaging tape to the box marked to be opened first and then gingerly prised the closure leaves aside.

The smell of old leather and paper was immediately apparent as McGeary looked down at a post-it note on the binding of the top volume. 'Read first' it said and McGeary picked up the book, removed the post-it note and turned the volume so he could open the front cover. He turned the stiff marbled front endpaper and jerked slightly as he started to read the clearly titled Prologue.

'Death can be creative in numerous ways and I have seen, experienced and delivered them all.'

McGeary declined to read further, he did not have to. It was clear from the first line that he was holding volume one of the complete works of Adam, the very books he desperately needed to find in order to remove anything tangible that could be used to support the heresy that Adam represented. McGeary started to shake lightly as he placed the book on his desk and began to pick up the others from the box. There was nothing by way of a separate explanation, only the books were within the box itself. He turned to see Father Bernard and the other four priests looking at him from the doorway.

"Was there any note?" he asked the assembled men, "anything at all to suggest who has sent these?"

"Yes your Eminence, "One of the younger priests piped up, "it was a normal carrier service. I signed for the delivery and asked them to stack the boxes here but there was nothing else delivered other than the delivery note. I left it on my desk if you will excuse me."

"Thank you Father Johan," McGeary replied to the inexperienced Austrian as he hurried out into the main office where his desk was based, "Do any of you know what we have here?" There were small shakes of the head all around. "What we have here my sons, are the actual volumes of the Beast. I have no idea how they arrived here but the fact that they are here can only mean we have been given a tremendous chance to vanquish him before he is revealed. Without these books, he has nothing but himself to offer.

"But Cardinal," Father Bernard started, "That is wonderful news but I am puzzled. Whoever sent you the books…. how did they know to send them to you?"

McGeary paused before answering. He had no idea what to say to answer the priest but he was right. How did whoever sent these know exactly who to send them to? McGeary suddenly realised that something was wrong and looked at each priest in turn, including the now returned Father Johan.

"Well Father Johan, what have you got there?" He pointed to the delivery slip that the young priest was holding in slightly shaking hands. "Does it state who sent the books to me?"

"It does your eminence," Johan said softly.

"Well?" McGeary asked impatiently.

"You did your Eminence," Father Johan exclaimed, "you sent these books to yourself," He crossed the room and gave the note to the astonished Cardinal. McGeary read the sender's details and his name showed in bold type above an address in Exeter, England that he did not recognise.

"Dear God," McGeary said quietly to himself. He ushered the five priests out of his office and shut the door behind them as their mumblings became louder. He walked back to the boxes and placed the books back in the open box before sitting down in his chair. Something, somewhere simply did not add up.

Chapter Twenty-Seven

19.51 20th September Present Day, Somewhere in England

Tall Man returned forty-five minutes later with a tray of food for them Jessica and Crowe. Cold cuts, fruits and cheese which they both ate greedily. Jessica was already showered and after eating, Crowe took his turn, relishing the stream of scalding hot water as it cascaded over him. After standing in the water for almost fifteen minutes he towelled himself dry and put on the remaining white robe. He re-entered the bedroom to find Jessica still in her robe and reclined against the bed head.

"Do you think there are cameras in here?" she asked with a half grin.

"Adam does not strike me as a voyeur but I would imagine so. It is a prison after all." Crowe replied before climbing on the bed beside her. "Does it bother you if there are?" he asked.

"A bit," she replied, "I guess it does not matter much if we are going to be killed tomorrow anyway."

"We are not going to die tomorrow," Crowe whispered as he leaned close to her ear, "I have been thinking in the shower and however much we may not like what is happening, we have no choice but to go along with it, at least it should look like that. Let us play his game and look for our chance. I have an idea what to do but it is risky."

"What?" Jessica asked enthusiastically.

"Shss," Crowe said putting his finger to his lips. "He may be listening as well as watching remember." He started to kiss her neck and ear lightly. "Whatever happens tomorrow, we still have tonight so let's no waste it."

"But the cameras," Jessica protested quietly, "I am not sure….."

"I thought it was your idea," he said with a smile, "Let us make sure we give them a good show then," Crowe replied as he started to slip his hand under the folds of the robe and onto her rapidly hardening left nipple as she let out a suppressed moan.

20.03 20th September Present Day, Exeter, England

Carol Davis was working late into the evening despite the fact that her shift had finished two hours ago. She read and re-read the email attachment that Thames Valley Police had sent about Jessica Russell and Michael Crowe. All the reports of the interviews they had concluded said practically the same thing. This was a couple that were, to all interested observers, entirely normal. Yes, he was a well-known TV personality and author. A handsome man that brought history to life through the ground-breaking series and one-off programmes that had earned himself the following of both interested historians and over-sexed housewives at the same time. Carol had viewed the latest programme on the on-demand service and despite having no interest in the history of the Dark Ages, she got more than an instant attraction to the man's chiselled features, she surprised herself by actually enjoying it and indeed, had learned something. One thing that came out strong from viewing the programme was the overwhelming gut instinct that this man would not have been capable of the sadistic murder of his own university professor, or indeed anyone. After fifteen years in the Force, Carol had learned by now to trust her instincts and as far as she was concerned and without anything to prove her deduction, he was not now the main suspect.

That left the woman's car that had been left opposite from the murder scene and who was now assumed missing. But Jessica Russell was a slight and relatively timid person according to the neighbours that had been interviewed as well as her colleagues at the primary school where she worked. Also, Carol surmised that she would not have the strength to hold the Professor down whilst torturing him, or the muscle to force a gun barrel into his mouth, breaking teeth in the process. Plus, where would she have got the gun in the first place? There were no indications that the victim had been tied down so his assailant would have had to be bulky enough for his bodyweight to pin the professor down in the chair as he was assaulted. Summing up, Jessica could not be the murderer either, of that Carol was sure, so that left only one more possibility, the murderer or murderers were separate from the couple and who they must have disturbed in the act, perhaps dropping by for an unannounced visit. If so, Carol surmised, there was a strong possibility that they were already dead also but as it stood, she was happy to extend the missing person case to include both of them.

The crime scene report also offered some strange possibilities. Had the victim been tortured for a reason or just because he or they could take advantage of an old man too weak to resist? Why were the man's valuables still left undisturbed? A sweep of the whole house revealed that no other room had been noticeably disturbed, no obvious signs of ransacking in search of loot. Could the intruder or intruders been disturbed after the killing but before they could search the house? Also, why the empty bookcase? Every other shelf in the study was over-filled with books at askew angles and lacking anything like a proper library system and yet the five shelves of the freestanding bookcase positioned in front of a larger wall-mounted one was completely devoid of books. Particular mention was made also of the heavy velvet curtains that were positioned on a runner at the top of the bookcase suggesting that whatever the books were, they had sufficient importance to need protection from the sun or dust. Apart from the victim, there were only a few fingerprints that were not his and did not match anyone on the records, thus meaning that the assailant or assailants wore gloves and the owner of the other fingerprints found was either unknown to the Police anywhere, or had never been arrested. The size of the prints suggested a man and Carol's gut instinct was that they would eventually be proved to belong to Michael Crowe.

So why steal books? It was this thought that confused Carol the most. As part of the calls and visit made to the University itself, DC Stone had got it confirmed that the Head had no reason to believe Wilding possessed extremely valuable books, quite the opposite in fact. The Head had confirmed previous conversations when visiting the professor that the quality of his research material was suspect at best and in very poor condition at worst. Why steal a range of books? A whole bookcase full? One book of value she could perhaps understand but scores? How would they transport the books in a hurry? It did not make sense,

She next started on the statements from the neighbours and others and was stopped in her tracks by the third statement she read, actually from the local postman who had made a delivery to the house in the afternoon. The statement read that the postman had not seen anything of concern in the house but had noticed that the curtains to the front study were closed and that there was a UPS courier's van in the drive. This was at two fifteen and the postman had confirmed that he heard movement in the house and that the back doors of the van were open but the van itself was empty when he posted the letters. He concluded by saying that on his return trip back to the sorting office he noticed that the van was still there but the doors were now closed. The curtains to the front study, he confirmed were also still closed.

Carol referred back to the crime scene report and it stated plainly that the curtains were open when the police arrived they had not been opened when entering the room.

Carol was now building a picture of likely events in her mind. It was possible that the assailant probably arrived in the early afternoon, potentially even posing as the courier. He would have gained entry by deception and will have closed the curtains to the study to prevent outside eyes from seeing inside. The poor professor will have suffered for a long time before he shot him. Again, she thought, why shoot him? Why risk the noise unless he wanted to be heard? Obviously, a blade would be silent and just as deadly and an assailant capable of inflicting gratuitous pain on the victim would certainly have one on his or her person. So why use a gun unless it was the last act of savagery in the hope that someone would hear the shots and see the murderer leave. Carol was convinced that was it. The assailant wanted to be seen but why?

Carol referred back to the crime scene report one more time and focussed on the one line of text that now made sense whereas before it did not. She read it aloud,

"Piece of brown parcel tape stuck in hanging position to empty shelf."

Carol realised that the books were not just taken, they had used the time to pack them and seal them in boxes, no doubt taking them all out to the van in the process. In the time it took the postman to complete his round after calling at the victim's house and returning past it a short time later, the books had been taken out into the van and the doors closed. Clearly the murderer had taken his time. Enough time to prepare the books for transit and had used a courier's van to complete the process. Carol looked for a statement from UPS but none had yet been presented. The hour was late but she felt she should try anyway and looked up the local office details before calling the number. She received an out of office message so she decided to go one better and call the Head Office number in the United States who would still be on open office hours. The conversation was brief but productive. If sent though the proper channels, they would respond to confirm if any collections registered at the Professor's address and, more importantly perhaps, where the goods were going. Carol considered that most likely it had not been an official collection but she had to eliminate the possibility so she researched the number again before picking up the phone to call the American Embassy in London.

She had been hanging on the phone for almost forty minutes when the gruff male voice started speaking at the other end to say that the enquiries had been made. She had already been informed that her personal status would be checked as would the origin of the phone she was using and that the response was being emailed to the address she gave as the man spoke. She thanked him and replaced the receiver before checking her inbox. The email arrived seconds later and she opened it to find an attachment in PDF format. Opening it, she was presented with a manifest for five boxes to be sent to Rome, the Vatican specifically, to a Cardinal Donal McGeary. Of greater surprise was that his name also appeared on the document as the sender, not Professor Wilding. The weight of each box was shown to be within the twenty to forty-kilogram range, thus giving further proof to the fact that books, large and heavy books at that, were the cargo. The use of express delivery showed that there was urgency in the transport required and which also meant that the likelihood was that the books had already been delivered but perhaps only just, the manifest did not include a time or date of delivery.

Carol now had her proof and UPS had some further explaining to do. Were their employees involved directly or simply used at the pick-up stage for the boxes that had already been prepared? Carol thought the latter as a sack truck would have been used to transport the sealed boxed from the house to the van in any event, and would have been a two-person job to lift them. That meant that the courier was inside the house before the Professor was murdered. They needed to speak to the courier driver used as soon as possible but realised that the lateness of the hour meant it would not probably be tomorrow.

Carol was overjoyed at the breakthrough. They now had a motive, whatever those books actually were. She also had a named recipient who may have ordered the delivery from an address that was not his. She had to find out what McGeary's movements had been over the last few days. Was he still in the country or back at the Vatican? There were still many unanswered questions but Carol now had the bit between her teeth.

20.47 20th September Present Day, London, England

Parkinson turned from the driver's seat to look at Stubbs sat in the back of the official Jaguar.

"The call has come through sir. Local plod have made contact with the Americans to follow up on the courier van from Exeter. They have been provided with the manifest so will know about the Irishman." He turned and started the engine whilst Stubbs smiled in the back. It had been ridiculously easy tying in the Cardinal's visit to England to meet Avery within twenty-four hours of the time of death of the professor. Now that the link had been made between the Vatican, the murder and the theft of the books of Adam, further proof of the secretive nature of how the Catholic church was trying to eliminate the threat would be exposed. Even though McGeary himself would not be proved to be the murderer, the fact that the link was there would be enough. Andrew Stubbs felt elated and energised by the events of the day and the vision in his head of the hapless Avery, his face purple and swollen, the eyes bulging as he swung gently from the banister stirred up other desires.

"Excellent, thank you," he said. "I fancy some dark meat tonight Chris. Take me to the Streatham house will you and call ahead. Have them send their best black girl round, something fresh. Newly delivered." Stubbs sat back with his thoughts relishing the pleasure to come. "You will join us if we order two, won't you?" he asked.

"Don't mind if I do sir, thank you," Parkinson said with a laugh as he engaged the car into first gear and sped off.

Chapter Twenty-Eight

06.37 21st September Present Day, Somewhere in England

The knock on the door was gentle but constant as if the intention was not to shock or surprise, but to convey an insistence that required attention. Jessica awoke first to the muted drumming sound and for an instant, searched hard in her sleep-addled brain to recover any sense of where she was. Seeing that Crowe remained asleep beside her, she gently probed his shoulder with her finger to make him stir. His reaction was immediate and he positively threw back the duvet to reveal their nakedness and had already slipped one leg out of the bed when Jessica held him back with a squeeze on his arm.

"Listen," she said quietly, "Someone is tapping lightly on the door."

Crowe adjusted his eye to the pre-Dawn glow that was rapidly increasing and gingerly got out of the bed. He reached for the robe and put it on before padding softly to the door and turning the handle. It was still locked but his movement stopped the constant drumming on the wood and a piece of paper was pushed under the door itself which he noticed as it touched his toe. He bent down to retrieve the note and beckoned Jessica to follow him into the bathroom which she did after also donning her robe. They huddled together as he put on the light in the windowless room and unfolded the piece of paper they had been given. They read the handwriting together.

'*They will come for you in a couple of hours. Be ready to run when you see me create a diversion. Friends are on their way but we need to give them time. When you run, head for the trees but split up and go in different directions as there are sensors and fences in the wood. You will be followed but hopefully at least one of you will make it. If you get out of the trees, head South. Keep the sunrise to your left until you hit somewhere to call for help.*' The note was unsigned and both Crowe and Jessica looked at each other in astonishment. Crowe moved to turn on the shower so that the noise of the splattering water could mask their muted tones.

"Could be a trick," Crowe said first, "another test to try us?"

"Do you have any idea who this is from?" Jessica followed, concern etched in her face. "Has anyone approached you before now?"

No-one," Crowe responded thoughtfully, "All I have seen since I have been here were the two goons who brought me, Tall Man and Squat Man as I called them, Adam of course, some guy who looked after the Segways and the kitchen staff who served the dinner. But I didn't talk to any of the staff, only the goons and Adam." He looked at the note again, "The hand looks light to me, possibly female? What do you think?"

"Yes, I already thought that but how many staff did you see in total and were they all male?" She sat on the side of the bath.

"Two female and one male server were at that dinner," Crowe said recalling the spread that had been laid on for him when he first arrived. "I can remember one of the waitresses looking at me in a furtive manner but just thought she…. well"

"Fancied you?" Jessica said in a matter of fact way.

"No, that she recognised me. I thought no more of it until now."

"Can you remember her?" Jessica followed interested.

"Young, dark, pretty. Slightly exotic," Crowe described, "But no words were exchanged."

"Well she is as good a candidate as anyone I suppose," Jessica followed, "But can we trust her is indeed this is her? And why would she help us in the first place?"

"I have no idea, seriously none." Crowe replied with a shrug, "but if we are intending to just show willing until we make our escape then perhaps this is the break we are looking for? If it is a trap, let us make the best of it anyway." He pointed to the main window in the bedroom through the open bathroom door. "Go to the window and look to the right, as far as you can," he said and Jessica started to move so he took her hand and raised his other to stop her. "I want you to look for a straight line in the turf going from just beyond the house to the trees. You may see the deer grazing for their breakfast on the far right and the line should just be visible as a break in the grass between the house and the herd. Okay, go have a look and then come back in here."

Jessica moved silently across the room and looked out of the window as instructed. She could see the deer majestically moving in a small herd between the house and the tree line. She adjusted her gaze into the foreground between the house and the animals and eventually could just discern a relatively straight line that cut through the grass. It was hard to see but looked like the ground had been raised slightly on the side nearest the house. She returned to Crowe who was still in the bathroom.

"Yes, I saw it," Jessica said in an excited tone, "what is it?"

"It's called a Ha-Ha," Crowe started to explain, "It is an old landscaping feature of an earthen wall supporting a rise in the ground itself and facing a deep and wide ditch on the other side. It is designed to keep livestock away from the house without destroying the vista through the use of a raise fence. I studied it yesterday before you arrived, at least as much as I could from the window and it extends from the side of the house to the trees. I would expect there to be a fence that then goes through the trees either side to create a partly wooded, partly grassy enclosure for the deer." He paused to see if he still had her attention, "I had already thought we should perhaps make a run for it if we could before getting on the helicopter and maybe this 'friend' will be our chance?"

"So, what do you think we should do?" Jessica asked plainly," once we start running that is?"

"Head for the Ha-Ha and jump in. The ditch will be low enough to hide our heads so we will have a short time to decide which direction we go and they will not know until anyone chasing also reaches the ditch and sees us." Crowe paused and looked pensive. "Actually, as the note said, perhaps we should split up anyway and go in opposite directions?"

"I don't want to be parted from you Michael," she wailed softly and squeezed his hand.

"Neither do I," he replied with a smile, "But if I go left towards the furthest trees, you can go right where the tree line is nearer so you will be the first to be out of sight. In any event, If Adam still wants to go through with this whole thing then it is me he will send the goons after, not you. Once you are in the trees, try and get over the fence and head in a straight line away from it. South will be to your left but I am guessing the fence will curl around towards me through the trees so go off at a tangent and when out of the woods, try and follow south then. I will get over the fence then follow it around before going off away from it and hopefully we should not be too far away from each other when we are free from the trees. Do you understand?" He held her head in his hands and kissed her forehead twice. She held him close and they just stood swaying with the hold.

After a few moments they parted and agreed to get washed and ready for whatever was going to come. Crowe still had his bag and clothes and went to fetch it whilst Jessica removed the robe and stepped into the still running shower.

"Fuck!" she heard Crowe shout and stepped out of the shower reaching for the towel to hold to her body as she came out of the bathroom.

"We must have been visited in the night," he said with a pained expression. "Clothes, wallet and even my phone is gone. Check your stuff," he followed.

Jessica moved to where she had left her clothes on the chair in the corner but it was empty. It was the first time she had noticed they were missing. A quick glance to the nightstand also proved that the phone was gone although her earrings that she had taken off before they settled down to make love properly were still there

"All gone," she said.

"Looks like they are not taking any chances," Crowe said meekly, "And neither of us heard a thing. Shit." He looked up towards the ceiling to look for any tale-tell signs of hidden cameras but could not see anything suspicious. "I guess we will have to wait until they come with whatever clothes they need us to wear," he said in a resigned manner. He looked down at the space beneath the balloon backed upholstered chair where he had placed his shoes and was gratified to see that both his and Jessica's were there, neatly placed in pairs, "well at least we have our own footwear" he said glumly.

Jessica went back into the bathroom and continued her shower, leaving wet barefoot prints on the carpet as she walked. Crowe went back to the window and looked again at the ditch line they would be heading for if given a chance. His run would be about two hundred yards he estimated. Perhaps a minute of hard sprinting once in the ditch itself he thought. Jessica would have, on the other hand, about seventy-five yards, perhaps thirty seconds if she pushed herself. It was potentially a big ask of them both but if the adrenaline kicked in, who knows what could happen. As for their new 'friend', Crowe hoped beyond all reason that whatever diversion she was going to pull would be timed exactly right for them both to make a run for it. But who exactly were her accomplices who need the distraction or delay to arrive? Were they here for Jessica and him, or Adam? His money was on the latter.

Chapter Twenty-Nine

07.42 21st September Present Day,
South London, England

The dead girl's eyes were wide and pleading but completely lifeless. The dark brown pupils were fully dilated and staring at Stubbs. She was on the floor of the dingy room on her back with both arms splayed out sideways, her head tilted to face the bed upon which Stubbs now lay. Her legs were straight so that she gave the impression of being crucified to the bare floorboards. The marks made by the ligatures that Stubbs had removed before arranging the body darkened the skin to her wrists and ankles and her young naked body bore the angry bruises of the night of torment she had endured. The cruel black slash across her throat and the dark dried pool of her blood that stained the wooden boards upon which she lay was copious and wide.

Stubbs had taken his time to arrange her body so that he could sleep on his side as he stared at the dead girl. He recalled her face as she recognised him as soon as she walked into the room twenty minutes after he and Parkinson arrived late the previous evening. She had attempted a smile but Stubbs had silenced her immediately with an aimed punch to her stomach that bent her double and left her breathless. He had been quick to slide the cable-tie that Parkinson had given him over the winded girl's wrists and then quickly followed it up with a piece of duct tape which he stretched over the mouth. The sound of screaming in the next room proved that Parkinson was also enjoying his entertainment for the night and Stubbs had smiled at the thought.

His abuse of the trafficked girl had been long and brutal. The rape itself was satisfying but too quick. He almost wanted that out of the way so he could take his time beating her. At first, she resisted as best she could but soon the constant weariness of the pain overcame her until she became limp and placid. Stubbs had soon tired of beating something that refused to participate and took the knife he always kept in the small cupboard beside the bed to finish the job. In any event he was tired and tomorrow was going to be the highlight of his life so he arranged her body as he wanted, lay down naked upon the bed and closed his eyes as he observed her, slipping into an untroubled sleep.

Now fully awake, he moved to the small en-suite at the end of the room and splashed water onto his face from the basin. He cleaned his bloodied hands and arms as best he could with the cold water and small dried bar of thin soap whilst looking forward to the hot shower he would be having soon. He heard movement in the room next door and went to see if Parkinson was awake. The driver met him as he reached his door and smiled broadly. Stubbs was amazed at the state of the man. His body was almost entirely covered in blood, even his hair was matted and hard as it had dried. Stubbs pushed past him and into the room Parkinson had slept in to see a sight even he could not have prepared himself for. Whatever was left of the girl that was thrown into his room the previous night was now scattered and plastered over the floor, walls and furniture. She had been dismembered, gutted and eviscerated so that her existence as being human had been almost eradicated. Stubbs turned back to the blood-covered man.

"For fuck's sake man, did you enjoy yourself or what! Clean yourself up as best you can, and I mean thoroughly. Call the Serb to send the usual team in and get the car from the garage. I want to leave in thirty minutes do I make myself clear?" Parkinson nodded in agreement and made for the main bathroom down the hallway of the safe house. "Oh, and tell the Serb that he excelled himself this time!" Stubbs called after the retreating man, "The best yet!".

07.49 21ˢᵗ September Present Day, Exeter, England

Carol Davis was up early and in the station before her shift start time was due. She laughed off her colleague's banter about not having a life outside of the force, however true that actually happened to be, and got straight back onto the case notes she had reviewed the previous night. She now had a name. A member of the Catholic clergy, a Cardinal no less! What he had to do with Wilding or indeed either of the two missing persons was unknown but apart from the UPS employee who was being collected for interviewing at this very moment, the Cardinal was now the main lead and the main suspect.

Carol did a Google search on the name and found the Wikipedia entry. If it was to be believed, then she now had the full biography, his age, place of birth and career to date culminating with his 'special secondment' to the Vatican of which there were no specific details. An email popped up within Outlook as she read the article and she noted that McGeary's name was in the title so she closed the Wikipedia tab and went to her inbox.

The email was the response from her enquiry the previous night as to whether there were any travel details for the Cardinal logged in the Border Force records. There were. McGeary was logged as having entered Britain only yesterday and through Exeter airport having travelled from Charles de Gaul airport outside Paris. He had returned later in the day so although she now had proof that the Cardinal had been in the UK, his arrival and departure were documented as being almost a day after the time of death. The timings were not in line with the afternoon of savagery that had befallen the poor Professor Wilding and the collection time on the UPS manifest for the courier, they were a day late.

Carol was troubled. She thought she had proof that McGeary could have been the murderer but not only was he not in the country at the time of the crime, he had visited and left a full twenty-four hours afterwards and was now back in the Vatican. But he had landed only a few miles from the murder scene. Why not Gatwick or Heathrow? Whatever his business had been in the country, it surely was more than coincidence that he had landed at the closest airport to the crime. Perhaps he had come to deliver payment to the assassin or to get a report back from the crime itself? The fact that the only things taken appeared to be the books themselves now had added weight if the main suspect was a high-ranking clergyman, if only by association. But why would such a man risk so much for a few books? Why add his name so obviously to the scene of a crime? The more Carol thought it through the more she knew she was missing something. This was all far too convenient. She needed the courier driver's statement quickly and without hesitation, she picked up the phone to call the detective constable bringing him in.

08.12 21ˢᵗ September Present Day, Vatican City, Rome

McGeary had chosen to spend the night in the small ante-room to his office that housed the single camp bed for occasions such as the one that was now upon him. He had sent the priests back to their lodgings just after midnight to give them a well-deserved rest but could not himself be parted from his work and continued to investigate far into the night, pausing only to select another of the volumes from the open box and pages at random to read.

In his mind, his faith was clear and unequivocal but he forced himself to read at least a page of the volume. In the end he read several pages finding the prose not too difficult and which flowed at just the right speed to keep his interest. It was volume seventeen that he had picked at random and the page he equally turned by chance took McGeary back to the Roman Empire and to the life Adam described of himself as Lucius Verus, Emperor. Adam described how he had been adopted by Caesar Marcus Aurelius who had taken him into his confidence as adviser to the obvious disdain and loathing of his natural teenage son, Commodus. How life had been fraught between the two young men, the constant arguing and one-upmanship culminating in the attempted assassination Commodus had tried against him when Adam as Caesar Lucius Aurelias Versus Augustus as the old man had named him fully whilst in office as his co-Emperor. Adam as Lucius described how his assailant tried to garrotte him and yet despite being a huge beast with numerous gladiatorial combat successes to his name, he could not find the strength to choke the life out of his victim. Adam's neck had hardened to the bite of the coarse roped knot pressed against his throat, preventing it to crush his windpipe and allowing him to slip the knife from his belt and gut the heavier man. The continued hatred between the two sons became so obvious that it troubled Aurelius greatly and as Adam was always in awe yet had genuine affection for the wise Emperor, he knew the time had come to move on. So, he described how he faked his own death through plague and his body interned, only to return as assassin himself twenty-three years later when he strangled Commodus in his palace dressed as a member of his Praetorian Guard using the same garrotte style that Commodus had ordered against him years earlier. Adam described the look of shock and horror on the face of the older Commodus as he fought for his last breath whist a man he had seen die choked him with hands that had not aged one day.

McGeary had read the section that explained all of this with actual interest. It was strange to think that the section he read described events that involved the very ground upon which the city around him now stood. The piece had shown the second century AD Adam to be both caring in his love for Marcus Aurelius as he had been ruthless against his errant son. Part of McGeary wanted to carry on reading, following the journey of the man that he was now pitted against but realised that to do so would question his own faith. If he was to accept what was written to be the truth and Adam was indeed the immortal son of creator's past, then he knew all was at an end. Instead the desire for sleep overcame him and he retired to his makeshift cot.

As the sun rose over yet another flawless Roman blue sky McGeary rose quickly and used the small bathroom reserved for him only. He washed and prepared himself as smartly as he could for today he would yet again have an audience with the Holy Father. Quite what the Pope was going to say to him he did not know although he suspected that the book delivery would have already been communicated to the Pontiff so he needed to have some sort of explanation ready as to why he had received the books and why, apparently, he had also sent them. He thought hard and considered what he would say as he dressed in his finest robes.

Outside McGeary's office, Father Johan arrived at his desk bleary eyed. The young priest had slept badly with much on his mind following the late-night research only a few hours before. The delivery of the books had unnerved him and his research had been interrupted by the Cardinal's return so one unresolved mystery within his findings had not been completed and had thus played on his mind, preventing sleep. As he booted his computer into life he once again started to scroll down the names seeking to re-discover the group of names that he had been working on before retiring. As he found the group he started to go through each one in turn using Google to fill in the gaps and in doing so, managed to whittle the list down to just a handful. Thirty minutes later, he was down to three possible candidates for the geographical area he had been assigned but something did not add up. By further applying all the filters he had used previously, he was now down to one name but realised he could not be correct. He must have made a mistake, surely, he could not be right? A thin bead of sweat started to form on his brow which he wiped away on his sleeve as he sat thinking in fear at what was now in front of him. He resolved himself to one course of action, the only one he possibly could do. He wrote the name on a piece of paper and started to rise to go and speak to the Cardinal who remained inside of his office. As he rose, a voice behind him boomed.

"Father Johan! You are early this morning. Could you not sleep?" Father Bernard said purposefully.

Father Johan turned to see the older priest framed by the doorway into the central office. He smiled and walked towards him.

"I see his Eminence has had similar night time issues Father," Johan said, crossing himself.

"As have we all in these troubled times," Bernard responded. "What have you there Father?" he said pointing at the paper he was holding.

"My research has uncovered something…odd," Johan said looking down to the floor.

"Let me see Father," Bernard said holding out his hand as Johan handed him the name. Bernard turned the blank side over to reveal the writing on the other side and laughed.

"Why Father Johan, you are making a joke surely?" he said strongly.

"I must be mistaken," Johan responded quickly, "I have made an error," he followed, visibly shaking now as Bernard held out his left arm and placed his hand on the younger man's shoulder, drawing him closer.

"Yes, Father," he said softly, "an innocent mistake surely?"

"But…. but I was so sure!" Johan said almost whimpering, "It was hard to find but the connection was there. The drugs, the Cartel, the family name, a coincidence perhaps?"

"Do not worry about it Father," Bernard said, "you can always rely on me."

With that Father Bernard quickly spun the younger priest around so that his head was caught in a lock between the two strong arms of the oppressive man whose face was instantly curled into a rage. With all his strength and with a swift and decisive twist, the slight man's neck snapped, his head lolling onto Bernard's arms.

Looking quickly around, Father Bernard pulled the limp body of Johan towards the storage cupboard to his right. Keeping the man restrained with one arm, he unlocked the key to the cupboard and opened the door, bundling the lifeless young priest with him. He arranged the boxes on the floor to form a temporary wall to hide the corpse and deposited Johan behind them. It would do for today, Bernard thought, after which it wouldn't matter anyway. He exited from the cupboard, shut the door and locked it putting the key in his cassock pocket and went to Johan's desk to wipe the computer screen of the data he had left on view. Finally, he took the piece of paper and shredded it before going to his own desk. A little complication easily overcome he thought as he stared his own computer and sat down.

Chapter Thirty

08.21 21st September Present Day, Somewhere in England

Adam rapped on the door with excited rapidity and let Tall Man turn the key in the lock to open it. Both men walked in to find Crowe and Jessica sat in their robes on the bed watching them. Adam smiled his usual beaming grin and held out both arms upon which two sets of boiler suit type garments were held, both sky blue in colour. Jessica looked down her slim and freckled nose at the clothes and wrinkled it.

"Not my colour I'm afraid," she said flippantly, "Do you have them in green?"

Crowe smiled to himself but was also resigned that these would be their only clothes to wear if they did not want to exit the building still in just their robes. He picked up the top suit and realised that between the two garments there was underwear and socks also. He picked what was clearly the man's choice and handed the rest to Jessica.

"Seriously Adam?" he questioned, "Why is this necessary?"

"My show, my rules," Adam replied taking a bit of the gloss off his smile as he did so. "I am sorry for the charade," he followed, "but I have to be sure you are both, how can I put it," he paused, "sterile?"

Jessica started to disrobe but realised that Tall Man's eyes were boring into her. She picked up the small pile of clothes and retreated into the bathroom, shutting the door.

"I will have some breakfast sent to you shortly," Adam said sharply, "please be ready to depart in thirty minutes would you? Can I just check you are still both committed to this? I would hate there to be any last-minute hesitancy from you Michael. Remember, Jessica will be in the good care of Pavel and Karl all the time you and I are in the public spotlight."

"I am ready," Crowe replied, "and what of myself? Am I still to be your sacrificial lamb after all has been done?" He looked up from his sitting position to the thoughtful would-be God before him. Adam resorted to his normal childish shrug of the shoulders and a thin smile.

"It would seem we may already have that offering but let us see how you do Michael. Remember, all you have to do is kill me. Do it right so that the world cannot but see my immortality and you shall both go free. Get in my way or try to sabotage this day and you will both die. Your life is in your own hands Michael, treat it with caution." Adam turned abruptly and left the room with Tall Man following swiftly behind. Crowe called immediately after them.

"I have one more question!" he said with a raised voice. Adam returned to the entrance of the room.

"Go on," he said impatiently,

All this," Crowe said waving his arms around to indicate the building they were in. "All this was for my benefit, I understand that. But how much of it made you hanker for what you did in the original? The rituals? The torture? How much did you want those days to come back? The return of the Hades Society?" Crowe stared straight into Adam's darkening eyes.

"Who said they ever stopped?" Adam said curtly, "There are those that support me in this country that have maintained the activities until even now. I got bored myself of course. When you have lived as long as I have done, there are seriously no pleasures left to discover that I have not already experienced so many times. But I always found that providing for even the most cruel and sadistic whims of others can guarantee loyalty. I do not question but I do understand." He abruptly turned and once again left the room, this time scowling. As he left Crowe's own fears were simply strengthened. Despite the advanced age and megalomaniac ambition, the man was clearly insane and undeniably evil. This was no longer just about saving their lives. Whatever the cost, he was going to do his level best to thwart him.

Jessica came out of the bathroom in the boiler suit which despite its drabness, complemented her quite well as she had tied her hair back in a ponytail using the ribbon that had been once been tied around a flannel. She looked at the now locked door and sighed but then smiled at Crowe and started to disrobe him.

"Come on, get it off," she said and he willingly agreed, dressing quickly in his own similar suit afterwards. They looked at each other and laughed but did so in a hollow manner knowing what lay before them.

"Are you ready for this?" Crowe asked softly.

"Just make sure you find me when we are out of the woods," she replied in a hushed tone before moving towards him and taking him in her arms. The kiss was long, soft and passionate and neither of them wanted it to stop.

The sound of the key turning once more forced them apart and they looked through the now open door to see Tall Man. Behind him, the young girl who had served Crowe dinner upon his arrival stood with another tray of food, bagels, fruit and a jug of coffee with two mugs. Crowe looked at the woman and realised that she was a bit older than he first thought, early thirties perhaps and tried to meet her eyes. Tall Man ushered her in and indicated towards the table for her to place the tray. She entered slowly but at no time did she meet Crowe's gaze. Perhaps he had got it wrong, Crowe thought. Perhaps she was not the one he surmised as he observed her place the tray and then turn to leave.

When the eye contact came it was for the briefest of split-seconds and would have been missed if Crowe was not looking for it. She simply widened both eyes whilst looking straight at him and although no words were said, they were not needed for the message was received loud and clear. She was the contact and the one who had passed the note. But who did she represent? Who were her friends, and could he now assume they would be their friends also?

"Eat", Tall Man barked and pointed to the tray as the woman left the room. He closed the door behind him and locked it again as Crowe glanced over to Jessica and smiled.

"It was her," he mouthed in almost a whisper, "it's on." He moved to the tray and took a bagel. A quick sniff indicated that it was an onion one with cream cheese and poppy seed, he took a bite. "Come on, it's good," he said and smiled. "We might as well eat now, I guess we may need the energy."

Jessica joined him at the tray and selected the other bagel. As she ate, Crowe poured two coffees from the jug, it was hot and steaming.

"Not too much perhaps," he said and selected the one that was half full. They ate and drank in silence for a few minutes and held hands without saying anything for a further period.

After ten minutes, the door opened again and Adam was standing there alone.

"It is time Michael," he said purposely, "time to change the history books!" he smiled and clapped his hands rapidly, "would you please both follow me?" He left the room with the door open and Crowe and Jessica looked at each other before following him. Crowe held out his hand and Jessica took it.

"When I start to run you run with me, as fast as you can," he whispered, "keep holding my hand to we get to the ditch and then you go right, okay?"

"What are you two love birds chatting about?" Adam said, "Ah love! I have seen so much love and so much pain come of it. I thus soon became immune to the pull of the heart and concentrated on just sating my lust. Such a more efficient view," he said as he skipped down the staircase.

"Where are we going?" Crowe said inquisitively not expecting an answer when Adam surprised him.

"I have something to say, so we go to where traditionally those with something to say may say it!" he answered, "Speakers Corner, Hyde Park. Where else! I need a big space for the crowds that will appear once the first videos are posted onto social media. They will come in their droves once they see me." He finished with a smile.

"And what of the authorities?" Crowe followed, "The police. What if they stop you?"

"They won't," he replied. "I have that covered already."

They walked through the ornate hall and past the entrance to the small gravel circle in front of the house. The helicopter was still where it had landed bringing Jessica the day before. Both Tall Man and Squat Man were waiting by the aircraft looking pleased with themselves. Squat Man in particular remained sneering at Jessica.

The pilot was just starting the engine when the explosion happened. Crowe, Jessica and Adam were all blown forwards by the force of the blast emanating from within the house. A huge ball of fire erupted from the rear of the building and extended to above the second floor. A canister of gas could be seen catapulting into the trees as a cloud of acrid black smoke started billowing from behind the staircase, across the hallway and out of the main door.

Crowe took his cue and recovered Jessica's hand before they started to run full pelt towards the direction of the Ha-Ha ditch. Adam was still sprawling in the gravel as they shot off but Tall Man saw what was happening and started to canter after them with Squat Man bounding up behind.

"Just Crowe," Adam spluttered after them, "I want him alive." The pilot got out of the cockpit but Adam waved frantically at him.

"No!" he shouted, "get back in and keep that engine going!" The pilot did as he was ordered as Adam stood up fully and dusted down his linen suit. The flames were already catching quickly to the wooden trusses in the half-completed house at the rear of the house and Adam caught a glimpse of the young waiter emerging from the blast in full flame. The man thrashed about in a crazy fire dance and screamed before the flames extinguished the sound and he crumpled to the earth. Adam looked towards where the fugitives were heading and realised that they were already half way to the ditch. He scowled and bared his teeth. How dare they humiliate him now!

Crowe shouted at Jessica to keep up. He was sprinting more than he had ever done in his life before but this time his life depended on every effort he could give so his laboured breathing cut through the pain. They could see the slight rise of the Ha-Ha coming quickly upon them and bounded as fast as they could for it. As the crest became visible Crowe turned to Jessica and nodded mouthing 'I love you' as they ran. She nodded back just as the edge was within a few steps and almost immediately, both were in the air, flailing their arms.

The drop was more than both expected and each landed heavily. Jessica turned to see Crowe get up and start to run towards the furthest trees keeping within the ditch. She turned the other way and started again, the trees in front of her closer than Crowe was heading for but still looked a long way away. Behind her she heard Tall Man as he grunted after leaping into the ditch and landed with a thump closely followed by Squat Man whose landing was heavier still. Both swore and paused momentarily before collecting their thoughts.

"You take the bitch!" Tall Man shouted, pointing at the fleeing Jessica and started to stride quickly after Crowe, increasing his speed as he did so. Squat Man smiled cruelly and started after the running woman. He had to catch her now. The thought of what he would do to her was as good as a shot of adrenaline as he increased his speed.

Crowe was willing the trees to pull up their great roots and march towards him to lessen the gap. His chest was heaving and his lungs burned as if he had breathed acid. A stitch was forming in his side but he knew that any chance of getting away was entirely dependent on his will to keep going. He really wanted both of their pursuers to follow him and now, with only Tall Man was hot on his heels, he knew that meant Jessica was at Squat Man's mercy. He prayed that her lighter frame would mean that the distance between her and the fat man would prove vital to her getting away. The trees looked to be a hundred miles rather than yards away but slowly, achingly slowly, he was making ground.

Jessica entered the tree line just at the retaining fence joined the ditch as Crowe had said it would. She afforded herself a quick glance behind and was aghast to see the monstrous form of the Squat Man bearing down on her. The fence was of steel mesh with a razor

wire top and about ten feet high. She knew that she
would not be able to jump or climb it so she just
carried on running as fast as her body allowed whilst
keeping the fence to her right. She remembered that
Crowe expected the fence to run in a big semi-circle to
encompass the deer park so she desperately needed a
way over. She looked ahead but the fence seemed to
just go on without anything to help her scale it until,
suddenly, the opportunity presented itself as she saw
the small gulley of a dry stream bed running under the
fence and providing just enough room for her thin
body to wriggle under. She dropped to the floor and
using her hands as paddles, she pushed back the leaf
mould and top soil behind her on both sides like a
mole to crawl through. It was working; slowly she
inched under the bottom of the wire ever thankful that
the razor edges were confined to the top only. She had
just managed to crawl through past her thighs when
she felt the weight of Squat Man's hands on her feet,
starting to pull her back. She screamed and clawed at
the earth to gain purchase on anything that could help
her from being pulled forcibly back under the fence
but her fingers found nothing but loose soil. Squat
Man laughed as he pawed at her legs and then her
thighs, always pulling. He inched his grasp up to the
belt that was around the boiler suit so he could have a
firm hold and made one last effort to reach it. As he
did so, he stopped suddenly and stared in shock. The
small hole in his forehead started to immediately issue
blood in a strong gush that soon covered his face. As
his head dropped onto the screaming woman's legs she
felt the warmth of the liquid soak through and did not

see the hands and arms of the man pulling her through
the fence and away from Squat Man's dead body.

Jessica stopped screaming only when she felt a hand
go over her mouth to silence her. She looked up into
the face of the camouflaged man who winked at her
and put his other hand up to his mouth with the index
finger raised to indicate that she should be quiet. As
she became accustomed to the fact that she had been
saved, she noticed the other figures appearing, all in
dark clothing and with streaks of black over their
faces.

"Shalom Motek," he said thickly, "You are safe."

Adam recovered himself sufficiently to remain steady
on his feet just in time to see the two fugitives
disappear from view as they jumped into the ditch.
Karl and Pavel launched themselves in the same
manner a few seconds later and then all four were
absent from view. He turned to see the back of his
house in full flame with huge billowing clouds of acrid
black smoke spilling into the air around the building.
Through the entrance door he could see the orange and
red flashed grow as the hungry flames reached out for
and overcame anything combustible. He was
witnessing the second destruction of the great house
although the first time around over two hundred years
ago it was in the original location and with one more
huge difference, this time Adam was outside the
building looking in, not tied to a chair in the library
looking out.

As he watched the mock-up of the original house burn wildly he heard the shot. It had come from behind the flaming house somewhere, from within the trees. It could have been either Pavel or Karl shooting in pursuit of either Crowe or Jessica and assumed it must have been to bring down the latter. A scream followed and then silence. Perhaps Pavel had indeed caught up with his prey and was finally living out his fantasies he thought. It was of no consequence as he only wanted Crowe back now but considered that he was already beyond further persuasion. So, his purpose would simply to assume the mantle of martyr after all, Adam thought. Either of the two men now chasing them can be Adam's executioner for the cameras and Crowe can be represented, just like Jessica, another disciple killed by the legions of the failing church. It was a crude end to his dream of academic acceptance before conquering through more direct and cruel means but it was too late to go back now. He knew the new Four of Twelve, no less than the British Prime Minister, would be announcing him in an hour from now. A live broadcast where Stubbs would claim both the murder of Wilding and the assisted suicide of Avery had been directly ordered by rattled major world faiths in the mission to find and destroy Adam. Both his proof of immortality and the endorsement of the highest political power in the country would be sufficient. The lower key populist endorsement from the academic world would still be used but, following Wilding's savage death, Adam would say that Crowe and his woman were 'missing' to allow for their bodies to be found a few days later adding further proof of the murderous role of the church to try and thwart the new Age.

Adam scanned the grassy fields for any sign of the pursuits but it was clear both fugitives had kept to the ditch below the eye-line until they had reached the trees. No matter, he was sure Crowe would be caught in any event. Adam turned to face the helicopter and was stunned to see the pilot clutching his throat and falling to his knees. He held his neck with two hands through which his life blood was gushing and Adam could just see the small hilt of a throwing knife protruding from the left side. He sensed movement to his left and spun around to see the men approaching fast. Weapons were raised but that troubled Adam not at all. Realising that he was unprotected and his only means of transport gone was the greater concern and he thought quickly if he had any options. Realising that time was extremely limited; he started to move back toward the house in some vain expectation that he could repeat the disappearing trick he had accomplished all those years ago. He could not. As he neared the main door a figure appeared from behind the entrance pillar and swung a large copper-bottomed frying pan so that it connected with the bridge of Adam's nose, pulping it in an instance to bloody ruin. Adam catapulted back with the blow and plunged heavily onto his back on the gravel. As the wounded nose already started to undulate as the restoration process commenced, the girl stepped out from the stone porch. Her blackened arms and face from fighting through the thick smoke looked menacing and with intent to take life, she raised the heavy pan above her head to deliver what would have been a mortal blow to any ordinary human. The pursuing attackers shouted and gesticulated to her to stop. She did as ordered, pausing in mid strike before slowly lowering the pan and dropping it to the ground by her feet.

The lead attacker reached her in time to catch her as she fell from the effects of her actions. He praised her slowly and calmly in Hebrew as he laid her head on his bended knee. She looked at him through scared, pleading eyes before coughing once and then the eyes turned glassy as her head lolled to one side. The man checked her pulse on her scorched neck and then closed the lids over her fixed stare before laying her fully on the ground.

"You will be remembered Miriam," he said softly and bowed his head.

Beside him, Adam was stirring. His nose was already healing before the Israelis eyes as they grouped around and gradually Adam regained both his senses and his wits. He looked up at his captors and gave one of his widest smiles.

"Jews!" he said with a half-laugh, "But of course, how apt! Of all the races, all the religions, it is most ironic that those who capture me first, the first time in many thousands of years are Jews!" He laughed loudly and without stopping as two of the soldiers pulled him up and applied a cable tie to his wrists. "It has been too long since I have been apart from Judea," he followed,

"Over two thousand years in fact. I shall look forward to returning."

"The only part of Judea you are going to see will be the walls of the deepest fucking hole we can find to throw you in," the Captain said with an American accent which indicated he was a later settler in Israel, "Let's see how long you can last in perpetual darkness with nothing to eat or drink? Eternity does not seem that attractive when all you can do is slowly rot but never die. Get this piece of shit back from the house and get ready to escort him back through the woods!" he growled and watched as the two men holding Adam started to frog-march him towards the trees.

Jessica came around the corner of the building to see the final act of Adam's capture being played out before her. The heat from the fire within was now emanating through the frontage of the house but she stood unmoved by it as Adam was dragged past. As his gaze met her eyes, he smiled a wide grin, his white teeth gleaming. She saw the intense bruising above the mouth restore the nose to normality and instantly felt sick. He seemed unconcerned, happy even and Jessica shuddered as the Captain followed and came up to her.

"Are you okay Ma'am?" he asked softly.

"Michael," she started hesitantly, "Michael, he ran that way," she pointed to the far side of the lawns. He was being chased like me."

"I am sure he is fine Ma'am but we will check on it. Levi! Stefan! Double quick!" he pointed to the tree line and the two soldiers immediately started to sprint in the direction he was pointing in the most direct route towards the far end of the ditch.

"How did you know we were here? That HE was here?" Jessica asked meekly, pointing at the retreating group holding Adam.

"Miriam…" the Captain started, pointing to the still form in the entrance porch, "Miriam had infiltrated his staff for a while but he never stayed in one place long enough to be sure of capture. Once she reported that Mr Crowe had come here we knew the time would be now to take him down. We just needed time to prepare, to infiltrate into the country without raising suspicion with the British authorities. Adam had already gained his supporters from within the establishment, were just not sure who until yesterday and once we did know, coming through anything officially was a no-win option."

"I don't understand, "Jessica said with a concerned look on her muddied face.

"You will by tonight." The handsome Captain said with a toothy grin and gestured for the nearest man to assist Jessica as they walked back to the trees. One of the soldiers took the key from the helicopter so that it finally started to reduce in noise as they walked.

"Michael?" Jessica said looking behind her.

"Don't worry," the Captain said with a reassuring hand on her shoulder, we will get him.

Once he was in the trees, Crowe relaxed his stride slightly. The last thing he wanted to do was trip on an unseen root or a fallen branch meaning that Karl would be on him within seconds. He allowed himself a short glance back through the trees to see that the Tall Man was indeed still hot on his heels and he was sure that the man was gaining ground. He turned just in time to avoid a young sapling in his way and swerved. The fence was taller than he had hoped for and he had not reckoned on the razor wire topping so he continued to run, keeping the fence on his left but knowing that just to continue in this fashion would lead eventually to the other side of the deer park and possibly mean literally bumping into Jessica and her own pursuer. As he heard the shot ring out his heart sank. Although nothing more than the aging duelling pistol had been seen by way of firearms during his stay at the mansion, he really had not accounted for the fact that both of the pursuers could be armed. Had he heard the execution shot for Jessica? He prayed there was another reason and just carried on running. He could now hear the heavy laboured breathing of the man behind him. He was close, closer than he had been throughout the chase and Crowe knew his level of fitness was going to let him down soon. As he ran through some coppiced saplings, Crowe took a gamble. He grabbed the flexible trunk of a young birch with his right hand and pivoted his run to go around the back of the tree, keeping the sapling as horizontal as he could. As he felt the tension from the trunk tighten to the point of complete resistance he let it go. His timing was perfect as the trunk arched upward and backwards to strike Tall Man squarely in the face. Karl screamed as the whipped sapling cut into his forehead, stopping him immediately and forcing him to put both hands to his face. Crowe took his chance. He stopped and doubled back three paces before thrusting his right fist into Tall Man's gut forcing the wheezing man to bend double. Crowe followed with a well-aimed kick of his shoe between Tall Man's legs causing him to scream and fall to his knees. Crowe finished the gasping man with another sharp kick to the chin which sent him sprawling into the leaf mould.

Crowe rested for only a few seconds before he saw the two men running towards him. He did not recognise them but his instinct was to keep on running. As he started the lead man, Levi shouted at him.

"No Mr Crowe, we are friends! Stay where you are!"

Crowe was too exhausted to really put up any more of an escape anyway and collapsed into the dirt wheezing. The two men walked up to the moaning Karl who was massaging his groin.

"Don't rub them, count them!" Levi said with a laugh as the other man, Stefan, applied the cable tie to the unresisting Karl.

"The lady is safe Mr Crowe and we have Adam in our 'care'. Are you fit to walk?"

Crowe nodded and took the outstretched arm that was offered to steady himself.

"This way Mr Crowe," Levi said and led him and the supported Karl directly out of the trees and across the lawns towards the opposite tree line. Crowe had a million questions but was too breathless to utter any.

The sudden sound behind him force Crowe to turn sharply. Karl had overcome the struggling Stefan and was holding him by the neck so that his back arched toward the ground. Despite using every ounce of strength he could muster, the Israeli was too overbalance to make it count and with his air flow restricted, he was losing the fight. Levi acted instantly and drop-kicked the pair of them so that capturer and captive sprawled heavily amongst the fallen leaves. Tall Man recovered first and made to grab the pistol Stefan was also trying to retrieve from his holster. The pair scrambled for the gun in unison before Levi took hold of Karl's head between his meaty hands and twisted it quickly, breaking the neck with an audible crack. Karl dropped instantly, allowing Stefan to regain his standing position, breathing hard.

"I really did not want that to be necessary," Levi said with regret, "We could have learned much from that piece of shit."

Chapter Thirty-One

09.07 21st September, Present Day, Vatican City, Rome

Despite the short struggle outside of his office, McGeary heard nothing beside that of the voice on the other end of the phone. The call had been unexpected and despite the early hour, the speaker seemed excitable and yet, austere all at the same time.

"I am sorry," McGeary said, "you are saying that you know where he is and at this moment, your assets are seeking to capture him?" The Cardinal had not fully processed what he had heard and the man's accent and low tone of voice made for additional difficulty.

"I am," the voice confirmed, belonging to Benjamin Dahan, the Israeli Defence Minister. "A squad of Sayeret Matkal should now be in position and will engage before he can move out."

"Sorry, Sayer…. I didn't catch that." McGeary asked

"Israeli Special Forces. These guys are trained to perform hostage rescue and other missions on foreign soil," Dahan clarified, "Following your request to our faith leader in the Paris meeting before you were caught up in that unfortunate car bomb, we employed our assets to help track this man down. Observers from our intelligence service followed a visitor, a Michael Crowe, after visiting Professor Wilding's house, the man you confirmed had received the books of Adam. We saw where he was picked up the following day and taken to a remote location in Britain for a meeting, we believed, with Adam who used a helicopter to leave the location. The registration of the aircraft was taken and we established, somewhat surprisingly, that it was part of the fleet for an American registered film company. Using a special GPS tracking system, we were able to pinpoint the locations it subsequently visited. One of those locations was an apparent film set to which there were several outsourced services, catering amongst them. We immediately infiltrated the catering company so that we had eyes on the inside. Crowe's car was abandoned at another remote location to where we tracked the helicopter landed so we were sure he was either a hostage or a collaborator. Our agent on the inside then confirmed that he was indeed a prisoner, as was his female partner who had been kidnapped shortly afterwards." The man paused and went silent.

"My God," McGeary said softly, "so you mean that the Beast may finally be in our hands at any moment?" he asked, almost hesitant for the response.

"If all goes to plan, yes" Dahan responded. "I wanted you to be aware but to also remain silent until I can confirm success. We can then decide what is to be done. Are we agreed?"

"We are agreed," McGeary said gleefully, "Thank you Minister."

The line went dead and McGeary replaced the handset and immediately clasped his hands in front of him praying hard. He had the books and now, just possibly, Adam would be captured. He looked up at the ornate frescoed ceiling and thanked God.

09.11 21st September, Present Day,
Winchester, Hampshire, England

Elizabeth Moon reacted to the sound of the letterbox flap being allowed to slam back against the front door. Post had been delivered.

Her eyes were still sore and itchy from a relatively sleepless night, her head still buzzing from the call she had received from the office confirming that Avery had committed suicide. Elizabeth rubbed her eyes but they were too dry to offer any relief and stung even more for she had no tears left.

She slowly got out of the bed as going to work was not something she was prepared to do this day and reached for her robe before going into the bathroom. Relieved and with splashed cold water on her face offering a degree of freshness to her tiredness, Elizabeth walked down the stairs and to the front door where the A4 brown envelope was sat on the doormat. She bent to pick it up in confusion and wonder at what it could be and then she recognised the hand that had written her name and address, it was Avery's. Trembling slightly, she turned the envelope over and started to open it. The seal had been taped for security so she walked into the kitchen and took out a pair of scissors from the drawer to make the process easier. Once open, she extracted the contents which comprised of a hand-written letter and a series of CCTV black and white photographs, each one dated and showing the same car emerging from a garage. In one of the photos, one of the men getting into the car was clearly looking up almost directly at the camera. She gasped as she recognised the face of Andrew Stubbs. Putting the photos on the kitchen work surface, she started to read the letter.

'*Dearest Elizabeth,*

I have many regrets in life, many things I would have changed with the benefit of hindsight for indeed, hindsight is a wonderful thing as they say....

I regret not spending more time with my boys. Something that now, looking back, was perhaps the worst failing in my life. I regret not paying more attention to my wife in her grief and not realising what she intended to do. Most recently, I regret not seeing the feelings you have for me and not recognising how I truly feel towards you. Of that I am particularly sad and in another life, I would not have hesitated to take you in my arms and love you.

It is because of how we feel, that I know you are the only person in this life I can trust but I do not want you to be in any danger so you must promise me that you will act upon what I am about to say to you and ensure the contents of this letter are with the press immediately. Do not hesitate or think to approach this yourself, please just make sure that you do what I ask and most of all, do not trust the police with this.

There has been a constant in my adult life that I have been tasked to ensure remains secret. I will not trouble you with what that is, suffice to say that it has dominated how I feel and think. I have hoped against hope that I would not be the one called upon to complete my duty but it appears I will now have to be that person. But I have grave doubts about the nature of my calling to the point that I do not think I can complete what I will be tasked to do. In admitting this, I believe I will be signing my own death warrant and due to the urgency of what is to happen, that my death will be very soon.

With that thought, I have decided to entrust you with the other great weight on my mind to which the enclosed photographs relate. As you know, Andrew Stubbs and I have been friends for decades. Our families have been close both as neighbours and friends for centuries. Andrew is my oldest and closest friend and so whilst I am alive, I cannot do what needs to be done with the enclosed. Should I die, however, I will no longer be troubled with the guilt of exposing my friend; to destroying him.

The photographs enclosed are from a security camera overlooking the entrance to a builder's yard in South London and the parking garage alongside. As you can see, they all show the same car, one of the official pool cars for the Cabinet which is why these photos ended up with me as Cabinet Secretary. All are dated over a period of a few months, all are late at night and those that show the occupants of the cars, clearly confirm that the Prime Minister amongst others is a regular visitor, not to the builder's yard itself, but to the house next door which is now known to be a location for trafficked sex workers. Most of the houses in that area are not occupied by regular families, but are mostly in multiple occupation by immigrants or squatters and the builder's yard itself is mostly disused but the cameras are maintained as a precaution.

It is my belief that Andrew is not only a regular visitor there, but a participant in the abuse of young women, some of which are merely children. The camera has captured other images of plain white vans arriving the day after some of the photos have been taken and groups of men in cover-alls going in and out. I cannot imagine what had happened in that house but what is clear is that Andrew is unfit for office and must be exposed.

Thus, my regrets also extend to not being man enough to betray my friend and to allow this to go on for far too long. Please redeem my weakness and expose this dreadful revelation after my death. I know you will do that for me.

Please forgive me Elizabeth. I wanted to be a stronger man, for Adam, for Britain and especially for you but I feel my life is worthless now and will soon be ended. The final insult to my despair is that I do not have the strength to do it myself. Even my dear wife was braver than me. No doubt, I will be reunited with her soon.

Yours ever,

Donald
Testbank, Stockbridge, Hampshire.

Elizabeth saw that she was shaking slightly as she finished the letter. It was a lot to take in and she sat down on the dining chair against the wall. She reached for the photographs and viewed them again. Yes, it was clearly Stubbs in one but what would it all mean if she simply presented these to the newspapers? And who exactly was Adam?

She re-read the last paragraph and was immediately struck by a line she had glossed over in the first reading *'I do not have the strength to do it myself'*. She accepted without question immediately that Avery did not kill himself. The caller she had spoken to yesterday was adamant that although it could not be officially confirmed how Avery died, they would most likely say it was suicide. If Avery did not have the strength to do it himself, then his prediction of being killed had come true. Elizabeth realised that the longer she had the contents of the letter without passing them to the press, the longer she could be potentially in danger. Who could know about his letter, about her? Her mind was made up. She would make some calls then wash and dress and get on the next train to London. These photos needed to be delivered in person but first she would scan both the letter and the photos and email them to the newspapers straight away.

09.22 21st September, Present Day, Exeter, England

Carol Davis sat opposite the bewildered courier driver in the interview room and passed him a plastic cup with hot coffee in it.

"Be careful it's hot," she said with a smile before sitting down. She pressed the record button on the tape machine and said the expected phrase about the time, date and occupants of the room. She paused and looked at the young man.

"When you approached the door of the house, was it open or closed?" she said plainly.

"Closed," he responded, "I rang the bell and knocked."

"Who answered it?" She followed and held up a photo of Wilding. "For the benefit of the tape recording I am holding up a photograph of the victim." She turned back to the man in front of her," Was it him?"

"No," the man said. Carol held up a photo of McGeary that she had taken from the internet., "For the benefit of the tape recording I am holding up a photograph of Suspect A," again she turned to the courier being questioned,

"Was it him?"

"No," the man repeated. "The man was short, a bit fat I guess. No neck, you know the sort?" He waited for an answer but none came so he continued. "Didn't say much, only to ask if I had a sack truck as the parcels were heavy so I went back to the van, took out the trucks and went back. The door was open so I called inside and he said to come into the room to the left."

"What accent did he have?" Carol asked.

"Foreign. Not English, at least not as his first language. I would guess East European, not sure where though."

"Did you see anyone else when you made the collection?" Carol asked.

"No, nobody. I could hear the radio on upstairs somewhere, it was quite loud but didn't see anyone."

"So, you would say it was a normal collection, nothing out of the ordinary?"

"Yes." The man sat back in the chair, slightly more relaxed.

Carol knew that at least the courier company and the man before her were simply caught up by way of doing their job. She had no doubt that the murderer, or murderers had kept Wilding upstairs whilst the books were loaded and had the radio on to stop any attempt by him to cry out. He had probably been tied and gagged but still alive. Forensics had not found any evidence of anything suspicious outside of the library itself which added weight to the theory.

"How did the room look?" She asked, "Was it normal? Tidy?"

"I think so," The man replied.

"Nothing disturbed or out of the ordinary?" she followed.

"I remember thinking that it was a strange place for the man to have as his home; didn't look the type, not academic like, but no, nothing else."

"So, he signed your tablet, you loaded the boxes and that was it?" she enquired.

"Well he just put a line on the screen with the stylus," The man said, "he didn't really sign. Looked nothing like McGeary and I assumed he was signing for somebody else anyway, as I said Eastern European, not Scottish."

"Irish," Carol responded, "Not Scottish."

"Whatever," the man said.

There was a knock on the door and the Detective Constable entered.

"Boss, you need to see this," he said and walked out. Carol terminated the interview on the machine, told the man to stay put and left the room closing the door behind her.

"We have been told to put this one to bed boss. To drop it."

"What the fuck?" Carol exploded, "Who said we have to drop it?"

"The Super boss, we are not to pursue this any further at this time. Apparently, there is going to be some Government announcement this morning, soon actually, and the case is involved. Sorry."

"Shit!" Carol shouted. "Right, let him go," she pointed to the interview room, "he's clean anyway and do the paperwork will you. Christ, this fucking job!" she stormed off knowing that there was nothing more she could do at this stage. The Detective Constable called after her.

"Oh boss! We found Crowe's car by the way. Valley of the Rocks, up on the North coast. Been there a few days according to the tea shop owner. Looks like we may have a jumper or another missing person after all! I have notified the Coast Guard" Carol did not respond directly but the DC heard her swearing as she walked down the corridor.

Chapter Thirty-Two

09.54 21st September, Present Day, Downing Street, London

Andrew Stubbs looked at himself hard in the mirror and adjusted his tie so that it was straight. He brushed his hand over the lapels of his electric blue suit and slicked back his hair. Satisfied, he left the bathroom with a spring in his step and with a determined stare which he kept straight ahead as he descended the portrait gallery staircase and across the floor to the front door. He paused slightly before the doorman and then nodded. The door of Number Ten Downing Street was pulled open and Prime Minister Andrew Stubbs walked confidently out into the morning light made even brighter by the hordes of press cameras flashing as he approached the podium in the middle of the road. He waited as he reached the lectern and looked down to his right where a monitor had been placed upon his own instructions. In front of him, the glass autocue was fired up and ready for him to push the button. He looked straight at the assembled journalists, camera operators and photographers and cleared his throat.

"Good morning," he began, maintaining his forward stare. "To the people of the United Kingdom I have a statement to make although it is perhaps not a statement for which you were prepared." His words were met by an increased number of camera flashes. "You will all be aware that the Cabinet Secretary, Sir Donald Avery, resigned a few days ago and that I reluctantly accepted his resignation. It is my duty," he paused, "my sad duty to now tell you that Sir Donald Avery is dead." He waited for several seconds before continuing to maximise the effect of the announcement. "He was found dead yesterday in his Hampshire home under suspicious circumstances. I have requested hourly updates from the investigating officers and it appears that whether he took his own life is questionable and remains undecided." Another pause, "My original purpose today was to make an announcement on the likely reshuffle of the Cabinet following his resignation but I now wish to use the opportunity instead to confirm the reason behind Sir Donald's resignation and what we are about to witness as a result." Another longer pause.

"Sir Donald met with me several days ago to confirm that he could not continue in his post as he was to commence a greater duty that eclipsed his responsibilities to this Government, to me and this country as a whole. He spoke of the coming of a great man. A man who would change the world for the better and one who would enrich all our lives for the future. Sir Donald thought he had been selected alone to bring this message to us all but he was wrong. Others also had knowledge of this man, including myself, and therefore I welcomed his decision as I knew he, like myself wanted what was best for this country and indeed all mankind. I cannot emphasise enough what this will mean and whom I speak of and therefore, so that we can all be astounded by what is to come, I have arranged for this man to be presented to you all and for him to be announced. He is, as we speak, preparing to do so at Speakers Corner in Hyde Park and I have asked the various television news networks, both domestic and some international companies to have their outside broadcast facilities ready in Hyde Park for this to take place after I have completed my message." He stopped and drew breath, relishing the confused faces of the journalists now silent and still before him.

"Before we switch to Hyde Park, I must make one more announcement about Sir Donald's death," he adjusted his shoulders before staring down the nearest camera. "As you will see and hear, the ramifications of what will be clear are questions that will be asked of all establishment thinking. There are forces in the world driven by religious ideology and fanaticism that will want to destroy what is heard. They will want to discredit all sources of dissent and eliminate those that spread it. I firmly believe that these forces were behind Sir Donald's death and indeed, are implicated in the gruesome murder of a well loved and respected Professor at Exeter University as well. A crime that also resulted in the theft of vital evidence as to the truth of what you will hear." He started to elevate himself as far as he could and remained impassive, his face a stony visage, "Many will disagree or even be frightened about what will be said and whilst I and many others can see what the future will hold in the new age, there will be thousands that will try to stop it. Believe me when I say that whoever you are, you will be hunted and the murderers of Sir Donald and Professor Wilding will be caught and will be punished." He stepped back from the podium slightly and pointed to the monitor to his side. "There will be no questions now but I will answer questions after what is about to begin has concluded."

The journalists surged forwards en masse but were restrained by the police on duty. All started shouting questions but Stubbs ignored them all. He stood rigid staring at the monitor which showed the makeshift stage in Hyde Park; an empty makeshift stage. Several journalists got the hint and started to look at their tablets to see what was happening whilst others were busy calling their offices for information. A few still shouted questions but Stubbs remained impassive. As the seconds ticked by, Stubbs started to get a gnawing feeling of doubt. It was not that Adam was late, it was the fact that there was no-one there ready to present at all. He could feel small beads of sweat start to form on his brow and he started to wiggle his fingers on his right hand, a trait that he had used all his life to show impatience. He glanced at the door of Number Ten but it remained shut. Several journalists were staring to look up from their tablets and at the Prime Minister looking for direction and one television reporter put her finger to her earpiece and nodded. She moved her microphone towards Stubbs, leaning as far as she could over the steel barrier and spoke.

"Prime Minister, I am being told that all the TV crews are there alone. There is no sign of anyone even approaching the stage area. No speakers and no assistants to help. There is no-one there Prime Minister so can you confirm what this is all about?" Other journalists started shouting questions again and Stubbs began to feel very uncomfortable. He decided to try and regain the initiative and moved back to the podium. There were no notes on the autocue to help him now.

"It appears there may be a delay and so not to keep you all waiting, I suggest we reconvene when it has been established what the issue is."

"Can you not tell us what the big announcement is?" Said one journalist, "who is this mystery man that will change the world?"

"Yes, come on sir, you whetted our appetite here. What is it that has your complete approval and for what others are apparently willing to kill for?" said another.

"Tell us!" shouted a third.

"Is it true about you and trafficked prostitutes?" screamed another, causing the other journalists to stop and look at the man who was bounding up and down with excitement. "We have the photos coming Mr Stubbs. Like them young, do you?"

Andrew Stubbs stood mouth open and staring with a face that expressed a mixture of intense anger and fear. His cheeks flushed red and he lifted his arm to point at the smiling journalist.

"How dare you! Do you not know who I am!" he screamed before bounding from the podium and approached the barrier to try and grab the man by his neck. He felt a restraining hand on his arm before he could get to the man as Parkinson also lunged forward and held him back before pulling him towards the now open door of Number Ten. The cameras flashed and clicked in thunderous rapidity as he retreated with now two security men shielding him into the relative safety of the building, the incessant calls from the assembled journalists hounding him as he disappeared.

"What the fuck just happened?" Stubbs said breathlessly. "What the fuck…...!"

"I think we need to go sir, "Parkinson said. "Let's use the tunnel exit. We both need to get away, at least until we know what the hell happened to Hyde Park."

"Yes," Stubbs said and started walking swiftly towards the tunnel entrance down the back stairs.

09.59 21st September, Present Day, Exeter, England

Carol Davis watched the Television with her colleagues, all in an almost unheard of state of total silence witnessing the complete public breakdown of the British Prime Minister. It was unprecedented that he first had seemed to undermine their whole case over the murder of Wilding by aligning it to the no-show of some sort of saviour, blaming world forces, which Carol quickly realised meant the Vatican with McGeary resident there, and then lashed out at a reporter asking if he was an abuser of trafficked women. The whole episode had become surreal, not true to life. Carol and her colleagues looked bewildered, their eyes straining at the news ribbon that skirted the base of the screen, waiting for it to give some explanation to what they had all just seen. Even the announcer was lost for words. He allowed long pauses to punctuate the inane, random words he was desperately seeking to fill the silences, to try and explain what had just happened. None of police workers in the room knew where to start but all of them realised with collective acceptance that nothing would be the same again.

"No wonder we got called off the case," Carol said suddenly and loudly, shocking those closest to her to involuntarily jump with the surprise, "and just how did they know about the Vatican connection? We have not made any sort of statement about it!"

"It's still our case," a voice said behind them, "but we may have to be patient to pursue it further." Carol turned to see the Superintendent standing in the doorway.

"I have news about your missing persons though Davis," he said, "Norfolk Police have them. They both walked into the station in Diss thirty minutes ago. Tired, dirty and disorientated but unharmed I understand. I am having them flown here this afternoon for interviewing." He smiled and Carol acknowledged the statement with a similar grin of satisfaction back.

10.07 Same Day, Winchester Rail Station

Elizabeth Moon put her face in her hands and cried as
the repeated video of Stubbs lashing out played over
and over again on the BBC news channel in full view
of the railway station's packed coffee shop occupants.
She tried to look away but became as transfixed as
every other one of the silent customers staring at the
screen, most with their mouths open in shock.

Whatever shame she felt for having given the story to
the newspaper was muted by the thought that Avery
had been right in predicting his own death and frankly,
Stubbs deserved what was going to happen to him. She
had already decided her only course was to resign her
position and give up her Civil Service career. It would
be simply too hard to try and carry on with so many
memories and regrets forever staining the walls of the
Cabinet Office. Elizabeth was genuinely sad that it
was ending this way but she knew that she had
absolutely no other choice, the die was cast. She was
sure that Avery was somehow involved in whatever
was going to happen in Hyde Park and if so then she
did not really want to know what that was. She needed
to hold on to the memories of Avery that thrilled her
and wanted nothing that would sully those precious
thoughts. Elizabeth Moon sobbed gently and quietly
using the napkin she had collected with her coffee to
wipe the moisture from her eyes. She was resolved and
knew without any hesitation that she had had enough.
The fallout from what had happened in front of
Number Ten would already be tearing through the

Cabinet Office and she wanted nothing of it. She drained the rapidly cooling coffee from the cup before her and started to rise. There was no doubt. The promise she was making to herself was going to be only course. After the newspaper interviews, she was going home.

10.09 Same Day, Vatican City, Rome

Cardinal Donal McGeary paced the last few yards to the Papal apartment with defined resolve. The call he had been waiting for had come through and the message it gave filled him with elation. He rubbed his hands together and clapped them once, loudly. They had him! Adam, the Beast, was now being smuggled out of Britain and as he walked McGeary beamed at the thought that his job was done. All that remained to do was to find the deepest, most secure location for Adam to be imprisoned for the rest of time, far longer than McGeary's or any human's own life span could witness. He now accepted fully that the only way you can kill something that cannot be killed is to deprive him of any reason to live. It was cruel but necessary for the sake of the faith, indeed for the sake of all faiths that this creature should never be allowed to roam free again. He looked forward to the next message from the Israelis as to where he was to be taken.

The Cardinal rounded the corner to the entrance to the Papal apartment and into the small waiting area. A thin wall mounted television was on in the corner and

McGeary gasped in astonishment as it showed what had happened in London. Dubbed into Italian, McGeary had some trouble in following the full speech given by Stubbs but he heard enough to realise that he had been played all along with regard to Avery. That it had been Stubbs himself who was to be on the Council of the Votary. Clearly the Israeli operation had successfully prevented Adam declaring himself to an audience of millions live in London and Stubbs had been exposed at the same time. It truly was a great day, McGeary thought but troubled at his own lack of foresight to see Stubbs for what he really was. Thinking back, perhaps it had been too convenient for the British Prime Minister to willingly effectively stop everything to see him as he did, to re-arrange meetings, even personal ones, to accommodate the Cardinal. As he reflected on what his interventions had resulted in for Avery in particular he heard the footsteps getting louder on the marbled floor from behind him and he turned.

Father Bernard approached the Cardinal as he looked at him and sat to his left.

"It seems our job is done," he said with a smile pointing at the television before turning to McGeary, "That your job is done your Eminence."

"It does seem that way Father and we must thank God for it," McGeary followed. "We have such good news to tell his Holiness!" he said with a beaming smile as the door opened and Pope Pius stood there with open arms.

"Cardinal McGeary and Father Bernard he exclaimed in perfect English but with an almost musical Mexican twang, welcome! Please come in!" The Pope turned and walked into this apartment followed by the two clergymen. Father Bernard shut the door behind him as they entered.

"So Cardinal, strange days are these," he pointed to the television which was on but muted.

"Strange days indeed," McGeary said before hastily adding, "Your Holiness."

The Pope held out his hand and both men knelt to kiss the ring before he retreated to an ornate baroque style chair and indicated the other two should be seated also.

"You are to tell me that Adam has been captured and his books are already in these buildings." The Pope said, not as a question which caught McGeary unawares that his thunder should be stolen, but as a statement of fact.

"Uh…yes your Holiness but how…?" McGeary started but the Pope ignored his question and began to speak again with a wry smile.

"You know Cardinal, you were a strange choice to lead this unit. You are old but you were useful. Of all the candidates that were presented to me I was firstly torn as to whom would be right for the position. I did not want someone too eager to make a name for himself; someone who might actually force what has happened today even sooner, way before the time was right. You were the steady choice Cardinal. Respected enough to put the doubters to bed. Of suitable authority to make sure those who may question the appointment could be tamed to the view that you could approach the question of Adam efficiently. Not a career man though, unless it was to this Holy office that you perhaps once day intended to fill?" The Pope gave a crafty look at McGeary and raised one eyebrow, "You were a convenience Cardinal rather than a first choice, I hope you realise that now?" His expression changed to one of pointed solemnity.

"I do not understand your Holiness," McGeary said slowly, "Did I not have your blessing to contribute to this great day? To see the vanquishing of the Beast?"

"My authority yes. My blessing no," the Pontiff responded. "Why would I want him vanquished? Why would I want something I believe represents the future of the church defeated?" Pope Pius rested his hands on his knees and bowed his head slightly.

"The future of the Church?" McGeary said with incredulity and paused. He looked at the Pope with narrowed eyes, his lips a thin line, "You mean you are a believer in him, in Adam? You are a follower?" The Cardinal's doubt showed plainly on his reddening cheeks.

"A follower no," Pope Pius followed slowly, "A facilitator perhaps?" He paused and looked up," Can you not see that with the rise of ever growing apathy towards religion, this very Catholic Church is under constant threat? We may be the largest faith but that does not make us the strongest. We continue to defend the old ways the old teachings but make no allowances for how man had progressed, how technology increasingly makes us look irrelevant and sterile. We resolutely debate such a simple thing as contraception and make no progress whilst the world moves on without us. We are constantly plagued by scandals of sexual deviance with children of stories of priests forming carnal relationships within their parishes. We expect men who take up the cloth to be celibate when every sinew in their mortal bodies strain their faith when faced with temptation." The Pope waved his arms wildly and McGeary noted that the tick in the Pontiff's left eye that manifested itself whilst under strain was already twitching rapidly, "These challenges test the church on a daily basis, causing many of the faithful to question that faith, to further eradicate the belief. The huge gaps we leave amongst the once faithful are eagerly filled by opposing faiths looking for new answers, sometimes by violent, barbarous means. We have nothing new to give whilst we as a faith refuse to modernise and move with how society evolves. We are gelded by science and progress and yet we assume that the faith of the devout will always be with us." He paused again and pointed to McGeary, "That is why Adam offers us; offers the church fresh hope. A new beginning or as is so commonly termed with the young of the twenty-first century, a re-boot of the faith"

"But everything he stands for is set to destroy the Church!" McGeary screamed, "Allowing his philosophies to take root destroys man's hopes, not enlightens them!"

"Think on this Cardinal before you become too excited," the Pope responded. "What if we were seen to first resist the new order but then be persuaded to embrace it? What if the message of God is simply put back in to distant history as the Creator of those that developed Adam. What if we position ourselves as those that praise Adam for his immortality, a sure sign that God still works in wonderful ways? What if what we now call Christianity is proved to be right, except we revered the later misrepresentation of the Son of God which had been based on the real Messiah, the real product of the Creators sent to Earth by God to improve us in every way? What if we accept the old scriptures are the work of many and subject to misrepresentation whilst the Books of Adam are all written first hand by the Messiah himself and prove that all subsequent religions have been nullified by his truth, the truth of the ages since the dawn of Man? Is that not such an exciting prospect? That only the followers of Adam can claim to be the true religion making all others void of meaning or trust? Most of all, how wonderful would it be that he still walks amongst us. That he has revealed himself like the scriptures state that he would. That he is the expected second coming of the Messiah! The Rapture we all preach about is the establishment of Adam! Tell me that does not excite you now Cardinal?"

"But that is monstrous!" McGeary blurted, "You are saying the Church has sanctified the death of countless people to just be able to morph into something more resilient to the march of technology and modern thinking? That my team and I have been played to represent a false objection to Adam only to be made ineffectual in the face of a greater enlightenment! That Christ in all his glory as we remember him was not the man from Galilee but must instead must be replaced by this abomination….this Devil! It is monstrous!" McGeary was almost purple with rage and was breathing heavily, using the back of a chair for support.

"You played you part Cardinal," Father Bernard said wistfully, "The Books of Adam will be associated with the savage death of the man who held them and now they are in your possession. We will simply say you acted outside of our expectations and exceeded your brief. That you proceeded without the blessing of the Church, but that now the Books of Adam are in our possession, that we will take the time to fully study them before changing the world."

"But Adam is captured." McGeary challenged with renewed strength, "The big reveal was thwarted. Have your plans not been destroyed with that?"

"No, merely delayed," The Pontiff responded with indifference, "An unfortunate state of affairs, but one which will be redeemed when the time is right. You see we are here for the duration Cardinal and we will protect what is right."

" Then you are of the Votary," McGeary said with scorn realising that his worst fears had just been realised.

"I am the Votary," The Pope said, "More specifically I am what you will recognise as One of Twelve. As Saint Peter was the principal disciple of Jesus. So it is natural for me to be so also of Adam. My family is the wealthiest in Mexico and it has been that way for hundreds of years, ever since my ancestors first looked to Adam for his financial help. With him, my family built an empire through trade and manufacturing and yes, whilst some would call us a cartel or even gangsters now, we have prospered since Adam first offered us the help we needed to become established when the first Spanish settlers conquered that part of North America. He was always there when we needed him and our loyalty was absolute. So when the day came for my father to pass his duty to Adam on to me, he was there. Yes, Adam himself was there as he had already decided that my role would be most important for what had to come. Young Father Johan discovered the link as his investigations uncovered my brother as the likely Votary member for Central and South America but that was a deliberate sleight of hand to protect me." The Pope rose and leaned on the table before him.

"So much has been in the planning Cardinal. Becoming a priest and rising up in the Church to Cardinal was all facilitated and planned. Becoming Pope required the demise of my predecessor but this was just as easy. The poison was undetectable and the effect on the heart was very quick and absolutely fatal. The conclave needed encouragement in some quarters and threats in others but the decision was made as I wished it. Thus, I am here as the ultimate authority in the largest World Church to be the greatest supporter of the Age of Adam. But that particular revelation must stay secret Cardinal, you do understand? Whilst the events in London have delayed the inevitable, it has by no means stopped it. So you must go with Father Bernard here please and try not to resist. Father Bernard has been my constant and loyal companion for many years and has done my bidding without question. Trust him now for if your faith is strong then you know you will go to a better place." The Pope finished speaking and walked towards the door.

McGeary felt the blade press hard against his ribs but Father Bernard kept up the pressure just enough to illustrate the meaning without piecing his body.

"If you please Cardinal," he said and McGeary started to walk under his direction towards the door which the Pope had opened as they passed.

"Goodbye Cardinal McGeary," he said, "We will not meet again", The Pope offered a cruel thin smile as Cardinal Donal McGeary left his apartments, accepting completely that this would indeed be true.

Chapter Thirty-Three

Michael Crowe and Jessica returned home the next day tired and grateful to see the familiar surrounding they had assumed they would never see again. Following their interviews at Exeter Police station, the story they told to Carol Davis had been full and detailed. Crowe confirmed the invitation to visit Professor Wilding, the conversations that had taken place over Adam, the Dartmoor rendezvous and subsequent journey to the replica Barnsford house. The firing of the antique flintlock followed by the imprisonment and subsequent escape. Jessica had also given a full statement about finding the deceased professor and her own kidnap, culminating with the reunion with Crowe and the death of Squat Man at the hands of her Israeli saviours.

The interviews had been long and cumbersome and Carol had followed procedure to the letter to tie all that had been said with the murder case. Although Carol had recorded all of what was said about Adam and after Crowe and Jessica had been taken out to the driver who would be taking them home, the Superintendent called Carol into his office. The conversation had been short but heated. The Superintendent had insisted that, as he had been commanded by the Chief Constable upon the demands of the Home Office that any reference to Adam and anything beyond the immediate requirements of the murder itself should be deleted. All transcripts and case notes were to be handed over and Carol had been made to sign the Official Secrets Act whilst stood at his desk. As far as the murder of the Professor was concerned, the culprit would be documented as being the Russian gangster whose body had been found by Norfolk Police in the middle of a large wood with the fire damaged remnants of a half-built mansion only yards away. The local police would supply the forensics to make the match with those taken at the Professor's house and with no-one left alive to prosecute, any further investigation would be futile. All references to Crowe or Jessica would be deleted.

Carol made her protests known but was slapped down by the Superintendent without discussion. Fuming, Carol also new that any enquiries to the Israelis would be fruitless and even the official enquiries to the Vatican produced nothing other than Cardinal McGeary was now himself, declared as 'missing'. As far as she was concerned, the case had nowhere left to go and neither had she.

Two days after the Downing Street meltdown, the bodies of Andrew Stubbs and his driver, Parkinson were recovered from the burnt-out shell of the official car after it plunged down the embankment off the M5 Motorway the day after the debacle in Downing Street. Witnesses said that it looked like the driver had lost control or that a tyre had blown. No-one expected that it had been anything other than a tragic accident that had deprived the country of a salacious trial for sex crimes committed by their own Prime Minister, a man who had clearly become dangerously mad in any event. There had been no expectation of a third party involved and certainly not from a sniper's bullet aimed at the tyre. The death had become necessary and inevitable of course. There could be no failure amongst the Votary.

Epilogue

In the absolute blackness of his surroundings, Adam sat motionless with his eyes closed. Making sure his mind and body were ready for the task, he slowly rose from his position of meditation until he stood erect and straight. He reached slightly behind himself to confirm the damp wall was indeed a few inches behind him and turned abruptly to his left so that the slimy stone was now touching his left shoulder. Using his left hand as a guide and reaching out fully before him, he let his fingers explore the first stone until he found the edges and continued to trace around the irregular outline. After he had completed the full circumference of the stone he grunted and moved forwards one pace so he could repeat the exercise and trace his finger around the new stone. This time he smiled in the darkness as he recognised the outline he had memorised, this was indeed the first stone. It was drier than the first which meant that the seeping moisture through the rocks above had not yet reached this part of his underground prison. The stone surface was relatively flat however, the product of hundreds of years of sweat and bloodied fingers as generations of miners had dug to find the ore they craved, hacking at the rock races with their primitive tools. What had been their place of industry was now Adam's place of eternal rest. Where no food was ever offered and the only moisture to soften his parched lips was the very same slime he was reduced to licking from the rock.

Adam had no idea how long he had been here now. It may only have been days or could have been decades, it was impossible to know as the light never entered the mine nor did a sound ever permeate through the metres of rock above and around him. All he now knew was total silence and total blackness, an everlasting night that only allowed his memories of past centuries to populate his mind. For a being that required little sleep, a continuous slumber to the end of time was all he could expect. A never-ending solitude where death itself could and would not intervene.

Adam continued his probing onto the next rock, memorising the outline, forming a picture in his head of each stone so that the full internal dimensions of his prison could be slowly illustrated, even in the all-consuming blackness that surrounded him. As he probed, the faint vibration was sudden and unexpected but it was there. He pressed his finger with renewed strength into the rock's surface but then withdrew it slightly so it was only just touching, an action which he realised made it easier to register the vibration, a singular throbbing that stimulated the most sensitive nerve endings in his finger-tips. It was the only sensation that had broken the monotony for as long as he could remember in the pit that he now called home. The throbbing became deeper, louder almost and rhythmic. Adam smiled to himself and sat down once again to meditate. It would not be long after all.

The End.

48269167R00240

Printed in Poland
by Amazon Fulfillment
Poland Sp. z o.o., Wrocław